Working Stiffs
Scott Bell

Working Stiffs
A Red Adept Publishing Book
Red Adept Publishing, LLC
104 Bugenfield Court
Garner, NC 27529
http://RedAdeptPublishing.com/

Dedication

To my wife, best friend, toughest editor, and partner-for-life, Margaret: this one's for you.

News Bytes

User CNN@cnn.com: #unemployment. Unemployment figures reached 30year high of 26.9%.

User roger626: @cnn.com must not be countin the ded. fukin revivents all got jobs

User plutoizzaplanet: @cnn.com hey, get a job loozers

User 489skittles: @pluto why?

One | First Class Felony

THE THREE DEAD GUYS on the freight elevator had a personal odor reminiscent of vomit with an undertone of road kill.

"You freaks need to stand in the rain, you know that? Take a shower."

My formerly living companions swayed with the motion of the elevator but kept their thoughts on hygiene to themselves. One of the three, whose name tag read "Larry," belched—an editorial comment or random gas bubble? Hard to say.

Sixty-seven more floors of asphyxiation. Why their owner didn't wash down his Revivants was a mystery. They didn't decay like regular dead people; if they did, body parts would be strewn around the city like the remnants of a jihadi bomb factory.

Take shallow breaths.

I adjusted my stolen waiter's jacket to hide Grandpa's old bullet-firing pistol. The weapon made my pants sag. Since I quit eating anything more solid than tomato soup prepared from ketchup packets, everything—including a sudden change in barometric pressure—made my pants slide down.

Dampness blotched the jacket's red sleeve from the cold sweat off my forehead. *C'mon, Joe, pull it together.*

Two of the Revvies rode in silence. Larry, the talker, vaguely resembled a classic comedian from the early 2000s. The hell was his name? A funny guy, I'd caught some of his stuff in all the old bootleg videos Grandpa made me watch.

Jay Leno.

Unlike Jay, Larry knew only one joke.

The dead comedian leered over my shoulder and, in a zombie voice, moaned, "B-b-b-brainssss!"

"That wasn't funny the last six times you said it. You're not a zombie."

Larry laughed, a sound like an old gas-powered car trying to start on a cold day. "*Hhnh-hhnh-hhnh.*" He wore a unisex coverall, once brilliant red, now faded to Pepto-Bismol pink. The nametag curled, unstuck at one corner.

"Keep your day job," I grumbled.

The elevator shuddered and clanked to a stop—the damned thing was older than Grandpa Warren's firearm—and the doors ground open. Larry, hit of the graveyard comedy tour, stayed aboard and bared his gummy teeth in a grin. Since Revvies didn't eat, I refused to speculate on what might be stuck in his incisors.

The two silent dead guys scuffed away in their worn shoes, heads canted to one side in that odd zombie-walk favored by the revived. Larry stayed with me on the empty elevator.

Me and the Walking Dud.

"*Hhnh-hhnh-hhnh.* Braaaiinnnss."

"Whoever programmed your nanos for comedy needs to be punched in the throat." I hit the up button and focused on the groaning doors.

The gun poked my testicles. Grimacing, I resettled it, finger most definitely *off* the trigger. The gun hadn't been fired since the second Ms. Clinton administration, but now was not the time to test it. Wish I'd thought of that before I left Ding's apartment.

Soon, though.

Thirty more floors.

I tugged at the damp collar of my white dress shirt with its built-in bow tie.

"*Hhnh-hhnh-hhnh.*"

"Shut up." I stalked over and stabbed a finger in Larry's chest. "Just shut up, okay? Every time I look at one of you, you know what I see? I see failure, asshole." I poked the gaping Revivant again. "I never would have been put in this spot if it wasn't for you!" I shoved Larry, and he swayed in place but didn't fall. "Fuck it. Why am I even talkin' to you?"

Larry grinned, his keyboard teeth spackled with mortar. "*Hhnh-hhnh-hhnh.*"

"Yeah, very funny. You don't have to eat, don't have to sleep... just work all day long without even a piss-break. You make people sick with your germs, give them fucking brain tumors... steal their lives." My mouth snapped shut.

And how stupid am I lecturing a corpse?

The elevator shuddered to a stop, the P button flickering on the panel. The penthouse.

Showtime.

I adjusted the pistol and waited for the doors to part. They clunked open, showing a dingy white service corridor. Another pink-suited Rev waited by the doors, placid as a cow, carrying a black plastic trash bag in one immobile hand.

"Tah-rash," it said.

The newcomer handed Larry the bag as I stepped around them.

"Tah-rash," Larry repeated. He leered at me, churned out another creepy laugh. The doors closed on his grinning pumpkin face, shutting Larry away. Gears clanked, a spark flared, machinery whirred, and the elevator started down.

The remaining undead janitor wasn't as chatty as Larry. He rotated in an old-man shuffle and tottered toward the door at the far end of the service corridor, his coverall yellowing under third-rate LEDs lighting the corridor. Who used LEDs anymore? Spared every expense, these guys.

Which is a good thing.

The financial straits of modern America in the year 2051 should work in my favor. For once.

Please.

Two doors flanked the service corridor on either side. One bore the label *Mantenimiento.* The other read: *Seguridad.* Security. Spanish language labels in Chinese-owned buildings. *¡Bienvenidos a los Estados Unidos!* Foreign spices seasoned the melting pot, sometimes creating a tasty stew, sometimes a bellyache.

"Well, let's find out if this works."

I fished the preprinted finger cot—it resembled a short condom—from my waistcoat pocket and slipped it over my thumb. Gingerly. Tearing it now would be bad. I had lifted the molded fingerprint from a Revivant in Moline, the former security chief of the Huateng Tower. Programmed to pick tomatoes, he kept trying to get back to the field, becoming more anxious the longer I held him down in the back of my van.

Which sounded pretty freaking sick, right?

When I let him go, he hustled off in jerky little steps, head cocked to the side, like the actor in the latest V-Real remake of *Rain Man III.*

"Thanks, Chief. I hope you're enjoying the afterlife." I placed my covered thumb against the biometric and held my breath. "All right, guys. Did you reprogram the locks, or were you having a sloppy day?" *Buzzz*-click. "Yes, baby! Score one for cheap and lazy."

I palmed the door to the security room, one hand on the pistol in my waistband. If they left a human guard to watch the cameras... "Nope. Too cheap for that. Heh-heh."

Monitors glowed. Light flickered. Computers hummed. Air circulated.

Anti-climax exhaled.

The main display fluttered to life when I pressed my fake thumb against the reader on the desk. Locking down the passenger elevators sucked up thirty seconds. Deactivating and memory-wiping the surveillance nodes took only a few minutes. The remaining building security devices went down one by one. Activating the signal-damping field required a little more time, but everything seemed simple enough. Tap-tap. Done.

Easy as pie. My comp sci minor, aborted upon my departure from college, would serve some use. At least I could find my way around a server.

"Time to get a little payback," I murmured, dragging the antique pistol from my waistband. Joe Warren, gunslinger.

The damned thing was *heavy*. Steel and lead and grim death, all in a hand-sized package. Bright nickel finish, wood handle adorned by a stylized S&W medallion. A revolver, Grandpa said when he showed me how it worked.

I settled the revolver in my waistband and buttoned my jacket over it.

Showtime!

Corpus Interruptus

"How far do you think he'll get?" Homeland Agent Maravich used his pinkie to circle the inside of his nostril.

Across the street from the Huateng Tower, in what was once the Magnificent Mile Marriott but was now a deserted hulk harboring junkies, alkies, and lice, Agents Ramirez and Maravich followed Joseph Warren's antics on a portable vid screen. Scratchy audio buzzed from tiny speakers. An inset window indicated the subject's position in real-time and read out his vital stats in a tiny scroll at the bottom.

"Far enough to hang himself." Ramirez leaned over the monitor, set up on what was once the circular bar in the Marriott's lobby. He refused to let any part of his body other than the soles of his shoes touch any surface in the derelict building. Water dripped and things skittered in the dark corners of the open space, long since stripped of fixtures and covered in a layer of filth deep as cake icing.

A team of six TAC officers in full gear held position near the boarded-up entrance. A chain hung from a hole in the plywood, its lock a thing of distant memory. The glut of street people lurking in the lobby had slunk away like feral dogs when Ramirez and his fellow agents shoved open the damp and rotting barrier and flashed lights around the interior. Ramirez perceived them hovering in the shadows the way a ship's captain sensed bad weather over the horizon.

"So what is it about this dingleberry?" Maravich studied the small screen, his Eastern European ancestry evident in the flat planes and angles of his face. "This Warren guy, he ain't much."

"He's going to get us in."

"You think?"

"Warren is the only person I've ever seen get close to MacCauley who wasn't one of her fanatics."

"And you think that's enough?"

On the screen, Warren accessed the security door, and the camera view switched to inside the room. Ramirez smirked as their subject tapped his way through the building's security features.

"There's more to Warren than meets the eye," he told Maravich. "He's a survivor. I get a lever on him; he'll do what we need."

"You say so." Maravich shrugged. He snorted and spat across the bar. "I think the guy's a chump."

"He is. But he's our chump. He'll get us in, and we'll run down these terrorist fucks once and for all. These assholes think they can tear down the foundation of this country and destroy the United States government. I will not, under any circumstances, allow that to happen. If I have to sacrifice a hundred Joseph Warrens, it'll be a small price to pay."

Two | Robbin' Hoodie Strikes

BACK IN THE CORRIDOR, the cool air chilled the sweat beading on my forehead. The door at the end of the hall led to the *Salón de Baile del Pueblo*. Ballroom of the People. The Huateng Tower: one of a few downtown skyscrapers still in use, an icon of the disparity evident between one block and the next, or, as I like to think of it, a proctologist's big middle finger sticking into the asshole of downtown, squeezed all around by cancer. The site touted a banquet room with elegant dining tables, a dance floor, gleaming silver and gold accouterments, and stunning views of downtown Chicago. The Haves arrived in armored limos and were escorted inside through bulletproof glass corridors so that none of the Have-Nots' cooties would touch them. Ballroom of the People. Yeah, right. What a joke. It should be named Ballroom of the Rich People.

There was no lock on the interior door from the service corridor. A lock would prove too challenging for the Revivant service staff.

Steamy air, smoky griddles, and the shouts of cooks and waiters greeted me on the other side. The kitchen staff barely glanced at me as I wove through them and shoved open the swinging door to the people's ballroom. Kitchen sounds dropped off, and a solid wall of voices, music, laughter, and clinking silverware slapped me in the face. Wall-to-wall people, elegantly dressed and sumptuously fed, crowded tables draped in linen. They lifted glasses filled with sparkling wine and toasted their mutual success and beauty.

I recognized an A-list actress whose most recent V-Real grossed over seventeen billion dollars. It involved interspecies sex with dolphins, I think.

At another table, a sloshed Democan Senator, Illinois's very own Hernando Martinez de Soto, eye-fucked the cleavage of the teenage hardbody next to him (I think she was an Olympic Nude Volleyball champion) while his wife glared *puñales calientes* at him. From the solar eruptions flaring from her eyes, it appeared the Democan Uni-party would have a vacancy to fill next term.

At the far end of the room, a low stage featured a spotlighted podium stationed in front of a blue velvet drape. On the drape, a graph glowed, gaudy white letters in Godzilla-sized font.

Renascentia, Inc. Where Death is but a Stage

Below that, with eye-watering visual effects, the text repeated the phrase:

Congratulations Renascentia Team for 10 years of Revivals and Rebirths. Thanks to you, being dead doesn't mean you have to stop living.

A table flanked the podium with twelve of the High and Mighty arrayed like a parody of the Last Supper mythos. The Jesus Christ figure in this tableau sat to the right of the podium—my left—and lifted a dainty forkful of veganibbles to his gene-spliced, ultra-handsome face.

Jamil Yamadut.

Twentieth-generation Kanyakubja Brahmin. CEO of Renascentia. Creator of the Revivant Nanobot.

Progenitor of the undead labor force. That stole Chelle from me. And started a chain of events that left me broke, homeless, and alone.

I felt like a Revvie myself, disconnected from my legs and moving in a haze; a shaking, buttery mess sliding around islands of merriment and witty conversation. The gun tugged at my britches; I had to keep my hands stuffed in my pockets to stop it from sliding into my crotch again.

The murmur of conversation bounced off my ears without penetrating.

"—then Daniel said—"

"—that's a great place. It has an underwater pool—"

"—cute dress! Where'd you—"

At the stage, the guy at the end of the head table frowned at me when I stepped up next to him. He made a sour face and pointed at his empty wine glass. His expression turned to shock when I said, "Get your own damned wine."

No tip at this table.

Jamil Yamadut never looked up from his plate of organically grown protein slices, sautéed with what resembled lawn clippings from a well-tended garden. The food left on his plate represented more than I'd eaten in a week. My stomach growled, and dizziness fuzzed my eyesight.

I sniffed up a lungful of air and stepped to the podium. As soon as I did, the AV system activated, and doll-sized replicas of me appeared in the middle of every table. The sight froze my jaw in the standby position, like an actor in a home V-Real, paused in mid-sentence.

Is that really what I look like? Hell, a Revivant dragged behind a bus looks better.

Two hundred guests saw a guy in a badly fitting waiter's tux, pasty white and glistening with sweat, standing at the podium with visibly trembling hands.

"I, uh..." My voice reverberated around the room, bounced back and trailed off into a high-pitched squeal. *Unbelievable. Two hundred years of technology and they still can't eliminate feedback.* "I... wait, no." *Concentrate, Joe.* "This is a stick-up!"

Grandpa was my live-in babysitter. We must have watched a thousand shows where people rode horses and shot it out in dusty streets or rode smoke-pouring autos and rattled off tommy guns. I steeled myself to be as ruthless and brutal as those long-ago actors—something unheard of in this day and age. *Thanks for the education, Grandpa.* I repeated it, louder. "This is a stick-up!"

The audience failed to react. A mild titter ran through the room. The clinking of silverware continued, some diners seeming not to notice, so involved in their own conversations even the threat of a man holding a gun...

Oh.

Note to self: Next time, draw the gun first.

"What are you doing?" Jamil Yamadut demanded. He rose partway from his seat, a napkin in one hand. "I did not order a comedian."

Really? Well, you should meet Larry.

"Laugh at this, Pilgrim." I tugged the revolver from my waistband after two tries—it snagged, of course—and pointed it at Yamadut's face. I'd never seen eyes get that big and round. "Now sit back down." Facing the audience, I said, "This, gentlepeople, is a stick"—I cocked the hammer, which required more effort than I expected—"*up!*"

I pointed the shiny Smith & Wesson at the ceiling and depressed the trigger.

BOOM!

The gun bucked so hard, I nearly dropped it.

Holy Mother of Unnatural Breeding!

Nobody told me how loud the thing would be. If a pair of brass cymbals had clapped my head, my ears wouldn't ring any worse. The shrieking and startled shouts of the dinner guests came from a deep pit, though I could read their expressions well enough. Most people looked only slightly less freaked-fucking-out than I.

"Okay, people, pay attention," I yelled. My magnified voice replicated across the Ballroom of the People, twenty miniature Joe Warrens repeating after me. I retrieved my bit-stick from my pants pock-et. The balance reading on the side, in glowing red numerals, in-formed me I had point-one-six bucks in my account. "Everybody get out your bit-sticks, bit-jewels, and other bit-currency devices. See my stick?" (I choked down a laugh.) "Key your balances over to me. If I don't see an acceptable number on this screen in ten seconds, the prick with the grass stain on his chin gets the next round through his head." I pointed the weapon's dead weight at Jamil's face again. "My receive code is 115698." I repeated the number three times.

"Are you insane?" he hissed.

"Yes, Jamil, I'm crazy as glue." I giggled. Really. I did. Twenty miniature Joes giggled with me. *Get control, you idiot.* I made an in-stant change in plan; the guy's healthy, well-fed face really got under my skin. "Get ready for a little trip, Yama-dope. You're coming with me."

"*What?*"

"You heard me." I turned back to the audience of stunned diners. Many of them pointed their sticks in my direction and subvocalized instructions. The balance counter fizzed in a red blur, numbers com-ing in faster than it could handle them. "Come on, get up."

I snagged Jamil by the fancy dress jacket—the material caressed my fingers like it wanted to blow me—and shoved him to the edge of the stage. Jamil's husband twitched as if he wanted to say something, maybe even get up. One glance froze him to the spot. Jamil's wife had already fainted. *So much for tonight's three-way.* I stifled another gig-gle.

The journey to the kitchen across the now-hushed Ballroom of the Frightened People lasted forever and passed in an instant. A few hushed comments drifted from the corners.

"—a real gun!"

"—must be a right-winger. I played one in *Die Bad III*—"

"—so pale. Is he sick?"

"Rebel scum."

That last one may have been my imagination.

The kitchen staff had vanished, probably scattering when I fired the Smith & Wesson. Oddly, now that the first surprise had worn off, I wanted to fire it again. I shoved Jamil between the empty grills and steaming dishwashers, propelling him with little shoves until he cleared the doorway into the service hall.

I closed the kitchen door and retrieved a simple wooden wedge from an inside jacket pocket, which I jammed in the bottom of the doorframe. "There you go, Jamil. I think we're alone now."

"At least there doesn't seem to be anyone around." The urbane Jamil had recovered some of his poise. He stood tall and aloof, sneering without moving a single facial muscle. "What do you plan to do now? You know you're at the top of a hundred and sixty floors."

"Please." I gestured to the end of the hall. "Your chariot, sweet prince."

The freight elevator promised salvation or destruction. My favorite death trap. At least Jamil would be going with me to meet the Grim Reaper if the thing crashed. Maybe we'd even be revived together, share a trash route.

Only when he'd stepped away did I focus on my bit-stick's balance indicator. Which had turned from red to gold. I'd never seen it gold before. It took me a frowning-damned-long time to figure out what happened. Had all those rich bastards screwed me over? No, wait...

The reader needed an exponent to describe the balance. That was... that was... a fuck-ton of money.

Holy Mother of Payday.

I followed Jamil on air-cushioned feet and directed him to push the arrow button. Familiar machinery groaned. Hopefully the elevator wasn't all the way down on the bottom floor.

"How do you possibly think you're getting away with this?" the CEO of Renascentia stated more than asked. "The elevator will go into security lockdown once the alarm is activated—"

"Uh-uh." I shook my head. "Deactivated the locks, cut the passenger elevators, activated the damping field, killed surveillance."

He sneered and crossed his arms. "All right, Mr. Gunman. What do you plan to do with me?"

I hefted the gun, let him get a good look at it. "You're along to make sure I get out of here. If I don't, I plan to use this weapon and blow your brains out the back of your head."

He blinked and let his arms fall. Some of the sneer left his face. "But... why?"

"Because, you bloodsucker, you invented this damned walking meat."

"Look... what's your name? What do I call you?"

"Joe." Joe the Moron, who is now getting chatty with the Architect of Doom. Insanity beckoned.

The AoD smirked. "Joe. Sure."

I ran a hand through my sweaty hair and paced the corridor from side to side. Where was that fucking elevator? "You think this was my first choice?"

We watched each other in silence, the elevator humming a one-note soundtrack. Jamil held my stare with coal-dark eyes under trimmed brows. My stomach grumbled, loudly enough that I winced. I jiggled in place and rolled my neck.

What was taking the damned elevator so long? Was it coming from hell?

"Look, Joe," Jamil said with a sigh, "I don't see how killing me helps you at all. I pay seventy-five percent of my income in taxes. I support charitable programs for the poor and the sick. I mean look, man, I sponsor a mating pair of humpback whales! I'm not the bad guy here, Joe."

The gun dragged at my hand, dangling loose, heavy, but not forgotten. He was right, and I knew it. The hate I'd held for Yamadut and his creations was too tenuous to hold on to; an ideal rather than something active and alive. My threats to kill the man were as empty as my head.

But I owed something to Chelle, didn't I?

The elevator thunked and thudded to a stop; in a second the doors would grind open. I cocked the hammer on the Smith. *Click-click.* "Let's go."

"Joe." Jamil shook his head, a picture of infinite sadness. "Joe, Joe, Joe. Who am I?"

"Are we playing games, Jamil? Stalling won't help."

"I created the Revivants, did I not?" The elevator doors split open. There stood my old buddy, Larry, his creepy grin fixed to his slack face.

"Well, yeah. That's what this has all been about, hasn't it?"

A smile I could only describe as condescending slithered across Jamil's face. "Revivant, code Alpha-Foxtrot-One-Seven-Niner. Execute."

"Doe-kay." Larry shuffled toward me and stretched his hands into claws. "Kill."

"What?" My feet rooted; I couldn't move. I had never seen even mildly threatening behavior from a Revivant. Larry left *mildly threatening* at the door and escalated to *scary as fuck* in the space of a heartbeat. "What is this?"

"I invented the Revivants." Jamil stepped behind the lumbering undead janitor. "Did you think I wouldn't build in some safeguards to protect myself? We look out for each other, the Revivants and I."

Oh. Shit.

I backed a step, leveled the revolver and triggered a round into Larry's chest.

BOOM!

My ears rang, and acrid smoke burned my nostrils. Larry jolted but kept moving, shrugging off the lead projectile like a mosquito bite.

"Ah, Revivant," I blathered, "code Alpha Foxtrot, ah, One-Niner-Seven."

"Wrong code!" Yamadut called out from behind the lumbering Revvie. "And besides, it only works once. The nanobots are dispersed through its body and are programmed to very strict parameters. You should have read the marketing brochure we printed for the Army. Revivant Soldiers. Harder to kill than herpes. So long, Joe."

BOOM! BOOM! BOOM! BOOM! Snap. Snap.

Six shots, Grandpa Warren said. Six shots and that's it. Show's over. Larry didn't have much of a head left. One eye dangled from its socket.

Cold steel greeted my back. The door to the kitchen, which I'd oh-so-intelligently blocked with a wedge. A graveyard chill shivered through me when Larry pinched the wet orb delicately between finger and thumb and pointed it in my direction. I kicked at the wedge I'd planted earlier, but the damned thing was stuck hard and deep.

How the hell had it come to this?

"I see ouuuu." Larry grinned past bloody teeth. "Braaaiinnnss. *Hhnh-hhnh-hhnh.*"

Three | I Can Quit Anytime I Want

User Renascentia.com: #retirement. New, from the company that brought you Revivants: An alternative to death. Don't be a burden to your loved ones. Be a Revivant!

User Spotacuss: @renascentia: Volunterry zombees?

User Berkin54: @renascentia: be all you can be, join the rvt.

User wingnut333: @berkin54: lol

Three Months Ago

C offee.

Coffee, coffee, coffee, coffee. Where was the fucking coffee?

We had coffee yesterday, didn't we? I rummaged through the last cabinet in the kitchen, the one where we kept the dishes, as if the packet of coffee might have snuck under a chipped plate or snuggled down in one of the three mismatched cups. All the other cabinet doors hung open, having been raided, pillaged, and left for dead.

No coffee in the plate cabinet, either.

It's a law—federal, state, and natural—when in doubt of an object's location, ask the woman. "Chelle!"

"Joe!" Her voice came through loud and clear from her permanent place of residence in the john. In a three-room government apartment with Xerox-copied walls, we did not need an intercom to communicate.

"Where's the coffee?" While the question traveled across time and space, penetrated Chelle's hard crust of annoyance and generated a response, I checked under the sink. Nothing except for a bottle of liquid soap (so old, it had cemented itself to the cabinet floor), some Drano, a can of unopened greenish powdery substance (for cleaning?), and an empty box of scrub pads.

Somebody should throw that out.

I tried the fridge next, in case I missed seeing the baggie of Folger's pellets the first three times I checked. Two pickles in a jar of green vinegar. Ketchup, nearly empty. Mayo, nearly empty. Can of Diet Dr Pepper, open, half gone. (Gulp. Oops, now all gone.) Pack-

age of cold cuts, one left. Takeout Beef with Broccoli in a paper car-
ton that... *ew*... had more green than broccoli alone could account for.

Chelle's response pinged back from the bathroom. "Coffee?"

"Yes! Coffee! Where! Is! It?" I scratched my bare chest, followed
by a spot on my ass—covered in gym shorts.

The toilet flushed, the tap ran, and Chelle wandered in, naked
from head to toe.

"Do you have to yell?" she asked. "Half the fuckin' building
must've heard you."

"I probably wouldn't yell, but I just got up, I haven't peed yet because you've been in the bathroom, and I can't find... the stinkin' coffee!" That last bit was accompanied by me slamming the refrigerator
door, cutting off the pleas from the pickles. *Eat me! Eat me!* the pickles cried. Yeah, well. Me first.

"You drank all the coffee yesterday, Joe." Chelle used that overly
patient tone women employed when they want to fucking piss you
off.

"No, I did not."

"Yes. You did."

I can recognize a circular argument broiling faster than you can
say *did not, did too,* so I tried a different tack. "Did you buy some
more?" Shopping was her chore, as bug killing and cap unscrewing
was mine. Which doesn't sound like much, but hey, in our apartment,
bug killing was a full-time job.

"With what, Joe? Your draw doesn't come 'til Tuesday. Food
stamps reload Wednesday. I spent all my paycheck on the light bill.
Should I fuck Chang so you can have some coffee?" She spread her
arms wide, as if holding up the world. Her small breasts perked up in
my direction, which distracted me. A naked Chelle was once the stuff
of my late-night, box-of-tissue fantasies. She'd zapped off her pubic
hair with a follicular laser and had an arrow tattooed from her navel

to the split of her vagina. Over the arrow, in stencil, were the words: Eat Here.

I once believed that was sexy as hell.

"Of course not," I told her. "I absolutely do not—most emphatically *do not*—want you fucking the grocer." I put on a thoughtful expression. "I think just a blow job would do the trick—Wait! I'm kidding!" But I was speaking to Chelle's jiggling derriere.

Slam!

Bathroom door. I recognized the sound.

"Hey, I still need to pee!"

The love of my life, the woman who once asked if she could hold it for me when I went to the john, voice muffled by one door and six years of emotional insulation, yelled back. "Use the fucking sink!"

"I need a cup of coffee," I muttered. "It's too early for this shit."

I found a use for the empty Dr Pepper can. Ahhh. One problem solved.

We lived in an apartment building off West 23rd Place, south of the Chicago River, in a rectangular block structure stacked between other rectangular block structures that, altogether, formed a mega-block. You put four mega-blocks side by side and you get a "neighborhood filled with diversity." Which is code for slum. It had been a slum in the latter half of the twentieth century and, through willpower and stick-to-it-iveness, was even slummier in the mid-twenty-first.

It used to be called Chinatown—before the Asians, being smart people, migrated to the North Side—and was within a quarter-hour hike of Lake Michigan. Not that we would hike it. If I wanted to inhale the aroma of dead fish and sewage, all I had to do was hang out in the alley behind the restaurant on Wentworth, the Frying Fresh (and try saying that with a Chinese accent).

My point being, if I wanted coffee, I had to put on clothes, boogie down three flights of stairs (the elevator shaft now being used as a trash chute), haul my ass through my "neighborhood filled with diversity" without getting stomped into glue by the thousand-and-one addicts and street people, make a right on Wentworth—opposite of the Frying Fresh—and waltz into Chang's store. Chang's ancestors had either been left behind during the exodus or they were the only dumb Asians in Chicago, remaining in place while everyone else boarded the proverbial Chinese Ark for the North.

No matter how intellectually challenged his ancestors may have been, Chang was sharp enough to demand payment for goods received (treacherous son of the Orient that he was), so of course I wouldn't be *buying* coffee once I reached his Asian oasis. Buying required money, and money required either a job, or government unemployment, or food-stamp deposit to my bit-stick.

Or performing oral sex on Chang, but I was pretty sure I wouldn't sink to that level.

News tweets claimed the government threatened to cut off unemployment benefits at two years if Congress couldn't get another tax increase passed. My unemployment had lasted two years and three months. So far. With no end in sight. If they cut off unemployment, I'd be eating gravel stew between food-stamp payouts.

Evil Joe whispered, *You need money. Ding's offering money.*

Shut the fuck up. I'm a working-class guy with no education. I'm not a crook.

If you can't find a job and have no income, how are you supposed to eat?

You have a point, but think about it. Ding. That dude ain't right. I get tied up with him...

Derisive laughter echoed in my head. *Can you imagine trying a felony on your own?*

Can you imagine my life in a detention camp, I fired back at me, *huddled with six other guys under one blanket, hoping that thing prodding my butt isn't what I think it is?*

Chelle came out of the bathroom, showered and dressed in ancient knee-length jeans and a split-front T-shirt. She had obviously decided not to press charges against me. Her attitude said, *Hey, I'll forget you're a jackass if you'll leave it alone and don't make me fucking come across this table and rip your nuts off.*

I can read a lot into women's body language.

"Are you going to get dressed?" she asked. The question weighted and freighted a very subtle undercurrent on six tiny words. Chelle busied herself at the kitchen counter, oh-so-very carefully not looking at me.

Tell her to fuck off, Evil Joe urged.

"Fuck off."

"What?" Chelle asked, a frown splitting her forehead.

"Nothing. Talking to myself. Yes, babe," I tried, "I plan to. Right now, in fact."

Chelle dumped her ass at the table, pouring the last of the gluten-free flax cereal in a bowl. I sensed her watching me even though she appeared intent on her breakfast. She appeared pretty pale and shaky.

"You do remember, right?" Chelle asked.

"Sure I do." My brain's electronic impulses shorted out in a frenzy of sparks. Oh... wait... "You want me to go with you to the doctor. You'll get your test results back today."

A sparkling smile lit Chelle's lips and touched her green eyes. I tried not to sag with relief. "I'm glad you remembered. We have to be there in an hour, so you might want to get moving."

"Yep. Will do. It's been, what? Six months since they sent them in? You'd think they cloned a whole new you to find out what's wrong."

I pushed back from the table and stretched. Checked around the kitchen in case I forgot something. Like where I put my balls. Oh, there. Hiding under the table; so small I couldn't see 'em. I headed for the bathroom.

"Oh, hey, Chelle?" I pointed to the Dr Pepper can by her elbow. "Don't drink out of that. I didn't want to have to clean the sink."

Four | Medical Malpractice

THE LINE AT THE CLINIC stretched along the sidewalk for half a block. Located on Wentworth, on the opposite side of the street from Chang's store, the clinic occupied a building that retained traces of the original Chinatown architecture. Faded, ratty signs written with complex Chinese characters decorated nearly every storefront. We joined the line in front of what was once a US Post Office, closed like the rest of them. Somebody had spray-painted the words, *Sorry, the rent check was in the mail.* Under that, another tagger added, *All postal employee termination notices sent by email. Thank you, USPS.*

A faded-out For Lease sign hung in the window, taped inside the glass. It had been there for all six years I'd lived in the neighborhood.

"What time did you say your appointment was?" I asked Chelle.

"Ten."

I reflexively glanced at my wrist before I remembered my IT service had disavowed all knowledge of me after the sixth disconnect notice. I asked a chubby guy ahead of me for the time.

"Nine forty," he said from behind his surgical mask. I nodded my thanks.

"Damn, Chelle, we'll never make it on time."

"I told you to hurry up and get ready."

My part of getting ready had taken all of ten minutes, thus screwing up the atomic clock by which Chelle ran her life.

At least we had nice weather for standing in line. Late April in Chicago was hard to beat, mid-sixties, blue sky, a few fluffy clouds...

26

What more could you ask for? In February we'd be standing out here turning to popsicles. The homeless and unemployed were out in force, droves of them meandering, begging, pilfering and picking through the trash lining the gutters. In other words, doing whatever it took to get through another great day in the Windy City.

Speaking of popsicles... My stomach grumbled, reminding me two pickles for breakfast was a rotten trick to play on it. I eyed Chang's front door and considered creative credit terms: zero down payment, two pocket spending limit, and a forever repayment term. Penalties may apply.

I didn't see the dead woman until she was almost on us. A Revivant, shuffling along the line of patients, handing out paper flyers. Female, about twenty or so when she died, dark-skinned and slender. Pretty once, I supposed, with a good figure, full lips, and dark, almond-shaped eyes. The owners had dressed her in a sexy maid's outfit with high heels and a higher skirt; the light breeze brushed it above her panty line every few minutes. The nanos running through her were having a hard time managing the heels, and she scuffed forward in wobble-steps in a parody of a sexy sway.

My empty stomach bubbled with acid.

"I hate those things," the guy with the mask mumbled.

"Yeah, me too." I accepted the flyer the Revvie handed me without looking at her. "They creep me out."

The man's mask crinkled when he grimaced. "What I want to know, how do they make them look so alive?"

The line had grown behind us. A couple of dropouts from the School of Morons had joined the tail a few minutes ago and entertained everyone with a steady stream of obscenities laced with curse words. Hey, I'm no saint when it comes to foul language, but still, there are limits, right? The taller of the two mental giants shouted out, "Woo-hoo, lookit dis fine bitch!"

"I hear dead pussy's mighty cold," his running buddy claimed.

Both of them were racially ambiguous teens (their parental gametocytes swam in a diversity stream) decked out in trendy grunge clothes and wearing the flat-brim, Amish-style hats favored by the discerning hoodlum. Without squinting, I could count another score of hoodlums exactly like them within a two-block radius, poised like IEDs, waiting for the unwary so they could explode with uncontained violence.

The taller one, in a Bears T-shirt, cupped the crotch of his basketball shorts and shook it. "Hey, Dead Mamma, izzat true? Lemme see how cold yo pussy is."

His buddy, in a green T-shirt and plaid boxers, reached out and clamped a hand on the dead woman's breast. "Oooh, Sanjay, you should be fillin' dis. It fills goooood," he crooned.

The Revivant woman stumbled and would have fallen if the one called Sanjay hadn't grabbed her around the waist. Her dull expression never changed. She wobbled in place the way a drunk might, if you squinched your eyes and pretended she wasn't dead and reanimated with a gazillion tiny machines running along her arteries.

"Fly-er, sir?" she deadpanned.

The morons laughed and pawed at the woman's chest, clawing at her top.

I ground my teeth and looked away. Don't get involved in fights you can't win. That was my creed, and I planned to stick to it. My new friend with the mask caught my eye and grimaced. His expression said: Look at what the world's coming to when dead people can't even walk the streets. Tragic.

The line crept forward a few feet, and I tugged at Chelle's hand. She didn't budge.

"Look at those two," she hissed. Staring at the twins from Stupidville, her jaw set in a hard line, Chelle sounded mad enough to chew nails and shit steel wire.

"Yeah, I see 'em. Let's go." I tugged her hand again, but she refused to budge.

"That's disgusting!"

The twins had the Revivant woman's outfit yanked down to her waist and were commenting—loudly—on the size, quality, and firmness of her breasts.

"C'mon, Chelle. It's none of our business." I pulled a little harder. It was like trying to move a fencepost. "Chelle..." I used my stern voice. "Don't start—"

"Hey, fucktards!" Chelle barked. "Leave that woman alone!"

"—any trouble."

The fucktards in question snapped to attention and pinned Chelle with twin feral stares. Werewolves, scenting new prey.

Sanjay shoved the Revivant. She fell in the street, landing awkwardly on her butt, hard enough to make me wince even though I knew she felt no pain. Her breasts bounced, and the flyers she carried scattered across the pavement.

"Who you callin' a fucktard?" Sanjay demanded. "You wan' me come up dere and split you open?"

Chelle glared at me with an *Are you just gonna stand there?* challenge. Her eyes narrowed when I failed to immediately leap into my Superman unitard and smack some ganstah ass. She snarled at Sanjay instead and pointed at his crotch. "You'd have to get it up first."

That did it.

Sanjay and his buddy stalked forward past a line of suddenly disinterested, blind, deaf, and mute people. I was not ordinarily a violent person. The reason I avoid fights: I learned at an early age everyone in an eighteen-square-mile radius—including grandmas and small children—could beat the dog snot out of me without breaking a sweat.

I gave Chelle a *nice knowing you* smile and prepared to die.

"Hey, Sanjay, look..." I started forward, hands spread in supplication. "You know they can't treat it here, right? This clinic doesn't do that kind of medicine."

"Da hell?" Sanjay's eyebrows twisted together in a knot. He and his pal were close enough, I could smell the stupid rolling off them in waves, like the smell of unwiped ass.

"They can't fix burst testicles," I said and kicked him with maximum applied force in the nutsack. When you don't fight well, you learn to fight dirty.

Sanjay folded like a cheap lawn chair. Which left Fucktard #2 to take the lead in beating the shit out of Mean Joe Warren. Within half a second, I ate three punches in a row, all of them hard enough to rattle my brain and loosen a few teeth. The world spun—*Look! Pretty colors!*—and tilted under my feet. Legs wobbling worse than the Revvie on high heels, I bumbled around in a dizzy circle for a lost moment in time, then *whap!-thud!-smack!* Three more punches knocked me to the ground.

Pretty ground. Concrete. Old chewing gum. I like it down here. I think I'll stay.

Some other Joe Warren living nearby reported that Chelle had taken a piece of the action and was going all Loud Bitch Kung Fu on the green-shirted gangster, shrieking and clawing and kicking and spitting. Probably biting too.

I hoped she had her tetanus booster.

This all happened from far away, in a distant galaxy, with swirling stars and muted sounds. The other Joe told me the female Revivant had gotten to her feet and was wandering away. Her maid's outfit hung from her waist, leaving her topless. She didn't seem bothered. ("Fly-er, sir?")

"Bye-bye," I muttered, my breath blowing dust and candy wrappers away from my face.

A shadow eclipsed the sun, and a pair of black boots stopped in front of my nose. The soles were really, really thick.

Whap!

The dull, meat-like thud of hard object meeting soft skull sounds like nothing else. Once you've heard it, you never forget it. The gangster fell on the other side of the black boots. His right eye appeared to bulge from its socket, and there was a crease on that side of his head.

I forced my blurry vision to track upward to the source of that sound. A couple of years later, I found the top. Black boots, as noted already. Black pants bloused into the boot tops. Belt with a hardware store and armory attached. Black shirt with bright-blue patch on the sleeve. Badge. Riot helmet.

Homeland Security, to the rescue.

Yay.

Night-night, Mr. Police Officer.

"ARE YOU SURE YOU DON'T want to go to Chang's and get an ice pack?" Chelle asked me for the third time.

"Doe. I'm fine."

"Joe, your nose is all swollen and bloody."

"But I really hurd his ha'd."

"Yes, you did hurt his hand. He won't jack off for a week, that guy."

We were next in line at the clinic door, and I knew if I left now, they'd call Chelle, and I'd miss the eight-point-six seconds the doctor would spend with her. The gangsters had disappeared, Sanjay dragging his friend away and limping. The cop warned both of us not to start any more shit or he'd bust us on general principles. I asked where that was in the penal code, and Chelle thumped me in the ribs. The only part of me that didn't hurt, up to that point, was my ribs.

"Fud me, Chelle, dis better be good news. Dese test resulds."

"I'm sure they will," she said and bit her lip. A tall woman, Chelle could look me in the eye, but this time kept her gaze locked anywhere else but on me. She'd tied back her blondish hair, and I could see how her skin had paled and how gaunt her cheekbones had grown. I tended to forget how sick she really was, especially while I endured her bitch mode on a pretty much constant basis. For which, I grudgingly admitted to myself, maybe she had good reason.

"How're you feeling?" I coaxed, softening my voice.

She grimaced. "Not so good, Joe. It gets worse all the time."

I waited for more, but that seemed to be all she wanted to say.

"Next!" the nurse at the intake desk yelled.

"Dat's us!" I chirped with my bright, cheery Disney voice. We walked in, holding hands for the first time in as long as I could remember.

Five | Answer My Questions Three

I WOULD SAY THE PERSONNEL (I won't call them people) who staffed the clinic treated their patients like cattle, but that would be a lie. No one treated cattle that badly. My buddy Ding once described a doctor's visit as bending over, spreading your cheeks, and being grateful when they jammed the broom handle in and broke it off. I told him he'd gone on a good day.

The intake admin lady at the Wentworth Clinic had a face only a blind dog could love. She guarded the Bridge of Medical Intake from behind a bulletproof glass shield. It was the same woman as last time, and my soul shrank at the idea of going another few rounds with this particular guardian. Cerberus, her nametag read. No, I'm kidding, it really said Cherise, but I believed nametags should reflect function over appellation.

"Name?" barked Cherise when we approached the window. She didn't look up from her screen. "Last name first, first name last."

"Schweitzer, Michelle," my girlfriend said.

"DOB?"

"November third, 2027."

"Social Security Number?"

She recited her ten-digit number.

"Thumb here." Cherise pointed to the bio-reader, and Chelle placed her thumb on it. Why did they go through the drill of asking the same questions your thumbprint could answer for you? Another medical mystery I'd never understand. Cherise stabbed us with the same kind of expression she might apply to a splattering of dog vomit on her shoe. "You're late."

The rule was, once you answered Cherise's "questions three," you were allowed to pass to the prison cell-slash-waiting room where you served your time with the other detainees—sharing germs in a friendly, relaxed environment—until the RN granted you parole. If you displeased the Cherise the Bridge Keeper, you were vaulted into the Chasm of Doom, otherwise called the "next available appointment."

"The line..." Chelle motioned vaguely toward the people standing behind us.

"You should account for that when planning your visit."

"I know. I'm sorry," Chelle groveled, as meek and humble as I'd ever heard her. "Please, we've been waiting six months for my test results to come back—"

"Method of payment?"

"Uh, Affordable Health Care."

"Of course," the Bridge Keeper said. Flat. Toneless. "What was I thinking?" She tapped on her virtual keyboard long enough for me to count to a hundred and forty-seven, if I'd started from the beginning, which I didn't so I estimated.

"Go through," Cherise commanded and stamped Chelle's hand with a number.

Our pent-up breath flushed out at the same time, and we escaped through the interior door when the buzzer sounded. On the other side: the anteroom of hell.

Ninetyish coughing, sniffling, sneezing, hacking, bleeding, miserable people stuffed a room built for a hundred, giving it a piquant charm all its own. Searching the ten rows of hard plastic chairs, we found two seats together. The vid in the corner was running last year's *Sports Illustrated Nude Gymnastics* issue.

Sweet.

The tote board at the end of the room read **NOW SERVING: 1238** in glowing red numerals.

"Whad dumber did you ged?" I asked through my thick sinuses and angled for a look at the back of Chelle's hand. She held it up for me to see.

"Oh," I said in a small voice. "Thirteen-thirteen."

"Uh huh. Good thing I'm not superstitious, right?"

"Dock wood."

IN THE EXAM ROOM, I used some tissues and blew the blood and snot from my nose until I could speak without sounding like Elmer Fudd. Chelle situated her fanny on the torture table's paper cover—it crackled when she shifted—while I squatted on the short stool doctors used when they wanted to see you at groin level.

I rolled up and put my face between Chelle's knees, leered. "Hey, you want I should examine you?"

Strong girl. Somehow she withstood the temptation.

A doctor I'd never seen before breezed into the examination room carrying a tablet and a cup of coffee. He was about five-four, and the sleeves of his lab coat fell to the tips of his fingers. Smooth face, clear skin, small stature. Chelle failed to prep me about the doctor's size, so I later blamed her for what popped out of my mouth.

"Hi there, little guy. Is your dad coming too?"

He had a thin plastic nametag with Dr. Kleszczynska printed on it. His eyes were red-rimmed, and his hair had last seen a comb when disco was king. (The second time disco was king, not the 1970s.) The smell following him into the room carried a combination of cheap aftershave and pot reek. By the time my brain caught up to my eyes, my mouth had already fired that opening shot, with no way to take it back.

"Oh, ah... sorry, Doc," I mumbled. "I thought you were someone else."

Chelle rolled her eyes, but the doctor only looked confused. I found out why when he tried using English for the first time—probably in his life.

"Who paychent?" His bloodshot eyes swiveled from me to Chelle and back.

"Uh... me, Doctor," my girlfriend said.

I wanted to say, *No, you paychent, he doctor*, but I managed to hold my tongue.

He studied his tablet and frowned. "You Marcha Wah... Way... Wyant?"

"No, I'm Schweitzer. Michelle Schweitzer."

The doctor tapped his screen and muttered in a foreign language something that sounded like *fucking computer piece of shit crap electronic bullshit no-good fucking system*. But I could have been projecting.

"Ah. Schweitzer," he sort of said. I won't attempt to reproduce the sound that actually came out as I think he made up some consonants. "Here we, uh, you, are being."

He leaned against the sink while I swiveled back and forth. Dr. Strangename jacked with his tool. Computer, I mean. Silence encroached. He frowned. Tapped some more and frowned really hard.

My palms were sweating.

"Ah, Mizz Schweitzer." The doctor cleared his throat and kept his eyes glued to his screen. "I am being sorry to tell you this. Cerebral amebiasis is diagnosis. Not long you have to live. Please see front desk for referral to hospital for treatment. Is best to do soon. So sorry. Good-bye."

I flew off the stool and slapped the door shut before Dr. Charm could escape. "What? Say that again. She has what?"

His eyes bugged out with fright. "Is... ah... how you say? Tumor brain. Meck very sick." He shrugged. "Is too bad."

"Too bad!" My voice climbed the register to Getting Pissed. Chelle sat on the exam table with a blank look, as though struck by a monkey wrench. "What the fuck? What about medication? Tumor? From what?"

He consulted his tablet, holding it up between us like a shield. "Is from parasite. You know *Entamoeba histolytica*?"

"Yeah, sure, we're old friends." The sarcasm was lost on the doctor. "No, I don't! What are you talking about?"

"Ah, how say... ah, parasite, yes?" He peered at Chelle and asked, "You maybe eat bad food? Work near undead people."

"Revivants?" Chelle said in a small voice. Her eyes were fixed on a point across the room. "Yeah, down at the factory. They're everywhere."

"Ah."

"Ah, what?" I demanded.

"Oh, is maybe nossink." The witch doctor busied himself with his tablet and started babbling about fecal this and parasite that. Brain abscesses. Lesions breaking open.

Chelle didn't seem to hear him, so I asked, "What's the treatment?"

"Many good drugs now." He bobbed his head like a chicken. "See desk, go hospital. Maybe cured"—he snapped his fingers—"just like that. Or—"

"Or?"

He shrugged thin shoulders and sketched a rueful smile. "Is tumors on brain. Very dangerous, not catched soon. Maybe we catch earlier? No problem. Now...?"

"What do you mean, catch it earlier?" Spittle flew and sprinkled his forehead in a saliva shower. I had now reached a full-on Screeching Fit, forcing Dr. K to retreat until his back hit the wall. "She came in here six months ago! Your tests took that long to run! Are you telling me she's dying because you people couldn't get a test done?"

The doctor's hand snaked into his lab coat, and he fumbled with something there. Too late, I realized it was an alarm button. The door slammed open from the outside, pinning Dr. K behind it, and two HSA goons in riot helmets invaded the room, carrying stun rods. Their rush threw me back against Chelle, who tried to grab me, but I had too much momentum. I crashed to the floor, upsetting a bedpan and a bottle of tongue depressors from the side table.

"What's the problem here?" said Goon One. I recognized my friend from outside at the same moment he recognized me. "Oh. You."

Things got hazy for me after that.

Later, I vaguely recalled jumping up and wang-chunging the living shit out of both cops, the doctor, *and* the bitch out front. My Frenzied Ferret Fu was strong. I dropped Goon One with the old classic, Drop-Kick to Nuts, followed by Spinning Bedpan and Dragon Tongue Depressor to the Throat. I chucked Goon Two through the wall using a combination of Gassy Tornado and High Karate Chop to the Spleen. I beat Dr. K senseless with his stethoscope.

On Cherise, I used a flamethrower. No sense getting too close to the dragon in her lair. Stand off and nuke 'em from orbit; it's the only way to be sure.

Later, Chelle shook her head and told me, "It didn't happen that way at all. Joe, they beat you like cake batter."

Texas Twang

"That the lot?" Homeland Agent Ben Maravich wiped sweat from his forehead with the tail of his black T-shirt. Fucking Texas. He hated fucking Texas at any time of the year as the temperature always seemed one degree warmer than hell. Hated Texas the state and Texas the attitude. Everything here, from the people to the lizards to the plant life, hated the federal government and its humble servants like Benny Maravich and his partner Angel Ramirez. Everything in Texas wanted to kill you or suck your blood, or both.

"That's all," the stubby Ramirez confirmed. "I'm going to call it in."

Six men, four women, and eight scruffy kids lined the fence in the front yard of the rural homestead in the Ass-end of Nowhere, sixty miles south of Fort Worth. Kneeling in the dirt, wrists plasti-cuffed behind their backs, they didn't look like much now. Certainly not the terrorists their activities revealed them to be.

Scrawny chickens head-bobbed across the yard, clucking and restless at the multiple vehicles and dozen team members of the Terrorist Interdiction Taskforce (and if Maravich could ever find the bureaucrat who came up with that name, he'd gladly turn the prick into walking dead meat), lounging in whatever shade they could find. They'd shot the dogs on the way in, and flies circled the blackened, glistening blood matting the dead mutts' fur.

A pencil-thin cat slunk under the house and disappeared before Maravich could draw and fire. He hated cats worse than Texans.

The patriarch of this little clan of anti-government libertines twisted his head around and fixed Maravich with a green-eyed glare of distilled bile. "You got no right to do this. We ain't did nothin' to you people."

"Learn English, ya mook," Maravich sneered. "Didn't they teach you nothing in school? And, yeah, you did do something. See that?" He pointed to a stack of illegally modified AR-15s. "And we got emails and voice recordings of you preaching sedition: overthrow of the U.S. government."

"Overthrow?" the man scoffed. "Overthrow? All we wanted was to be left alone. The only thing I preached was to get out from under Uncle Sam."

"That's not what you said when the farm subsidies payouts rolled around. I noticed you lined up with your hand out like all the rest of your backwoods motherfuckering buddies."

"You tell 'em, Benny!" one of the gathered taskforce officers called out. He and his buddies lounged in a circle in the meager shade of a lightning-cleaved oak. Dressed in black TAC gear, the men dripped sweat, spat nicotine-free dipping tobacco, and waved at the flies and mosquitoes dive-bombing them from the air.

"Shut up, Daniel," the woman next to the green-eyed farmer hissed. "Keep shut, or no tellin' what these sunsabitches will do."

"Listen to your woman, Farmer John," Maravich warned. "I'm hot, I'm pissed, and I hate this fucking state and all you people in it. No telling what I'll do."

"Understood, sir. We'll make it happen." Ramirez came back at the end of his call, tapping the connection off.

"So?" Maravich asked with a raised eyebrow.

"The evidence is clear." Ramirez kept his voice pitched low so only Maravich could hear. "We have a green light for summary judgment, based on Executive Order 22666."

"Cool." Maravich eyeballed the oak branches overhanging the yard. He called out to the leader of the TAC agents lounging in its shade. "You think that tree will hold the weight?"

The lieutenant squinted, considering. "Not if we do them all at once. Maybe three or four of the adults, do them first. The kids will go in a batch."

"Finest kind," Maravich said. "Get the ropes, boys. It's piñata time!"

Ever serious, Ramirez frowned. "That's not funny, Agent Maravich. These people will be relocated to Camp Dakota for reform and cultural alignment."

"You're right, amigo. No doubt." Maravich grinned. "But I do so enjoy hearing the rope twang when a Texan drops. It's music to my ears." He sighed. "But the bounty's higher for live bodies. Let's get 'em loaded, boys!"

I STIFLED A SCREAM and only whimpered a little when Chelle applied the ice pack to my head. I'm manly that way. We were back in our palatial apartment, where I reclined on our single piece of living room furniture, an antique (curbside pickup) sofa. The cushions smelled faintly of urine.

"So what'd Dr. Buyavowel say after I mopped the floor with him and his goons?"

Chelle slouched on the floor next to me. Her forehead glistened with sweat. She was the one dying, and here I was, taking my leisure on the only cushiony thing in the living room-slash-dining room-slash-kitchen.

Real manly.

"After they zapped you unconscious—you peed yourself, by the way—"

"Oh. I thought that was the sofa making that smell."

"—the assistant searched for a hospital with an opening. Everything's booked up for months." She choked up, and her voice roughened. "Any minute I could start having seizures, or go into a coma and never wake up again." She snapped her fingers. "Dead. Just like that."

"Don't worry, Chelle." I patted her shoulder. "Tomorrow morning I'll get up early, go down there and put my foot down. We'll find a way through the red tape and get you cured."

"Sure," she said, without a shred of emotion. "They gave me a pamphlet. I can opt to become a Revivant before I die, which will mean I can continue to be *a productive member of society*." Chelle grunted with the effort of getting off the floor and wobbled toward the bathroom. "I need to throw up now."

I watched her backside and tried to feel the spark that view once inspired. It didn't even flicker. We'd had something once, but it was the classic story of high school boy meets high school girl, knocks her up, they move in together, she miscarries and they live together long enough to hate each other. Or at least to not love each other the way they once did. Funny how life jerks your chain. Before the doctor's visit, I'd been planning to break up with Chelle and give us both a chance to move on, but dumping her now would be a really shitty thing to do.

The door thunked closed, and minutes later the sound of muffled sobbing trickled through the apartment.

I stayed on the sofa and pretended I couldn't hear.

News Bytes

User CNN@cnn.com: #entitlements. HHS Secretary Marciela Zapata said there would be no cuts in Medicare, AHC, Social Security, or any other entitlement for the foreseeable future.

User tom_T_baker: Who's paying for that?

User gran75015: Better not b any cuts. I need my pills.

User BaronDlight: @tom_t_baker. Fuckin natzee assw-hole. STFU an pay you're taxes.

Six | A Series of Seriously Fucked Up Events

PRE-DAWN IN ARMOUR Square. A magic hour when the addicts nodded over their needles, and dreaming ganstahs rode the Scarface Express to the top o' da world. Morning sun bled into the sky, its ruby light sparkling on streets salted with broken glass. Dew frosted rows of silent cars parked in lonely rows, and feral dogs boldly roamed the sidewalks, baring their teeth in reflexive hatred at any challenger. Football-sized vermin rattled through overflowing dumpsters. A growling mongrel crouched over a fur-and-blood... something... in the doorway of an abandoned office building.

A chilly, cloudless morning found me huddled in my peacoat, yawning and shuffling my way the hell down Michigan Avenue, north of 13th Street. Having missed the five a.m. No. 24 bus, I had hoofed it all the way from the apartment, working loose the kinks from a night of half-sleep and bad dreams.

Window reflections showed me a face painted with bruises and contusions. My jaw was sore and flared with pain every time I yawned, which was, like, twice a minute.

I waited in line for an hour to hit up the kind folks at Mission Mondrigal for breakfast—powdered eggs, toast, and weak coffee—for which I was appropriately thankful. I asked for some take-out for Chelle, but they didn't have to-go boxes.

After that, I made the epic trek to the Office of Benefits and Welfare on Roosevelt. It didn't open until eight, but when I turned the corner, I found the line stretched the entire block between Michigan and Wabash.

The wind off the lake made me shiver, despite the sun crawling higher, and it whipped empty paper cups and fast-food wrappers around my ankles. I joined the line behind a woman in an ankle-length granny skirt made of sheer white lace. Underneath the skirt, she wore a thong and goose pimples, and had her arms wrapped around herself, chafing her biceps. I pictured Chelle and decided to withhold from this frozen waif the warmth of my embrace.

The OBW office opened at eight fifteen instead of the promised eight o'clock, and I followed the line through the security scanner—the Homeland guys ran a wand over Ms. Thong but ignored me—into the waiting room, took my number, and hung out until they called me to Room 2, Cube 502. I found 502 in a maze of cube walls, in Row 5, believe it or not, between cubes 501 and 504. No sign of 503.

Bureaucrat 502 was an eager puppy named R. Killingsworth—it said so in magic marker written on a masking-tape label under the cube number placard. He pumped my hand like he wanted top billing in my Last Will and Testament, and told me the R stood for Rogair. He spelled it for me, in case I missed the nuance of pronunciation.

"So what brings you in today, Mr....?"

"Warren. Joseph Warren."

"Mr. Warren, how can we help?" He used the royal "we" to indicate he and the rest of the federal government, I supposed. Rogair was my age, or thereabouts, somewhere between twenty-four and twenty-eight, with a flattop and long sideburns, a bright-pink shirt, and a complexion of innocent happiness. He had a thin, perfect nose and a delicate jaw and the most hazel eyes of any human I'd ever met. I couldn't decide if I wanted to hate him or date him.

"I, uh, I..." Now that I was here, my brain slogged to a halt. "I've never done this before, Rogair. I mean, gone on the dole, so to speak. I've got, uh, you know, food stamps and unemployment on account of losing my job, and all, but..."

"There's no shame in coming to the OBW for help, Mr. Warren." Rogair's expression of sympathetic caring could have cured cancer. "Millions of people need help these days, and that's what your tax dollars are for, yes?"

"Uh. Yeah, I guess so." Seeing as how my income had been so low, I hadn't paid taxes in two years, I had to admit the rationale tasted a little flat. "I've never really thought about it."

"No problem, no problem. Think of me as your coach, Joseph. May I call you Joseph? I'll be showing you the ropes and getting you hooked up with all the services to which you're entitled. Before we begin, place your thumb here." Rogair held out a wireless biopad the size of a cube of pool chalk. The finger spot was worn from hun-dreds—thousands—of previous applicants for federal assistance. I touched it briefly, and a green light indicated a solid read.

"Awesome." Rogair beamed. "Just awesome."

I rubbernecked while my coach fiddled with his computer screen. The inside of Room 2 had the charm of a cell block. Institutional, featureless walls painted a dull white and hung with motivational posters and government edicts, the room was filled with a warren of identical gray cubicles. Rogair had decorated the inside of Cube 502 with wall-mounted pictures of his (I assumed) parents and girlfriend, and, in a desktop viewer, a 3D shot of him and a tabby cat held near his face. The cat looked highly pissed.

I occupied one of two straight-back chairs designed by a sadist for maximum butt pain, whereas Rogair wobbled back and forth in a squeaky roller chair. In addition to the aforementioned portrait of Rogair and Cat Killingsworth, the desk sported a healthy potted ivy, a desktop monitor, and a basket of pens and styluses—styli? A squeezy stress ball hid under the ivy.

"Ah!" Rogair made a noise like he'd discovered masturbation, his eyes lit by the glowing screen. His chair cried out when he moved. *Squeak-squeak.* "Here we are. Joseph Adam Warren, age twenty-six, Caucasian male, one-point-seven-five meters, seventy-three kilos. Born to Denise and Ross Warren at Mercy Clinic in Napier, Illinois. Completed two years of college at Northwestern before quitting. Why was that, I wonder? Test scores in high school, college prep exams, all in the 97th percentile, so you were certainly bright enough. Hmm." Rogair seemed lost in the digital me, having forgotten the real me sitting across from him. *Squeak-squeak.* He crossed his arms and tapped his cheek with one finger. "Super-high scores on aptitude and achievement tests... last employed as a, oh my, at SteelWerks CNC here in Chicago, operating a High-Output 3D Tool & Die Printer. Laid off—what?—two years ago and a bit? Unemployment drawn biweekly since that time. Enrolled in SNAP. That's okay, Joseph, no shame in food stamps. We all have to eat. What else do we see here...? Appendix removed, age twelve. Living with Michelle Schweitzer, government housing project on 23rd Place, for the last six-plus years. Phone disconnected July of last year. No TV, no Internet. Good gracious, how do you live, Joe? That sounds like hell on earth."

He contemplated me for the first time in his long soliloquy and blinked, maybe surprised I was still there. *Squeak-squeak-squeakle.*

"Library," I said. "I spend a lot of time at the library."

"My goodness, I'll bet you do. Have you tried submitting a 2214-C? You can get a free netphone if you meet the requirements. Are you bi-gendered in any way? A victim of attempted denial of entry into this country? No? Pity." *Squeak-squick.* "Let's see here... High school disciplinary action for behavioral issues... altercations with police one, two, three... good gosh, how many times? Eight times, Joseph? My you have been a bad boy."

"I have a big mouth and issues with authority." I shifted and cleared my throat. "Two things that don't go over well, huh?"

"No, I would say not." Rogair pursed his lips and ooched forward in his chair. *Screech-squawk.* He tapped his touchscreen monitor a few times. "Your record shows both parents deceased, and you have a sibling, Marissa, age twenty-two. Does she still live with you?"

"No, she's married. Lives in Baltimore."

"Too bad," my coach mused. "You might have qualified under the Americans with Dependent Siblings Act. I don't suppose you have any children?"

I hated to dash Rogair's hopes. "No, sorry."

"Any children you can claim as yours not living with you?"

"Huh-uh."

"Oh, well. Can't be helped." *Squeak-squawk.* "Okay, then, this all looks good. Let me run your income tax returns."

Ah. Shit. "Um, do you have to?"

Coach Rogair frowned. A ray of darkness had pierced his silver cloud. "Of course we do. Sub-section C of Chapter 22 of the Federal Code of Managed Benefits. We need to establish your earning history and your fiscal standing in order to assess what benefits might apply." He tapped and squeaked without looking up. "Why? Is there some—oh, my."

"Okay, that's not me. I had my identity stolen when I was sixteen and—"

"This says you have earned in excess of twelve million dollars last year."

"—and when the Social Security Administration fixed it, they got my records—"

"And nine million the year before that. Why would you be applying for government assistance with that kind of wealth at your disposal, Mr. Warren?"

"—crossed up with a pharmacy chain out of Dearborn called Warren's. It's in the IRS database now, and I can't—"

"Fraudulent claims for benefits is a serious crime, Mr. Warren. Do you know how many people try and scam us every day?"

"—get the IRS to fix it. I've been down to their office in person like eighteen times in the last ten years. I keep—"

"Dozens, Mr. Warren. Dozens of people try and scam us every day." Rogair practically vibrated with disapproval. His arms were crossed, and his mouth crimped into a thin line. Two red spots glowed on his cheeks, and more red flushed his neck.

"But I'm not one of them, Rogair," I maintained. How many times would I have to tell this story? Every time, apparently. "Not a scammer, I mean. Literally, I'm telling you, the IRS database is screwed up. I can email you my W2's... well I could if I had a netphone—but I can bring them to you. Today. Look, you said it yourself, I was employed as a CNC Printer. How much do you think that pays?"

"I don't need your W2's," Rogair said with a sniff. He twirled his monitor around to show me the screen. "It shows your earnings records right here. That's your name, correct?"

"Yes, but—"

"It was your fingerprint ID that pulled up these records, yes?"

"Yes, but—"

"And that's your income, right there on Line 16. Twelve million, four hundred and sixty-one thousand, eight hundred and eight dollars." He sniffed again and leaned back. *Squeakle-squark.* "And fifty-two cents."

"None of which is mine. I'm telling you, the IRS database is wrong."

"The IRS?"

"Yes."

"Is wrong?"

"Yes, exactly. I had my social security number stolen and—"

"I think you'd better leave now, Mr. Warren."

"—when I tried to get it fixed, the lady at—"

"You need to leave, Mr. Warren."

"—the IRS office got in a hurry or something, you know how these things go—"

"Mr. Warren! Leave! Now! Before I call Homeland and have you arrested for fraud." Coach Rogair's face had gone beet red. People in other cubes were craning their heads out, like turtles with square shells. The only sound in the office was the ringing of desk phones going unanswered.

Humiliation flourished.

I left.

Squeak-squeak. Not Rogair's office chair—that was the sound of my ass puckering up as I walked.

I clattered down the stairs rather than wait on an elevator, crossed the lobby past the homeland cops screening and patting down the supplicants, and shouldered through the glass doors onto Roosevelt.

And stumbled smack into a street riot.

Seven | The Government is my Shepherd and I Shall Not Want

WELL, OKAY, MAYBE "RIOT" was an exaggeration.

Forecasters say conditions are right for a tornado when they see rotational patterns forming along the leading edges of an apocalyptomous wall cloud. That's what we had here. A solid wall-cloud of protestors lined the sidewalk along Roosevelt, marching in a rotational pattern in front of the OBW office. Surrounding them and blocking the street at both ends were platoons of HSA storm troopers (*storm troopers...* heh) in full riot gear and ball-crushing attitudes.

The marchers chanted, "We. The. People!" in cadence as they looped an oval track along the sidewalk. I bumbled through the office door and straight into a college-age scruffball with a monster beard and thick, black-framed glasses who carried a sign reading, "Life, Liberty, Pursuit of Happiness." Each word was crossed out in bold, red strokes.

"Sorry." I staggered back into the doorway—a space large enough for one anorexic ferret—avoiding collision with the next protestor, whose sign said, "Land of the Freeloader." At the bottom edge, the words "Children of Liberty" were printed in block letters.

Ah, hell no.

The next person in the parade, a dumpy, plain woman of thirty or so, lifted and lowered her poster in time to the chant. A snicker bubbled up my throat when I read, in green-lettered words: *Choked by the Yolk of Tyranny.* The lady glared ice picks into my brain without breaking stride or losing her place in the chant when I asked her, "What have you got against eggs?"

"We. The. People!"

Protestors. More irritating than a salty ass-crack.

Argh, I so hated politics.

Any kind of politics was a waste of time, but especially fanatical politics—always so fucking earnest, always so fucking sure about everything... It made me sick, the way they acted, as if they held the One Truth. *Here*, their recruiters said, *sign on the bottom line; check your brain at the door*. The acolytes of the Children of Liberty were the most bug-eyed zealots in the Wacko Parade, an anti-government gaggle of anarchists and extremists bent on tearing down the protection and safety guaranteed by the Constitution. What a crock of shit. These people were worse than Jehovah's Witnesses, who would at least dress nicely before allowing their dogma to hump your leg.

"We. The. *People!*" The chant had grown stronger as the police completed deploying at both ends of the block. The protestors' faces were red and sweaty with effort and enthusiasm. Or maybe orgasmic release.

The Homeland troops appeared a little edgy, slapping palms with riot sticks and fiddling with face masks. I breathed in a strong odor of Head Busting tinged with Whip Ass. I was allergic to that scent. The revolving idiot line crammed me into the shallow portico of the OBW offices; I could shove my way out, go back inside to Rogair's warm embrace, or don my Cloak of Invisibility and sneak away.

"*We!* The. *People!*"

The damned chant sanded my last nerve and squeezed lemon juice on it.

Blue sawhorses barricaded Roosevelt at both ends, and blocky vans with light bars and shiny black sides waited behind them. I counted six of the brontosaurus-sized trucks and a plethora of smaller squad cars. No gas rationing for the police, now was there? A small army of riot-suited robots cracked their knuckles and grinned with fangs dripping venom. No, I'm joking; what they really did was form up in lines from one side of the street to the next, in front of the barricades, and lift shields like some medieval line of pike pokers.

"*We! The! People!*"

Match, meet gasoline.

Time to scoot.

"Excuse me!" I shouted and shoved into the deck full of jokers, knocking a skinny true believer out of line and interrupting him the middle of "PEE-pull."

"Hey!"

I ignored him and squeezed past the next guy in line, a balloon-shaped dude with frizzy hair, not old enough to shave.

"*We!* The! *People!*"

Holy Mother of Thesaurus, couldn't these fuckers find another three words?

I bumped and tussled, bouncing between protestors and the concrete wall, making my way upstream, which in hindsight, seemed a poor choice of direction. I had come from Michigan Avenue, so like a salmon returning to his home stream to get laid, I went back the way I came. It would have been better to use the line's momentum to shoot me out toward Wabash and go south from there. Hindsight is a brass-balled bastard.

"*We!* The! *People!*"

A few more Children of Little Brains and I'd be in the clear. The cops, I hoped, would ignore me as small beer and go for the brewery of demonstrators. I could slip away and head for the clinic and my date with the dragon lady, Cherise.

A body blocked the sun and cast darkness across the land. I flattened against the wall to avoid being crushed under the mighty heels of the biggest human I'd ever seen. This seven-foot giant strode the earth in tan shorts and a blue jersey with the number twenty-seven stitched to it. The jersey's sleeves strained against the pressure of arms bigger than my waist, and each of the man's legs must have weighed more than I could lift. Red-haired with a light, freckled complexion, he was jock handsome, with a square jaw, straight nose, and green eyes. He didn't bother carrying a sign, merely thrusting one sledge-hammer fist into the air at every word.

"We! The. People!" Thor thundered as he passed.

Holy fee-fi-fo-fum, the guy was huge. I blinked and drew a shuddering breath. Back plastered against the wall, I slid toward daylight. Escape. Freedom. Happiness. A few more meters would do it.

A can bounced and rolled under my feet, spewing smoke.

"Oh, hell no." Tear gas, or vomit gas; either way I was fucked.

The once-orderly lineup broke apart, flying into a demolition derby of scattering, panicked humans.

Now, it was a riot.

The first taste of gas hit my nostrils and burned my eyes from their sockets. No shit. On fire. Like hot pokers jammed in my face.

"Get out of my way!" I screamed. Blindly, with acid fear squeezing my throat, I stiff-armed the milling, formless, shrieking crowd. Gibbering in the back of my brain, my own little panic-monkey rattled the bars of his cage and threw turds against the wall, threatening me with eviction from Planet Sane if I didn't get out of this scrum of... stupid... *assholes*!

The crowd decompressed for a heartbeat, and I made one violent push between two unseen bodies, breaking into the open. Blinking streams of water from both eyes and coughing up bits of lung, I caught a glimpse of clear pavement ahead... for a meter... until a wall of police black filled my blurry vision.

"Wait," I yelled between coughs, "I'm... not with... them!"

Whap!

The dull, meat-like thud of hard object meeting soft skull sounds like nothing else. Once you've heard it—

COLD FLOOR.

Smell of vomit. Blood.

Crying. Low-pitched voices. Muttering. Bitching. Pleading.

Jail. I was in jail again. I'd recognize the *je ne sais quoi* of the atmosphere anywhere. Aromas of industrial cleaner and human waste. Greenish fluorescent lighting (which I avoided by keeping my eyes firmly shut) and gray iron bars everywhere. The technology of jails hadn't really changed in nine hundred years: you built cages, you shoved people in, and you locked the doors so they didn't wander off.

Incarceration ensued.

"Fuck me," I grumbled under my breath. How did I get in these situations?

I opened one crusty eye, and a shoe filled my entire range of view. I cracked the other eye, doubling my perspective and adding stereoscopic depth, and it helped not at all. Shoe. Athletic. One. As seen from the side.

I lifted my head, peeling one cheek from the slick tile floor with a sound like ripping masking tape. "Ow."

The shoe stirred, and a voice rumbled from above, "Are you all right?"

I tracked the sound up one tree-trunk leg, over a bowling-ball-sized knee, and found a cheerful, freckled face looming over me. The giant from the protest march. I deduced he was seated on a bench while I, on the other hand, abided in peaceful repose on the floor, along with enough germs to take down a bull elephant.

"Mmurphh," I grunted and sat up. "Oh, shit, that hurts."

"I believe it." The giant spoke with a deep, resonant voice, with very distinct enunciation. No accent I could detect, which made him a freak in more ways than his size. Who grows up without an accent?

"My ribs." I winced and probed the tender spot under my arm, where it felt like—

"Yes, they kicked you after you were down."

"Oh, you think?"

He nodded gravely. "I do. I saw it happen."

My head chose that moment to remind me of its recent meeting with a hard object; pain lanced from one temple to the other. "Aw, jeezus-pleezus, that feels like a knitting needle through the brain."

"The brain has no nerve endings," Gargantua informed me. "It would feel nothing."

"Thank you, Mr. Literal."

"You're welcome. But my name is John."

"Of course it is. You wouldn't happen to be Vulcan, would you, John?"

"No, I'm from Idaho."

"Good. Good to know."

John the Prodigious Pedant and I inhabited one corner of a ten-square-meter holding cell occupied by two dozen fellow prisoners. I recognized Bearded Guy and Yolk Lady among the detainees. Three solid brick walls and one of bars surrounded us. A tile floor and a gray concrete ceiling capped top and bottom. If I stood on John's mighty shoulders, I might've reached the steel mesh cover that protected a bank of fluorescent lighting. Not that it would help, but it was nice to know I could.

"Because it's there," I grumbled.

"What?"

"Nothing, just babbling."

"That's typical of head wounds," he cautioned me with the seriousness of a mortician. "You should see a doctor."

"First thing on my to-do list, Little John."

John smiled and reached out a frying pan with fingers to help me up. "Everybody calls me that."

"Hnhh," I grunted and let him haul me to my feet. Swayed there. Examined the pretty colors in my head. "Imagine that. People have no creativity these days. What the hell happened?"

"We got arrested for protesting."

I could see I would need to phrase my questions more precisely with John. Standing—listing—in front of the big man, I could zero in on his earnest green eyes without getting a crick in my neck. "John. Pay attention. Why did we—meaning you, since I was a by-stander—get arrested? Didn't you have a permit?"

John's mouth thinned out, and his pleasant expression evaporat-ed. "We couldn't get a permit. Every time we tried, it was denied, so we decided to practice our right to free speech without it." He shrugged. "You see what happened."

"Well, yeah. But permits are sort of required—"

"We—"

"Hold that thought." I held out a palm to stop whatever cocka-mamie protest would come out of his mouth. Debate lunatics and you become a lunatic debater. Besides, a commotion at the cell doors stirred the crowd; everyone bubbled up for a look-see, including me. I left John and joined the group close to the front of the cell.

A pair of guards flanked a white-haired sergeant, who held a key fob in one hand and a tiny reader in the other. The guards carried stun batons and wore flak jackets and helmets with face shields, and the sergeant displayed three stripes on his sleeve and a chunky belly over his belt. His nametag declaimed Ledbetter in bold white letters.

Sergeant Ledbetter consulted the reader before he regarded the prisoners. "Warren, Joseph," he yelled. My heart seized up. "Warren, Joseph, front and center. Agents want to see you."

My feet froze in place, and intelligence derailed from the main line, crashing into a steaming pile by the gateway to coherent thought. A metallic taste invaded my mouth, and I clenched up to avoid an embarrassing accident. It was never-ever-and-for-all-eternity *bad* to come to the attention of the Homeland Security Agency's higher echelons. Get ass-kicked by a cop? Sure, any day. Get noticed by the guys in suits? I'd rather stick my dick in a disposal.

After the Department of Homeland Security had transmogrified into the Homeland Security Agency and swallowed up the FBI, ICE, and the DEA, they'd become more powerful than an avalanche and equally as likely to bury you alive if you didn't get your miniscule ass out of the way. Local police departments had been absorbed into the collective as the HSA seeped across the country and assumed a greater role in law enforcement. Cities went broke, and the feds swooped in, amalgamating their infrastructure along with the commensurate budget required to operate them.

I'd come close to serious encounters of the judicial kind more than once, scraping by with help from Lucky the Leprechaun and a lack of real interest by the Men in Black as my crimes were juvenile in scope and pathetic in execution.

I had the feeling my little friend Lucky was running for his life, hands over his charmed green hat, headed for the nearest bomb shelter.

News Bytes

User CNN@cnn.com: #deficit. US budget deficit growth slowed to $442 billion per month, remaining steady for the last quarter, according to the GAO.

Eight | Jailhouse Rock

THE OLD JAILER AND his Robocop pals led me to a sterile white interrogation room containing a battle-scarred table and two straight-back chairs. The A/V recording equipment was discreetly hidden, high in opposite corners of the room, two tiny bulbs the size of scarab beetles, as white as the surrounding walls. I only noticed because I notice things like that. It gives me an illusion of control.

"Will you be serving lunch while I wait?" I asked. "I have low blood sugar issues."

"Fuck you." Ledbetter didn't bother looking up from the vid playing on his reader.

"No thanks, but a hand job would be nice."

The guards used a teeny-tiny bit more force than absolutely necessary to get me in the prisoner's chair and snap a shock collar around my neck. They removed the wrist cuffs and left the room without speaking, though the sergeant communicated a warm sense of human compassion with a single-digit salute. I was A-number-1, according to him.

Interrogation rooms were something else that hadn't changed in hundreds of years, except now they had a video terminal on the prisoner's side of the table. If you had a substantial bank balance, you could plug your bit-stick into the terminal's port and have an attorney present via web conference. If you had a medium bank balance, you could use the terminal to access one of a hundred automated services that dispensed legal advice in a series of yes-no questions. (Have you been charged with a crime? For Yes, click here. For No, click here. Was this a felony? Do you wish to plea bargain at this time?) They claimed they had a legally binding response programmed for every possible situation and could present advice in multiple languages and countless dialects. My close brushes with the law had given me some insight into the legal system—that and I watched a lot of vid.

If you had no bank balance—and time on your hands—you could hold out for a public defender. May God rest your soul. I'd met PDs who might have slept with a law book under their pillow once, but the rest had as much chance in a real courtroom as I would winning at blindfolded grenade catching.

The door opened to admit a hobbit in a shimmery gray satin suit, polished black shoes, and a bloodred cravat. This guy should get together with Chelle's doctor and play racquetball; they could use a curb as a backstop.

"Hey," I said before he took his seat, "if you hook up with John the Giant back there in holding, you could sit on his knee and make a great ventriloquist act."

"I am Agent Ramirez," he intoned. "You may call me Agent Ramirez."

"See, you already talk like he does."

Ramirez studied me the way a surgeon examines colon polyps. He had a smooth face, hooded eyes, and slick jet-black hair. And a nice suit, or did I mention that already? He carried a handheld reader—must be department issue, to sergeants and above—and consulted it while giving me a chilled shoulder to not cry on.

Do his feet touch the floor? I held back my impulse to check under the table.

"Warren, Joseph Adam," Ramirez began. "Born 14 July—"

"Not this again? Coach Rogair already told me who I am, do you have to do it too?"

Ramirez plowed over my outburst, reading off my vital statistics with the enthusiasm of a corpse. He raised his hooded eyes to me when he finished.

"Will there be a test later?" I wondered.

Ramirez said nothing. He made a production out of unwrapping a piece of Doc Smith's THC chewing gum and popping it in his mouth. No wonder he had sleepy eyes; chewing cannabis gum will tend to do that. He offered me the pack.

"No, thanks. It makes me ill."

After he got his gum settled, Ramirez said, "How long have you been associated with the Children of Liberty, Mr. Warren?"

"Whoa. Hold on there, Agent. I'm not with those people. I was applying for benefits when your goons snagged me. See this? This knot on the side of my head? I'm seriously thinking about bringing some kind of formal complaint for excessive force and false arrest. However... if you let me go now, I'll consider that an apology, and we'll be square." I leaned back and crossed my arms.

"When did you first join the Children of Liberty?" The expression on the detective's face could have been cast in bronze. The man never seemed to blink. Maybe he was a new-model Revivant—one that didn't smell and chewed pot-laced gum.

"I'm telling you, I'm not one of them. Never have been. I hate politics of any form."

"Do you hate the government, Mr. Warren?"

"No! Well... I'm a little pissed at it right this minute, but overall, no. I think the government does a great job." I started ticking things off with my fingers. "I live in a HUD project apartment, I draw unemployment, SNAP, free health care... I live in a safe and secure community thanks to dedicated officers such as yourself." That last may have been spreading the icing too thick, so I leaned back and threw up my hands. "I mean, shit, think about it. I could be living in Russia, or Venezuela, or some other communist hellhole and be ten times worse off. No, Agent Ramirez, I love America, just the way it is."

Other than his jaw working his gum, the stubby cop didn't twitch a muscle. A cold bead of sweat ran down my spine, and a whopping-hard pulse thumped my neck. Every beat stabbed a painful shock through my head. Fuck what Literal John said, my brain had nerve endings, and they were all singing the same hymn, "Oh Woe is Me."

"Who recruited you to join the CoL?" Ramirez asked without inflection.

Seriously? Was this guy from a different planet?

"I was an *innocent... by... stander.* I was coming out of the OBW on Roosevelt when I ran into the parade. I tried to tell the moth-erf—the riot control officers, but they wouldn't listen."

"The OBW?"

"Yes, the Office of Benefits and Welfare."

"You said you were coming out?"

"Yes. Exactly."

"Who did you see?"

"Excuse me?"

"Who did you meet with at the OBW?"

Oh, fuckadoodle. Rogair would confirm I was there, but would he feed the cops his attempted fraud fantasy? Would he jam me up for something else I didn't do? The answer: Yes, in a heartbeat. And when he did, how long until all that got sorted out?

Forever.

"I, uh... I don't remember his name." I touched my scalp and winced. "Head injury, you know. It's all fuzzy, that time there in the actual office."

"Fuzzy."

"Yeah. Hazy, y'know." Inspiration struck. "Hey, don't I get to have an attorney present? Isn't that in the Constitution somewhere?"

"Mr. Warren." The agent's face locked down, tightening to a latex skin mask like it was heat-sealed. "I got back from an assignment in Texas late last night. I'm not in the mood for flippancy. You have been arrested pursuant to an investigation of a known domestic terrorist group. Under the Homeland Protection Act of 2024, all your Miranda rights have been suspended until such time as you are cleared of any crimes against the state." Ramirez leaned forward and put his face as close to mine as his stubby body would allow. The sickly-sweet smell of THC gum puffed from his mouth as he spoke. He never raised his voice above a monotone when he said, "In short, Mr. Warren, I can throw you in a deep, dark hole and have six guys with batons do unspeakable things to you for as long as I want. Your skank girlfriend will die of a brain tumor long before you ever see the light of day, and your asshole will be as big as a freeway tunnel when you do. I will fuck you over until you die if you don't stop fucking with me right fucking now. Am I making myself perfectly clear, Mr. Joseph Adam Warren?"

Which was worse? That I could be subject to this guy's homosexual fantasies, or that he knew Chelle had a terminal disease? We only got that diagnosis yesterday! How was that poss—?

"Am I clear, Mr. Warren?"

"Crystal," I rasped through a sandpaper-dry throat. "Ah, very crystal. Sir."

He leaned back, gum grinding with regular, measured flexes of his jaw. "Good. Now, start from the top and tell me your bullshit story. But remember... if you waste one tiny fraction of a second of my time, I will bury you in the basement of this building, and rats will eat you down to the bone."

"Uh... sure. No problem. Could I, uh... could I get some water, please?"

THE CHUBBY SERGEANT and his twin satellites escorted me through the booking process. I got the full spa treatment—strip search, delousing shampoo, cold shower, quick medical check, and a stiff, chemical-smelling orange jumpsuit to wear. I was so numb, I tottered through each stage like a wind-up toy with a bad spring. Every so often, a guard would need to shove me to get me moving again.

They didn't seem to mind. The shoving, I mean.

Ramirez had wrung me out so thoroughly, a dead man's dick had more spunk. I told him everything from that day, including a vivid description of Thong-Woman's butt. I started with what I had for breakfast, segued to what I said to Rogair, the IRS mess I was in, what I felt about the Cubs' shot at repeating as world champs this year, and how often I clipped my toenails. He never wrote a note, nor did he comment beyond asking for an occasional clarification. When I ran out of things to talk about, the agent spit his gum into a trash can, got up, and left. I slumped in my chair until the three amigos showed up for my trip through Jailhouse Funland.

A long corridor of cell doors waited at the end of the ride. Somewhere along the way, Sergeant Ledbetter had dropped out of the procession and left me to the tender mercy of Frick and Frack. They, at least, seemed more ambivalent than hostile and only got worked up if I moved too slowly or didn't understand the instructions they recited in monotone without punctuation.

They stopped me in front of a cell midway in the row on the left and waited. A buzzer blared, the lock snicked, and the door grumbled open. With a flourish, Frack invited me to my new room, wished me a pleasant stay, and said to call the front desk if I needed more towels.

Inside I found a four-person cell with two bunk beds on each side, a toilet, and a sink with a steel mirror. Three of the four beds were occupied, leaving only the cot on the lower left available. I guessed that was mine.

My enormous buddy from holding owned the top right bunk.

"Hey, Literal John, how's it hanging?"

John's legs stuck off the end of the bunk all the way to the knee. With his hands locked behind his neck, he reclined on a pillow two sizes too small for his head. A twinkle lit his eye, but he said with a straight face, "They're hanging off the edge, thank you very much."

"Har-har."

A blonde pixie popped up from the bottom right bunk and regarded me with bruised, narrow eyes. "Who're you?" she demanded. She worried a thumbnail between her two front teeth.

"What? You don't have all my vital statistics too?"

Her eyebrows drew together. The pixie had a bobbed haircut with bangs and diamond-blue eyes, a button nose, and full lips. She was a dozen donuts shy of being too heavy—not stocky but not skinny either. Sturdy.

"Watch out, Millie," said the other bunk-dweller with a laugh in his voice. "He could be a government plant."

"That's what I'm thinking." Millie crossed her arms and scowled. It failed to make me quiver since the pair of shiners and the split across the bridge of her dinky nose gave her the face of a ferocious raccoon.

"You've gotta be kidding me," I moaned. "You guys think I'm with the cops, and the cops think I'm with you. Listen, do me a solid. If you see Agent Ramirez, tell him I'm not one of you. Can you do that for me? You can recognize Ramirez by the bloody chunks of my ass hanging from his teeth."

Millie's glare eased up a notch. She pursed her lips, cocked her head and studied me as if she were a triage nurse trying to decide if I was worth saving or should go out with the trash. "All right, guys," she admitted with a sigh, "nothing we can do about it one way or the other. Just watch what you say. The place is bugged anyway."

"Yes, Mom," they chorused.

The man in the upper left bunk sat up on his elbows, and I got my first real look at him. Normal height (for a change) and medium build, he flashed a happy smile through split and bruised lips. I suspect he was model-handsome before he took his lumps, with wavy black hair and dark eyes that matched his tan complexion.

"I'm Alex de Galvez," he said. "The little fireball is Millie, and I gather you've met the big fellow over there."

"In holding, yeah," I said. "Hey, John, how come you aren't beat to shit like the rest of us?"

"I don't fight," he informed me. "At my size, if they think I'm resisting arrest, they'll just shoot me, so when the cops come, I drop to the ground and surrender."

You're a giant vagina, is what I thought. "Makes sense," is what I said.

My bunk invited me to collapse. I fell into it with a sigh like air escaping a balloon. Millie resumed her position on the bed across from me, sitting on the edge and chewing a thumbnail. The weight of her scrutiny washed over me at regular intervals, as if her eyes were searchlights, and when they turned in my direction, invisible heat waves shot out and pinged off my cheek.

Alex loomed over from the top bunk and said, "I don't like to fight either." He grinned with puffy, bruised lips. "But I haven't learned to surrender as fast as John."

"Sometimes it doesn't matter how fast you surrender," I told him. "If it's your day for a beating, there's not much you can do about it. That sums up my week so far."

As sure as they made super-hot tacos in hell, I did not—most emphatically did *not*—want anything to do with these people ever again. All I wanted was to get out. Chelle needed a hospital bed and a fighting chance to survive. Being locked up did nothing to advance the cause.

Hospitals and clinics once existed on practically every street corner, with hordes of trained nurses, doctors, and medical techs. My impression was only the well-to-do had easy access to those facilities, while everybody else had to mortgage their lives for the same level of treatment. At least today healthcare was free for everyone; no more of that bullshit double standard. They wanted government out of our lives, right? What did they think would happen if the feds walked away from healthcare? The system would collapse and millions of people would die, that's what would happen.

Idiots.

Of course, Alex had a lecture for any anti-government topic in the *New Revolutionary's Handbook.* Chapter Seven: Revivants are Like Undocumented Workers.

"One," he said, "the feds get a surcharge on Revivant labor for social security and healthcare—that they never have to pay out to the quote-unquote worker, because Revivants don't retire. They're already dead. Two, it means less drain on resources like schools, hospitals, and jails. As each successive generation of Revivants gets better programming, they can do higher-order tasks. Gen Four Revivants are almost fully functional as humans, and we think they're not even dead before the conversion these days. Our source tells us one day soon—"

"Alex," Millie warned. Her eyes said *shut up in front of strangers.*

"Whatever." I shook my head to let everyone see my disgust and rolled over to cut off further bullshit. "Conspiracy nuts," I muttered. "They're all the same. Stale and salty."

I shifted to get away from a dip in the mattress that hurt my back. My bunk creaked worse than Rogair's office chair. Millie and John spoke to each other in a low murmur. I couldn't hear what they said, nor did I try to listen any harder. I let them fade into the background noise of other jail sounds.

There was no way these guys would keep me long.

They couldn't, right?

Nine | You Say Terrorist, I Say Tomato

TWO GUARDS CAME AT sporadic intervals, stopped in front of a random cell, called a name, and carted that person away in cuffs and a shock collar. Those people did not come back. As a consequence, the inmate population dwindled, sometimes by only one per day, occasionally as many as three. No schedule, no order, and no reason given for the removal.

It was the same two guards every time, or clones from the guard factory, wearing black pants tucked into jump boots, flak vests, and helmets with black visors. We called them the Ushers of Doom.

By the end of the first week, only forty-two of the original sixty-odd CoL prisoners remained. Some cells were empty, some with only one or two occupants, and others—like ours—were full. With nothing to do but sleep, eat, and talk, my cellmates speculated for hours about where their friends were going, and what was happening when they got there. We couldn't get anything out of the ushers or the regular guards. The only thing they ever said to prisoners, beyond commands to go here, sit there, and stop, was "fuck off."

They said that to me a lot.

It got to where those chosen by the ushers would make their final march between the cells calling out to as many of their friends as they could, saying goodbye and remember me to my kids, and keep your chin up, keep fighting. Rah. Rah. Rah.

I stayed mostly to myself, crammed into my bunk while John counted off a zillion pushups a day before he flipped over to crunch his abs into chiseled marble. He had the right idea, using the enforced idleness to exercise. I considered it, I really did, but in the end, staying in my bunk seemed wiser. Exercise would be good for me, but it also meant displaying my pathetic lack of strength in front of Millie and the guys. I could do... ten, maybe twenty, pushups? The comparison would not be flattering.

We measured time into sections, divided by events: lights up, breakfast, lunch, dinner/TV time, lights down.

After breakfast and before lunch, on day seven by my count, the ushers escorted another prisoner to the exit. It was Goldie, the dumpy woman with the yolk poster I'd laughed at. A mother of three grown children, she liked horses, quilting, and cooking. She owned twin Pomeranians named Snowflake and Aster. Snowflake had bad hips, but Aster seemed okay and would probably outlive her sister.

Hey, it was a small lockup and sound traveled well, what can I say?

"Bye, Millie!" Goldie called as she passed. "Bye, guys! Don't worry about me; I'll see you soon! Oh. You too, Joe."

Millie, John and Alex crowded close to the bars and called out encouraging, platitudinous vomitus regurgitatus until the orange metal door at the end of the hall buzzed and Goldie disappeared.

The blond munchkin put her back to the corridor and slid down the steel bars to slump on the floor. She wiped a sleeve across her eyes before burying her head between her knees. John patted her with a hand big enough to hold a watermelon, leaning way, way over to do it.

"I'm sure Goldie will be just fine," he crooned.

"No doubt," Alex agreed. His tone suggested rainbows and picnics for lunch, with a chocolate fountain for dessert.

Millie's voice, muffled from between her knees, floated out. "But where are they going? What's happening to our people?"

The trio had worked hard to keep me from learning much about their organization, but I'd picked up enough, through body language and half-heard comments, that Millie—formally known as Millicent Margorie MacCauley (Yeah, no kidding)—held a leadership position in the Chicago Children of Liberty Secret Decoder Ring Society. She might even be the group's top dog. Well, not dog, exactly (one would not use the word "dog" in association with Millie), but head honcho, grand poobah, and Ultimate Supreme Leading Chief MF in Charge.

"What are you people so worried about?" I asked her. "It was just a freakin' street protest. That's like, what, a fine? A slap on the wrist? It's not like you people were sneaking pocket nukes into the Kluczyn-ski Building." Meaning the John C. Kluczynski Federal Building in downtown Chicago.

"Just a street..." Millie gaped at me, her blue eyes outlined in red. "Joe, tell the truth, are you an alien from the planet Delusion, orbiting the Black Hole of Ignorance?"

"Third rock from the dumb," Alex threw in.

"I—What the hell, de Galvez? Thanks, buddy, love you too," I said. "No, Mini-Millicent, I am not—Look... a bunch of people with plastic signs holding up traffic, that's what? Disturbing the peace? Obstructing traffic? Violation of grammar rules on protest posters? A misdemeanor, at most. You people act like you're being held by the Spanish Inquisition."

"If it's such a small deal," John chimed in, "why are you still here? You're not even one of us, and you've been in jail a week now."

Millie held her palms up, as if in appeal to a higher power. "Yeah, Joe, why is that? Why do you think they grilled you about the orga-nization? Why did they invoke the DTA to arrest you for a misde-meanor? The Do-*mes*-tic Ter-ror-ist Act, Joseph. Think about it."

"Hey, but they still have to prove it," I argued. "They can't just take you out back and shoot you."

"There's worse things than getting a bullet to the head."

"Yeah, right. 24-7 in a teeny cell with you people, for one. Don't you have lawyers lined up? A bunch of ACLU-types ready to file motions and whatnot?"

"Gosh." Millie's jaw dropped in mock astonishment. "I wish we'd thought of that."

"Yes, we have lawyers," Alex explained. He paced the narrow runway between the bunks, from the toilet to the door and back. "And I'm sure they're causing a stink right now, and that may be why our people are being taken away, going to bail hearings and being cut loose." He directed that last part at Millie. She nodded with a distinct lack of conviction. "But the feds have all the cards in this game. You may not know it, but they can hold someone indefinitely on suspicion of terrorist activity, US citizenship notwithstanding. It started after the terrorist attacks around the turn of the century—"

"Oh God, please no," I moaned. "No more lectures."

"—when the police needed more investigative authority to find the jihadists operating inside the borders. In response, the fanatics invented more devious methods to kill innocent civilians. Most attempts were foiled, but a few got through, and people died in attack after attack. Pinpricks, really, unless you were one of those pricked. Scared people want safety and security, not some esoteric concept of individual liberty, and so we have the DTA and other laws that broadened police powers and curbed our constitutional protections."

"What do you do for your day job, de Galvez?" I said. "The way you can spin anything into an anti-government rant, you have to be an advertising exec or lawyer."

"Heh, no, wrong on both counts." His white teeth flashed in a smile. "High school history teacher."

"That was my third guess." I turned my back to him. "Look, no one has to explain jihadists to me; my parents were killed by a suicide bomber. On their first vacation in thirty years, in London."

After that, no one said anything else. John practiced isometric exercises on the bars, pushing and pulling like he would bend the steel with his bare hands, then turned around, grabbed the bars over his head, and started vertical knee raises. Millie crawled back to her bunk and flopped on the thin mattress, one arm over her eyes, while Alex wandered around the tiny cell, poking at this and that.

I drifted into a doze and didn't notice when the ushers showed up. A collective feeling of *Oh shit* charged the atmosphere in the cell; a sensation I couldn't describe, but one that my survival instincts recognized and jolted me out of my snooze. *Wake up, dummy, the lions are here to eat you.*

"Oh hey, look, guys," I chirped, "the Rainbow Rangers are here for a visit. Let's have a tea party."

"Fuck off," said one of the ushers. With facemasks on, it was hard to tell which one.

"Alexandre Favio Martinez de Galvez," said the left or right usher. "Step forward."

"Favio?" I asked. "Seriously?"

"It's a family name," Alex told me. He grinned and shook my hand, back-slapped John, and hugged Millie. "See you guys on the other side."

They went through the handcuff drill, buzzed open the door while staying well back—after, I might add, telling John to stay waaaay the fuck over *there*—and led Alex out, hands on their stun rods the entire time. The cell door closed with a buzz-click, and a moment later so did the exit door.

And then there were three.

"I SPY... SOMETHING brown."

"Dead roach by the toilet," said Millie. "You did that one already."

"Oh." I squinted. "I don't think it's dead. It moved under the sink."

"And you're telling me this why?"

Day 13, and Millie and I were all that remained of the original fantastic four. Of the other prisoners, sixteen CoL protestors occupied nine cells. We still had no idea where their friends went: if they were dancing in the streets free as birds, moldering in a damp basement torture chamber, or decomposing in a lime pit somewhere.

An influx of new prisoners added to the cellblock population—all of them low-priority burglars, muggers, dopies—another baker's dozen inmates. They all sang the same song of the incarcerated, *I Didn't Do It,* off key, but with feeling.

None of these maligned citizens had a clue about the fate of the people whose cells they now inhabited.

In my little corner of paradise, Millicent Margorie MacCauley (or 3M, as I now called her) and I had the cell to ourselves. The ushers came for John—who I now knew as John Carter Marsh (I think they made these names up)—the day after they hauled Alex away. We two remaining musketeers had reached an accord whereby I didn't bring up certain subjects, like say the benefits of free healthcare, and Millie didn't call me "a brainwashed product of the modern no-education system." Everything else was fair game.

Like when I said, "What do you do when you're not tearing at the foundations of our government and economy?"

"I sew clothes for orphan children and bring food to the homeless."

"Bullshit."

"You're right, I'm kidding." Her nose crinkled when she grinned. It was... it was cute. "No, I train dolphins to swim into the Potomac carrying sea-to-ground missiles, which they fire at the White House."

"Hah! Don't even joke about that in here. Besides, you can't fool me; I know nothing can swim in the Potomac and survive."

"You're too sharp for me, Joe. So tell me about Chelle. What's she like?"

That was... when the hell was that? Six days ago? Five? One day blurred into the next, and I only knew the total number from the hash marks I made in the brick mortar with a chip of stone I found. Thirteen total. Longer than I'd ever gone, post-puberty, without an erection. A novel experience for me, having a conversation with a woman where the objective wasn't to score.

We just... talked.

It was weird.

MILLIE'S VOICE, FROM the other bunk. "Do you think they feel anything?"

"Who?"

"Revivants."

"Sweet Mary, I hope not."

"What about traces of their old personality? Memories? Would they remember who they were?"

"You're killing me, 3M."

"If you saw someone you knew on the street, someone who's, y'know, an RVT, what would you do? Would you try and talk to him... it?"

"I—I honestly don't know."

"I think I'd try to communicate. If I were a Revivant, would you talk to me?"

"Oh, hell no."

"WERE YOU AN ASTRONAUT?"

"We don't have astronauts anymore, Joe. NASA was scrapped in the 20s, and all the private stuff is unmanned."

"I knew that. A pilot then?"

"I have a hard time reaching the pedals on a car—you think I could fly a plane?"

"What? They don't have booster seats? You're pretty smart under that blonde disguise you wear; I'm thinking something pretty technical."

"And you? You put on a good stupid act with all your wiseass, and you've been brainwashed—"

"By the no-education system, yeah, yeah, yeah."

"—by the no-education system, but you let slip some almost bright ideas once in a while. Did you go to college?"

"I was in my second year at Northwestern, taking Advanced Electrical Engineering, when Chelle got pregnant, and I quit school to be a daddy."

"She got pregnant? How the hell did that happen?"

"Well, when a man puts his penis—"

"No, I mean with all the birth control available today..."

"Which only works if the stuff they give you at the pharmacy isn't too out of date."

"Oh. Shit."

"Exactly."

"I SPY SOMETHING BROWN..."

"Joe, please. Find something else."

"Crawling up the side of your bunk."

"Oh, fuck! Where? Get it off! Don't just lay there... wait, why are you laughing? You asshole. I'm going to cut your balls off when you go to sleep tonight."

"Eh. I'm not using 'em anyway."

ON DAY 22, THE USHERS came for me.

Ten | Where I Get on Agent Ramirez's Christmas Card List

"WARREN, JOSEPH ADAM," said Usher One.

A wild frog jumped inside my chest, and all the snarky remarks I had stored up against this moment hit a brick wall and died hideously. Millie's blue eyes rounded as though a woodland creature was dying right in front of her. Maybe a bunny, or a chipmunk.

I slipped on my brave face and stood on quivering legs. Made sure they'd support me before I tried anything rash, like moving. "I spy two big, ugly things dressed in black." My words came out steadier than I expected.

"Oh, Joe." Millie stood and hugged me.

"Don't forget to turn out the lights when you leave. And be sure to clean up, or we'll never get our deposit back."

She sniffed into my chest, and I was surprised to feel dampness there. Millie shoved away and brushed the front of my orange jumpsuit, as if straightening it. Her eyes were red and watery, her voice husky. "Take care of yourself, Joe. Good luck."

"And to you."

"And good luck with Chelle." Millie spun away and crossed to the sink. Turned on the tap. "I hope you find her a good hospital and she gets well soon."

Usher Two grumped, "Come on, darling, we ain't getting paid by the hour."

"I'm sure that's true." My legs carried me to the cell door without collapsing, and I put my hands through the slot for the shackles. "I'll bet you guys get paid by the soul. Am I right?"

"Fuck off," said Usher One while his pal clamped the cuffs on.

The door buzzed, and I marched outside. Prisoners lined up at the doors of their cells, those farther away pressed right into the bars so they could see. The combined impact of their sympathetic hang-dog faces nearly dropped me to my knees right there. I drew a shaky breath as the door clanged shut behind me.

"Don't be sad, people," I called out. "I'm sure my new family will have a nice mommy and a daddy and new toys to play with and—"

One of the ushers shoved me. "Shut the fuck up and move."

At mealtime every day we were marched through the door at the end of the hall for chow, so I should have been used to hearing it close. This time, when the cellblock door slammed shut behind me and an empty gray corridor stretched ahead, my knees wobbled, and I almost asked to be taken back inside. Almost.

I strode forward instead, keeping ahead of the ushers and walking like I knew the way. At the T-junction, I turned left—right went to the mess hall, so it was a safe bet—and earned a growl from the ushers to slow down. We tramped through sparsely populated corridors, meeting few people and talking to none. We trundled up metal stairs and maneuvered through electronically locked doors that opened by some unseen magic. I suspected the guards wore a microchip that allowed them to access doors without stopping and fiddling with keys or cards.

The guards halted me at a room with a number—602C—and Usher One said, "Here."

Two comfy chairs and a table occupied the center of the room, with a desk and office chair against the right. Bookcases lined the walls. Done in institution off-white, the room left a lot to be desired, but it was a few notches better than any other part of the lockup

I'd seen so far. A coffee service waited on the table, and the smell of roasted java brought tears to my eyes.

"Sit." Usher One pointed at the comfy chairs.

I sat. And stared at the coffeepot the way a dog watches a rare steak on the floor.

"Go ahead, have some," said Usher Two with a wave of his hand. The pair stationed themselves by the door and didn't budge again, switched into a power-down mode common to robots of their model. C3P-Asshole.

I slugged back the first steaming cup without pausing for breath. I didn't offer the guards any. The dark roast hit my tongue, and I shivered. Had I not been dosed with anti-libido pills, I'd have gotten off right then and there. I folded back into the cushions and sipped until the second cup was empty, poured a third, and killed it too.

An old-fashioned clock ticked somewhere, and the armchair was soft as a cloud's butt. I sank into the cushions and closed my eyes...

SMACK-SMACK-SMACK!

"Mr. Warren?... Mr. Warren?"

Smack-smack-smack!

"Chelle?" I popped open my eyes, the last traces of a dream scattering away, and found Agent Ramirez slapping my cheek. I blinked and shoved upright from where I'd sunk into the cushy chair. My eyes were sticky, and my mouth tasted like I'd drunk a bottle of glue.

"I'm 'wake," I mumbled, waving off the gnome with a badge. "Gah." I smacked dry lips and rubbed my eyes. "How long was I out?"

"Not long, Mr. Warren." Ramirez perched on the opposite chair and poured coffee from the thermos on the table. The smell alone made me salivate. How much coffee can one person crave? "Not long at all. Would you like something else to drink? Some food?"

Was he kidding me? This from the guy who threatened to have me butt-fucked with batons? "Who are you? Where's Agent Ramirez?"

Ramirez cracked a tiny smile. World of wonders, I had no idea his smile muscles were connected. "No need to be concerned, Mr. Warren. You'll be happy to know your story checked out, and we'll be letting you go soon."

"Seriously?" I made a point of examining the industrial-grade office. "I'm not the expert on getting out of jail, but I don't ever remember it being quite like this."

"Normally, no." Ramirez perched on the edge of the chair, feet together on the floor. He set his cup on the table and leaned forward with (what I think was) a sincere expression. Fear trickled back into my veins and zipped around in panicked circles in my chest. "I had the guards bring you here first. There are a couple of things we need to discuss."

"Things?" I had an itch in the middle of one of my shoulder blades, in a place that was a real bitch to reach. I twisted this way and that, scratching around it, but never quite getting it.

"Yes, Mr. Warren. Things. You see, I learned early on that you were exactly who you said you were; that you had nothing to do with the so-called Children of Liberty. I had a nice long chat with your case worker, Mr. Killingsworth—"

"Wait." I rubbed my back into the seat cushion, scratching like a bear. "How long ago did you figure this out?"

"Oh, almost immediately."

"Almost... *What?* You left me in a cell for three weeks, knowing I didn't do anything? My girlfriend—"

The Nice Ramirez flushed from the detective in a heartbeat. Without moving anything more than a few muscles in his eyes and cheeks, the earnest and sincere look vanished and Evil Ramirez, Agent of Darkness, appeared. I couldn't prove it, but I suspected the temperature in the room dropped several degrees. He held up one finger, and my mouth snapped shut, just like that, and my anus puckered so tight, I couldn't pass a pin.

"Mr. Warren, you were arrested"—his words frosted the air—"with a group who strives to overthrow the lawfully elected government of the United States of America. We had to be sure you were exactly who you reported yourself to be before we could release you. We listened very attentively to the recordings of your conversations with your cellmates before deciding you were a person we might be able to trust."

"Uh... thanks?"

"You're welcome," he said with all due gravity and not a hint of irony. His predatory appearance faded, and he resumed his earlier personality. I wondered how many shades of Ramirez were in there. "It is because of this fragile bond of trust that I have asked to speak with you." He sipped from his coffee and placed the cup exactly where it was before. "You see, I would like you to do something for us. For your country, Mr. Warren."

"I see," is what came out of my mouth—flat, neutral and noncommittal—while screaming inside my head was, *The fuck kind of moron are you?*

"You seem to have bonded in some small way with the people in your cell, especially Ms. MacCauley. It's why we separated out the other men early in the process; we wanted you and her to spend some time together. Had there been a way to conveniently do it, we would have taken the anti-androgenic out of your food and disabled the fraternization analytics so the two of you could have engaged in sexual intercourse. Unfortunately we could find no way to effect that outcome without tipping our hand."

"Yeah," I murmured, "too bad." Jesus, Joseph, and Moses, were these people for real? I didn't know whether to laugh aloud or run screaming from the room. *Agree with everything. Shut up and get out of here.* "Yeah, we got to know each other a little. I mean, how can you not, locked up with somebody?"

"Exactly." Ramirez seemed pleased I was with the program. Good doggy. "What we would like, Joseph"—apparently we were on a first-name basis now—"is for you to take advantage of that budding friendship and strive to get to know Ms. MacCauley a little better. Look her up, have coffee, gain her trust..."

"Spy on her, you mean."

"Hmm." He shrugged, frowning as if I'd used a naughty word. Bad doggy. "If you want to put it that way. Joseph, the Children of Liberty are a dangerous group, and we need to keep tabs on them. We need somebody... on the inside, so to speak."

A dangerous group? Yeah, I could see the yolk lady knitting suicide vests for her dogs Goldie and Snowflake. Millie tossing fish to her missile-shooting dolphins for every successful launch. De Galvez might bore a man to death, but armed rebellion? Who was this guy kidding?

To badly paraphrase Dorothy Parker, *What fresh pile of dogshit was this?*

"You'll be that somebody," Ramirez continued without a glitch. "Nothing too sneaky, nothing dangerous. Get to know a pretty girl and ask questions. Pretend to be interested in the answers and even boink her if you want. Act like a convert, in a manner of speaking. Once a month or so, come back here and tell me what you learned. Simple as that."

"Simple as that." Was this guy for real? Did he even stop and listen to himself? *Keep your cool, Joe. Just get through it.* I refilled my coffee cup to buy time to think, and to wash the gummy taste out of my mouth. I had two choices: Go with the flow and sign up to be Ramirez's happy little snitch, or go all fuzzy batshit crazy and throw this coffee in his face and see how much punching I could get in before the ushers came over and stomped the multicolored steaming guts right out of me.

"Well, Joseph, can I count on you?"

I sipped coffee and said, "Well, you know, Agent, I may have a little problem at home. I live with a woman who's not very forgiving, you know? I mean, I come home ten minutes late and *bam!* she's all over me. What's going to happen when I sneak in late at night, smelling of some other female person? She'll bust a two-by-four over my head."

I had him now. No need to tell Short-Dick Ramirez I planned to break it off with Chelle once she was cured and things weren't so life-and-death. All he had to know was I couldn't play Romeo because my Juliet had a temper and wasn't afraid to abuse it. I could picture the look on her face when I told her: *Hey, you know, the feds want me to seduce a cute little seditionist. I don't want to, but hey, it's my duty. I regret I have but one penis to give for my country.*

"That brings up the other thing I wanted to talk to you about, Joseph."

"Yeah, sure, what else you got?"

He cracked that tiny smile again and said, "I'm sorry to be the one to tell you this, but Ms. Schweitzer has passed away. She opted for early Revivant conversion rather than wait for the disease to kill her. She stipulated her mother as the Early Option Bonus recipient. I know that's shocking news to hear, especially now, but I wanted you to know before you went home. It seemed the least I could do."

Eleven | Death and Taxes

Afraid of being a burden to your loved ones? Of the pain and expense associated with a terminal illness? Renascentia has the answer. In a quick, painless procedure, nanobots can assume all bodily functions on your behalf. Why, you can even remain with your family if you wish!

—Myths About Early Revivant Option, *A Patient's Guide to Their Choices*

THE KIND AND TENDER people at the Cook County jail buzzed me through the final door onto the street at six minutes after noon, on Wednesday, April 16th. I knew this from the clock on the outtake office wall. The time felt right, but the date seemed off. Somehow I must have miscounted a day while locked up, or the day-night cycle was different inside than out. By my count, it should have been the 15th.

Tax day.

A poster from the OBW came back to me: "Even if you don't owe, you have to file. It's the Law!"

Yeah, I'll get right on that. Hate to make the feds mad now, wouldn't I?

My 1040 would be pretty interesting this year. Income: Zero. Tax owed: One human female, paid in full.

Chelle was dead. Dead but shambling around. I shivered, thinking how I should have asked where they put her. How freaky would that be, having her pass me on the street? ("Fly-er, sir?")

Rain beat down on slick pavement, and brown water rushed beside curbs and overflowed the street drains along California Avenue. Midday, and it was dark as night. I stood in the downpour, cold but grateful for the sensation of weather, the smell of fresh rainwater mixed with the sour reek of trash floating along the gutters, the pounding of the drops battering my face, and the taste of salt on my lips as water washed my eyes clear. I teetered as cautiously as an old man without his walker, feeling like any sudden motion would break the thin glass shell holding my insides together, ripping me open from the inside with razor-sharp fragments.

I tottered north, toward 26th Street. Home—or what was home when Chelle was alive—was about eight kilometers east. An hour's walk? I checked my bit-stick, which said I had $57.14. Enough for a bus ride or a McDonald's cheeseburger, hold the fries and drink. My stomach rumbled. I'd been programmed over the last three weeks to eat at the same time every day. My empty belly didn't seem to care that the woman I once loved, the woman I almost had a child with, was dead. Ish. Dead-ish. A new RVT, according to Ramirez.

The thought skittered through my mind that maybe Ramirez helped things along, merely to get me where he wanted me, next to Millie. No, it didn't feel right. I had the strong suspicion I was little more than a bug under a magnifying glass. Interesting, potentially useful, but ultimately not very important.

How important was it for him to get inside the Children of Liberty?

"Shit, Joe," I muttered. "You're getting as paranoid as de Galvez."

I made the corner and turned right on 26th. A bus swooshed by in the opposite direction, throwing up rooster tails as it crashed through the deeper pockets of running water. The lights were on inside it, showing the seats were filled with weary people focused on their own problems. A few cars hummed past, splashing the sidewalks with dirty-brown tidal waves. I stayed well back from the curb and tucked my chin into my collar. The street people were gone, huddled somewhere dry. I had the sidewalk to myself.

What would they have her doing?

Did Chelle choose to become a Revivant because she believed I'd abandoned her? Alone in our stinking apartment, probably sick, probably hungry, with no one there to take care of her. I knew Chelle well enough to know that, despite her tough exterior, she was really still a little girl inside. Afraid of bugs. Afraid of the dark.

She would have been terrified of death.

And I should have been there.

Wind gusted and threw cold pellets of water in my face that stung, but I didn't flinch. I deserved the pelting, and much worse. In fact, if I saw another bus coming, it wouldn't be a bad thing for me to step in front of it, get everything over with in one shot. Lose the guilt, lose the pain, and find my own place in that undiscovered country.

Wouldn't Ramirez be pissed about that, huh?

"Fuck Ramirez," I told myself. He wanted me to play his game, get close to Millie MacCauley and her friends. "Well, fuck him in his short little ass. I'm not playing, no matter what I said."

Get close to Millie, he told me. Learn what they're up to. Come back and we'll have a nice little chat, just two amigos shooting the shit. As if. The last group of people I wanted anything to do with was the Children of Liberty. If it wasn't for them, I wouldn't have been arrested in the first place. The last three weeks of my life wouldn't have been wasted in a cage.

Chelle might still be alive, or if not, at least I would have been there for her.

I glared at the leaden sky and shouted, "You hear that, Ramirez? I'm not *playing*!"

Thunder rumbled, as if God approved of my decision.

"Well, fuck you too, God!" I screamed at the sky. Cars passed, the drivers taking one quick glance before finding something else to focus on besides the crazy bastard yelling at the clouds. "Where were you these last few weeks, huh? Where were *you*!"

I shivered, not getting an answer from any form of the Almighty—God, Yahweh, Buddha, Jesus, Mohammed, or Krishna—all of them remained silent, playing their celestial poker game, with people as chips and no pot limit.

A possibility jumped up and slapped me in the face. I missed a step. I had read in the pamphlet Chelle brought home from the clinic that sometimes people opted to stay with their family. What if she was still in the apartment?

That thought had me quickening my pace. Crazy as it seemed, I couldn't shake the idea. What would be waiting for me? Empty apartment or robot girlfriend? By the time I turned onto 23rd Place and my apartment building came in sight, the fantasy had taken on weight and substance and grown to almost concrete surety. I pushed through the gate with the perpetually broken lock, entered the vestibule, and climbed the stairs, dreading what I would find.

Boxes lined the hall in front of my door, which stood open. The smell of cleaning chemicals hit me first, followed by the sound of Tejano music playing from an iPlant implant with external speakers.

"Chelle?" I stepped into my apartment and froze. The place had been stripped to the walls. All the furniture, fixtures, posters, and bric-a-brac—gone. Miguel, the super, spritzed something harsh and chemical onto the walls and swiped it off with a dirty rag. He saw me at the same moment I saw him.

"Joe!" he cried. He tapped his ear, and the music shut off. "Where you been, man?"

"In jail, *compadre*." I glanced around, feeling dread ball up in my stomach and take root. "Where's Chelle?"

His eyes told me before his words did. "I'm sorry, bro. She's, y'know... gone, man."

"How long?" I choked out.

He wagged his head in sadness. "She leff mebbe a week ago? I had to clean up in here because, y'know"—he winced—"it was vacant."

"It's okay," I said, though it was anything but. "What about our stuff? Why'd you put it out?"

"Oh, man, I'm really sorry, man, but the manager? He leased the place out."

"Leased it? The fuck you say. I live here."

"Not no more, my frien'. The manager? He say the apartment was in Chelle's name, and since she's... dead and all, he can lease it back out. He say to me, 'Clean that fucking place out, right now, Miguel, I gots a list of people waiting.'"

"Well, not anymore, Miguel. Put my stuff back in here while I go speak to this manager. Who is he, and where can I find him?"

Miguel scratched his head and shifted from one foot to the other. "He don' live here, Joe. He live somewhere, y'know, out there, in the burbs, man. And besides, I can't put your stuff back, because we done..."

"Done what?"

"The manager, he say, give it all to Goodwill, man. So I did what he say, y'know? I have to; it's my job. Except I kept a box of your personal things in my apartment, in case you came back. It's downstairs."

"What's all that shit in the hall, then?"

"That all belongs to the new people. They moving in later today."

I slumped in the doorway and dripped water on the cracked flooring tiles. Ramirez was telling the truth. Go figure.

"Hey, y'know," Miguel said, "I could put in a word with the boss for you. Get you on the waiting list for the next place to come open."

"How long's the list?"

He winced again. Wagged his head some more. "It's long, man. I don't know, six months mebbe, we can fine you a place."

"I'll be dead before then." I huffed a short laugh. "No, don't worry, Miguel. I'll find something."

"You sure? You can bunk on my couch tonight, you need a place to sleep. I'll move my brother to the chair in the bedroom—"

"No, it's okay. Thanks anyway." I waved and stumbled to the stairs. I had one option left open to me. One that I'd dreaded while I still had pride and a little hope that things would get better, but now...

It was time to go see Ding.

THE RAIN LEFT SOGGINESS behind. A damp wind blew in from the lake, ruffling puddles and flinging drops from trees and awnings. It didn't matter to me; I couldn't get any wetter. I squished north to Cermak and headed west, toward the river.

Ding lived in a crusty redbrick building overlooking the Chicago River. I crossed the Cermak Bridge, one of the few "rolling lift" bridges in the city, which split in the middle and allowed river traffic to pass. The lift mechanism broke when I was in high school, and the city didn't have enough money to fix it, effectively shutting down the trickle of commerce that once used the river to move goods. Since the only businesses in Chicago by that time were a very few retail stores, Chinese-owned banks, and law offices, the clogging of this artery went unnoticed.

Chilly drips plopped from the bridge's iron trusses with pinpoint accuracy down the back of my neck.

Two guys lounged at an umbrella-sheltered patio table, playing a holo-game that involved a lot of miniature explosions and shouting. They reminded me of bridge trolls, all brute muscle and an appetite for skinny white goats. I didn't believe for a second the game occupied their entire attention; no doubt they spotted me before I made it halfway across the bridge and, before I stepped off the end, probably knew more about me than Ramirez.

Was Ding's open invitation still good? I hadn't spoken to the man in more than six months—the last time I turned him down for a job. Words were exchanged, and we hadn't parted on the best of terms. "Kiss my fat black ass," was used, as was "Suck me, Jabba the Hutt." (Star Wars was playing on TCM at the time.)

Ding was short for the type of cream-filled chocolate cupcake Marion "Ding-Dong" Winston ate by the gross. When I met Marion in high school, he was already a BMOUS—a black man of unusual size—with an IQ so high, they didn't make tests to score it. Ding started life plump and never looked back, and what's more, didn't seem to care. In high school, he earned a lot of shit for being a chubby nerd, as much as I did for being a skinny nerd, and we bonded, the way nerds do, spending our middle teen years devising and executing elaborate revenge plots against our tormentors. Senior class fuckwad Billy Moss to this day had no idea who secretly recorded him masturbating to an epic conclusion in his mom's underwear, or who set it to music (Ravel's *Bolero*) and released it to all the big social media sites.

After high school, I went to Northwestern, and Ding went to the Graham Correctional Center in Hillsboro, Illinois as a guest of the state. His habit of cracking secure servers for amusement and profit landed him in the crosshairs of the Homeland cops, who had zero tolerance for identity theft and credit fraud.

Somehow, he gained weight in prison.

He also got sneakier and learned to protect himself behind layers of cut-outs and fall guys and firewalls and, well, thugs.

"Hello, gentlemen," I said to the examples of thuggery under the umbrella. "Can you let Ding know Joe Warren is here to see him?"

"He know," rumbled one troll. He had a brow ridge thick enough to use as a diving board, a scoop nose and jowly cheeks. "He say to ax you what you want."

"Tell him I'm here about a job."

Both trolls examined me for tasty bits while my words were no doubt transmitted via hidden microphone up to the, er, big man himself. I shifted my feet and checked for escape routes. I didn't *believe* Ding would be pissed enough to have his loyal henchmen beat me like a foster child, but I wanted to be ready for anything.

When the henchman with the eyebrows smiled, the breath I'd been holding vented like a tire deflating. He gestured to the metal door behind him. "He say go on up."

"Thanks."

"Have a nice day."

Even thuggish bridge trolls could learn good customer service.

A MINIATURE HOLOGRAPHIC projection of Joseph Warren slogged across the Cermak Bridge and approached the two guards in front of the non-descript building. Ramirez fiddled with his vid player until the sound quality improved. The internal mic buried in Warren's jawbone required some adjusting before Ramirez could filter out the ambient body noise—heartbeat and stomach gurgles—and clarify the subject's speech and hearing.

"Thanks."

"Scritch-crackle—ice day."

Maravich entered the conference room where Ramirez had set up shop for the duration of the Chicago Children of Liberty operation. He held up a generic, untraceable bit-stick. "Your cut of the Texas job. My contact at Renascentia paid top dollar for the fresh meat. Yours if you want it."

The short agent's nostril twitched, and his eyes narrowed. "You know I don't take blood money. Those people were citizens, misguided though they may have been."

"Yeah," Maravich huffed, "you're a true believer. It's all about saving the world for you, isn't it?"

"Not the world. Just America."

"Prick," Maravich mumbled under his breath.

"What was that?"

"Nothing. Finest kind." If the little hobbit fucker was too sanctimonious to keep the bounty, it was okay with Maravich. *More for me, right?* The tall, blond-haired agent pocketed the bit-stick and jerked his chin at the 3D representation of Warren on the screen. "You think he knows he's been chipped?"

"This guy? Not a chance. He's dumb as a box of donuts."

"You think he'll do us any good?"

Ramirez pursed his lips and shrugged. "It's a long shot. They've got some good tech; so far they've killed all the chips we've planted on them. I suspect they'll find this one. But if Mr. Warren here can give us some good intel, we could wrap up a bunch of terrorists in one strike."

"Heh. Wouldn't that be funny?"

"What?"

"We send these fucking anti-government types to the camp, they get reprogrammed and wind up serving in the army after they're dead. Now that's funny."

"Hysterical."

"Jesus, Ramirez, lighten the fuck up, dude. You're so serious, you're making this like work." Maravich drew back a chair and plunked down, opened his own 3D vid player, turned it on and found a porn channel. Naked people of various sexes and ages writhed over the top of the conference room table. He tilted his head to one side and cocked an eyebrow. "I think I'll upgrade to the interactive player. That looks like fun."

Twelve | Necessity is the Mother of Groveling

FROM THE OUTSIDE OF Ding's building, you'd never suspect a polished marble floor and a lobby bigger than a downtown bank lay on the other side. Granite columns in two rows led the eye toward the far wall, where the burnished-nickel finish of the single elevator door gleamed under muted overhead lighting. I could never spot the cameras covering the lobby, though I knew they existed. I suspected poison gas vents, anti-personnel laser beams, and a shark tank hidden under the floor, though Ding always denied it.

"You fed the shark today?" My voice echoed off the marble walls.

Nothing happened, so I squeaked across the floor in my damp shoes, and when the elevator door swished open, I slipped into a space as inviting as a woman's arms. Teak walls, brass accents, offset lighting, orchestral music so soft it made love to my ears... no buttons, of course. The elevator went from the lobby to the third floor with no stops; it whispered upward with barely a sigh.

I skulked into an open loft filled with stack after stack of hard-shell moving boxes. Elephant-sized crates lay scattered across the floor. Sawdust, packing materials and bits of trash covered the glossy hardwood finish in a dusty rime of filth. The bare walls revealed faint outlines where pictures and panels once hung, a ghostly afterimage of technology burned onto the textured finish.

I didn't have to be Agent Ramirez to figure out Ding was moving.

A woman swayed through the row of boxes. Calling her a woman was like referring to crème brûlée as vanilla pudding. Sheathed in a pale-cream dress that flared from opaque to translucent as she swayed, revealing hints of her sepia-toned skin, Aphrodite twined through the clutter and debris as if it didn't exist. Diamond-studded hoop earrings glittered against her straight black hair, setting off almond-shaped eyes, a flaring petite nose and the reddest, fullest pair of lips I'd ever seen.

Phasers on stun.

"Mr. Warren?" Her voice glided across the floor, slid up my leg, and caressed my ear. "I'm Deandre, Mr. Winston's assistant."

Only the aftereffects of the erection-killing drug in my system allowed me to speak at all. Sort of. What came out of my mouth was "Gahp mullaka borrun."

She understood me perfectly. "Right this way. Mr. Winston is expecting you."

With a tilt of her head, the goddess swept her hand and led me through the box maze to a stripped-down version of Ding's former office, against the middle of the back wall. At every slinky movement of her hips, Deandre's creamy dress material flashed erotic images of tawny flesh. If the track-switching mechanism between Joe's brain and Joe's penis were functional, the express train to Hard-On Junction would have left the station like a rocket-sled.

She glided to one side when we reached a pocket of open floor. A battleship-sized desk hogged the bulk of the space. Ding had his desk made from the outer layer of polished Whipple shields recovered from the International Space Station after it splashed into the shallow waters off the coast of Bermuda.

Behind it, using a privacy-shielded 3D projection monitor that cost more than the gross domestic product of Norway, Marion Winston tapped a virtual control pad and made things happen on his screen that I couldn't see.

"Joe," he said. He didn't look up, but I didn't expect him to. Ding had a problem with eye contact. He also hated to be called by his first name.

"Marion."

There were no visitor chairs. Deandre joined an equally stunning woman on the cream-puff sofa against the wall of stacked crates to my right. Her friend had milky skin and blond hair so pale it was almost white. Topaz-blue eyes regarded me over a straight nose and Nordic chin. Where Deandre's cream dress contrasted with her cinnamon skin, this woman's pale complexion was offset by a black dress of the same peekaboo fabric. She ran a hand through her hair, and I caught a glimpse of an impossibly pink nipple.

"You met Deandre," Ding said. "Say hello to Signe."

"Hello, Signe." I hitched my chin at the blonde, whose pale lips curled in a wicked smile. The dynamic sexual voltage of the two women nearly shocked all the anti-androgenic out of my system and left me a helpless puddle of goo.

I cleared my throat and addressed my old pal, who'd grown to the size of a baby hippo, with jowly chins and a Hershey's Kiss-shaped body. Have I mentioned he hated to be called Marion?

"So, Marion," I said, "where'd you meet these two lost souls? Bingo night at the Ladies of Nocturnal Emission?"

"What do you want, Joe?" Ding had a eunuch's voice, lilting and soft. He once confided in me that he lost interest in sexual contact—with men or women—not long after puberty, about the time his belly eclipsed his equipment. Sort of an *if I can't see it, it ain't there* philosophy.

So why employ female assistants who could cause a contact ejaculation? "Because," he once explained, "they distract the opposition. Their undiluted pheromones make men dizzy, and dizzy men think only about their dick. Can't bargain for shit."

"I'm in a bind, Ding," I admitted, standing in front of his space debris desk, a supplicant in the court of the King of Last Chances. If I had a hat, I'd twist it in my hands. "Chelle's... dead. I'm flat broke and homeless—" Something cracked in my voice, and I focused on the watery drips sliding down the high window behind Ding's head. "Shit, man, I don't know what else to do."

Ding glanced up from his display, shooting a peek at me before jerking his chin at Signe and Deandre. "Ladies, please give us the room. Joe? Over here, Joe. Sit down. Tell me what happened."

I sank into the warm depression the blonde left in the sofa as the women swished away, butt cheeks flashing. Signe tossed a look over her shoulder, the wattage of her crooked smile lighting the power grid throughout the South Side. Any other day and my hair would've spontaneously combusted. I studied my hands, curled into lumps of water-wrinkled flesh in my lap, and ignored her.

"What happened?" Ding's eyes—although not his attention—had returned to his display, safely hidden in the world inside his computer. Somehow, that made it easier... Ding not watching me, I mean. More like a confessional, where the priest stayed behind a screen while you spilled your guts, allowing you to open up without judgmental faces adding to the misery.

I sucked in a deep breath and said, "Chelle and I went to the doctor..."

SOMEWHERE IN THE MIDDLE of my story, the rain started again. Drops ticking against the window provided the only sound in the cavernous room. I cradled an empty beer bottle with a strange label. Something foreign, with a strong scent of barley and a smooth finish. When Signe brought it to me, I was telling Ding about Rogair Killingsworth, OBW Employee of the Month. She gave me the cold bottle without a word, holding my hand a beat and a half too long, her eyes promising, lips parted. She slipped away with a lingering look, and I waited until she'd gone before I asked Ding what the fuck that was all about.

"Pay her no mind," he told me. "That's her job, but Signe doesn't know when to turn it off."

"It's... disturbing."

I wished now she'd come back with more beer. I hadn't tasted real beer in ages, and I'd inhaled the first one with barely a tickle of a taste bud. My story finished—Chelle getting sick, the street riot, jail, Ramirez—I waited for Ding to render judgment.

"You're about four months too late." Ding sighed, and his eyes flickered to me and away, in less than a heartbeat. "Look around, Joe. What do you see?"

"This a trick question? A bunch of boxes."

"I'm getting out of here while I have a chance." Ding tapped a key, and a panel display lit up on the wall behind him. A news feed crawled up the screen, one headline clicky after another. Back when I had a working phone, I used a similar feed to keep up on baseball scores; if I wanted details on a game, I could tap the clicky, and the screen would fill with a summary and highlights. Ding was the only person I knew who kept a running feed from Fox, CNN, and ABS. "You see these headlines?"

"More trick questions? Jeez, no, Ding, all I see is a bunch of squiggly lines." I glared a *fuck you*. The dipwad was always on me about getting my head out of my ass and paying attention, as if my awareness of current events would make a difference. "What about the headlines?"

"If you read them very, very carefully"—another eye flicker—"you'll see the pattern. Not here, right this second, but if you follow the newsies every day, read what they say, and—more importantly—what they *don't* say, the pattern emerges."

"Now I know you're shitting me. How do you read what they don't say?"

Somehow he communicated with his female assistants by secret button, or telepathy, or hell, I don't know, maybe they were programmed to know what he wanted. Deandre brought me another beer and refreshed Ding's bowl of cupcakes and glass of whole milk. Her delivery was less sexually charged than Signe's, but that was like saying a Jaguar was slower than a Ferrari. My hand tingled where she touched me.

Chelle is a Revivant, wandering the streets somewhere with a vacant expression.

I shuddered and sucked out the top third of my beer in one swig.

"How do I read what they don't say?" Ding continued talking throughout Deandre's appearance, and my brain caught up in a rush as she departed. "Simple. You were involved in a police action in downtown Chicago approximately three weeks ago, correct? You were there. You got arrested. You know it happened." An eye flicker of slightly longer duration. About the lifespan of a quark.

"True."

"And yet, when I search for the information on the *official* news sources"—he sneered at the word "official," his light voice rising to falsetto pitch—"I find no mention of this riot. So what they didn't say, very loudly, was that a group of citizens called the Children of Liberty were protesting the pervasive and invasive nature of the United States government and were arrested under provisions of the DTA."

He let that statement sit there in the quiet room and allowed me to examine it at my leisure. My leisure decided it didn't want to examine shit.

"Your point, Ding?"

"The press doesn't report what the government doesn't want reported."

I slapped my forehead. "Holy-fucking-cow! I never would've guessed!"

Ding's lips twitched in a smile, and he almost peeked at me again. "I forgot how sarcastic you could be. Let me try this one on you. What if I told you I'd learned through non-news sources that ninety-three percent of the current and former high-ranking executive, judicial, and legislative members of the federal government owned estates in mainland China, Bermuda, India, or South Africa? That I could prove it to you? And that no news agency anywhere has mentioned even one tiny hint of it. What would you think of that?"

"I... I have no clue what that means." I drained my beer and slapped the bottle on his desk with a clang. "Why don't you cut to the chase, buddy. It's been a real fucked-up day, and all I want to know is do you have something I can do for money, or not."

"It's simple," Ding said. "They're running for the hills, Joseph. And so am I. In two days, three at most, I'll be on board a sixty-foot yacht with Signe, Deandre, my two muscleheads, and any significant others those folks want to bring. I've liquidated my assets, and I'm getting the fuck out of the United States of America before the bottom falls out."

"Bottom falls out?" My clothes had nearly dried, but a few damp spots left me itchy. I scratched my shoulder blade, twisting one arm over my head to reach it. "Explain it for the dummy in the room."

Ding met and held my eyes for a full second. Then another after that. Unnerving. "In a few months," he said, matching stares with me, "maybe a year, at most, the USA won't draw enough taxes to service the interest on the debt. News sources have stopped reporting the actual debt itself. A CNN tweet hit the wires a few days ago about the rate of the deficit at $400 billion per month, then it disappeared from the feeds." Ding sighed and looked away. "Stay with me for a second here, okay? In 2014, the average deficit added around $80 billion per month to an $18 trillion debt. Annual interest on the debt was around $230 billion. Today, the interest payment is *two trillion dollars*, which sucks out over half of all tax revenue. When tax revenue can no longer pay the interest and maintain daily operation, the government goes into default. The military will not get paid. Grandma's social security draw will bounce. Food subsidy programs, social services, government housing, the FDA, the FBI, and the US Forest Service will have no money. Government bonds, which prop up a huge segment of the financial market, will be worth less than toilet paper. Everything from the Department of the Treasury to the goddamned Bureau of Indian-fucking-Affairs will have... no... money!"

Ding settled back in his chair and mopped his face with a handkerchief. He popped a cream-filled chocolate pastry in his mouth and chewed on it while I digested what he told me.

"So," I said into the silence, "does that mean you got something for me, or not?"

Ding said, without hesitation, "You can have everything, my entire operation, wall to wall, floor to ceiling."

"Even Signe?"

"Not Signe."

Thunder grumbled, rattling the window. Night had snuck in early, and the lights inside Ding's loft flickered whenever lightning danced on the other side of the dark pane. I considered myself duly impressed that his power stayed on; he must have greased the right palms at the electric company to keep the juice flowing.

"You want to be a crook, Joe?" My friend's chair creaked as he settled back and rubbed his bald head with both hands. He seemed tired. "I'll give you my How to be a Crook starter kit. Fingerprint replicator, ID creator, hidden bank accounts, secret decoder ring, and all."

My face scrunched in suspicion. "Why so generous?"

"Not generosity. I told you, man, I'm out. The United States is done, and all this stuff in boxes is headed for a shipping container.

When I find a place—probably an island, somewhere cool—I'll have it shipped there and set up house again. Who knows? Maybe I'll go on a diet, get buff."

I pinched my nose to stop the snort. "You and the Pheromone Fillies, living the dream."

Ding shrugged. "Why not? Seriously, man, listen... I'm doing you no favors." Ding reached into a desk drawer and removed a small plastic box. He popped the top and dumped out a half-dozen snack-size baggies, each with a white label printed in black ink. "Here, pick one."

I snagged a baggie at random and read the label: **Johnson, D'metria T.**

Below that, in smaller print, was a laundry list of vital statistics. I opened the bag and found a clear latex-like finger cot, larger than a thimble, smaller than a condom. Nothing else.

"Okay, I give," I told Ding. "What's with the rubber?"

"It's a replica fingerprint of"—he read the label—"D'metria T. Johnson. D'metria passed away and became a Revivant at some point in the recent past, and we were able to obtain her fingerprint without too much trouble."

"And this gets you...?"

"Any and all benefits to which D'metria was entitled during her life, up to and including social security and unemployment compensation."

"But... she's dead. Don't they—Doesn't the government keep records of dead people?"

"Sure they do. But Revivants aren't registered as officially, quote-unquote, *dead* until their body is retired from service. Supreme Court ruled on that in '43. There's paperwork to prevent fraud, but it's easy to get around if you know how."

I sank back into the sofa and tried on D'metria's identification. It fit like a one-finger glove. "So now what do I do with this?"

"With that? Nothing. Those were made for welfare scams." Ding flicked his hand in my direction. He extracted a shiny metal cube from his desk drawer and slid it over to me without looking. "Fingerprint replicator. Use it wisely. If I were you, I'd work on one big score, something involving a corporation. Scam a pile of cash and blow town. Head for greener pastures, dude. When the government shuts down, things will get ugly, fast. You don't want to be anywhere around when that happens."

"A big score, huh?" My mind was totally blank. "Help me out here, Ding. I'm not the huge—pardon the pun—criminal mastermind in the room. I—" A headline in the crawl caught my eye. "Freeze that!"

Ding tapped a key, and I read the clicky twice more to be sure I had it right. A static charge sizzled from my cold heart all the way down to my fingertips.

"That's it," I said.

"What?" Ding frowned and followed my pointing finger. "Renascentia," he read, "inventor of the Revivant app, will be holding a dinner event honoring the tenth anniversary of their signature invention Wednesday, May 30th at Chicago's Huateng Tower."

"Click for details, man." A fever burned bright in my face; my eyes simmered, hot and moist. "I'm going to get the fucks took Chelle away. That's gonna be my big score."

Foundered Fathers

Ramirez ran the history of the chubby fraudster, Marion Winston, and opened a file on his criminal activities. Already Warren's bug was paying dividends; Winston was a good catch. A felon with a short record but a lot of suspicious activity. The government had been after Winston for a long time. Maravich had even switched off his porn video to follow the Joe Warren Saga playing on the table-top monitor.

Air stagnated inside the conference room at Cook County Correctional from the remains of their takeout burrito-and-bean dinner. The lights flickered, and thunder reverberated through the thick walls.

"Big score," Maravich snickered. "What a putz. This guy has a snowball's chance of hurting Renascentia."

Ramirez rested his chin on his tented hands, face inches from the fuzzy display. The rain and Winston's building infrastructure were playing hell with the pickup. A tiny reflection of Warren and the chubby crook danced in the agent's dark pupils. "Shut up. I'm trying to listen."

"You think he's right?" Maravich punctuated his question with a rumbling belch. "You think the government's going tits up?"

Whap!

Ramirez slammed his fist on the table, making his video display jitter and fizz out for a moment. His mouth slit into a scalpel-cut gash, the senior agent pinned Maravich with a freezing glare. He seemed to have to pump his lungs full of air a few times to get the words out, and when he did, they chipped out cold as a corpse buried under Arctic ice.

"No, Maravich, I don't believe a goddamned word that little faggot Winston says." Pump, pump went the HS agent's lungs. "This nation's government was founded to take care of its people. We have a covenant with the American people to protect them from harm, to provide for their well-being, to feed them when they're hungry and paddle them when they're naughty." Pump-pump. "We are of the people, for the people, and by the people, and we shall never perish from this earth, Maravich. Never."

"Whoa, little buddy." Maravich held his palms out. "Calm down, man. I'm on your side."

The shorter man visibly shook himself back to calm. The bitter cold seeped out in small degrees, and his lungs slowed their furious pumping. "Sorry, Maravich. I, uh, I can't help myself sometimes. These ungrateful bastards make me crazy."

"Dude, I get it, I swear."

"All the things this government does for these people... it is insane anybody would want to overthrow it, or tear down its institutions." Ramirez resumed his seat like a deflating balloon. "We take care of the American people. I mean, that's our sworn duty, right? Level the playing field, even out the highs and lows, make it fair for everyone? Why can these bastards not see how much we do for them?"

"You got me, Ramirez." The junior agent rolled his eyes when he was sure his partner wasn't watching. "But you know, you need to unwind some, my friend. I'll tell you what... we bust Winston and his crew; we'll make a deal with my people at Renascentia to test out the Gen Five bots on the two chicks. I'll get the tall one, Deandre, and you can have the little blonde for yourself. Deal?"

Thirteen | Bad Boys, Whatcha Gonna Do?

DEANDRE AND SIGNE MATERIALIZED through a gap in the crates. Signe's eyes grew wide, and she gasped a breathy little sigh when she spotted me holding my latex-coated finger to the light.

"Is that for *me*?" she gushed.

"Down, Signe," Ding said. "The man found out today his girlfriend died. He doesn't need your teasing."

"Who said I was teasing?" She pouted. Men would crawl barenaked over steaming-hot, broken glass to taste her lower lip.

"Signe..." Ding warned.

Deandre said, "It's after five, boss. Do you need anything else before we get out of here?"

"No. Thank you, Dee." Ding glanced at the women for a nanosecond. "Have the boys walk you home."

"Of course. Mr. Warren, I'm sorry for your loss." Deandre took the blonde's hand and led her away. "C'mon, Signe. I have back-to-back interviews for companions tonight, and I need your help with the grading process."

"I like the front-to-front kind of interviews..."

Ding spoke as much to himself as me, "This says the dinner will be invitation only... a quote-unquote who's who of politics, entertainment and industry... keynote by Jamil Yamadut, CEO of Renascentia... hmmm ... Top floor of the Huateng Tower, that'll be a minor bitch to get in." Louder, he said, "What do you plan to do here, Joe? I don't see any easy way to peel money out of this deal."

Plans fired off and died like fizzy rockets. What would hurt these people the most? I was categorically against acts of violence; arson, bombing, and poisoning were out the window. For one thing, I didn't have the stomach for it, and for another, the point was to score some cash. I ran through a list of major felonies—

"Robbery," popped out of my mouth.

"Say who?"

"An old-fashioned stick-up," I told Ding. "I'll hit that crowd right where it hurts: in their bank accounts."

"Like Jessie Ventura, with a mask and a gun...?"

"You're thinking of Jesse James, but yeah, essentially." The idea scared me and excited me in equal parts. "I sneak in—we'll have to get the plans for building security—and I stick a knife in old Jamil's face and threaten to cut his nose off if he doesn't fork over his bit-stick."

Ding's heavy brows drew together, and his puffy eyes scrunched up until they almost disappeared. "A knife?"

"Or, you know, a gun." I imitated a pistol with my index finger and thumb. "Bang-bang. Gimme your loot or you're dead!"

"You've watched too much late-night vid," Ding snorted. "And where are you gonna get a gun? You know the feds have that shit locked down."

"I... I don't—wait!" I snapped my gun fingers together. "My grandpa's things. He left a honking big pistol with his stuff, said he hid it during the registration drives of the 20s. It was in my stuff—oh, fuck."

"What?"

"Miguel gave away all our shit to Goodwill, except for a box of my personal things." I covered my eyes and fell back into the sofa. "Argh! Was Grandpa's stuff in there? What time is it?"

"After six."

Lightning flared outside the window, followed in seconds by a rattle of thunder. Rain washed the glass in sheets. It didn't appear to be a good night to hike back to 23rd and find out if my grandpa's ancient firearm was in with the box of crap Miguel kept for me. How stupid could I be, leaving my things behind? What if he decided to dig through the boxes and found a pistol tucked inside with my old family photos and birth certificate and whatnot? A working firearm was worth its weight in gasoline these days. If I'd remembered I had it, I probably would have sold it myself by now and had enough for a few weeks' grace before poverty set in.

"Can I stay here, at least until tomorrow?" I asked Ding. "On your sofa? I'll go see Miguel in the morning, find out if I'm armed or not. If I am"—I snarled a shark grin—"then it's on. My next stop will be the top of the Huateng Tower on May 30th and a date with the fucker who raised the dead, Mr. Jamil Yamaha."

"Yamadut."

"Yeah, him."

Tuesday, May 29th.

I went over my list for the tenth time in the last hour.

Gun. Check.

Bullets. Check. (*Cartridges, goddamnit!* I could hear my grandpa's voice in my head every time I said bullets instead of cartridges.)

Ding had coded me into the loft's access system before he left, so I had the run of the vacant, three-story building, rattling around like a BB in a cup. He took all his furniture, so I scavenged a mattress and some blankets, as well as some odds and ends to use as chairs. I hit the thrift store for some spare clothes and recovered my personal stuff—including Grandpa's shiny steel pistol (*revolver, goddamnit!*)—from Miguel, and made a cozy rat's nest in a corner where Ding once kept a bed the size of a ferry boat.

Untraceable bank account. Check.

Bit-stick keyed to said account. Check.

One good thing about hanging in Ding's vacant loft: the shower ran hot water as long as I wanted, and the soap dispensers were full. I used it two, sometimes three, times a day. It was a strange sensation, lathering up under a fine spray of hot water, butt-naked in an open space big enough to park a fleet of cars. Decadent? Sort of. But more like I was being watched from the shadowed corners of the echoing room. Creepy, bad V-Real type of stuff.

Waiter's uniform. Check.

When Ding left, he slipped me a few thousand on an open stick, for operating expenses. I'd burned through some of that laying my hands on a genuine Huateng Tower catering staff uniform and the ID card that went with it. The rest was eaten up running down the current whereabouts of Chuck Simmons, former Huateng Security Director and current undead picker of tomatoes in Moline, Illinois.

Coercing Chuck to stick his finger in the replication device... Not a pretty sight.

What little money I had left went toward food, which ran out a week ago. Since that time I'd rummaged through empty shelves, hoping to discover something I might have previously missed, and haunted the food pantries and missions. Made soup from ketchup packets filched from fast food restaurants.

Twenty-four hours before the big day. Check.

Electricity-generating bugs crawled inside my stomach and zapped me when I least expected it. My fingers tingled at odd moments, or a ball of dread would curl up in my chest and block the oxygen from my lungs.

The last thing Ding said to me before he left?

"Joe, you weren't cut out to be a crook, you know that, right? High school pranks are one thing, but a true-to-life outlaw..." He patted me on the shoulder while staring at a portable holo-projector strapped to his wrist. His high voice failed to echo as we stood next to the elevator in the loft. "You're straighter than a metal ruler, man. You understand this adventure you're on, it won't come to a good end."

"Thanks for the pep talk, coach."

"A real criminal," Ding continued, "has to accept the consequences, which in this case would be some heavy jail time. You're not good with consequences, Joe. You never have been. Besides, you told me you didn't love Chelle anymore. Why risk going to jail for her memory?"

"Hey, I've done jail. It wasn't so bad."

"You did three weeks in a county lock-up with some political activists. Think about twenty-plus years in a state penitentiary with three-strike killers and maximum-sentence mobsters. Dudes with the moral code of a pile of snakes. Give this up, man, and come with us. There's plenty of room."

"And be a deckhand on the SS Narcissism?"

Ding shrugged one shoulder. "There're worse things in life. Worse places, for sure."

I had laughed my friend off and watched him go, later wondering why I'd been so stupid, turning down a cruise on a luxury yacht with Deandre, Signe, and one of the smartest guys I'd ever met. Why stay here and risk everything, sticking it to the company responsible for a product that, in all likelihood, killed my high school sweetheart? Would it bring her back? Not as a Revvie, I mean.

No, I'd bought a one-way ticket on the Guilt Bus, and I was staying on it until the crazy-mad driver plunged over the cliff.

Pling!

I jumped at a tinny sound from the far side of the vacant loft. It was well after sunset, and about two-thirds of the lights were off, leaving an island of light where I lived and worked. Darkness owned the remainder of the third floor. It wasn't the first time I'd heard something up here I couldn't explain. Buildings settled, right?

From the day after Ding and his people left, I'd been completely alone in his loft, which was the first time I could ever recall being truly and totally without another person living in the same space.

It creeped me the fuck out, big time.

Things flickered in the corner of my vision, disappearing when I looked. Noises. Clicks. Pings. Plops. I got to where I half-expected one of Dickens's freaking ghosts of Christmas whenever to show up and rattle some chains at me and show me my dark and scary future in an Illinois state correctional facility.

Ding had paid the power bill through the 30th, but some innate sense of conservation and frugality had forced me to leave the lights turned off at night. The switches were way the hell over by the elevators, on the Dark Side, where boogeymen dropped their keys and snickered, waiting for hapless dolts like me to come get their heads chopped off and their bodies used for puppets in hell.

"I have a gun. I'm not afraid to blow your spooky balls off, Mr. Boogeyman."

No sound came back. Nothing giggled, tittered, or chuckled.

I strained my eyes for a while longer, trying to see beyond the circle of light that made up my makeshift bedroom and living quarters. Ordinarily, I'd hop on over to the switches about now, turn off all the lights and go to sleep without any problem. Which was exactly what I should do right now. Yes, sir. Hop up. Go turn off the lights. Climb into my cozy, mildew-reeking mattress, and get some much-needed rest. Tomorrow was the big day, after all.

Yep. Get right on up and turn off the lights like a big boy.

. . . or not.

I found the list and reviewed it again.

Gun. Check.

Cartridges. Check.

Waiter's uniform. Check.

Creeeeaak.

"You've gotta be shitting me."

I SLEPT WITH THE LIGHTS on.

RAMIREZ ENTERED HIS office at 7:05 a.m. and started updating paperwork at 7:06. At 7:07 he glanced at the left corner of his desk and frowned. A chip in the wood veneer the size of a man's fingernail had popped loose. It stuck up three or four millimeters, enough to snag his attention... or anything else he might brush over it, like a suit jacket. Ramirez squeezed it down with his thumb.

It stayed put until 7:09. Ramirez squeezed it down and held it for a count of five. No good.

He owned no glue of any kind. Tape would look like shit. Ramirez huffed a curse and left his office to rummage in the department admin's desk. She wouldn't be in until nine, at the earliest, which forced him to dig through unruly piles of junk in her drawers, until he located a half-expended tube of Super Glue.

When he got back to his office, the phone was warbling a business-like tune. Ramirez punched the answer button without checking the incoming caller display. "Ramirez."

"Hold for Director Proctor."

Ramirez stiffened. His boss, the Director of Homeland Security, rarely called; when she did, the news was never good.

Techno-punk hold music played while he waited. And waited some more. During the pause, he mastered the glue's stuck cap and dropped a tiny crystal pearl of adhesive under the chip. Pressed it down. A thin bead squeezed out around the edges, which he swiped away.

"*Tu madre*," he hissed when the sticky crap smeared his thumb.

"Excuse me, Ramirez?" Proctor's thin, nasal voice whined over the speakerphone. "Am I interrupting your day, perhaps?"

"Ah... no, ma'am, I was not referring to you. It was another irritation. I mean, an irritation not related to you in any way." Ramirez winced and shut up. Better to throw out the shovel than keep digging, he decided.

The director held the pause for a ten count. "We have a problem, Agent Ramirez. I understand you currently have an operation underway regarding the so-called Children of Liberty."

"Yes, ma'am." He rubbed absently at the tacky gunk on his thumb, trying to scrape it off with a fingernail. After another long pause, he added, "They are a group of subversives who have taken their name from the pre-Revolutionary War group, the Sons of Liberty. They were—"

"Enough, Agent. I'm fully versed in the Revolutionary War."

Because you no doubt lived through it. Ramirez said only, "Yes, ma'am."

"They have a mole inside the cabinet," the director continued. Her querulous old-maid voice made every pronouncement sound like it was coming from a crazy neighbor lady who lived in a house everyone avoided.

"A mole?" Ramirez repeated, picturing at first a small varmint in the furniture. Then it clicked. "You mean an informer? In the president's cabinet?"

"Exactly that."

A sick feeling eeled up from his stomach. How? How could such a group get someone so highly placed? The glue on his thumb had shredded like so much dead skin. He picked at it, removing bits smaller than a pinhead.

"Could be a staffer," Proctor was saying, "or it could be one of the cabinet members themselves. There's forty-two of the damned people to vet, not counting their gaggle of staffers, so it's taking some time to find the leak."

"How can I help?" Ramirez scrubbed his tacky thumb on the desk's rough underside.

The director sighed. "I'm going to give you some background here that you're not cleared for, Agent Ramirez, because sources tell me you're the right man to get this done." The line went silent, and Ramirez held his tongue. "The mole managed to plant a button-cam inside the cabinet meeting room minutes after the counter-electronics sweep. They recorded a very... um, sensitive meeting. The video file from this meeting has been delivered to Millicent MacCauley, of that we can be sure. Electronic traces and drone surveillance confirm she picked it up from an Internet café in downtown Chicago. From there, we of course lost her."

Ramirez winced. MacCauley. "I had the little bitch in jail. We chipped her, but..."

"They killed the chip."

"Yes, ma'am." He drew a deep breath and asked, "Am I allowed to know what was in the file?"

Director Proctor told him. Ramirez grew colder as she spoke, to the point he had to repress a shiver.

"*Madre de Dios*," he breathed.

Ramirez checked the progress of his Super Glue removal and hissed in pain. Somehow he had managed to scrape the pad of his thumb so raw, droplets of blood seeped through the skin. Bits of glue hung in ragged shreds.

WEDNESDAY, MAY 30th.

The big day.

I rode a bus downtown, dressed in my waiter's uniform, three pounds of pistol tucked into my waistband, its hammer digging a crater in my gut. I kept one hand wrapped around the bit-stick in my pocket.

The Huateng Tower occupied two blocks along Michigan at Grand. One of the thirty or so Chinese-owned buildings in downtown, the Huateng featured one hundred and sixty stories of office space, with ground-floor restaurants and a high-end fitness club. The top floor was given over to a ballroom of epic proportions—or so claimed the web info. Renascentia's corporate headquarters occupied eight of the floors, between 101 and 109.

When I hopped off the bus in front of the skyscraper, I craned my neck like a tourist and tried to see the top of the building, but low clouds blocked my view. I had learned through recon (we super-criminals use terms like that) that to reach the service entrance, one had to go through the lobby doors, turn left, and follow the outer wall around to a nondescript door with a card reader access panel. On my dry run several days ago, I tested my ID card on the reader. The door clicked open, and I ventured inside far enough to find the elevator before I backed out. So much for their high-class security.

Now it was time for the real thing. My feet stuck to the sidewalk and refused to stir.

A lake breeze brought a cool, humid touch to the springtime temperature, a comfortable 70 degrees. The city smelled of concrete, dust, and open dumpsters. Downtown was a ghost town at eight p.m., with the exception of the ubiquitous street people. Every third building was either closed or condemned and boarded up, and more trash rustled through the street than pedestrians. For the first time in a while, I wondered if Ding might have been right. Maybe the money was drying up and the country was headed for bankruptcy. I'd seen pictures of a vibrant and active downtown Chicago taken less than fifty years ago, with people jamming the streets, cars everywhere, and shops, restaurants, and theaters going full bore.

What's more, why was I standing in front of the Huateng with a pistol sticking down my pants like some solid-steel erection, instead of marching inside and fulfilling my destiny? Now was not the time for philosophical discourse. Now was the time for *Grand Theft Automaton*.

Get going, Joe. You ain't got all night. I glared at my right foot and forced it to move. *There ya, go. One foot in front of the other.*

I entered the Huateng and followed my route to the service entrance. *Click.* The door opened. Sixty paces later, I arrived in front of the freight elevator. Three Revivants joined me when the doors clattered open. They stank like they'd wallowed in dog shit.

I stabbed the button for the top floor and waited while the steel doors groaned and slammed shut.

One of the Revivants grinned at me and said, "Brainsss. *Hhnh-hhnh-hhnh.*"

Oh great. A comedian.

Cops and Robbers

In the deserted, urine-soaked lobby of the once-magnificent Mile Marriot, the HSA TAC squad had taken to Tasering rats for entertainment. There was no shortage of targets, so size counted, with the biggest prize being ten points for a Godzilla rat, all the way down to five points for a baby rat. Anything smaller than a cat didn't count, and ten bonus points if the Taser put them down with one jolt.

So far, no one had collected the bonus.

"I think he'll shoot his dick off before he makes the top floor." Maravich idled against the bar, dividing his attention between the 3D antics of their subject and the competition in the lobby. "Hey, Duvall! Nice shot, *compadre*." To Ramirez, he said, "Man, this is a waste of fucking time. Let's go pop the guy now and get it over with. I mean, think about it, if he actually hurts somebody up there, it'll be our ass."

"Your ass, you mean," Ramirez scoffed. "You afraid you'll lose your payday, Big Ben?"

"Fuck you, Beaner. You know how much Renascentia pays for a fresh, *live* body in good shape, with all the right paperwork attached. Duvall, you jackass! That wasn't a rat, that was a homeless guy."

Duvall cackled. "My bad."

Fourteen | In Which Things go to Shit Again.

FOR MY FIRST ROBBERY, I'd grade the attempt a C-plus, or maybe a B-minus. From the beginning, everything went down slicker than melted butter on a waxed floor. I was one short ride away from freedom and a life of self-indulgent sloth.

It was at that moment my captive, Jamil Yamadut, CEO of Renascentia, activated a hidden protocol in the Revivant programming, and Joker Larry turned into Killer Zombie Larry. My straight flush busted with one turn of the river card, accompanied by a dangling eye and a bloody grin.

"I see ouuuu." Larry burbled past bloody teeth. "Braaaiinnnss. Hhnh-hhnh-hhnh."

"WELL," MARAVICH SAID. "He almost made it. Should we go get him, or let the sap earn his reward the hard way?"

Ramirez frowned at the display showing the hapless Joseph Warren in the service corridor at the top floor of the Huateng Tower, blazing away with a six gun at the advancing Revivant and having all the effect of pissing at an avalanche. The jittery, frizzy image left a lot to be desired. Warren's microchip could use the feed from the nearby security cameras—even though he had cut the signal to the cameras' head end—and bounce the reconstructed picture off a cell tower to the Homeland field monitor. It didn't have much juice, however, so the action appeared as if broadcast over an antique TV with rabbit ear antennae.

"I have a lot invested in this prick," the dark-eyed agent mused. "If Yamadut kills him now, we may never get close to MacCauley. Not in time, anyway."

"We should get up there and yank his skinny ass out of the fire?"

"Agreed." Ramirez shut down the player and stuck it in his pocket. He whirled one finger in the air. "Let's move out."

THE OPEN FREIGHT ELEVATOR door yawned at the end of the hall, its horizontal metal doors retracted into the ceiling and floor. Between me and it stood a shambling zombie assassin and a sexually ambiguous CEO. It occurred to me—in the timeless moments between seconds, when the brain either produces a brilliant plan to keep you alive or folds up into a quivering blob of Jell-O—that ol' Larry the Killer Guy had a problem. He held his one functional eyeball in his right hand, so whenever he tried to let go and use both hands to throttle me, the eyeball plopped onto his cheek and the Revivant lost sight of me. When he picked it back up, his free hand wasn't enough to pin my throat for a terminal date with Mama Thumb and her four fingers.

Ordinarily, that would have been funny as hell.

We danced the Macabre-erena around the confines of the hallway for a few sweaty, cursing seconds: me ducking away, Larry one-handedly spotting me again, followed by me ducking the other way.

"Hode stih," he grunted.

"Hold still?" I wheezed, already out of breath and lathered with sweat. "I don't think so, Lare ol' buddy."

With panther-like agility, I slipped past his grasping hand, executed a balletic triple-Lutz pirouette in the tradition of Spider Man and James Bond. (It only *seemed* like I ducked, fell on my ass, rolled like a bowling pin past Larry, and scrambled away like a six-legged crab on meth.) I bounced up next to Jamil, who cringed and squeaked a full-on girlish squeal.

"Oh fuck, Jamil, grow a pair," I rapped out. In a fit of meanness, I swung the nickel-plated Smith & Wesson at his head.

He ducked.

I missed.

I hot-footed for the elevator, trailing heated curses. My black work shoes slapped the tile floor in a staccato beat—*blap-blap-blap-blap*—and I lunged into the steel elevator car well ahead of the Revivant. Jamil was out of the action; he sprawled on the floor after whacking his head on the wall, dizzy if not unconscious.

"Waiiiiii—" cried Larry. Nano-soaked blood the color of strawberry paste streaked the floor behind the shambling, pink-suited janitor. He held his eyeball to see where he was going. Gore dripped from the crater where the top of his head once covered his brains. *Braaai-innnss*, that is.

I shot him the finger with one hand and stabbed the Down button with the other.

Bad noises happened, nothing else.

"*Hhnh-hhnh-hhnh.*"

"Oh, give it a rest, Larry." I finger-punched the plastic Down button like a demented woodpecker. Something groaned and clunked. A smoky reek of burned plastic filled the air, and the floor juddered. The doors most emphatically did *not* fucking close. "Ah, come on. This is bullshit."

I scanned the interior of the car, hunting for anything. A breaker box, a switch... a bazooka... anything to keep Larry's cold-sausage fingers from clamping around my throat. Loose papers and splinters of long-lost pallets littered the floor; other than that, the elevator was empty. I had about twenty or thirty scuffing steps before Larry would have me pinned. Doing the duck-around game again would only delay the inevitable. I had to get out this hall, and out of this building. In my favor, I had an expensive paperweight—without ammunition, the Smith & Wesson wouldn't do the job.

"I need... I need a goddamned flamethrower, that's what I need. Take this, you putz." I threw the revolver, and it thunked off Larry's chest and clattered to the floor. If I had access to the Net, I could enter the search term: *How do I kill somebody who's already dead?* What would Google do with that? "Hey, Larry? Can't we all just get along?"

More from prayer than practicality, I jammed my index finger into the Down button so hard, the plastic cover cracked and sliced my fingertip. Machinery whined, the clamshell door burped a few centimeters and froze, straining against an invisible force. I jumped up, snagged the upper half of the two-part door and chinned up, lifting my feet clear of the floor. The door shifted another few centimeters and groaned to a halt.

My sweaty fingers lost their grip, and I fell on my ass. Larry's clawed hand swung through the space over my head, and he tottered, stumbled, nearly fell. His turn to growl. I kicked him in the shin from my seated position, and something cracked in his leg. Of course, the Revivant didn't feel a thing.

I scrambled along the door jamb, fighting for space to get off another solid kick. If I broke Larry's legs, it wouldn't matter how little pain he felt, the sonofabitch would be stuck on the floor where I could stomp him to glue. A splinter stabbed my hand.

"Fucking ow!" is what I screamed. What I thought was: *Holy shit, there's a splinter in the door jamb! Fucking ow, that hurts.*

I focused on the nexus of my elevator-door problem—a chunk of wood about the length and shape of a kitchen knife had fallen in the crack between the steel door and the floor plate of the elevator, wedging it open in much the same way I blocked the kitchen door from this side. I tore at it with ragged fingers, worming the bloody tip of my index finger under the thick end and prying at it.

"God ouuuu," Larry gurgled. His heavy body fell on me with a linebacker's passion and a cement bag's finesse. *Fffump!*

"Jesus, Larry," I huffed, nearly cackling with hysteria. "At least buy me dinner first."

I elbowed the Revivant in the chin with a dull smack. Liquid bits splattered over me from his gaping cranial cavity. He *oomphed*, and his crawling fingers squiggled over my shoulders, seeking my neck with the single-mindedness only the dead can bring to a job. The wedge shifted a millimeter, and the doors promptly shifted enough to jam it in tighter. I turtled my neck into my shoulders and shoved the door edge down with one hand—pushing against the mechanism that wanted to close it, heaving for some slack—and dug at the embedded stick with scratching fingers.

Larry's stink, coupled with his morning breath, made breathing a chore. Or maybe it was all his, ah, *dead weight* crushing the air from my lungs. Either way, my vision darkened at the edges, and my sweat-slippery fingers slid away from the chunk of blasted wood time and again. Every time I worked it loose enough to grab, the door mechanism caught up with my effort and jammed it in tight again.

"God! Damn! It!" I stabbed the fingers of my right hand so deep in the crack, skin tore and bones bent in odd places. "Come! Fucking! Loose!"

"*Hhnh-hhnh-hhnh,*" Larry churned out. I bowed up under him and tugged at the chunk of wood, cramming the fingers of my other hand in next to the first. Things tore... I'm not sure if it was muscles, skin, my clothing, or the fabric of the universe. The bloody stick shifted and popped loose, flying free and skittering across the floor without a care in the world.

The door mechanism chunked and moaned. It shoved up under us, threatening to pin me and Limpet Larry in a meaty sandwich. Without a handy wedge, it seemed quite happy to squish us.

I howled, a primal scream that tore the back of my throat and shattered star systems in distant galaxies. With both hands free, I bent Larry's fingers back until they crackled like kindling wood. He moaned something an awful lot like "Aw shit," but I could be mistaken.

"Take that, you fucktoad," I bellowed. And heaved. Larry rolled outside the elevator doors, and I rolled inside. "Hah! I win, cocksucker. Bite me, Larry! Bite! Me!" The last I saw of him, he was trying to catch his dangling eyeball with bent, splayed fingers and having as much success as a duck playing trombone.

The doors clamped shut, and the elevator gasped and clanked to life, the floor dropping under my panting back with a blessed motion indicative of a descent to safety. Like the reverse of a trapped miner, I rode the shuddering elevator toward freedom and life, fresh air, and salvation.

And I was rich. I patted my jacket pocket. All I had to do was take my bit-stick and—

"Where'd I put the thing?"

The jacket pocket where I'd stuck my bit-stick was empty. I tried my pants, my shirt, my underwear... my jacket again... my pants. I danced up and down, thinking maybe the stick had rolled loose and gotten caught on my clothes. Nothing fell out. I scrabbled around the floor at bug level and scuffed my sore and bleeding hands across the diamond-patterned steel. I sifted bits of paper and smaller bits of wood and other trash.

Then I did it all again.

Somewhere between floor number fifty and floor number ten, the realization sank home. The bit-stick containing all the raw, untraceable cash I'd just stolen was gone.

I considered the Up and Down buttons—the latter cracked and stained with my blood—and dithered. Should I go back up? Duke it out with Larry long enough to find the missing stick? And the real question: could I manage to go another few rounds without getting my head popped off at the shoulders?

Did I have the time? The security measures I'd shunted wouldn't last forever. Somebody may have figured out they could take a hundred and sixty flights of stairs and walk out. The cops could already be on the way, making any rematch with Larry a lost cause.

But the money!

Without burning a single brain cell, I punched the Up button with a swollen knuckle. "Fuck it, how hard could it be to get past one broken-fingered dead guy?"

The elevator shuddered, gears churned and bumped while cables twanged over my head. With a wordless protest the car shifted momentum, paused, and started back up. Based on past experience with the elevator's blazing apathy, it would be another ten minutes before—

Ka-thunk!

The elevator jerked and stopped. I punched the Up button, and nothing happened. I punched the Down button, and nothing happened. I punched both buttons together and—

The lights went out.

Fifteen | When the Lights Go Out in the City

BLACKOUT.

If you lived in Chicago—or anywhere on Planet Earth—in the last twenty-plus years, you became inured to random and frequent losses of power. At the most maximally inconvenient times. Individual buildings used solar or wind (in some cases gasoline-powered) backup generators to power essential functions during these glitches. Essential functions like servers and emergency lights and dialysis pumps.

Freight elevators were not on that list.

I stood in the middle of a silent metal coffin, its dead, dark air pressing against my lungs and invading my eyes.

Claustrophobia compressed.

A rosy flush seeped through the door joint as the building's emergency lights flickered to life in the hallway outside. At least I wasn't stuck between floors. Probably. Maybe. The power of positive thinking. "I can get out, I can get out," chanted the Little Engine Joe in my head. I had fought a cage match with Larry the Fatal Guy to get these doors closed. Could I pry them apart without power?

Well, let's find out.

The joint where the doors came together left a fingernail-wide gap, enough for a few brave photons of light to make it through, but too narrow for my fingers to get a grip. I put a palm on each side of the gap, set my feet, drew a deep breath and *pressed*!

127

And nearly fell flat on my face when the doors *whooshed* apart without a hint of resistance.

"Well, that was easy," I whispered. *Too easy*, something cold and evil whispered in the back of my mind.

"Shut the fuck up," I told it.

My ride had frozen one long step below floor level. The emergency light revealed a vestibule stacked with boxes and trash bags, mop equipment and shelves of acidic-smelling cleaners. A metal plate riveted to the doorjamb told me I was on the 9th Floor. I hiked my leg up and climbed out of the elevator. I found a box, sat on it, and rubbed my face with tired, sore hands.

As a felon with no money, no home, no transportation, and no friends that I trusted, I could count my options on one hand and have enough fingers left over to play darts. Run for it, or go back and rummage for my missing bit-stick. Up one hundred and fifty-one flights of stairs. Yeah. Sure.

"Move, Joe," I said. "Time's running out."

I jumped off the box and navigated through the cluttered maintenance room to the only exit. On the other side: vacant space. The entire floor had been cleared of all walls and furnishings. Overhead, a metal grid that once held ceiling tiles crisscrossed the room, and cables hung through the empty space like dangling vines in a techno-jungle. Scattered emergency lights, aided by the glow of the city through the windows, left the entire floor clouded with deep pools of primal darkness.

Something clinked in the distance.

"Well, this ain't spooky at all." My shaky voice echoed, and sweat dripped from my nose. I combed the hair back from my forehead with a jittery hand, and it came away soaked.

A meter away, an exit sign dangled from a loose conduit at head height. I quick-marched that direction, following the solid wall on my left. A low-hanging coil of wire brushed my neck. Nothing makes you a karate expert faster than a snake-like object touching your neck in the dark.

Five meters beyond the next exit sign, a metal door labeled "Fire Escape" in bold red letters appeared. Shouldering open the door, I discovered a short landing and utilitarian concrete stairs that zigzagged into the darkness above and below. Weak light flickered from orange bulbs at every zig. Mostly. They grew dimmer as I watched.

"Oh shit," I muttered. "The generator's going out."

With a glance upward, I said a mental goodbye to my billions of dollars and bolted downward, feet pounding, with one hand on the rail for balance. One flight, two flights... three flights... four... flights. Where I drew up and sucked wind like an overridden horse. You'd think going *down* would be easy.

I bent over at the waist and panted until the blackness around my vision receded, then started down again, at a more measured pace. At the first floor, a rail separated the stairs, preventing anyone from accidentally going to the basement in case of a fire. A metal door with a push bar opened—I believed—onto the building lobby, from which the average escapee would flee to safety from the fire, or Godzilla, or crazed waiters with revolvers, or whatever chased them from the Huateng in the first place.

I put my hands against the cool metal and tried to extend my Spidey senses beyond the surface. Had the cops beat me here? Something... tingled. Maybe it was only gas, or maybe it was my nerves acting up, but I really didn't want to go out that door.

I vaulted the rail and jogged down another flight of stairs to the basement level. There was no emergency light at this landing. No light at all except what filtered from above. Another door, another push bar, this one so shrouded in darkness, it appeared black rather than gray. I touched it with the same superstitious belief I had relied on earlier.

This time: nothing.

"Fuck it," I said under my breath. I hit the door with my shoulder and the push bar with my hip. It screeched open, bottom dragging across the concrete. Light spilled from the other side; at least here they'd not scrimped on emergency bulbs. I shoved my way through and—

"Hello, Joseph," said Agent Ramirez. "Glad you could join us."

Behind Ramirez stood another agent, with blond hair and a chiseled face. Two more goons in black flak jackets held spotlights, which they now chose to shine in my face. Blinded, I threw an arm over my eyes.

"No!" Anger from losing my newfound wealth clicked with fear of imprisonment, and a switch tripped in my brain. I lashed out at the backlit, blurry targets, powered by the uncontrolled fury of a tanker-truck explosion. One fist connected—hard and satisfying—a dull, meaty thud that jolted my arm. Someone snapped out a bark of pain. I'm pretty sure it was Ramirez. Rational analysis drowned under a haze of red. Rage burned hot.

I was screaming.

Something jabbed me in the ribs. A billion bees stung me at once, all over. My muscles locked up, and fire exploded from my scalp.

Floor.

Ceiling.

Feet.

Lights.

Nothing.

RAMIREZ PROBED HIS split lip with the tip of his tongue. Every time he touched it, his annoyance with Mr. Joseph Warren clicked up one notch. The next few minutes would give him the greatest satisfaction he'd experienced in a long time. He occupied one of two seats in a room the size of a modest kitchen; the chair across the table from him waited for the arrival of the little shit in question.

Maravich leaned against the interrogation room door, not bothering to hide his amusement. "The goofy little shit tagged you a good one, didn't he?"

Ramirez ignored the taller man and brushed at a dust smear on his faux silk jacket. The jacket cost more than Warren earned in six months of unemployment assistance; dirt and grit were embedded in the fabric after Warren punched him. Ramirez had tumbled across the dirty floor, more from surprise than the power of the blow.

Oh, yes, the next phase of this operation would be a pure joy.

The door opened, and two guards carry-marched their prisoner into the room and plopped him on the vacant chair. Warren slumped in his seat, hunched over, ankles and wrists cuffed and chained to a waist belt, wearing an orange jailhouse coverall and sporting a puffy, bruised eye. Lank, mousy hair fell around his face, and five o'clock shadow stubbled his hollow cheeks. Pale, thin and undoubtedly malnourished, their soon-to-be snitch reminded Ramirez of a thousand similar small-time crooks.

Pathetic.

"He looks," Maravich drawled, "like something the cat vomited up. Tell me how this little puke knocked you down again, Agent Ramirez?"

Ramirez leaned forward and snapped his fingers under their prisoner's nose. "Joseph?" Snap-snap. "Joseph, you in there?"

One brown eye glared through a tangle of greasy hair. "No, I'm at your mother's house, watching her crap out more kids like you."

"Hah!" Maravich barked. "I like this guy."

Warren's good eye flicked to Maravich and back to Ramirez. "How'd you find me?"

"Does it matter?" Ramirez unwrapped a stick of gum and popped it in his mouth. He needed some real calm to keep from snapping this little prick's neck. "Let me lay out the charges, Mr. Warren," he said once he got the gum going. "First, we have armed robbery, followed by conspiracy. Then comes fraud, then comes kidnapping, then we'll probably add malicious destruction for shooting up the Huateng's Revivant." Ramirez worked his jaw and let the seconds tick past. The prisoner failed to react. Surprising. By this time most of them were squirming in their seat. "Joseph, remember the story I told you about being buried in a hole somewhere, never to see the light of day?"

An eye-flicker answered him.

"There are worse things, Joseph," he intoned with as much menace as he was capable. "Much worse things."

"Like for example," Maravich chimed in, "have you seen the Gen Five nanos?"

Warren's good eye slitted tight. His mouth stayed clamped in a grim line. Ramirez wanted to Taser him again and wipe that truculent expression away in a blaze of electricity.

"Nah, of course you haven't. It's top secret shit." Maravich shuddered. "It ain't pretty, dude. They call 'em Behavior Modification and Control Devices, and they're used on live people, not the dead ones. The nanos, they, like... take over... the person from the inside and make 'em do whatever the controller programs them for."

"What do you federal cunts want?" Warren gritted out. "I'm done playing the game."

"Hardly done, I'd say." Ramirez sniffed. "Why, we have lots for you to do. You failed to carry out my simple request from the last time we spoke. What was that, Joseph? What did I ask you to do?"

"You... Get close to the CoL people. Spy on them for you."

"Very good, sir, very smart of you to remember. And did you do that simple task? No," Ramirez continued without pause, "you did not do what I asked. Instead, you went off and committed numerous felonies. Let me ask you: do you consider yourself an American?"

The sudden shift seemed too much for Warren at first. "What kind of question is that?"

"Humor me. What do you think of being an American?"

"What the hell—"

"Humor me," Ramirez repeated.

"I... I guess I never really thought about it. It's just the place I was born. I mean, in school they taught us the white Europeans came here, obliterated the Native Americans, and stole their land. I've read a little bit, and I know it wasn't all that cut-and-dried, but that's kind of... you know... if you stretch it, that's kind of our history. So is slavery and segregation. That part of being an American sucks more than a little." Warren drew in a breath. "But I would say I'm better off than, for example, those people in China dying of bird flu and winding up in mass graves. Or any part of the radioactive dust swirling over the Middle East."

"Yes, you are much better off than those people." Ramirez leaned back and popped his gum. Behind him, Maravich shifted, and Ramirez could almost see the man's eyes roll; he hated it when Ramirez went into an All-American rant. Warren stared at his hands with a sour expression. "This is a land of law and order, Joseph. As this nation has grown up, we've learned to do the right thing more and more often. We made reparations to the Native Americans you spoke of—what?—fifteen years ago. EEOC mandates have leveled the playing field for African-Americans. We've put the reins on un-bridled capitalism and forced businesses to toe the line; they either do the right thing—for the environment, their work force, and the community—or they get de-privatized. We've built the biggest per capita government infrastructure the world has ever known for one purpose: to take care of the citizens of this country."

"Ramirez?" Warren peered with his one good eye from under shaggy bangs. "Are you running for office? If you are, not a chance in hell you're getting my vote."

"No, sir. I am only a working stiff like you, trying to do the right thing—"

"Hah! Don't make me laugh; it hurts my face from where your goons kicked me."

"—and the right thing in this situation is to find the Children of Liberty. Dig them out by root, branch, and twig. They are a dangerous group, my friend, attempting to overthrow the United States government."

"I'm not your friend, Ramirez."

"I think he's got that right!" Maravich crowed.

"No," Ramirez said. His insides frosted over, and his face tightened. "You are most definitely not my friend. I, however, am about the only thing close to a friend you have in your pathetic little life, maggot."

Digging out a small vid player, Ramirez placed it on the table and keyed it on. In a tiny, lifelike display, a scene popped up showing Marion Winston in a jail cell, wearing coveralls and socks but no shoes. He lay on a bunk with an arm over his eyes, but everyone in the room could see it was Winston.

"We caught your only friend, Joseph. And thank you, by the way, for leading us to him. We never would have found this character without your help."

Warren slid forward, putting his face within centimeters of the diorama playing on the screen. "You're saying you caught Ding? And I'm supposed to believe this because you show me some doctored-up video?"

At a signal, Maravich opened the interrogation room door and said, "C'mere."

Ramirez watched his prisoner's face go from a sneering, ferrety kind of bravado to gape-eyed surprise, followed closely thereafter by something like real horror.

"You didn't," he breathed.

"We did." Maravich shoved the Revivant who was once Signe. The woman stumbled forward in a petite, see-through teddy and nothing else. Maravich grabbed the other Revvie, formerly Deandre, and dragged her next to the shorter blonde. Deandre was dressed in stockings and garter, with a push-bra. Both had vacant expressions and shiny, unwashed skin. "Gen Fives, buddy. Finest kind. Living, but, ah, reprogrammed. I did both of these gals, back before we turned 'em over. The blonde took it like a champ, never even cried. The black one, well, she fought it like a wildcat." The agent touched a scratch on his chin. "Anyways, after that, we injected both these gals with the Gen Five nano, programmed as sex toys. Now they beg for it."

Warren threw up on the floor.

After the prisoner finished retching—and it didn't take long as he had nothing much to expel—Ramirez snapped his fingers to get the man's attention. "Listen up, boy. Here's what's going to happen. This time, you will follow my instructions. You will find the group known as the Children of Liberty. You will report to me this success within five days. If you do not succeed in five days, your friend goes the same way as these two women. *Comprende?*"

A bit of drool hung from Warren's lip, and when he nodded, it bounced but didn't break.

"Second," Ramirez continued, "you will infiltrate this group and find a file—"

"A what?" the prisoner croaked.

"Shut up. Once you have found this file, you will report back to me immediately on its location. Failure in this matter will be dealt with even more severely. Not only will your friend become a Gen Five

Revivant, you will follow him in his fate. I will program your body to teach knife tactics at the Academy. Do you understand these instructions?"

The prisoner whispered something.

"What was that?"

"I said," Warren rasped, "how can you get away with this? Creating slaves?"

"Lady Liberty gives me a lot of latitude in how I pursue my protection of her." Ramirez smiled. He knew from previous testimony his face resembled skin tightened over a skull when he smiled. "It's not all stick; here's the carrot. Succeed in helping me recover this file, and the nanos in these women will be deactivated. Your friend goes free." Ramirez sat back and let his face relax. "Now, do we have an understanding?"

In the center of the table, the holographic representation of Marion Winston remained alive. The corpulent crook had shifted to his side, curled up in a fetal ball. He appeared to be crying. Warren stared at the holograph of his friend. As Ramirez opened his mouth to ask again, the goofy little shit across the table stirred and looked up.

"You'll let Ding go?" Warren asked. "You'll fix Signe and Deandre?"

"Of course. I don't want Winston. I want the video file in the possession of Millie MacCauley and her band of troublemakers. Nothing else matters to me at this point."

Warren paused for a long ten count. "I'll do it," he whispered.

Sixteen | Secret Agent Joe

THE BROKEN PLASTIC sign in front of my lodgings read Turn-berry Terraces, and, for a mere $850 per night, I could recline on a reeking, yellow-stained mattress in a room smaller than the Huateng freight elevator. I mean, if I swung my feet out of bed too careless-ly, they whacked the wall. This little slice of heaven was located so deep in the South Side, the Homeland cops traveled in up-armored squads, and the cockroaches carried blades.

It was nasty, dangerous, and cramped, but at least it was monu-mentally inconvenient to everything.

I missed the ghostly deserted atmosphere of Ding's place, but a crew of meth cookers had occupied the first floor and turned it into an explosion waiting to happen.

Three nights after my aborted robbery, I rode the Metro from the Ptomaine Terraces Hotel, boarding the bus at Washington Park and—two transfers later—got off a block short of Lincoln Park. Elapsed travel time from presidential park to presidential park, one hour forty minutes. Long enough to damned near reach Canada.

Fifteen, twenty years ago, the Dive In bar on Wells Street would have been part of a trendy neighborhood filled with boutiques and stores called shoppes. Clean, maintained streets filled with urbanites mingling over coffee. The bones of that neighborhood remained, like a picked-over turkey at Thanksgiving. Iron bars had replaced the cof-fee bars, and dress shoppes had morphed into head shops. A few small businesses held on by grim determination. Squatters had invaded some of the vacant spaces, selling whatever they could scrounge or steal, the landlords either out of business or too afraid to evict.

The folks with money stayed in guarded high-rises, well above the stinking stew, or in gated communities so far into the suburbs, even mass transit wouldn't reach them. These were not circles I traveled in, but I'd seen the pictures.

On the gritty streets, the new urbanite—known as the Homeless—wandered the streets in droves, about as lively as the occasional Revivant shambling by on its programmed task. Were the Revvies dead, or Gen Five? I couldn't spot the difference.

Walking from the bus stop, I imagined myself the only living person in a bad zombie flick.

This was Tuesday, making it my third attempt to spot one of the Children of Liberty. I claimed my favorite corner stool at the Dive In and ordered a beer. While in jail with Millie and her pals, I picked up a whispered reference to this bar that made me think they met here on a regular basis. It wasn't much to go on, but I had to start somewhere. Ramirez's threat squeezed my throat with invisible hands. If I didn't bring him something tomorrow, Ding's life would be the first penalty, and mine would be the second. Deandre and Signe would continue to be sex slaves for as long as they lived, or until their bodies wore out.

From my stool at the corner of the L-shaped bar, I had a good view of the room while remaining inconspicuous. Dim light helped, as did my fellow barflies hunched on their stools, and the waitresses and patrons who came between me and the main floor to place orders. I could hide in plain sight and practice my detective impersonation.

"'Nother beer there?" The bartender watched me like I'd steal his hoarded supply of stale pretzels without constant vigilance. Made of grease and black hair, the guy resembled one of those cartoon characters who gets hit in the head with a frying pan, compressing the hairline into the eyebrows.

"Beer?" I considered the suds in the bottom of my glass. "That what this is? Hmm. I thought it was fermented goat piss."

"Hey, you don't like the beer, go take up space somewhere else, big spender there."

I motioned for another. In fairness, the guy had a right to get snippy; three nights running I'd taken up a stool and had two beers in three hours. I was a lousy tipper too. And if I didn't find a clue, or a lead, or whatever the detective types called it, I'd have to crawl back to Ramirez and beg for more time. And money. More humiliating than wetting my pants in third grade while giving a presentation in front of Ms. Webster's class at Rahm Emanuel Elementary School and having Tamesha Davis point and shout, "Look, Joey peed hisself!"

Not that anything like that ever happened. I'm just saying, if it did—

Oops. *I spy something hairy.* Bushy beard at the two o'clock position. I'd seen the guy before, at the Children of Liberty protest march, holding a sign with the words Life, Liberty, and Pursuit of Happiness crossed out. Ran across him while in jail too, though he kept to himself. Medium height, medium build, and enough thick black hair he could be stunt double for a bear. He must have slipped in while I bantered with the flat-headed bartender. His name was... Tony? Tommy? Something like that. In jail, he stayed in a cell at the far end of the row from mine, and he was one of the first released, so I never got to know the guy.

But he was one of them. A Child of Liberty.

Beardboy huddled across a table near the door with a dark-skinned guy, one who had been there earlier, a bald man with hoop earrings the size of hubcaps and a bone through his septum. I couldn't decide if he was going for pirate or Zulu warrior, but either way, the guy could scare a freight train onto a dirt road. The pair of them had their heads close together, all serious and sincere, and anytime a server or patron passed too close, they would go quiet and watchful.

Intrigue smoldered.

My original stakeout plan involved me "stumbling" upon my jailhouse companion and leading off with, "Hey, I know you! It's Joe, from jail. Remember me?" and from there working my way into the group. I scrapped that idea two minutes after spotting Beardboy and his pal. If ever two guys were involved in skullduggery, it was these two, and I sensed dropping in on them unexpectedly would end badly for me.

Plan B: Follow Beardboy when he leaves and see where he goes.

I didn't have long to wait. The waitress, in tan super-short-shorts and a mesh top (I checked her out meticulously for concealed weapons) brought him an amber drink in a shot glass, collected payment, and swivel-hipped away. Beardboy knocked back the drink, and his face twisted in disgust. His companion flashed yellowed teeth in a laugh and slapped palms with the CoL member, who pushed back from the table and made for the door.

I chugged my beer and followed.

Beardboy headed south on Wells. I hung back under the awning, amid the outdoor tables occupied by the pot and tobacco smokers, risking a contact high while I waited. My guy wore navy trousers and a white-and-blue striped shirt, which showed up nicely under the rare streetlight. I let him get half a block away before I left the hazy atmosphere in front of the Dive In and trailed after him. I figured he shouldn't be too hard to follow; the guy probably left a trail of hair everywhere he went.

At an hour before midnight, many of the homeless had gathered in doorways and sheltered alleys, like human snow drifts. The weight of their watchful eyes pressed against me as I passed. If Ramirez hadn't slithered into my life, I'd be one of them about now, huddled with my back to a solid surface, prowling for a meal... Maybe I should thank the half-pint prick, next time I saw him.

A bundle of rags with scarecrow hair vaulted out of a dark nook. My heart seized, and I flinched back.

"Hey, sugar," the tatterdemalion rasped, "a hunnert bucks and you can use any hole."

"Ah, no, thank you." I hurried past her and nearly choked on the smell while she complimented my parents, my manhood, and my love of small animals. Seconds later, I had a panic attack when I failed to spot Beardboy, who had disappeared while I was occupied with the harpy hooker.

I hustled to the corner and picked him up again, strolling west along Evergreen Avenue, acting without a care, hands in his pockets. I turned up the collar on my lightweight jacket, stuffed my hands in my pockets, and trailed my subject with the guile of a highly trained secret agent.

The streetlights gave out once we passed under the L, pitching the sidewalk into near-darkness. I had to pick up the pace to keep Beardboy in sight, closing the distance to twenty meters while trying to keep quiet and not scuff my shoes on the ground, or kick a bottle in the dark. The guy never looked around, not once. He kept up a brisk but not hurried pace, ignoring the street people, moving at a steady cruise.

Beardboy crossed to the south side of Evergreen, and I kept pace as he turned left on Sedgwick. It wasn't until I passed the dead body hanging from an old-fashioned light pole that I realized where we were.

Cabrini Territory.

Oh.

Fuck.

Me.

I stopped in my tracks. To hell with Beardboy, to hell with Ramirez, to hell with Ding. There wasn't enough incentive in the universe to make me stroll into Cabrini-held turf without air cover and a battalion of homicidal maniacs at my back.

The schools closed in 2030, after the rape and murder of an eighth-grade teacher... by her class. She was the fourth teacher in the area killed that year. The union had called a strike, and the administration had no choice but to pull out. Ten years later, the authorities—from the city to the national level—had washed their hands of about ten square kilometers surrounding the area where the Cabrini-Green housing complex once stood.

Nowadays, the kids ran feral, and order was maintained by the Gangster Disciples, who sold everything from drugs to heavy weapons. They were fiercely opposed to anyone not-black entering their area. Unless you could prove at least one black parent, you ran the risk of being strung up like this poor dumb fuck hanging from the light pole. How in the hell did a white man like Beardboy stroll so casually into an area patrolled by the most vicious gang in Chicago?

And how fast could I run away?

A throat cleared behind me, and my blood chilled.

I turned to find a gathering of shadowy figures materializing from the depths of the night. Two, then four, then six. They shuffled into a loose ring around me. All of them were armed, holding everything from handguns to wicked-looking rifles with extended magazines. I found myself unable to swallow, a cold sweat washed over me, and I needed to pee.

"Uhhhh," I stammered, "one of... one of you guys order a pizza? I gotta pepperoni-extra-cheese for Tyrone. Is Tyrone around?"

"A pizza?" the banger directly in front of me asked. Taller than Stonehenge, with oiled coal skin, he had a gold coin embedded in his sternum and wore a satiny-black shirt open to the navel to show it off. "You got it in yo' pocket?"

I patted my jacket. "Damn, I knew I forgot something." I made as if to edge past Stoney. "I'll go back and get it. No wonder my tips are always so—"

"Hold up, Pizza Man." No less than three firearms were pointed at my face. I didn't check behind me, but I suspected those were as well. Nothing as quaint as my (former) Smith & Wesson, these weapons were matte black with levers and buttons and bores big as subways. "You wanna 'splain why you followin' my boy?"

An aircraft passed overhead, winking red and white lights, the muted roar of its engines rumbling across the sky. One of the bangers behind me had a bad case of allergies, or was in the latter stages of co-caine-related rhinitis; he sniffed more than a church full of mourners.

"Your boy?" I spread my empty hands in a show of good faith. "I didn't know he was your son, but now that you mention it, I see the resembl—No! Wait!"

Next thing I knew, I was on the pavement, tasting blood from where Stoney hit me in the face. He loomed over me, grim as Stage IV cancer, a malignant darkness blotting out the midnight sky.

"What you want we should do wit' him?" He wasn't speaking to me.

"I know this guy." Beardboy leaned over next to Stoney and squinted. "Joe? Joe Warren?"

"Hey, Tony!" I gushed. Never was I more glad to see someone so hairy. "How's it been, man?"

"It's Tim."

"Yeah, that's what I meant. Sorry, my head's a little rattled."

"Why were you following me?"

"Following...?" I let my mouth gape open. "Why would you...?"

Stoney screwed the muzzle of his pistol into my left nostril. He cocked the hammer. "Say goodbye, muthafucka."

"Wait-wait-wait! Okay, yeah, I saw you in the bar, and I wanted to see, uh, see Millie again, so I thought you'd lead me to her. I didn't mean anything by it, I swear. I just... I just got to like you guys in jail and all—"

"Lead you to Millie, huh?" Beardboy—no, Tim—jeered. "So why? You could let the cops know where she lives?"

"Doe, mahn." Stoney had driven his pistol barrel even farther into my sinuses. "I sweah, I jus' wanded do see hehr."

"You a lyin' scrotal sack o' shit," Stoney said. "I bes' kill you now."

"Hold on." Tim frowned, making his bushy eyebrows twist together like a fuzzy, black caterpillar. "Millie needs to decide what to do with this guy. He was in jail with us, so he's probably been chipped. Can you wand him and find out?"

"Easy."

The gun left my nose, and one of the other bangers produced a device the size of a chapstick tube. He ran it over me from head to toe. Rough hands grabbed me and flipped me onto my belly. A few seconds later, a high-pitched beep sounded.

"Yep. Chipped."

"Best cut it out. Domino?"

"On it."

A third banger knelt beside me and removed something from an inner pocket. *Snick!* A bright surgical steel blade popped out, longer than a woman's memory and three times as sharp. My shirt split with one long rip.

"Hey," I said, "what the hell—"

They stabbed me in the back.

Irony's a bitch.

Seventeen | Roses are Thorny Bitches

Generation V Revivant B-Mod CD

To: Proctor, Eliza<eliza.proctor@dhs.gov>

From: Bernstad, Maurice<mgbernstad@renascentia.com>

CC: Yamadut, Jamil<jyamadut@renascentia.com>; Pulte, Laura<lpulte@renascentia.com>; Scott, Newtria<nkscott@renascentia.com>; Broward, Kent<kjbroward@renascentia.com>

Eliza,

Attached please find the test results on the Gen V B-Mods, v6.71. The subjects in the test group retained a great deal of motor skill and verbal ability, though self-awareness and cognitive ability were somewhat impacted. None of the subjects were able to reject their programming or refuse the orders of the controller. You will note that all six test subjects became non-viable once the B-Mods were rendered inactive. On the bright side, these subjects were successfully resourced as Gen II Revivants and returned to a state of usefulness, although in a non-breathing capacity. The Gen V process is irreversible, though we believe this will be addressed in future revisions.

The Gen V tests prove the decay and short-lived usefulness of the Gen II model can be addressed by bot injection prior to the subject's separation from a living modality. Using the enhanced formula, Gen V-Plus, pre-injection terminal illness progression can be suspended, prolonging the subject's utility.

We are very excited by these results and believe they fully comply with the directives of the RFP. Renascentia stands by, eagerly awaiting the go ahead to enter mainstream production of the Gen V product line.

Sincerely,

Mo

Maurice Bernstad

VP of Global Sales

Renascentia, Inc., Chicago, Illinois

~Death is but a stage~

I WOKE UP ON A COT. In a room. On my stomach. Standard issue cot, metal-framed, white sheets, lumpy pillow. Standard issue room, clean and well-maintained, four walls, two doors, two windows, one chair.

My back hurt. My head ached. I was drooling. Standard issue drool.

How the hell did I get here?

Gray sunlight filtered through the bars on the windows, secured by a shiny new padlock. The closet door stood open; it contained nothing bigger than a dust mite. The other door was closed, a meter away, on the same wall as the cot. I could see the handle in profile if I craned my head back far enough.

Where the hell—?

Memory oozed back in a series of images.

Gangster Disciples. Hairy Tim. Big fucking knife. Stabbed in the back. A gaping wound radiating more sullen pain than a Jewish grandma.

Stoney's voice: "You get it?"

"Yep." Crackle of plastic. "It daid now."

"Hit him with the trank so we can take him in."

"Are you shitting me?" I complained. "Now you decide to use a tranquilizer?"

"You lucky we used a knife." A sharp prick and consciousness slipping down the drain...

Brighter squares and rectangles on the carpet revealed where things had recently been moved away. Dents were pressed into the weave where furniture had resided, and tiny holes in the drywall indicated where pictures had once hung.

It was peaceful, in a way, lying on the bed under a cotton sheet. A Sunday morning, I-don't-have-to-get-up type of feeling. I drowsed off again for ten minutes or an hour. I had no clock, and the cloudy skies concealed any movement of the sun. Time passed without me, and I couldn't work up one single damn to give.

Some things never change, however, such as the need to pee. After ignoring the protests from my bladder for as long as I dared, I gave in. Groaning, wincing, and hissing, I crunched up and waited for my head to stop trying to fall on the floor. In a giant leap of faith, I stood upright. Wobbled. Steadied. Shivered.

Naked. No clothes in sight.

This did not bode well for my chances of escape.

Dragging the sheet from the bed, I wrapped it around me, toga-style, and tottered to the door. To my surprise, it opened. Beyond the doorway, I discovered the foyer of a modest two-bedroom apartment. To my left, the front door, to my right, the bathroom. Straight ahead, the main room decorated in Early American Comfy, with a stuffed print sofa and a matching easy chair, complete with a chubby grandmother knitting a... knitted thing. Behind her, the door to—I presumed—the second bedroom. When I slunk out, the old woman raised her eyebrows in a silent question, regarding me over glasses perched on her nose.

"Uh," I motioned to the bathroom, "need to..."

"You g'head, chile. Take yo' time."

Gathering the trailing sheet into my arms, I shuffled into the narrow room and shut the door. I clicked in the cheap thumb lock, feeling silly even as I did it. *What? You think the nanny's going to pop in on you unexpectedly?* Embarrassing enough, they left an eighty-year-old woman to guard me, now I was worried that she might sneak a peek at my winkie?

The bathroom might have come out of "Granny's Boutique Bathrooms" magazine. Molded to resemble shells, guest soaps in a scalloped dish complemented the hand towels. A white ocean motif dotted the blue wallpaper, and more fishy stuff covered the plastic shower curtain. Bare metal peeked through the chrome from age and handling, although the fixtures gleamed. A fresh, powdery scent filled the room. It was, by far, the cleanest toilet I'd ever seen. I urinated with greater-than-normal precision, avoiding my usual overspray, and washed my hands in the sink.

A Revvie appeared in the mirror and startled me, until I recognized Joe Warren. Man, I looked like hell. Nobody ever wanted money from me badly enough to call me handsome, but I once had a passable face, with strong cheekbones and a straight nose. Hooded brown eyes that some—okay, one or two—women found attractive and mysterious. Now, gaunt, pale, and healing from a layer of bruises, I could have played Frankenstein without makeup.

After a quick search I found a brush in a drawer. I dampened my hair and currycombed it into shape, falling from the natural part in the middle. The beard stubble would have to wait, but I swished out the gummy taste on my tongue with a bottle of blue mouthwash. There were no cups, so I poured a splash in my palm and sucked it up before it could dribble away, leaving my hand minty-fresh.

I twisted around to see the hole in my back, discovered somebody had dabbed a Band-Aid over it. The area appeared a little swollen, but not too bad.

"Well, Joe," said the ugly bastard in the mirror, "time to face the firing squad."

In the living room, the old lady clacked away with her knitting needles and spoke without taking her eyes off her work. "I laid out some clothes, yonder on the bed. Yo' pants is washed, but them boys done tore yo' shirt so bad, I had to throw it out. I found you some of my oldest boy's things that'll probably fit you."

"Thank you, Mizzz...?"

"Precious Rose Dalrymple," she told me. "But you can call me Momma Rose. That's how people know me best."

"Well, uh, thank you again, Mizz—Momma Rose." I clutched the folds of my sheet to my chest. Checked the front door. The deadbolt knob was turned up, and the chain dangled loose. "Aren't you guys... you know, worried that I'll run away?"

Momma Rose's needles froze, and she narrowed her eyes at me the way my mother used to when I tracked mud on the floor. "I thought you wanted to see Miss Millie and them other folks?"

"I do, but... I don't know, I assumed with getting knocked out and all, that your people might not... trust me?"

"Hah! No, Mr. Joe Warren, I don't believe anybody be trusting on you just yet." The old lady set her knitting in her lap. "But near as we can tell, you ain't a killer. Are you, Mr. Warren?"

"No, not a killer. Apparently I'm only dangerous to myself."

"And besides"—she grinned like a shark—"you in the middle of the baaaaad ol' Cabrini-Green. Where you gonna run?"

"Good point." I shifted in place. Something about Momma Rose made me think she was more than a little old lady with a cute bathroom and a knitting hobby.

"So you go on, get dressed now. Once you're decent, I'll fix you some breakfast, and we go see some people."

"Okay."

Dressed, I could manage. Decent, not so much.

Coituum More Capra

Maravich found Ramirez in his office doing a deep-background profile on the MacCauley woman. It did not surprise him to find his partner had collected a mammoth amount of data on the suspect, everything from her birth certificate and property tax records to her private emails and net search history, including texts from phones she once owned.

"Anything?" Maravich jerked his chin at the screen.

"Nothing."

"Hey, I came by to tell you, our guy's telemetry went dark last night. Fast, like the chip blew, not like he died. I checked the logs a few minutes ago."

"I know. I got the ping." Ramirez didn't look up from the search string he was typing. "They pulled the chip, so he must have made contact."

"You think he'll come through?"

The shorter agent sneered. "Joseph Warren is a cowardly little shit who'll sell his mother's ass on the street if he had to. He'll come through; he's too scared not to."

"We should just snatch up one of them Children. Beat the shit outta him until he gives up the file. Then we can roll in the front door, pop everybody, and be done with it."

"And what if they've made copies? It would be the smart thing to do. We can't assume they're stupid simply because their belief system is screwed up."

Maravich shrugged. "They can't get it on the news or the Net; we've got that shit locked down. We get a sniff of that file hitting the ether and *bam*! Phone, pad, or server, that IP is toast."

"Agreed. I suspect they will attempt to copy the data on hard media—wafer or chip—and distribute it manually, like they do their flyers. They'll need a lot of them to make a dent in the public's apathy, so that means mass production. I told Warren to find where they're replicating the files. We find that, we net the whole operation."

"Suit yourself." Maravich turned away, calling over his shoulder, "As long as I can have 'em when you're done."

Ramirez's voice followed Maravich down the hall. "Of course."

TRUE TO HER WORD, MOMMA Rose fixed scrambled eggs and warmed a plate of cornbread muffins she removed from the fridge. The latter she cut in half and layered with a chunk of real butter. I ate three before my stomach reminded me I'd had little in the way of solid food for the past couple of weeks, and it wouldn't tolerate another bite without open rebellion.

"No, thank you, ma'am," I told my hostess and... jailer?... when she asked if I wanted any more. "My stomach has shrunk to the size of a peanut over the past few months. Another muffin would be suicide." I eyed the plate of beautiful yellow-gold muffins. "Although it would be a good way to go."

"Well, here. I'll put some in a poke for you to take with."

Like the bathroom, everything in the kitchen was at least sixty years old, but every bit of it was spotless. Momma Rose opened a wooden drawer next to the sink and popped out a paper bag, into which she dropped the remaining three muffins. Twisting the sack closed, she handed it to me.

"Best you hold on to that. I don't know if you comin' back here or not."

"That sounds ominous." I put the sack in my jacket pocket.

She put a hand on a prodigious hip and frowned. "Now would I waste food on a dead man? Won't nobody do away wit' you, Mr. Joe Warren, as long as yo' intentions on the up-and-up."

"Well, yes ma'am," I told her with a straight face. "They surely are."

"Mm-hmm." She didn't seem convinced. "Well, daylight's wastin'. Let's go."

"Where are we going?"

"This way." Momma Rose trundled to the front door and waited for me to catch up. She didn't lock the door behind her when we left the apartment.

The hallway was nothing special: a central light strip, ten identical doors along each side, stairs at either end, and a landing in the middle where the elevators were located. Momma Rose's apartment was the third down from the middle, on the side opposite the elevators. I expected to find that Precious Rose Dalrymple lived in an oasis among the destitute. That somehow she'd carved out a corner of normalcy in the middle of the toughest ghetto, the meanest of mean streets, and the territory of the most vicious gang-riddled, drug-addicted, pee-in-the-hallway tenants that a negligent god could spew from the asshole of the world. After all, like she said, this was bad old Cabrini-Green.

My expectations failed to be met.

Clean, well-lit, and neatly painted, the hallway breathed a sense of self-possessed, middle-class pride. I followed Momma Rose like a baby duckling on its first trip from the nest. What the hell kind of alternate reality had I fallen into? Did they pop me with some psychotropic drugs and implant a V-Real viewer in my head while I slept? Where were all the savage bangers with dead eyes and burned-out souls? What happened to the shit-stained and graffiti-covered walls? So far, nothing I had seen jibed with the stories circulating about the Green and its inhabitants—its inmates, I should say. Last night, it was Stonehenge and his five carbon copies, the true-to-life bangers who held me down and stuck a knife in me. They were the reality I expected, not this make-believe scene from daytime vids.

The elevator dinged, and we rode in silence from what turned out to be the top floor (15th) to the 4th. The elevator opened to a landing much like the one we left, except this one had signs on the opposite wall pointing in each direction, with labels like: BLDG REP and COUNCIL. We turned right toward CMD CTR. I followed Momma Rose past open office doors, beyond which uniformly dressed black men worked on data terminals. Each wore a black shirt and khaki pants. Everyone was clean, apparently healthy, energetic, and efficient.

Just your typical gang-ridden cesspool.

The door at the end of the hall stood open, and Momma Rose waltzed in without knocking. I tagged along in her wake, slowing at the doorway and stopping inside the threshold as the man behind a mahogany desk stood up.

"My Precious Rose," the man boomed with a laugh. "How good it is to see you again."

"Franklin Rogers," she scolded, "keep that devil's tongue in your head and don't try and sweet-talk me. It won't get you nowhere in Council, y'hear."

I'd heard of people called dynamos before, but I'd never seen one until I laid eyes on the man in the corner office. Franklin Rogers and I shared the same height, at a goose bump under two meters. And that's all we shared. Where I had a vampire's complexion, his face was a warm chocolate tone. Steel-belted muscles wrapped his iron frame, whereas my build resembled a men's room symbol. Energy radiated from Rogers, while I radiated only body odor and frustration.

"Yes, ma'am," the powerful, vibrant Rogers lamented, "I am properly chastised. I shall speak no more of your winsome beauty." They hugged, a clash of titans, the grandma and the aging middle line-backer.

Either Rogers worked from his living room, or he decorated his office like a living room. By the far wall stood a desk the size of a pool table. Behind it a window showed gray sky and the red brick of a far building. Bookcases bracketed the desk, each shelf packed with real paperbound books. Lamps lit the room. Paintings and photographs of famous African-Americans hung on every spare bit of wall space. The caption on the painting nearest me said, "Frederick Douglass, Emancipation Memorial, April 14, 1876" and depicted a lion-maned black man delivering an address to a crowd of whites.

"Is this the condemned?" Rogers' voice penetrated my woolgathering, and I nearly snapped to attention.

"It is," Momma Rose admitted. "He says his intentions are pure, but I'm not so sure. I can't get a good read on him."

"That's not like you, Rosie. What's wrong?"

"Mixed signals, is what I'm getting."

"Well, we'll soon see." Rogers clapped the old lady on the shoulder in a friendly way. He pinned me with narrowed eyes, and the bonhomie slid away to be replaced with a cobra's death stare. "You understand, Mr. Warren, that if Millicent MacCauley does not vouch for you, a squad will escort you to the most convenient light pole, where you will be hung by the neck until dead. Are we clear on that?"

I tried to swallow past a tightened throat and nodded rather than attempt speech.

"Good," Rogers said. His eyes released me, and he hugged Momma Rose with an arm draped over her shoulder. "Rosie, did you bring any cookies? Company will be here shortly."

Eighteen | Thoroughly Mordant Millie

MOMMA ROSE PATTED ME on the shoulder and said, "Good luck," which sounded more like "My condolences," and left the room. Franklin Rogers invited me to sit in one of two chairs while he dropped into a seat on the couch facing me. The leather creaked when I shifted, but the cushions cradled my ass with tender, loving care.

"So tell me about yourself, Joe." Rogers crossed his legs and lounged one arm on the back of the sofa. His attitude indicated he would find every word I spoke fascinating, and there was no one else in the world he'd rather hear from right now than Joseph Warren.

"Nothing much to tell." I gave him an edited version of my life to date. I left out the major felony at Huateng Tower but included the bit about being arrested and jailed with Millie and her gang. I stumbled a little when I spoke of Chelle's death—or conversion to Revivant. I wrapped with, "So that's how I wound up enjoying your hospitality."

Before he could ask another question, I hit him with one of my own. "So what's the deal here, with this place? You... your guys out front all dressed alike... this building... I mean, it ain't exactly how I always pictured Cabrini-Green."

"The short version or the long one?" Rogers pursed his lips and consulted a real old-fashioned wristwatch—a timepiece and not a netphone—with a steel band and a complex face, filled with dials. "The short one would be best."

He cleared his throat and tilted his head to study the ceiling. "What you see today is the result of a two-hundred-year-old attempt to free my people from slavery. The Civil Rights movement, desegregation, and an enlightened population sowed the seeds of true freedom for the African-American. And then..." Rogers aimed a forefinger at me like a gun. "We got the Great Society, which added some addictive drugs that destroyed the black family, destroyed our incentive to better ourselves, and created a cycle of dependency. You don't believe me?" he asked before I'd said a word. Rogers bounded up and sprang to a bookcase. He ran his finger along a row of books before selecting the one he wanted, which he brought back and dumped in my lap. "Here."

Rogers and de Galvez were made from the same cloth. Born lecturers.

"*Black and Tired*," I read from the spine, "Essays on Race, Politics, Culture, and International Development."

"Dr. Anthony Bradley. A prophet. And here's another: *Liberty Versus the Tyranny of Socialism* by Walter Williams." Rogers resumed his seat after dropping another book in my lap. His butt barely touched the edge of the couch, as if he would leap into action at any moment. "So what happened to people of color?"

Something Alex de Galvez said during one of our jail-time debates came back to me. "They voted for the party that would give them the most stuff."

"Hah! True that. No, the cycle of dependence began. No fathers in the home, generation after generation of restless, angry young men in gangs. Drugs, violence, and ignorance characterized neighborhoods like Cabrini-Green for many years thereafter. To the point that here, at least, the authorities have written us off. Sealed the border and said, 'You stay there and we'll stay over here.' 'Let the inmates run the asylum' was their new motto. Well, we did."

Rogers' eyes glittered. It was obvious he'd been dying to tell someone this story. *Oh, lucky me.*

"Generalize much?" I quipped.

"A small group of my people," Rogers continued past my question, "grew disenchanted with the promises and the lies and—guided by thought leaders like Ben Carson, Thomas Sowell, and Walter Williams—developed a new paradigm for the black man. We gathered our resources behind the scenes, consolidated power and made plans. Thirty years ago, I was a major in the US Army and one of twenty such men hand-picked by our leaders to reclaim our people's dignity. At the right time, we invaded Cabrini-Green, Mr. Warren. Infiltrated it, set up an ops base, brought in logistical support, and we kicked the living shit out of the bangers, building by bloody building. Since we began, we have taken over two-thirds of the C-G Zone of Operations. We established our own democracy, elected leadership, created jobs, laws, and the infrastructure to put my people back on their feet."

"Democracy, huh?" I couldn't keep the disbelief out of my voice. "Sounds more like a military dictatorship."

"At first it was," Rogers admitted. He didn't seem bothered by my challenge in the least. "Order and safety were more important, as was changing the culture to one of self-sufficiency and enlightenment. The process is far from over, young man. Even here, where we have held elections for the past fifteen years, our people sometimes revert to their old habits. However..." He held up a finger to quell my objection. "However, I have relinquished my authority to our duly elected leadership. They decide what happens in matters related to internal discipline, law enforcement, and what have you. In fact, you had the pleasure of enjoying the company of our highest elected official, the Honorable Ms. Dalrymple."

"Momma Rose? Momma Rose is the... what?"

"Mayor."

"Mayor of Cabrini-Green?"

He grinned, well-pleased with himself and my surprise. His eyes shifted to a spot behind my head. "Yes?"

I twisted to find a young, fresh-faced man in the doorway, wearing the black-on-tan uniform of Rogers' soldiers. "Visitors, sir," he said.

"Excellent, son, thank you. Please, show them in."

Rogers stood, as did I. My heart thudded, and I had to put my hands in my pockets to control a small tremor. I wished I'd asked Momma Rose to let me take a bath; I was keenly aware of my own sweat. Footsteps and murmured voices sounded from the hall.

Millie came in first, followed by the giant, John Marsh. Tim, the walking hairball, brought up the rear.

"Hey, Millie!" I plastered on a megawatt smile and held out my hand. "Great to see you!"

Millie paused in the door, scanned me from head to toe, and ignored my hand. Her mouth pinched shut, like a woman who'd bitten into a sour apple and didn't know where to spit it out. "Joe Warren," she said. "They told me you were here, and I still didn't believe it. What possessed you?"

"I'm... I, uh—"

"We were waiting for you, Millie," Rogers interjected, "so we could address that very subject." To the soldier by the door he said, "Bring some coffee, would you, Mr. Perkins?"

"Hello, Sasquatch," I greeted Marsh, who at least acted glad to see me and shook my hand. Tim glowered with radioactive distrust, and I left him alone.

Millie circled the long way around me and hugged our host, telling him how wonderful it was to see him again, and how much she'd missed his company. Rogers returned her warmth with a charming line of bullshit. Together, they gave off uncle-and-favorite-niece vibes. I studied her while they spoke; this was the first time I'd seen Millie outside of county lockup.

Tinkerbell leads the resistance. This is who Ramirez is afraid of?

The top of her blond head didn't reach Rogers' chin, and wearing a short-waisted denim jacket and a white T-shirt and jeans, she could have doubled for a high school teen playing hooky. Or a gymnast, as her sturdy, compact body exuded vitality and athletic strength. Maybe because all the jailhouse drugs were out of my system, it came as a surprise for me when I noticed the round firmness of her ass filling the cotton seat of her jeans. A mental image of that same butt, naked and wet in the communal shower, flashed into my head. *Oh, hello.* My dormant dick lurched awake. Lucky me, with my hands already in my pockets, I could shift my badly timed interest to a safe place.

"Sit, sit, sit," Rogers commanded when Perkins brought a carafe and cups, along with sweetener and creamer packets, and deposited everything on the low table between us. "Coffee, anyone?"

I settled into my chair, Rogers settled on the couch. Millie sat beside him with John anchoring her left side. Tim plopped his hairy butt into the chair next to me, on my right. Nothing was said as we all went through the sacred ritual of coffee preparation. In my jacket pocket, the sack of cornbread muffins crinkled. Should I offer everyone a Momma Rose treat? There wasn't enough for everybody; however, I was not above bribing the jury. Since sexual favors seemed unlikely, maybe food would work. I opened the sack and found a pile of broken muffin crumbs.

Maybe not a good thing to share. It's back to offering sex.

"All right, Joe." Millie's blue eyes examined me over her cup. "Why were you following Tim?"

I sipped a hot shot of courage, gathered my wits, and launched into my story. "It's like this. Ever since jail, I've been knocking around the streets, living hand-to-mouth, you know? Chelle... died... while

I was locked up. That sucked because I lost her, but it also left me homeless. Suffice it to say, over the past few weeks, I've taken a real strong look at how things are being run these days."

I collected reactions. Mild interest from Rogers, a twinge of sympathy from Millie when I mentioned Chelle, an encouraging smile from John, and glaring mistrust from Tim. Mixed signals, Momma Rose would say. Time to ham it up a little. "Add to that, I'm disappointed in the current, uh, political environment. Unemployment's off the charts, right? The media says seven percent, but it has to be more like thirty. There's, like, no small businesses opening up anywhere. A friend of mine told me he thinks the government's going tits up—pardon the expression there—and all the politicians are bailing out like rats leaving the Titanic."

I had worked on this little speech in my head for a few days now. Once I got rolling, it sounded good, and I had John bobbing his head at the right moments, so I kept on. "So I'm in an alley one day, off Wentworth, hunting a safe place to sleep among all the other homeless people, when it hits me, what you folks were saying. About how the government caused all this with their deficits, and how they killed the marketplace with regulations, and that they... that they restricted our liberties in the name of security, and so on and so forth." I waved at Rogers. "Then Franklin here, he tells me about how the government just about destroyed his people with their giveaway programs and constant meddling, and that cemented it in my mind even more." I stopped and held my breath.

Wait for it.

John bailed me out.

"What's that, Joe?" he asked. "Cemented what?"

"That you guys were right, of course." I wanted to show some passion at that point, so I jumped to my feet and my voiced kicked up a notch. "We need to get the government monkey off our backs! We need to keep the goddamned Homeland fucks out of our business! We need to *take back this country*!"

And the crowd goes wild! I deserved an Oscar.

Chest heaving with drama, I settled back and swigged another slug of my coffee, waiting for the applause.

I waited... for... the... applause.

"What a crock of shit," the human hairball said. "This guy was chipped. The feds had him on an electronic leash the whole time. He was following me all the way from the Dive. The only monkey on his back is how much he can score ratting us out."

"I don't know," Millie said before I could work up a reply that would leave Tim crippled for life. She sighed and leaned back. "You never said anything like this while we were locked up together. You were all, like"—her voice acquired the jut-jawed cadence of sneering sarcasm—"hey, you guys are nuts, you're a bunch of conspiracy freaks, leave me outta dis, blah, blah, blah."

"But that was before," I jumped in. "When I was in jail. Before I knew Chelle died. Before I figured some things out."

"Yeah," Tim sneered, "figured out how to sell us to the cops."

"Hey, look, Fuzzy." I glared at Tim over my pointed finger. *Dial it back, Joe. Don't try to sell you're suddenly a true believer.* "I ain't saying you guys have all the answers, okay? I'm just saying I don't like where things are going, and I want a chance to hear more about what you're doing to fix it. Until I met Franklin here, I didn't think anybody had a plan, and you seemed like a good place to start."

So far Millie wasn't giving me much beyond a steady appraisal. Those clear blue eyes unnerved me with their intensity, so I scanned back and forth between the four people in the room, as if speaking to everybody instead of only her. I clamped down on the impulse to keep babbling. I had a sense overselling the political side would back-fire, so I waited out the silence.

"Are you working with the feds, Joe?" Millie asked me, straight up.

"What? No!" I snorted. Guilt reared up, and I squashed it back down. *Ding. Ignore the implanted tracker and think about Deandre and Signe and Ding.* "I hate those bastards after what they did to me and Chelle. Keeping me in jail like that. Hell, no." It wasn't hard to sound sincere; I really did hate Ramirez and that clown, Maravich. Holding eye contact with Millie was harder. If she didn't look so much like a sweet girl-next-door type, it would be easier to betray her and her friends. She had a habit of worrying a thumbnail between her two front teeth while thinking, and it gave her the appearance of a sixteen-year-old waiting for a date. I teased her about it when we were cellmates.

"Didn't I tell you to stop nailing your teeth?" I grinned, and she broke eye contact. A self-conscious smile of her own teased her lips, and she folded her hands in her lap.

"All right." Millie's bosom swelled with a deep breath, which triggered another shower memory I didn't need. She checked with Rogers, who lifted his palms in a shrug. John gestured encouragement. Tim, the fuck, shook his head.

One yes, one no, one abstention. Millie had the deciding vote.

I tried really hard not to crawl over the table, plead like a baby, and bury my head in her lap. Her lap... *Another* goddamned shower memory popped up. *My life at stake and all I can do is have sexual fantasies about my judge.*

"All right," Millie repeated. "Here's what we're going to do. Joe, you're on probation." Tim snorted and crossed his legs. I may have levitated out of my chair, I'm not sure. Maybe peed myself a little. "You will need to complete your probationary period, which will last as long as I want."

"Fair enough," I acknowledged, and it was. Beat hanging from a lamppost any day.

"Franklin," she continued, "can you put Joe up somewhere? Find him something useful to do."

"Sure we can. Always things need doing around here. Joe, you any good for anything?"

The challenge in Rogers' voice stung my pride—what little I had left. "I'm pretty handy with tools. My dad had his own construction company, and I helped him build houses in the summer. It's why I went to school...I wanted to be an engineer." I refrained from asking if I could work in the secret video-copying lab.

"Well, okay then. I'm sure we can find you something to do, if you're willing to work."

"Of course," I said.

"Good answer." Rogers chuckled. "Around here, unless you're old or ill, you work to eat."

"Thank you, Franklin." Millie addressed me directly. "We have an operation on tonight—"

"Millie!" Tim barked.

She cut him off with a raised hand. "We have to get him involved sooner or later, Tim." To me, "Joe, the Secretary of the Treasury is giving a speech downtown tonight. It's a fundraiser for the president's reelection campaign, disguised as a talk on economic policy. A group of us plan to be there, in front of the building, when he arrives. We want to ask him some questions about"—her eyes shifted away, and she stumbled over her words—"ah, about the solvency of the Treasury. We intend to *peacefully*"—this was delivered with a meaningful glower at Tim—"block the entrance to the venue in hopes the media will record and broadcast our protest."

She stopped, and I waited. Interesting stumble there. What did they really want to ask the Treasury Secretary? When she said nothing, I raised an eyebrow. "Okay?"

"Do you want to go with us? Be part of the protest team?"

Did I want another chance to get my head beaten in by angry police officers in riot gear? Why, who wouldn't? *Jesus on a cracker, these people are loons.* "Sure. Sounds like a great plan."

"Millie, come on," whined Tim. "This guy's a plant. He's gotta be."

"You can't know that, Timmy," John spoke for the first time. "Innocent until proven otherwise; isn't that the rule?"

The hairball inspected me with the disdain of a dowager passing a hooker. "I wish I'd let Dante kill you last night."

"Well," I said with a shrug, "you wish in one hand, I'll whack off in the other, and we'll see which one smells more like your mother's crotch."

"You little—" Tim shoved out of the chair, and I snatched up the carafe, ready to slam him in the shaggy noggin.

"Tim! Sit down!" Millie barked. "Joe, behave!"

He sat, and I behaved. Millie glared, and John hid a smile.

"This," Rogers proclaimed after a chuckle, "should be fun."

"My thoughts exactly," I said. "When do we start?"

Nineteen | If Zombies Attack, I Just Have to Run Faster Than You

"SO WHERE ARE WE HEADED?" I spoke to the back of Millie's head as we filed east on Oak Street, headed toward the lake. A stiff breeze whipped my hair back, and I was glad for my jacket. As night came on, the temperature dropped faster than a whore's pants at a political convention.

"The Drake," Millie called over her shoulder.

"It's a hotel, by the lake," John informed me. He kept pace on my right, having to shorten his stride to do so. "A fancy one."

"Really? What do they do about the smell from the lake?" I liked John, but I'd forgotten his tendency to state the obvious. The giant would lull you into thinking he was dimwitted while secretly having fun at your expense. My neck cramped trying to read his face for signs of humor. "You ever stay there?"

"No, I can't afford it."

Behind us, Tim kept quiet. I could feel his eyes boring into my back, giving me an itchy-crawly-millipede sensation down my spine. We crossed Wells, and I glanced north, toward the Dive In. Hard to believe I was there only last night, sipping cheap beer and waiting for one of my current companions to show up. Too bad it had to be Tim and his pal, the Zulu warrior king.

I swiveled my head around. "Hey, Timmy, who was that you were meeting with last night? He looked scary as hell."

"None of your business," he growled.

"Oh. Okay, thanks." *Dickhead.*

This part of downtown, propped up by Gold Coast money, had weathered the economic storm that gutted chunks of downtown farther south, like around the Huateng Tower. Expensive, trendy stores lined the street with window displays behind bulletproof glass, and fewer homeless wandered about. More cops patrolled in flak jackets and helmets, keeping the well-dressed shoppers safe from panhandlers, pickpockets, and rebels like us. Armed guards, stationed under apartment building entrances, tracked us as we passed, their hard eyes cold enough to freeze my balls.

"Hey," I said loud enough for Millie to hear, "isn't the Drake on Walton?"

She glanced over her shoulder. "The front entrance, yes, but Secretary Nguyen will come in through the back. We have a couple of folks out front, in case they pull a last-minute switch, but I'll bet he comes in the rear."

I resisted the obvious joke about *coming in the rear.*

Foot traffic thinned as we crossed Rush Street. Two guys I didn't know joined our parade on the east side of Rush, exchanging silent signals with Millie and John before falling in next to Tim. More Children, I guessed.

The scent of grilling steak caressed the air and flooded my mouth with saliva. Hunger hit me so hard, my knees buckled and I almost fainted. Two bouncers, titans in tuxes, flanked the entrance to a steakhouse, the name Olympia scrolled in glowing crystal on the frosted glass door. A 3D graphics board on the left tantalized with displays of sumptuous meals, the food appearing so real, my hand twitched before I controlled it. Below each dish, numbers appeared. It didn't take long to figure out the numbers were prices. My gut wrenched when I calculated one dinner here would cost more than a year's rent for the crappy apartment I shared with Chelle. Once upon a time.

"You coming, Joe?"

John's question penetrated, and I realized I'd stopped in front of the display. The bouncers were giving me the fisheye, and the other Children of Liberty were staring. "Yeah, no problem. I'm coming. Just trying to decide between the porterhouse and the ribeye. It's so hard to know how hungry you'll be after a police beating."

I offered John some muffin crumble from my sack. He declined, so I finished it off myself. I gulped the cornbread in a rush and of course couldn't swallow for the next ten minutes.

Oak Street crossed Michigan where it changed into one half of North Lake Shore. The two halves of North Lake Shore came together somewhere up north, after diving through tunnels and doing all kinds of crazy things that made drivers scream obscenities and shoot themselves. In the triangle created by the two sections of Lake Shore on the sides and Oak Street at the base, a patch of greenery with trees and benches had survived years of urban decay. Here, we were right against Lake Michigan; if we kept marching east we'd get very wet.

On the other side of Oak, the Drake reared up against the Chicago skyline, giving tourists a nice place to sit and admire the aging beauty. The Drake used the same red neon sign for the last hundred years or so, believing it gave the place a sense of old-world tradition. I sensed old-world tacky instead. The building was lit up like kilowatt hours would build a stairway to heaven.

A gaggle of people approached Millie, and it took a second, but one of the faces clicked and matched a memory. "Goldie!"

"Hello, Joe." The white-haired woman waved and smiled. "I'm surprised to see you here."

"Everybody is," Tim muttered behind me.

"How's Snowflake?" I said. "Her hips still bothering her?"

"The vet tried her on some new medicine," Goldie confided. "It's helped her a lot, but poor dear, she gets tired so easily now."

"Joe," Millie snapped. "Catch up on the pets later, okay? Anything yet?" This last she addressed to Goldie.

The seventy-year-old Child of Liberty shook her head. "Nothing, dear. More patrols, though, and the security people are wound up tight. Oh, and more cops are showing up. Any minute now, I'd say."

"Good." If I had any doubts Millie held a leadership position, they dried up in the next few minutes. Speaking to the group around her, she issued orders like firing bullets. "John, you and Joe take that bench and keep watch. The cops may come and roust you along; if they do, go ahead and move, but stay in sight of the service entrance. Tim, Sterling, Ramon, do the same on that bench across the way. Goldie, take your people and keep circling the park. Do not use your phones. I'll pass the message along to the rest of our people scattered around the park in person. When the security team gathers at the doors, that's our cue. Everyone rush across the street, line the sidewalk and link arms. Got it? Go."

The clump of people scattered, and I hunkered into a seat next to John. Millie strode away, her short legs pumping, a blond pixie on a mission.

"She's something else, ain't she?"

"Yes," John grunted. "Millicent is amazing."

I slanted a look at him. "Do you and she... have something...?"

He frowned for a moment, then his face cleared, and he smiled. "No. I'm married and have two kids back in... back at our home base. Millie doesn't date. Says she doesn't have time for it, but I think there's another reason."

"Such as?"

"I think..." John paused. "I think she's afraid they'll use anyone who gets too close against her."

He didn't have to explain who "they" were. Ramirez and his pals in the Homeland Security Agency. Two months ago I would not have credited the idea that the feds would resort to blackmail to reach their objectives, but that naïve ideal shriveled to a crisp the minute I saw Signe and Deandre turned into living slaves.

"I don't like the looks of this," John said. He hunched forward, eyes fixed on the activity to our right, along the western half of North Lake Shore. Our vantage point had an excellent view in two directions: North Lake Shore in front and Oak to our left. We could watch both streets without turning our heads more than a fraction. We were set back from the street by a short patch of grass, concealed by the darkness under the limbs of a billion-year-old oak tree. In the length of time since we'd arrived, six sedans with Homeland markings had parked along North Lake Shore, and seemingly at John's words, all the doors popped open, and men wearing dark suits boiled out.

I scanned to our rear; more Homeland guys piled out of cars there as well. Three black, boxy panel trucks with HSA emblems screeched to a stop behind the line of sedans. A covey of Homeland agents clustered at the back of each truck.

"Is this normal?" I asked.

"No."

"Somehow I knew you'd say that. Look." I pointed. "Millie and the other folks are moving. We have activity at the Drake."

A phalanx of six Drake security men spilled through the double doors and deployed around the service entrance. No weapons that I could see, but the guys appeared tough enough, bullets would bounce off their chests. They wore suit jackets over collarless shirts, black slacks and mirror-shined shoes.

"Nguyen's coming," John stated. He divided his attention between the Drake and the street behind us. "But something's not right. The cops are here in force."

"Should we abort?" *Abort. Listen to me, I'm a covert ops guy.*

"I... don't know." The big man bit his lip and twisted to check behind us. I did the same. The doors to panel trucks hung open, and ramps lay against the rear decks. A clot of men in black tactical gear milled about, some barking orders, some standing around in typical thumb-in-butt posture, and others trotting up and down the ramps.

Millie and a group of twenty-plus Liberty people lined the Oak Street sidewalk, their backs to the hotel, facing the park. Hopefully, they saw the same thing we did, which was a bunch of nasty-looking Homeland troops deploying on the far side of the green space. Millie must not have seen the deployment; she and the would-be rebels linked arms and lifted their chins, appearing as though they'd wait through Armageddon for this Nguyen guy to show up.

"Come on, John." I hopped up, trying to see in all directions at once. This most definitely did not feel like a good place to be. I shivered from more than the chilly wind blowing in off the lake. "Let's get Millie and book it outta here."

John dithered. "She's in charge, Joe. What if she doesn't want to go?"

"Hey." I clapped the big man on the shoulder, injecting some *badass mojo* into my voice. "You're six times bigger than she is. She don't want to go, you pick her up and carry her midget ass. You gettin' me?"

His eyes tightened, and his head bobbed in agreement. "Let's go."

We loped across the grass, hopped a low, decorative fence, and jogged to the other side of Oak Street. A small part of my—admittedly—small brain noted all the civilian vehicular and foot traffic in the area had mysteriously dried up. And oh-deep-fried-shit, the hotel's security guys no longer stood at the service entrance. They had vanished.

It turned out the blond leader of the rebellion was way ahead of me. Her blue eyes narrowed, studying the distant activity.

"Something's not right," she said. "I've never seen this kind of response."

"There's a couple of battalions of Men in Black on the other side of the park," I said, "and more on east and west. They're unloading some big-ass trucks, something needing ramps to get down. I don't know what, but I'm thinking tank."

"A tank?"

"I'm just saying, it's something big as a tank if it needs a ramp. That, or Godzilla."

The Children on either side of Millie who were close enough to hear traded glances. Some craned their necks or hooded their eyes like Apaches to get a better look. A low murmur ran along the line.

Her jaw clenched. "I don't like this at all. We need to abort."

"What is that?" someone muttered, and the others joined in.

I spun around to follow the pointing fingers.

The intensity of light behind us created deep shadows under the trees. Sporadic landscape lighting hindered more than helped, as the lights always managed to be in the exact wrong place. Shapes bobbled in the darkness. Awkward-looking. Shambling...

No way.

John said, "Are those...?"

"They can't be," stated a guy farther down the line. I think it was the one Millie called Sterling.

"They're—"

"I don't believe it."

Wind whipped my hair into my eyes. I shoved it back with a curse and cupped my hands around my eyes like I held binoculars. It didn't help me see, but by that time I didn't need to. The figures were close enough, I could confirm my earlier guess as to their identity.

"Revivants. Shit."

A marching line of eight, no, ten Revivants shuffled through the park like a squad of wind-up toys let loose on the lawn. Dressed in flak jackets and black parachute pants, they were a mockery of tactical cops, stumping around obstacles with a side-to-side, stiff-legged gait. The middle group passed through a floodlight, revealing a tubular contraption wrapped around their heads. The device resembled a neck cushion people used when they flew, a collar around each dead man's skull, blunt ends pointing forward, glistening of metal and plastic. I had no idea what they were for.

More disturbing than the silent march of zombies with headgear, each one of the revived carried a—

"What is that?" Millie said in disbelief. "Are those *guns*?"

"Yes, Millicent," John the Literal stated. "The Revivants are armed with automatic weapons."

"I would like to run away now," I said.

Magnus Imperium Sugit

Ramirez had just jerked the heating tab on his Swanson GMO-free frozen meal-for-one and set the boxed dinner on his kitchen table when the phone bud in his ear warbled.

"Never fails," he muttered and tapped it on. "Ramirez, go."

"Agent Ramirez? This is McKissack in Ex-Pro. Got a sec?"

"Sure. What can I do for Executive Protection?"

"Well, you have a flag on a, uh, a Millicent MacCauley. Is that correct?"

"Yes." He drew the word out as a band tightened around his gut. "She's mine, why?"

"One of our drones over Chicago picked up a suspicious gathering outside the destination venue of one of our protectees, Secretary Nguyen. Facial rec picked out some folks tied to a terrorist organization in the crowd, so we mobilized our Armed Response Team to the scene. Since the initial hit, FR's tagged a dozen suspected terrorists drifting into proximity of the target site."

"Don't tell me," Ramirez growled. "MacCauley is in the group."

"Plus your CI, a guy named Warren. You have him in the system as hands-off."

Warren's with MacCauley. At least something is going right. "Okay, then. Let me know when you get them processed through booking. I'll be down to have a chat." Ramirez reached to disconnect.

"Ahhhh," McKissack said. "Not that simple, Agent."

"No?" The knot in his stomach cranked tighter.

"My boss... he, uh, he's been wanting to play with his new toy for months now. A credible threat on the T-Sec was enough, so he punched the go-button and turned loose the Z Squad."

Ramirez had to think for a second before it clicked. *Zombie Squad. Gen II RVTs with remote-control collars.* "Oh, you are fucking kidding me."

"Not a bit, bro."

"Call 'em off, McKissack."

"Sorry, but they're already deployed. Even the director himself wouldn't get them called off in time. I'm afraid MacCauley and your CI are about to get shot to shit."

Twenty | Shoot Low Sheriff, They Might be Wounded

THE RVTS ADVANCED IN a staggered line—or a staggering line, depending on your perspective. By my estimate, they were fifty meters and closing. Wind chilled the sweat on my forehead, and my teeth chattered. The lineup of Children shuffled and murmured, breaking into nervous clusters.

"Are those things going to try and arrest us?" Goldie clenched her hands together as if praying.

The Revivants halted with a ragged thumping of mistimed stomps.

"Millie..." I warned. "I think it's time to leeeeave."

"Agreed." Snapping into command mode, Millie yelled, "Everybody! Scatter! Now!"

In a rippling crackle, like a thousand hailstones battering a tin roof, the Revivants opened fire. Dozens of copper-jacketed hornets *zip-cracked* past me, a tsunami of deadly force. Goldie jerked, and the back of her head came apart. She crumpled like a used napkin. Millie made a small "oh" sound, though I heard it distinctly over the snap of passing rounds, and stumbled to one knee. Shrieking people scattered in every direction, some holding their hands over their heads, as if that would protect them from the storm of bullets.

A round plucked my sleeve, and another burned a groove across my ear before my survival instinct kicked in. I grabbed John's shirt and dragged him down behind a parked car while pushing Millie to the ground under me.

"Get behind the car's battery," I demanded. We piled together on the sidewalk, shielded for the moment from incoming fire by a solid wall of Ford batteries.

Bullets cracked and zinged on the concrete. Chips of brick spewed into the air, fine as dust. Glass shattered, metal pinged. I tasted copper and smelled blood.

People screamed.

The guy I thought was Sterling lay a meter away, his mouth working like a landed fish. Blood spurted from his neck between clenching fingers, and his eyes dimmed. The flood dialed back to a trickle, and he died without another sound.

"We have to get out of here," John panted. His breath smelled of spearmint gum.

"There!" I pointed to the hotel's service entrance. Double steel doors inside a utilitarian alcove. Between us and the alcove, six meters of open sidewalk.

The vehicle we huddled against shuddered as bullets flayed it from the other side. Pock marks peppered the hotel's wall, and more rounds shattered against it every second, like so much deadly sleet. Chips of glass rained down from the car's windows, some of them trickling under my collar or sticking in my hair.

"It'll be locked!" John yelled over the clamor.

Shit.

My kingdom for a crowbar. The stuttering ripple of incoming rounds tapered off as the RVTs' magazines ran dry. I popped my head up for a look through the car's shattered windows. "Fuck me, they're reloading. How'd they learn to do that?"

"How'd they learn to shoot?" Millie said.

I hunkered next to her. "Are you okay?"

"No." She snorted. "I'm fucking shot."

Sure enough, Millie wrapped both hands around her upper thigh, where blood soaked a patch the size of a sand dollar. She hissed through gritted teeth, and cobalt fire flared in her eyes. She was tough enough, no doubt. I'd have curled into a ball and whimpered like a baby by now.

John told me, "We need to make a run for it."

"Where?" Millie asked him. "We go east or west, we're exposed the whole way."

"Some made it."

John spoke the truth. Of the twenty or so original protestors, eight lay prone along the sidewalk. Moans and small movement attested four were wounded. Goldie stared at the sky, an expanding pool of blackened blood under her head and soaking her gray hair. That the spray of bullets from ten automatic rifles had accounted for only six hits was a miracle.

"The service entrance is closest," John said. "We'd need a thumbprint to open the—"

"Wait," I said. "Did you say you had people around front?"

Millie frowned. "Yes, but..."

"Can you contact them?"

"Sure, we could, but they can't—"

"Would you shut up a minute?" I snapped. Being under threat of imminent death made me surly. "Get someone on the line. I need them inside the hotel, right fucking now."

"*Excuse* me?" Millie's face changed to mule-hard and thunderous.

"Please, Millie! Listen to me for a second. Tell them to find a fire alarm and pull it." When she hesitated, I grabbed her shoulders and locked eyes. "Trust me."

John said, "We don't need the fire department, Joe."

"Not the point." At that moment, the line of Revivants opened fire, the din drowning out my words at first. I screamed it out so they understood. "The locks open automatically in the event of a fire. It's a safety precaution built into the old mag locks. Assuming they haven't upgraded in the last dozen years, the service doors will pop open the minute that alarm goes off."

Millie grunted acknowledgement and touched the bud in her ear. She started yelling instructions to someone on the other end of the connection.

John crouched even lower as more shards of glass sprayed from our barricade. "And if they have upgraded?"

I shook my head. Some things weren't worth thinking about.

"Okay," Millie shouted, disconnecting. "It'll be a few minutes."

The battering ram of sounds made it hard to think, like somebody put a metal pail over my head and beat on it with clubs. Rounds thudded into both the living and lifeless bodies on the sidewalk, smacking flesh with a gruesome, meaty sound. Wounded people screamed again, or convulsed. My guts clenched with every impact. Millie's eyes glittered, either with pain or anger, I couldn't tell. Maybe both. She mumbled something I couldn't hear; when I bent closer, I understood it to be the Lord's Prayer.

"We may not have a few minutes," I said to myself. Pretty soon, these pricks would advance and find us cowering behind a beat-to-shreds Ford Future.

Firing ceased as the remaining protestors stopped moving. I risked a quick glance and found the line of Revivants advancing again, line abreast. One got tangled in the low-hanging branches of a tree. In his dogged movement forward, a limb scraped the gizmo off his head, and the instant it did, the Revivant halted and froze. I ducked back down.

"I think they're being controlled," I said. "Revivant nanos are not the most versatile beasties in the tech world, so this level of coordination has to be driven by some other... thingy."

"Ooh," Millie crooned. "I love it when you talk techno-speak."

"All right, John." I clapped the big man on the shoulder. "When that alarm goes off, you grab Millie. It's your job to carry her out of here."

"No, leave me." Millie squeezed her thigh with both hands. Sweat damped the hair on her forehead. "I'll only slow you down."

"Got it." John seemed happier with a plan laid out in front of him. He patted Millie's shoulder. "You won't slow me down one bit."

"I'ma gonna hit those doors like a jackrabbit—"

"A scalded-ass jackrabbit," Millie reminded me.

"I think she's getting loopy from shock," I told John. "We should find something to wrap that leg so she doesn't bleed out any more. I'll run interference, but anything bigger than a fruit fly is gonna give me trouble. We may have to switch off on the other side if security is there in force."

"Yup." John busied himself stripping off his outer shirt and ripping a sleeve loose to use as a bandage. He wore a white tank top undershirt, leaving his upper arms bare. His biceps were bigger than my waist.

Another quick glance and my stomach sank. The Revivant line had reached the other side of the street. Nine stiffs in black uniforms, spread along fifty meters, four one way, four the other, and one directly across from our fucked-up Ford. At this range, they'd blow us apart like confetti from a cannon, if they had time to aim. There had to be some lag between the controller and the—what?—Revivant drone. Didn't there? If I led the way, they probably (probably!) wouldn't have time to nail me, but anybody behind me...

"Change of plan." The words were out before I realized what I'd said. "You're going first, Big Guy. Grab Millie, throw her over your shoulder—" The fire alarm shrieked, a warbling scream so loud, they probably heard it in Canada. Even knowing it was coming, I nearly shit myself.

"Go!" I shoved John, and bless him, he didn't wait to ask questions. He snatched Millie off the ground as if she were a plastic doll and bolted for the alcove.

Instead of following him, I hopped up from behind cover and did jumping jacks in the other direction. "Hey, you ugly dead sonsabitches! Over here! You pud-knocking thunder-cunts couldn't hit the ground with a turd!"

What are you doing, Joe?

Nine sets of dead eyes swiveled onto me. Nine rifles rose to nine shoulders, and nine muzzles rotated toward little Joe Warren and his bag of endless insults. Out of the corner of my eye—John and Millie ducked into the alcove. I had to keep the Revivants' attention away from them for another couple of seconds.

"Yeah, you're a bunch of crusty scabs on a dead dog's dickhole. You—Oh, crap!"

I dove into the concrete behind my favorite Ford with an impact that knocked the wind out of me. Overhead, the world blew apart in a holocaust of incandescent chaos. Light strobed the back of my eyelids, and giant hammers pounded my eardrums. The world shook and shuddered and rang. Concrete, glass and steel—chewed up by copper-coated lead and spat into the air—speckled me in tiny patters of falling grit.

"Fuck! Me!"

Concentrate, Joe. Figure out how to get out of here.

Whoever controlled the line of dead soldiers didn't have a terrific grasp of tactics, or else trigger pull on these geeks was either on or off. They seemed to blaze away until empty, reload, stomp, repeat, which meant, if the pattern held true, I would have a few seconds of breathing room after they ran dry to make a run for it. The way they acted in concert made me think only one person controlled the entire batch. (Government think: Spend a gabillion dollars on robots, cheap out on the human controller.) If they'd been able to pin us down with one group while another advanced, they'd have killed all three of us by now.

Which way to run, now that was the question. Simple answer: the nearest shelter.

The fire hose of incoming hell slowed, died.

Now.

My legs refused to budge. Without the percussive battering of automatic weapons, the wail of the fire alarm registered over the ringing in my ears. Beyond that, an emergency siren in the distance. The fire department, I supposed.

A clattering of metal on pavement—nine empty magazines dropping to the ground—made my ass pucker. I wanted to curl in a ball, tighter and tighter until I disappeared into an atom with the mass of Joe and sink into the pavement.

Move, goddamnit!

This time the body obeyed. I bolted for the service entrance.

Quick glance left. Each Revivant poked full magazines at the weapons they carried. Some had trouble with the process, stabbing away at the receptacle like a teenage boy trying to jab his pecker home. Others were ready, but apparently had to wait for their slower cousins. *Design flaw, you twerps.*

I hit the alcove at a full sprint, hooked the corner to change trajectory and smacked the doors face first, expecting to burst right through. Note to self: Doors in public buildings open *out*. Fumbling at the handle delayed me a few centuries. Behind me, a collective ratcheting told me the Revivant soldiers were all loaded and ready to fire. I gripped the handle and jerked the door open, nearly slamming it with my face, but the motion threw me back, and I lost my grip, sending the door swinging shut. I snagged the edge as it was easier to grip and flung the fucking thing out of the *way*, leaping through the opening into the cool light of a receiving area filled with supply boxes, and electrical switches with lever handles longer than butcher knives.

I juked right the instant I cleared the door. A spattering of angry wasps zipped through the space formerly occupied by my skinny white ass and smacked into a mountain-high stack of toilet paper supplies against the opposite wall. Cotton puffed from a score of holes punched into the cardboard boxes. Tissue-paper snow drifted down.

The door swung shut. My head spun, and I held onto a shelf to keep from face-planting. My heart jackhammered away, and I couldn't get enough air. A single thought kept running in circles on the hamster-wheel in my head: *How the hell did that work?*

A vicious pelting hammered the other side of the door, as if the bullets were pissed they couldn't get in. "Yeah, well," I shouted at the door between pants. "You missed."

Until the bad guys cross the street and open the door, Joe. Use your head for more than a hair display. In a matter of minutes, the feds would waltz in right behind me, stick a gun up my nose, and paint the ceiling with a fresco *de la Joe*. I needed to lock the door.

The room turned out to be more of a corridor than an actual room. A floor-to-ceiling cage blocked off the left side, full of packages with shipping labels. A thumb-key microlock secured the cage, so there was no joy there. In the opposite direction, stacks of supplies (now perforated) lined the back wall, and electrical service junctions ran down the other. Silver snakes of conduit flowed upward from the electrical boxes and disappeared into the ceiling. At twenty meters, the hall turned left and went... somewhere.

I needed tools. A chain and padlock would be nice. While I was at it, maybe an arc welder and a fucking jetpack to fly me out of this shit. What I really needed was for the freaking *fire alarm* to stop for ten *freaking seconds* so I could *think*! I needed...

A ladder.

Thank you unknown maintenance man, whoever you were, for leaving your two-meter stepladder parked right between two electrical boxes.

The exit doors were hinged on the side and joined in the middle. Crash bars opened both doors from the inside, levering down to disengage Mr. Tongue from Ms. Strike's warm slot. The feet of my new stepladder fit into the space between the bar and the door, one foot on each side, jamming the crash bar in place.

"There. Take that, you ass-boils."

Bam!

The doors jumped as someone jerked the handle from the other side, and I leaped about a meter straight back. The ladder held. I paused to find my heart, as it had exploded from my chest and bounced off four walls and a box of double-ply toilet paper.

Bam!

The ladder rattled but didn't fall out.

Bam! Bam! Bam!

"I think it's time to fly, little jackrabbit," I told myself. I ran.

I sprinted along the maintenance corridor, hooked a left at the turn and ran for a single door at the end of the hall. This one had a crash bar as well. I hit it at approximately Warp Factor Five Hundred, almost blowing the door off its hinges...

. . . and whacked the back of a security guy holding a gun on John and Millie.

Twenty-One | Frenzied Ferret Fu

DING ONCE SAID MY STYLE of combat reminded him of a ferret with his dick caught in an electrical outlet. I admit I'm more of a hair-pulling, nose-biting, eye-gouging, ball-kicking kind of fighter, completely untrained in the martial arts. I believed a crazed ball of fury beats a karate expert once out of a hundred fights, and the odds were bound to roll in my favor soon.

When the door caromed into the back of Mr. Security Goon, he *woofed!* and his handgun spiraled across the room. Whiplashed, he stumbled forward and collapsed to one knee, giving my brain time to process the scene (John, holding Millie, both gawking), compute the odds of running away safely (zero to abysmal), and decide to unleash my Frenzied Ferret Kick-Ass all over the guy before he could recover.

I kicked him in the ass as hard as I could.

"Uh!" he grunted and flopped onto his hands and knees.

I kicked him again, aiming for the nutsack, except I missed as he rolled away. The guard bounced to his feet in the confident, athletic way of a highly skilled fighter (after enough beatings, I recognized the signs) and bared his teeth in a grin.

"C'mon, pussy," the security man growled. Blond hair, blue eyes, and a strong chin, the guy wore a cheap tux stretched across an acre of shoulders. A nametag pinned to his breast pocket read Wasserstrom. He beckoned me with a *come on* gesture. "Let's dance."

"Sure," I told him, "I'll lead," and threw a fire extinguisher at his face. It had hung from the wall next to the door and weighed as much as a microwave. *Clang!* Wasserstrom batted it away with a forearm, Terminator-style. He crabbed forward, arms extended in some GI Joe action stance.

We were in a laundry room, reducing the available weapons to towels and carts. I snagged a cart and shoved it across the room; the guard flowed to one side and let it roll past. Behind him, John Carter Marsh imitated a statue, with an expression that indicated his internal debate on whether to shit or go blind. Millie's head lolled. She appeared to be close to passing out.

"Get him, John," I yelled.

Wasserstrom glanced over his shoulder. I rushed him, slapped a sheet from a folding table as I ran past, and flung it over the guard's head in the instant before he realized he'd been had. The sheet settled on him like a ghost costume.

"Fuck!" Wasserstrom flailed his arms and tore at the cloth. I reared back and side-kicked him in the ribs, followed with a double-fisted overhead blast to the round lumpy spot I believed was his nose. I smacked home an axe-swinging shot to the side of his head.

Wasserman grunted and ripped the sheet free. Murder ran amok in his eyes, and blood trickled from a new, tomato-shaped nose. "You—"

I didn't wait for the insult. I launched into him in full ferret frenzy, punching, kicking, screaming, biting, and clawing. At one point I stuck a thumb so deep into his eye socket, I touched the back of his head. He absorbed it all, covering up with both hands and weathering my onslaught for three seconds, four, six, ten—*Bam!*

I floated in time and space for a long, peaceful moment before the floor hit me in the back and air punched free from my lungs. I spat out a piece of ear when I landed.

In a long stride, Wasserstrom loomed over me and latched onto my throat with one hand. A huge right fist wrecked my face. My head bounced off the floor, and things like sight and hearing disconnected as a barrage of lights flared behind my eyes. Breaker boxes in my brain overloaded and tripped off in a shower of sparks.

Then he hit me again.

Two blond, heroic-sized fellows occupied the sky above me. Both of them dripped blood and hatred. A vise clamped around my throat, and the giants lifted me to the atmosphere... no, higher than that. My feet danced on outer space.

My hands—I'm pretty sure they were my hands—swatted at the clamps around my windpipe with the strength of a ferocious kitten. My lungs heaved, but nothing happened. No air rushed in to fill the vacuum. Dizziness replaced double vision, and a red sea swallowed me, closing in around my eyes...

I gathered all of the table scraps of willpower I had left. Cupped my hands and clapped them over Wasserstrom's ears like a pair of cymbals. It stunned him. The clamp around my throat eased. I did it again. The blond he-man scrunched his eyes shut in pain and doubled over. He dropped me to cover his ears.

Beautiful, sweet air. *I will never take you for granted again.*

The red sea faded, and I shook my head to clear the cobwebs, holding the top of a washing machine to stay upright. Wasserstrom lurched around like a wounded bull, imitating my head shake, clearly dealing with some fuzziness himself. Behind him, John the Gentle Giant (having finally pigeon-holed Millie) danced around as lost as a man trying to grab a snake without getting bitten.

"Little help here, John," I croaked.

Jaw clenched, he rushed in and wrapped Wasserstrom in a bear hug from behind, lifting the security man off his feet and squeezing. Wasserstrom's eyes bulged, and his face dialed up to an interesting shade of red.

I stepped forward, and my toe hit something metal that rolled. The fire extinguisher. Thank you, God of Kung Fu, for this gift my enemy is about to receive.

Thunk!

Wasserstrom's head flinched to the side, and his eyes rolled up like cheap blinds.

"Let him go, John."

Wasserstrom timbered in a sweet crashing catastrophe of upturned laundry carts and floating cotton sheets. I dropped the dented extinguisher with a clang. This time it wobbled when it rolled, disappearing under the equipment lining the wall.

The room spun...

"Joe? Joe?" Big John shook my shoulder and knelt next to me with his eyebrows knitted in a deep frown. The cold floor chilled my back. How'd I get down here? "We have to go, Joe."

"Go. Joe," I wheezed. "Funny."

"Huh?"

"Nothing... Help... me up."

John brought me to my feet. The floor spun a little, but not as badly as I expected. Angry, broken glass scoured my throat when I swallowed. John kept one big paw clamped around my bicep while my vision cleared. Again. Black sea this time, not red.

"Where's—oh." I spotted Millie in a laundry cart, bedded on a cloud of folded sheets. Her feet hung over the edge, and she'd passed out. Wasserstrom sprawled at my feet, a pool of blackish blood growing around his head. "Is he dead?" I rasped.

John placed two fingertips against Wasserstrom's neck, paused. "I... don't think so. No, there's a pulse."

"Shit. Where'd that fire extinguisher go? I need to hit him again."

"Joe!"

"Don't worry, John." I patted the big man's shoulder. "I won't break the extinguisher."

John condemned me with a glower. I relented. "All right," I sighed. "Tear up some of these sheets and tie him up. Throw him in one of those dryers while I mop up the blood. C'mon, we need to hustle."

I patted Wasserstrom's jacket and produced an old-fashioned key card from an inner pocket with the Drake logo and the word "Security" printed on it. I tucked the card in my back pocket.

John levered the trussed-up security guard into an industrial dryer, folding him like an accordion. I tossed the bloody towels in after him, and a few more sheets to cover everything up.

"Now, set it on Permanent Press and let's get out of here."

"Joe..."

"Not even a quick tumble dry?" But he'd already left me to gather Millie and head for the exit.

At some point during our tussle, the fire alarm had shut off. My ears rang in stereo at full teenager death-rap volume. A crash-bang echoed from the hallway back toward the street doors, loud enough to overcome the whine in my head.

"The feds are coming." I dodged around John and led him into another corridor. This one ran left and right from the laundry room, and the décor was an upgrade from the maintenance area. Brocade carpet in red and gold tones lined the floor, and wood paneling covered the walls. Pictures of historical scenes, guys with swords on horseback, and of women in long hooped skirts dotted the walls. John and I paused as the laundry room door swung closed.

"Um." I checked both directions; no flashing ESCAPE sign lit up to guide me. With a mental coin toss, I picked left. "This way."

The hallway remained empty, but not quiet. From somewhere, the susurration of a milling crowd filtered through the halls. Guests, I imagined, coming back into the hotel after evacuating. Chattering voices, wry laughter, shuffling feet. We didn't have much time before someone spotted us. Or the feds sniffed us out.

"Where are we going?" John wanted to know. And so did I.

"I... Here! We're going right here." I said it like it had been my plan all along. In a recess to my right was a pair of utilitarian elevator doors. "I don't have great luck with freight elevators, but beggars can't be choosy."

"We're going up?"

"Yep," I said. The doors slid open when I punched the button. "The street'll be choked with people waiting to get back in. If we go out now, someone will report us to the cops." I made a point of hitching my chin at Millie, cradled in the giant's arms. Blood soaked the bandage around her leg. "We need to take care of that too."

I picked a floor at random—three—and waited while the doors closed and the elevator whisked us up. It was a far cry from the clanking, wheezy elevator in the Huateng. This one ran silent and smooth as a silk robe sliding off a woman's shoulders. I glanced at Millie again. Her head rested on John's chest, and a twinge of jealousy pricked me.

You dope, what are you thinking? You're gonna have to give her up to the cops soon, so don't go getting any ideas.

We got off the elevator in a utility room, a five-by-five space with stacks of sheets, towels, shampoos, soaps, and other supplies. "This place uses a helluva lot of toilet paper. Wait here," I said, and ventured into the hall.

Empty. So far, our luck—such as it was—held. Guest rooms lined the corridor on either side, numbered with swirly characters on fancy gold plaques. Using Wasserstrom's keycard, I opened one door after another. The first six I checked contained personal belongings and showed signs of occupancy. At lucky number seven, I hit pay dirt.

I hustled back to the supply closet. "C'mon, John. I found an empty room."

"Empty?"

"Not rented." I led the way back to Room 309. For a place as high end as the Drake, I expected to see an emperor's suite, with a foyer, a Jacuzzi tub, and slave girls standing by the bed with a bucket of grapes. The reality? Two beds, a desk, and a chest of drawers made up most of the furniture, along with a couple of guest chairs and a coffee table. I'd seen bigger rooms in a Holiday Inn.

"At this time of night," I said, "it's not likely anyone will be checking in, but if they do, we'll have to deal with it. Get her on the bed and get her shoes off. Throw all the blankets you can find on top of her. I'll be right back."

I didn't wait for John to get Millie settled. Bracing the door open with its hook, I trotted along the hall, opening every guest room on the floor with Wasserstrom's keycard. Maybe, if they ran a search on his card's activity, they'd be slowed down having to hit all the rooms on the third floor, instead of zeroing in on 309.

By the time I made it back, sweat drenched my collar, and I panted worse than an asthmatic dog. Adrenaline burn-off rattled through me in pulses, and I clenched my teeth to keep them from chattering. My cheek throbbed where Wasserstrom punched me, and I had collected a few dozen scratches that burned from sweat.

"How is she," I asked once the door locked behind me.

"Not so good," John intoned. He patted Millie's head with a damp cloth. Swaddled in blankets, she seemed very tiny, more of a schoolgirl than a fierce resistance leader.

"Do you know someone with a car?"

John considered the question. "Yes."

"Can you call them and get them down here? To the street outside, I mean, not to the hotel itself. We don't want valet parking, that's for sure."

"Yes." John frowned and touched his ear bud. He murmured to whoever picked up while I went to the bathroom and washed my face. Tenderly. The flesh had swollen around a cut over my left cheekbone, pinching the eye to a slit. Red and angry-looking, experience suggested the lump would turn a livid purple very soon. I picked some glass out of my hair and finger-combed it straight back.

"Let's check that leg," I told John when I came out. "Lift the covers up from the bottom and untie the bandage."

John exposed Millie's legs. Her small feet poked from denim jeans, cotton socks rumpled.

"Give me a hand," I said. "We need to shuck these jeans."

Millie's eyes opened the second I unbuttoned her pants. "What'reyoudoin'?" she slurred.

"Relax. We need to take a look at your bullet hole."

"Oh. 'Kay."

"John, bring me some towels." I tugged under her ass, and the pants came loose. So did her panties. Oops. I tugged the underwear back into place (they were white with a lacy waistband), very carefully not touching anything I wasn't supposed to.

A blue-tinged hole in Millie's upper thigh oozed blood. I slipped one hand under her leg, and it came away sticky and red. Millie moaned and shifted away from my touch.

"Appears the bullet went all the way through. No spurts, so maybe we got lucky and it missed the artery. Good thing too. I'm not much of a surgeon."

"You're not even a doctor, Joe." John handed me a stack of folded towels.

"I played doctor before. That counts. Can you rip up some sheets? Let's pad both sides and wrap it up tight. I assume you people have a physician on call? Dropping her off at the emergency room..." I shrugged at the stupidity of that idea.

"Yes, we have a doctor back in the tun—back at base camp."

"Good." I pretended not to notice his near-slip. Tun? What was a tun? And he said 'in,' which would indicate—"*Shhhhh!*"

Voices, in the hall. Male, young and gruff. Approaching... getting closer... at the door... right outside...

Going away.

The breath trapped in my lungs wheezed out.

"How long," I whispered, "until the car gets here?"

John handed me a wad of strips torn from the hotel's bed linen. Nice sheets. Eight-hundred-thread-count bandages. "Ten, maybe fifteen minutes."

"We need some way to get her downstairs. Lift her leg, would you?"

Millie hissed and her eyes popped open as John did what I asked. She bit her lip when I placed a washcloth against the nasty-looking exit wound in the back of her thigh. I motioned, and John eased the leg back down while Millie panted through clenched teeth and gripped the blankets with white-knuckled fingers. I folded another washcloth for the entry wound and laid it on the injury.

"This part's going to hurt, I imagine," I told her.

"This part? *This part?*" Millie snarled.

"Yeah, this part. Think about ponies and rainbows for a sec, 'kay? John, I need you to lift again so I can wrap this in place. Ready? Go."

John lifted, Millie growled, and I wrapped the strip of cloth around both makeshift pads as tightly as I could manage without cutting off the blood flow to her foot. The last half meter of cloth, I split down the middle and used it to knot the bandage.

"Jesus-be-damneded!" Millie snapped at me when I snugged the knot tight. "Where'd you learn your first aid? The Spanish Inquisition?"

"Nobody expects the Spanish Inquisition, MacCauley." I plucked the blankets down over her bare legs. No way was I going to try and get her jeans back on. "You could've been shot in the butt and had your brains blown right out."

"Fuck you, Joe." Her head flopped back, and she groaned.

"Nice of you to offer, but I demand dinner and a movie first. Hand me those pillows, John. Let's prop this leg up."

"You're pretty good at this," John told me. "Where'd you learn to take care of bullet wounds?"

"Not so many gunshot wounds, but working construction has its hazards. Guys on my crew did everything from cut their thumbs off to staple their foot to the floor with a nail gun." I found a vid remote on the nightstand and clicked on the screen, surfed for news. "We can't hang out here long, buddy. We need to figure a way to get her downstairs."

John frowned for a moment before his face lit up. He snapped his fingers and said, "I'll be right back."

"Wait," I said. "What...?" but he was already gone, the door closing behind him. "Well, okay then. We'll wait here."

The news came on screen. I turned up the volume.

Twenty-Two | The Bare Truth

I PERCHED ON THE END of the bed and tried to concentrate on the babe reading from her teleprompter. Not even her outfit—a thigh-high sheer teddy with postage stamp panties and no bra—could keep me focused. My ears picked up sounds from everywhere, and each ping, click, squeak, and hum prickled my skin and crawled into my skull, demanding attention. Was it the cops? Had they found Wasserstrom and figured out we were on the third floor? Was that the creak of an old building, or the stealthy footsteps of a TAC team about to bust in the door?

"Now for today's headlines," said the smiling blond anchor. "In Hollywood, actor Ryan Meers was seen with his co-star and leading lady from the film *Yeager's Law VII: I Reckon So*. Meers and M'Keya Newsome have denied rumors of a romance, but were spotted at a posh Beverly Hills restaurant with their heads *very* close together. Maybe they were 'collaborating'"—the news babe winked and made air quotes—"on their next box office smash."

"Jeez," I muttered, "I hated the first six movies, why would I watch another?"

The anchor's face shifted to a sad pout. "In a breaking news alert, Danion Carter and his long-time companions, Ja'Quille Bordelon and Abundancia Munoz, entered into a three-way marriage contract at their Newport Beach residence today. The seven-time Emmy-winning Carter, best known for his prime-time comedy hits *Suck It Up* and *Dynamite Blows*, said it was the right time for the trio to lock in a commitment and raise their five children in a three-parent household. Sorry, all you admirers, the delicious Mr. Carter is officially off the market." The blonde sad-vibed so hard, her moue could cause suicide rates to climb.

Millie groaned and shifted. "Wassat?"

"Nothing, 3M. Rest up; John'll be back soon, and you'll need your strength."

"Mmm."

". . . turn to local news," the babe said. It must have been cold in the studio; her teddy made a couple of significant points. "Homeland Security foiled an attempted assassination—"

"A what!"

"Huh?" Millie mumbled.

"Sshhh."

"—of Treasury Secretary Cho Nguyen in downtown Chicago tonight. We go now live to our reporter on the scene, Manila Carpeta. Manila?"

The scene cut to a view of the park where John and I had waited earlier. In front of the camera, a reporterette with a skintight body suit posed in the harsh light of a handheld vid camera. Behind her, the twinkle of expended brass littered the ground.

"Well, Daneace, here behind the Drake, a group of terrorists known as the Children of Literary made an attempt to kill Ambassador Nguyen and..." She touched her ear, and her eyes lost focus a second. "Sorry, that's Secretary Nguyen, and they, they were intercepted by elements of Homeland Security. Agents tell us the group refused to surrender when confronted and opened fire with automatic weapons, including banned energy rifles." Manila fixed on a serious expression. "Homeland had no choice but to use lethal, uh, sorry, legal force."

"Oh, holy megaballs of crap." Cold water poured over my head wouldn't have stunned me any more than the "news" spewing from the screen. The camera panned away from a saddened Ms. Carpeta and swept in closer to the sidewalk behind the Drake. Tarp-covered forms littered the ground, amidst a field of shattered glass and broken concrete. The camera operator made sure we all got a great view of the blackened blood leaking from under the tarps. Technicians in coveralls operated among the corpses, photographing and tagging and writing on pads.

In a voice-over, Manila Carpeta said, "In speaking with Special Agent Forrester, he informed us that, that uh, the terrorist group is one of several anti-government groups in operation around the country. They are to be considered armed and extremely dangerous, and for citizens to contact Homeland Security with any information on this or any other extremists. Drones with facial recognizance software will be operating—recognition software, sorry—in continuous surveillance over the entire area until—"

My stomach roiled, and I made it to the bathroom seconds ahead of throwing up, returning all my corn bread muffins over the next few moments. When I finished, I leaned on the sink and splashed water on my face. Swished my mouth and spat out the taste of used muffin.

I DRANK A BOTTLE OF overpriced hotel water and shared a second one with Millie. When the door chime dinged ten minutes later, I had managed to wash up and pull myself back together. I activated the touch screen door monitor; it showed a picture of John Marsh's chest. It had to be his chest; no one else could be that tall.

I blew out my cheeks with a heartfelt sigh and opened the door. "What took you—who's this?"

John entered, followed by an average-size fellow with a swarthy complexion and rich black hair, carrying a satchel over his shoulder.

"Joe, meet Sal." John dragged a wheelchair in behind him.

"Har-ya-doon?" Sal extended his hand and pumped mine with a calloused grip. He bypassed me and went to Millie. "Da-hell-happen-ta-ya?"

Millie winced and struggled to sit up. "I got shot, Sal."

"Does he speak English?" I asked John in an aside.

"Sal came with the car," John explained. "He brought some things we need."

I cocked an eyebrow. "The wheelchair? How'd he manage that?"

"No, I got the wheelchair." John dragged the chair next to the bed as Sal shuffled aside to give him room. "From the front desk. I told them my aunt got really tired from all the excitement and needed a wheelchair."

"Your aunt!" Millie stared blue daggers at the giant.

"John," I said. "You... *lied*?"

I could swear the big man blushed. He ducked his head and said, "Let's get you in the chair, Millicent."

"Hang on a sec." A memory pinged and demanded attention. "Facial rec drones will be in the air. What if they have—no, strike that, they're bound to have our faces, from when we were in jail."

"That's why Sal's here," John confided. He lifted Millie under the arms and helped her into the wheelchair. She bit her lip and scrunched her eyes closed. A small red blotch dotted the bandage around her thigh, so the bleeding had slowed.

Sal dug in his satchel and laid bits of cotton-swaddled objects on the bed. He unwrapped one and brought it over to Millie. "Here-ya-go."

Millie held still while Sal pinched her nose. A long second passed before I realized he was sticking something on it. When he stepped back, I whistled. "Neat trick!" And it was. Millie now sported a longer, straight snout, totally different from her dinky fairy nose. And the dark wizard wasn't finished. He worked on adding bits and pieces to each ear, her cheeks, and the corners of her eyes. The finishing touch was a black wig of long, straight hair.

"Great job, Sal," I said. "She's pretty now. That's, like, a miracle."

"Probation, Joe," Millie warned me. "Remember you're on probation."

"Siddown," Sal ordered Too-Tall John. "I canna-richupat-high." *I can't reach up that high.* I was starting to catch on to the swarthy man's staccato speech.

While Sal worked on transforming John's face, I stripped the blanket from the bed and tucked it around Millie, then I figured out how to extend the chair's footrest and get her legs straightened out, wrapping them in blankets as I did it. "Nobody's gonna believe an auntie taking a wheelchair ride in her lacy panties."

"It hurts to sit," she said. Sweat shone on her face, and all the color had drained from it. She seemed halfway to dead, with a ticket to go the distance.

"If I didn't know any better, I'd swear you were a Revivant."

"Not funny, Joe," she mumbled and closed her eyes.

"Okay," said Sal. He moved away, having worked the same miracle transformation on John's face. "I-dunalla-can." *I've done all I can.*

John stood up and I asked, "Can you take two feet off the top?" Sal packed things in his satchel without answering. "Hey, what about me?"

The makeup artist glanced at me, shrugged and said, "Nuttin'-left."

"Great."

John gripped the chair's handles and wheeled Millie to the door. "Come on. Homeland is all over this place. It is only a matter of time before they find the security officer in the dryer."

"Dryer?" Sal's bushy black eyebrows shot up.

"Long story," I said. "John, you guys take Millie and get to the car. She needs that doctor ASA-fuckin'-P. We need to split up, 'cause if they snap on my face, I don't want them to get you as well."

After a long moment, John nodded and laid a hand the size of a catcher's glove on my shoulder and held out his other for a shake. His paw was so big, it felt like I was six years old again, shaking hands with my dad.

"If anything happens," he started, then added after a pause, "I'll never forget what you did."

"What I did?" I blinked. "I've been trying to save my ass, you big goof. Now, get movin', before you get me caught. If I don't get busted, I'll make it back to Rogers' place. Tell those bangers not to shoot me, okay?"

"Okay, Joe. Good luck." The big man nodded again and walked away. Sal held the door and followed the wheelchair as John steered it out. The makeup man saluted me with a nonchalant two fingers to his forehead and left. The door automatically shut behind them.

"Well, shit. Now what?"

I surveyed the hotel room, which exhaled an odor of blood and puke and fear. I perched on the edge of the bed. What if I were to lie down, right here, right now, and draw the sheets over me? I could wait for the Homeland troops to come get me, at which point they'd either shoot first, like they did downstairs, or they'd arrest me. Arrested would be nice. I'd get a cozy cell and probably a long chat with my buddy Ramirez, who would offer me tea and cupcakes, and a nice massage. On the rack.

Getting shot might not be so bad after all.

The glowing numerals of the bedside clock told me an hour (an hour!) had passed since we lined up on the pavement to wait for the Treasury Secretary. I had to shift my ass, get to Rogers' place—no, wait a minute. Stop and think, Joe. I perched on the end of the bed curled into a Thinker pose. (Hands pressed against temples, in my case.)

The Cabrini bangers had cut the fed's tracker out of my back; I still had the ache to prove it. That meant Ramirez couldn't find me. Rogers and his people couldn't reach me out here, away from their territory. The only tie I had back to my old life was Ding Winston and two women I barely knew. They were as good as dead. The feds would never let them go; I was smart enough to figure that out.

If I cut and ran, would their fate be any worse than it already was?

It struck me, how alone I really was. Both my parents were gone, killed on vacation in London by a jihadist asshole with an explosive-packed vest. Chelle was gone. Ding, in jail, never to see the light of a free day.

Who else did I have?

Good question.

"You're a self-absorbed prick," I said to myself. "It's no wonder you have no friends."

Myself concurred.

"A sarcastic, crabby asshole who pushes away everyone and everything. Crass, vulgar, and annoying."

Agreed.

"A cowardly little fuck who stands for nothing and refuses to take a side, that's you."

No argument there.

I could see the future as a physical manifestation of two roads, splitting apart right now, from this room in the Drake hotel. Highway to Hell lay on the left, the one where I snuck back to Cabrini and picked up where I left off, worming my way into the Children of Liberty and, eventually, betraying them for a pat on the head from my owner, Agent Ramirez.

Journey to the Unknown split off to the right. On this road, I ditched everybody. I left this room, turned south, north, east, or west—well, not east, big stinking lake that way—and started walking. Disappeared into the shuffling herd of unemployed migrants, traveling from place to place like a modern-day hobo, working with my hands and living off my scant wits. It might kill me, but I'd die with maybe a tiny shred of dignity.

Why not? whispered a voice in my head.

"Why not, indeed?" What was the worst that could happen? Ramirez catching up to me, of course. Now that would suck. Maybe I could make it to Canada, where Ramirez had no authority, cavort with the caribou and the Eskimo and shoot the finger at the miniature little turd. I chuckled, almost sensing the chains falling away. "Why not? No fucking good reason I can think of."

I slapped my thighs, jumped up, and headed for the door. U-turned and raided the honor bar for all the snacks and goodies I could rake out and stuff in my pockets.

"Put it on my bill," I told the room and closed the door behind me. People filtered back into their rooms along the hall, engrossed in personal conversations with their electronics. So much for raiding some clothing or makeup for a disguise.

A short elevator ride later, I hit the lobby of the Drake hotel, a place more opulent than a dictator's palace and richer than a cherry cheesecake. I crossed the room in long strides with my head down, very conscious of my tacky clothes and pockets of loot. I tracked people with my peripheral vision and breathed a little easier when no one paid any attention.

"Have a good evening, sir," said the guy in a Beefeater costume at the door.

I kept my head down and waved. A second later and I was through. The night air bit my lungs with a chilly snap, and I paused to suck in a deep chest full. It would be even colder up north, but what the hell. I'd kill a bear and take its coat.

I turned right on Walton, hands stuffed in my pockets and feet barely touching the ground. Other folks, hotel guests or sightseers, milled around the entrance. I nudged through all of them and strode away, breaking into a clear patch near the end of the block. Behind me, nothing but trouble. Ahead of me, a wide-open future. All I had to do was reach out and grab—

"Hello, Joseph," Agent Ramirez said from behind me.

Twenty-Three | The Path Not Taken

"NO, JOSEPH," RAMIREZ said, "don't turn around."

I aborted mid-spin and wound up in a spastic shuffle-step. The night air, which had seemed so bracing and cleansing moments ago, now chilled like the breath from an open tomb. I faced the road in front of me. My new Journey to the Unknown was being swallowed by Hell's Highway. The miniature bottles of alcohol clinked in my pockets, creating a strong urge for a drink.

"Hey, Ramirez. I was about to call you."

He snorted. "I'm sure that's true."

"Well, I admit, I was a little distracted by your guys trying to *shoot my ass off.*"

"That was," he deadpanned, "unfortunate."

We traipsed to the corner of Michigan. I joined a group of people waiting for the light to change and sensed Ramirez slither up behind me. He stayed quiet, a pause that allowed me to rack the scattered pool-balls of my thoughts into a tight triangle. Keeping my head still, I studied the area: Homeland guys flitted around the Drake like a swarm of bugs circling a light. If I ran, Ramirez wouldn't have to raise his voice, and five agents would drop on me with excruciating suddenness and wanton vigor.

He had me. Any way I looked at it, Ramirez won. My window of opportunity to run for Canada had slammed shut. For now, at least.

The light changed, and the walk signal chirped. Our little cluster of pedestrians crossed the six lanes of Michigan, many of them chattering about the police activity.

"—was fifty terrorists—"

"—In downtown! Can you believe it?—"

"—you see the shooters? I think they were Revvies—"

"—sad about Danion—"

"—I know! I wanted to scream when—"

I lengthened my stride and distanced myself from the clot of nattering idiots, smiling at the image of Ramirez having to double-time to keep up.

"Turn in here," the agent ordered.

Here turned out to be an alley between a chic clothing store and a sandwich shop franchise, both closed for the night, but lit up on the inside. The alley, on the other hand, was dark as six feet up a black cat's ass. I barked my toe on a pallet and stifled a curse, picking my way with extra care until Ramirez commanded a halt.

"You made contact with MacCauley," Ramirez said. As my eyes adjusted, his short silhouette materialized, haloed by the light spilled from the street.

"I did, thank you very much." My tone was both bitter and reckless. Truth be told, I was tired of dangling on this asshole's strings. "And your people nearly managed to kill us all on the first night."

"Did you find the replication site?"

I shook my head before I realized he couldn't see the gesture. "No. She came to me at... at, uh..." I didn't want to give up Franklin Rogers and Momma Rose to this scumbag. "At the... at the place where I waited."

"In Cabrini-Green?"

Shit. So much for playing coy. "You know about Cabrini?"

"About Franklin Rogers and the cult of rebels he controls? Of course. Their time is coming, believe me."

The absolute-zero chill in his voice left me no doubt that Rogers was deluded in thinking the feds had forgotten him and his people.

"Yeah, well." I shuffled in place, the junk in my pockets clinking. "That's as close as I can get right now. I'm not exactly high on the guest list."

"But you will be, Joseph. Correct?" Ramirez didn't wait for an answer. "And when you are, I expect to hear about it. Much sooner, and in a more effective manner, than how I heard about this." The outline of one hand stirred in the darkness. I couldn't read the gesture.

"Uh, yeah." A thousand objections flitted by. I wanted to whine about how hard it was to get as far as I did, that they'd nearly killed me, and that I was still on probation with Millie. In the end, I kept that to myself, exactly like I kept to myself John's slip of the tongue about a *tun*, by which I inferred he meant a tunnel. "I'll have my people call yours. We'll do lunch."

Ramirez slithered closer. The sweet smell of cannabis-laced gum wafted from him. "Joseph, you are not a funny man. I do not appreciate your flippant attitude. You will contact me as soon as you've located the Children of Liberty's computer lab, office, or workshop, and you will locate that very quickly. Your friends' lives are forfeit, as is yours. Are we clear?"

I stared at the outline of the Homeland agent, unable to see his eyes in the dark. Just as well. I expected I'd see those dead-shark eyes of his. "We're crystal."

"Good." He paused. "I have another item for you to consider."

"Hmm?"

"We have located Ms. Schweitzer."

I blinked. Twice. "Chelle?"

"Yes, look." Light bloomed from a handheld vid display. It showed a silent movie of Chelle, working in some office building, pushing a cleaning cart through cube-lined rows. Her slack expression showed none of the spark I'd come to associate with my one-time fiancée.

"She's a Revivant."

"For now."

"For now?"

The agent's footsteps clicked as he minced away. "Nothing is permanent, Mr. Warren."

I MADE MY WAY BACK to Cabrini. Gun-toting bangers picked me up at the border and escorted me to a furnished, unoccupied one-bedroom apartment in Momma Rose's building. In daylight I saw the sign out front. Oak Street Apartments. Unoriginal, yet mundane.

People came at six o'clock in the morning, bearing a dry biscuit and cold coffee, which I finished as they marched me to Rogers' office.

"So what are you good for?" Franklin Rogers demanded.

My legs wobbled, and my stomach churned, the aftereffects of slamming back three packages of roasted almonds and a small arsenal of miniature liquor bottles the night before. No matter how much I drank, sleep had refused to come. Every time I tried, Goldie's exploding head, or Chelle's smooth blank face, showed up on my internal screen.

As a result, I swayed a tad as I contemplated Rogers' question. "What am I good for?"

"Yes, son, what use are you?"

"Umm."

"Do you cook?"

"If you put me in a big enough pot."

"Can you shoot a gun?"

"Hah!"

"Unarmed combat? Martial arts?"

"I'm pretty good at Frenzied Ferret Fu."

Rogers blinked. "Do you have any skills at all, Mr. Warren?"

"Building things," I said, after pausing for a fiery ball of stomach acid to slide back down my gullet. "I worked construction. Went to college on an electrical engineering scholarship, coupled with the insurance money from my parents' death."

"Interesting." Rogers leaned back in his chair and scratched his chin. I stood—more or less—in front of his immaculate desk, its surface so clean, a dust mote would die of shame. Where did he hide his computer and screen? Where—

"How are you with solar inverters?" the ex-Major asked.

"Umm, I can't build one from scratch, but I can add one into a building's power supply without frying myself to a crisp."

"Excellent." Rogers bounded to his feet. "Walk with me."

I tagged along after the energetic dynamo as he strode from the office. I caught up to him at the elevator, where he punched the button and bounced on his toes, clearly impatient.

"What we have," Rogers explained, "is a powerful, ahem, a *powerful* shortage of trained electricians."

"Powerful shortage. Got it." Great. Suddenly Rogers wanted to be a comedian.

"Parts we have. Inverters, wire, panels, batteries—"

"How old are the batteries?"

"Ahhh, good question." Rogers flashed a grin. "Maybe too old, huh? Well, you'll sort that out for us."

He said no more, and I didn't feel like talking, so we rode the elevator to the ground floor and exited the building in silence. I flinched when the morning sun beat me over the head. In contrast to the chilly night breeze off the lake, the day had broken out sunny and hot. I shaded my eyes as I kept pace with the shorter man, not really bothering to keep track of our route.

We turned this way and that until Rogers stopped in front of a metal door in a grimy, three-story brick building. To the left, a rollup door rusted in silence, and on the right, chicken-wire-reinforced windows clung to wood-rotted frames. Crud crusted everything like icing on a decomposing cake. Rogers touched his thumb to a nearly new thumb reader. A lock hummed and clicked.

"We'll get this keyed to your print."

"Okay," I said.

Inside, lights flickered on, revealing an aircraft-hangar-sized space crowded with benches, racking, shelves, and towering piles of equipment. Every shelf, rack, and square inch of floor space was covered with components, boxes, dangling wires, cable spools, and tools. I almost swooned when I spotted a red tool chest higher than my chin and wider than a city bus, parked against the left-hand wall by the door.

"Is it...?" I crept closer, not daring to hope, and slid open a drawer at random. "Oh, sweet Holy Craftsman."

Rows of old but cared-for screwdrivers in every conceivable make were aligned in descending size and arranged by type. From stubbies to crowbar length, Phillips to flathead, power to manual.

In another drawer, wrenches. Another held sockets. Pliers. Hammers. Conduit tools. Crimpers and splicers. Saws.

"I think I love you, Rogers." My fingers flexed, and I caressed a set of perfectly aligned hex bits.

He bellowed a laugh. "I wondered what it would take."

"Take?"

"To claim your soul, boy!"

"Where do I sign?"

"Take a look around, figure out what's here. We have an inventory of buildings that need converting to solar power. I have them prioritized from most important to least. We should have enough parts to do many of them, if not all."

"Where'd this stuff come from?"

"Mostly government grant money, help the *po' folk* become self-sufficient, that type of thing. Per usual, money spent equaled no results. I'm going to go get that list now. I'll bring it over when I get your students."

He was halfway through the door before my brain caught up. "Wait, my what?"

Rogers paused in the threshold, the sun backlighting him so I couldn't see his face. Was he kidding me?

"I told you," he said. "We don't have any trained electricians. I need you to show some kids how to not kill themselves when you're gone."

I let the student part slide past. "When I'm gone?"

"Somehow I don't see you staying here in Cabrini forever, Mr. Warren." Rogers tossed off a casual wave and tugged the door to close it. "I expect Ms. Millie's gonna want you to join the pack, sooner or later. G'day, sir."

"Yeah," I said, but he was already gone. The door shut with a thunk and a click.

I turned in a slow circle, taking in the floor-to-rafters piles of equipment. Sooner or later, he'd said. Sooner or later I'd have the chance to betray 3M and John. Kill their dreams and destroy their hopes.

My voice sounded flat in the cavernous warehouse. "Yep, can't wait."

I STOOD KNEE-DEEP IN inverters by the time Rogers came back, towing a troop of young men and women. I recognized Domino, the kid who'd performed street surgery on my back with a wicked-sharp knife, but the other five were strangers. All black, all dressed in work clothes and boots, and carrying sullen the way a person carries a heavy sack.

"Joe, meet your students," Rogers announced. Pointing at each one, he rattled off their names, none of which I remembered two seconds later. He slapped a piece of paper down on a nearby table and said, "Here's the list of buildings. These guys can show you where to start. Good luck!"

And he left.

Six pairs of dark eyes studied me the way a wolf pack regarded a limping sheep. Only with less compassion.

"Hey," I said. "I'm Joe."

Crickets.

"What do you guys know about electricity?"

Domino put his hands in his back pockets. One of the other guys crossed his arms. Somebody sniffed.

"That much, huh? Okay, then." I gestured at the pile of equipment stacked around me. "Before we start on the hard stuff, we need to get this organized, find out what we have. You plug the wrong thing into the wrong hole, you get a popping sound and a barbequed electrician. Heh-heh."

No one laughed with me.

"Well, let's get started." I pointed to a kid in the middle with shoulders big enough to pick up a dumpster. "What's your name again?"

"Mycroft," he rumbled. "But people call me Bears."

"Bear?"

"Bears. For the Chicago Bears."

As in all of them, I supposed. "Gotcha. All right, Bears, you're with me. We need to sort out these inverters by wattage and start making stacks along this wall. One of you grab a broom, somebody else get some dust rags and cleaning supplies. Take everything off the shelves and dust it down. We're going to do this, we're going to do it right, which means a clean workspace, and an organized, efficient plan of attack." I met each of their eyes in turn. "Well, okay then, let's get to it."

I turned my back to the predators and went to work. To my everlasting surprise, so did they.

Although Domino sidled up to me five minutes after we started. His voice hissed in my ear. "I cut you once, asshole. You fuck up, I be happy to do it again."

Bears rumbled, "And I hold you down."

Tempus Fuckus Fugit

Agent Ramirez jumped on a shuttle flight to DC from O'Hare at 6:00 a.m., spilling coffee on his hand while trying to juggle the cup and his briefcase down the aircraft's narrow aisle. The advantage to being small-statured, he figured, was that plane seats didn't present the same problem for him as they did for others. Unless he managed to draw the short straw—he smiled at his own pun—and be seated next to a mastodon in a flower-print dress. The woman overflowed her armrest like shit stuffed into a Hefty bag, and Ramirez spent an uncomfortable hour jammed into a corner of his seat. Even so, the woman's flabby arm touched his, and he flinched away.

He endured this aggravation because the current Director of Homeland Security, Eliza Proctor, failed to embrace technology. There was nothing wrong with V-meetings—the participant's avatars looked almost real these days—but the fossilized old bitch didn't like the occasional time-lag that chopped up dialogue, or that some putz inevitably forgot to unmute their microphone. No, Eliza Proctor didn't get to where she was by suffering—at least not when she had minions to do that for her.

Ramirez rented a car and exited Washington National at 8:20 in the morning. At 8:25 he rolled to a stop behind a line of jammed traffic trying to cross the Potomac. Fifty-seven minutes later he inched five miles and arrived at the old Treasury Building on 15th, which Homeland had taken over in 2031, remodeled, and expanded it to fit their growing needs.

Proctor's admin told him the director was in the National Press Conference, taking place in the Rayburn building, and would he be so kind as to meet her there. Well, of course he'd be so kind, wouldn't he? He had no other choice but to be so kind.

Fuming, Ramirez recovered his car and inched through masses of pedestrians, many of them holding signs for one dippy cause or another, and bullied his way into an access-controlled parking lot a block away from the Rayburn office complex. He took the longer way around, via Independence Avenue, because the sight of the capitol dome never failed to inspire him. The icon lifted his spirits. Ramirez jogged up the few steps at the Rayburn's entrance and badged past the metal detectors and X-ray units. He asked directions from the Federal Protection Officer and quick-marched through marble halls to room 2168, the Gold Room.

A guard in front of the conference room stopped him. "Sorry, sir, this is a press conference; it's not open to the public."

Ramirez flashed his shield. "I'm not the public."

Inside, the press conference was going strong. The Director for Health and Human Services, Doug Atkinson, stood in front of the mic. Seated along either side of the podium were directors from a baker's dozen federal agencies and offices. Eliza Proctor anchored the far left, as weathered as a redwood forest. *If she dies*, Ramirez mused, *they will have to cut her in half and read the rings to tell how old she was when she fell.*

The crone met his eye when he sidled into the room and tilted her head in a microscopic dip.

A long, narrow room full of reporters, both physically present and projected avatars, jotted quick notes and composed one-hundred-and-forty-character news blips to post. None of them looked old enough to buy a legal drink.

"In summary," Director Atkinson stated, "there will be no entitlement cutbacks as a result of the current fiscal crisis. We are confident Congress will reach a budget deal which will raise the debt limit and allow for an injection of much-needed currency into the economy. Everybody get that down? Excellent. We shall now move on to—"

"Excuse me." A ditzy blonde stood with a finger raised. She was present in person, so Ramirez couldn't tell which news outlet she represented. Obviously a newbie, heedless of the protocol for the National Press Conference. "Excuse me," she repeated.

Atkinson raised an eyebrow and uttered a tentative, "Yes? Mizzz, uh..."

"Cheryl Henderson, Midwest News Service." The blonde's hand tremored ever so slightly, but she stayed on her feet. "A follow-up question, please?"

Atkinson double-blinked his surprise but nodded.

"Ah"—the ditz ducked her head to check her tablet—"oh, here it is. You said 'inject currency into the economy.' Can you clarify where that money is coming from? Will it be new taxes, or will the Treasury, ah, just, ah, print more money?"

Atkinson shifted his feet and glanced at Undersecretary Sethi, the delegated Treasury representative. The woman, wearing a green sari with gold trim and a translucent gold uttariya covering her head, leaned into the microphone in front of her. "The government will do the responsible thing first, that which benefits the greatest number of people at the lowest cost. We will employ a multipronged approach to this situation and have developed a number of contingencies to meet our fiscal obligations."

"I see," said Henderson, although clearly she did not. She scratched her head with her stylus. "Um, follow-up question? What about inflation? I've heard that's really bad. Would you say your policies will help or hurt inflation?"

Atkinson leaned on the podium with both hands. A thick game-show-host helmet of white hair set off his reddening complexion. Ramirez suspected Ms. Henderson's press credentials would soon be revoked—or the IRS audit team would come knocking on her door.

"The only thing that will pull us out of this economic slide is jobs. Jobs, jobs, jobs. The government creates jobs by pumping money into the system. Surely you learned the phrase 'prime the pump' in school? Of course you did." The director leaned back, lips compressed. "Trust us to know what we're doing and report the news accordingly."

"But Director Atkinson—"

"That will be all for today. We will email everyone the remaining headlines for distribution." The white-haired man gestured, and the audio pickups clicked off; he then leaned into Proctor's ear for a quick word before stalking away.

The Director of Homeland Security joined Ramirez as the remaining reporters filed out. Proctor sneered at Cheryl Henderson, one of the last to leave. "Where do they find these puppies?"

"I do not know," Ramirez said. "The pound?"

Proctor buzzed a dry, raspy laugh. Broom thin and dried to the consistency of a cornhusk, Eliza Proctor would stand a head taller than Ramirez if her back wasn't bent by osteoporosis. "You were down in Texas recently, right? A little matter of an unruly family?"

"Yes, ma'am."

"You pick up any rumors of another secession attempt?"

"No, ma'am, not a word."

"Well, our sources are saying they're at it again, the dumb hick bastards. Tried it in '26 then again in '32. Getting whipped like stray dogs didn't teach them a thing."

Ramirez wasn't sure how to respond, so he signaled agreement and kept pace with her glacial shuffle steps. In two minutes they had covered less distance than a first down in football. Why didn't the slab of beef assigned to her protection detail simply pick her up and carry her in a backpack? They would at least move faster.

"Anyway," Proctor wheezed, "I need you to wrap up that Chicago thing, PDQ, and get down to Texas. Turn that little ferret nose of yours loose and find the damned rebels. The last thing this town needs is another damned civil war. Hell, we'd have to have a bake sale to fund it."

"Yes, ma'am."

"Where are we on finding that file?"

"I have a CI embedded with MacCauley's people who is tracking the copying facility. The work can be done in a single room, so I'm not convinced he will be able to find it in time. We have placed surveillance cams on every street corner in Chicago, and doubled that in the area of Cabrini-Green, which is where we think she went to ground."

"With the spooks?" Proctor's lips compressed even tighter.

"Probably." Ramirez hesitated before continuing. "We have a hard time infiltrating C-G territory, and the locals counter-sweep for electronics regularly. To counter this, we have blanketed the area with numerous drones. The database of every known terrorist has been refreshed, and FR will bingo them the instant they show their face."

"Results?"

Ramirez clamped his hands behind his back, squeezing them as if Proctor's neck were between them. "Negligible. We have spotted a few low-level players, and our CI has shown up frequently. He appears to be engaged as a rooftop electrician."

"Sounds like a complete waste of resources."

"Which is why we are also working the other channels, such as monitoring the purchase of data wafers and other media for spikes in shipments. We are also working our informants hard and have staked out all of MacCauley's known associates, past residences, and family members. Drones are patrolling for any street distribution of media. Active sniffers have been programmed by the NSA to patrol all phone, Internet, and satellite communications."

Proctor's querulous voice echoed from the marble halls as she shuffled. "We're feeling the press of time on this, Ramirez. Frankly, I expected more from you by now."

"Has the video become public?"

"You know it has not."

"Then our tactics are working." Ramirez tilted his head to take the sting from his words. "Results are forthcoming, Madam Director. Please be patient."

"Patience has a limit, boy," Proctor snarled. She sniffed and waited for a gaggle of lawmakers to bumble past. Pinning him with her watery-green eyes, the director said, "One way or another, Ramirez, when this is over, I expect that bunch of chickenshit motherfuckers to be *gone*. Are we clear on that?"

"Crystal, ma'am."

After another two meters, Proctor glared at him sideways. "Well, what you hanging around me for? Go to it, boy."

Twenty-Four | It Ain't No Picnic

DAYS BLED INTO WEEKS, which morphed into a month. My secret mission to infiltrate the Children of Liberty and find their secret lab faded to background noise. I worked like a diesel engine from before dawn to well after dark, six and a half days a week. (Momma Rose insisted my crew and I take a break for church on Sunday mornings, which was a whole 'nother subject.) In those four weeks, I cut, drilled, hammered, cabled, sweated, cursed, argued, and laughed. The juvenile delinquents managed not to get burned to a crisp. Some even learned to wire solar panels to an inverter and integrate it with a building's power supply.

After about day three, they reluctantly accepted I knew my ass from a hot stove. The sullenness wore away day by day until they forgot about playing tough and disinterested and started pitching in.

It was like the plot of a Disney movie. Very touching.

On a particularly hot Saturday, a rail-thin girl named Monique and I labored atop a building roof, installing panels in parallel rows. With my head buried under a rack of panels, I was cursing a connection into place when Monique sang out from the other side of the roof. "Hey, Joe!"

"Yeah?"

"Somebody here."

"If it's not Bears with that goddamned pair of linesman's pliers I wanted, feel free to throw 'em off the roof."

Sweat drizzled in rivulets, stinging my eyes and splattering the hot tar surface near my face. I needed another six centimeters of wire from the end of the conduit to reach the spot where I could attach it, and the flipping wire would... not... come... *through*!

"Shit!" My needle-nose pliers slipped, and I skinned my knuckles on a sharp metal J-box. "Son of a stiff-legged-whore-fucking-dickless-goat-sucking-shit!"

"Wow, Joe," said a woman's voice. "Do you kiss your mother with that potty mouth?"

"Is that—?" I scrambled up—*Thonk!*—without looking. "Ow!"

"Watch your head, Joe," she called.

"Millie?" I rubbed the forming lump on my skull and squinted at the woman standing by the roof hatch. She wore a summer-weight pastel-blue dress and leather sandals. Her blond hair had grown out and now curled under her ears.

For a long second, I found it hard to breathe. Must have stood up too soon. "How, uh, how're you doing, Millie? How's your... uh..." I waved vaguely.

"Good, Joe," she said. "I'm good. The doc says my leg will be fine. See?" Millie hiked her skirt and showed me a red, puckered scar on her thigh. "This side's not so bad, but..." She twisted and showed me the back of her leg. The exit wound was three times the size of the puckered dimple in front, a jagged, ugly mess of scar tissue, which I noticed did nothing to detract from her shapely thigh.

"Joe? Hello, Joe?"

I snapped back to the present and realized Millie had been calling my name. "Yeah, sorry. I'm here. Touch of heat stroke, is all."

"Well," Millie said, skirt back in place and facing forward again. "When you get through saying magic words over that panel, can you come to Franklin's office?"

"Uh, yeah," I told her. "Sure thing. Half an hour?"

"That'll be fine." Millie smiled and climbed back through the roof hatch, flashing a wave before her head disappeared.

A subsonic jet climbed out of O'Hare, leaving behind a muted roar. Pigeons strutted on the hot tar roof, careful to maintain their distance from the crazy humans invading their territory. I caught sight of Monique, standing hipshot beyond the roof hatch, whirling a crescent wrench by her index finger through the hole in its handle. Her lips twisted in a smirk.

"What?"

"Uh-huh," she grunted.

"Uh-huh, what?"

"I saw the way you lookin' at her. Like she a bowl of vanilla ice cream and you the scoop."

"Hah! Very funny, Moanie. You know you're the only one for me." I slapped the useless needle-nose pliers into the tool belt at my waist. "Just drop that loser, Domino..."

"You be de las' one I call," she promised. "You jump right over my pussy, get to that white chick. I see how that is."

"You're a hard woman, Monique. Finish this up? I need to take a shower."

"Uh huh, you sure do."

"JOE!" JOHN MARSH—TALLER than a sequoia and stronger than day-old coffee—bear-hugged me the second I filed into Franklin's office. Spinal joints crackled in my back. "Man, it's good to see you."

"Oof. Agurble-mestsed-utooh."

"What?"

"Put the man down, John," Millie said. "I think you're strangling him."

"Oh." John released me and pounded my back with a meaty hand. "You okay?"

"Yeah," I wheezed, holding up a hand to stall any more help from the big man. "Good to see you too."

"Man, you filled out," he told me. "Got some sun too, it would appear."

"He's right." Millie sat on the couch, in the same spot she'd occupied a month or so before, when first pronouncing judgment on me. "You don't look nearly as much like a Halloween decoration as you did before."

"Hard work and Momma Rose's cooking will do that," I said, not without some pride. They were right too. I had gained weight, gotten thicker through the chest and shoulders, and working rooftops had darkened my normally pale complexion to the point I could pass for one of Alex de Galvez's countrymen.

Speaking of Alex de Galvez, he was sitting to Millie's right until I came in, and now extended his hand. "Joe, it's been a while."

"It has, Alex." I shook his hand, realizing as I did how genuinely glad I was to see him.

Franklin Rogers waved everybody to seats. "Let's get started, shall we?"

"Started?" A coffee service beckoned from the table, and I helped myself. I made a point of examining the room. "And where's that lovable furball, little Timmy?"

"Tim didn't want to come," John said.

"He thinks you set up the Revivants to hit us at the Drake," Millie explained. "He... he can't accept that you're not a government informant."

I snorted. "Yeah, I tried to get myself shot. Makes sense." I lounged back and crossed my legs, hiding my face with a sample of hot coffee.

Millie shrugged. *What can you do?*

"More importantly," I asked, "have I passed my probationary period?"

"Take a look." She placed a palm-sized vid player on the table next to the coffee pot and touched the screen. A projection appeared above the unit, rendered in full color, four dimensions, and five senses. A chilly breeze ghosted from the display and washed over me, and when I recognized the scene, something twisted in my stomach. The coffee I'd swallowed turned to acid.

"We had one of our people hang a LiveCam in the trees that night," Millie explained. "It took some time to retrieve the unit, but this is what it captured."

In perfect scale miniature, the Children of Liberty lined the walk behind the Drake, shuffling and shifting in place. Near the middle stood Millie, arms linked with Goldie on one side and Sterling on the other. From the lower right, John Marsh and I ran into the picture. Our voices were muffled by distance and wind noise, I couldn't make out what we said. At this moment, I couldn't even remember those words.

The massacre played out on the tabletop, as if we watched a video game with a grisly cut scene. Shrieks and gunfire blasted from tiny speakers. Hell's soundtrack, recorded in stereo for the torment of the damned. My companions in Franklin's office leaned forward, frozen by the drama; all of them appeared as incapable of speech as I. When Goldie faltered and dropped, shot through the head, I wanted to reach out and stop the playback. Freeze time so that her death never happened.

Did the unseen recorder happen to catch my conversation with Ramirez? It happened on the other side of the Drake, down a dark alley, but still...

Tears traced Millie's cheeks, and I realized my face was wet as well.

"Here." She touched the screen, and the image slowed. Some idiot jumped from behind a car and waved his arms like a jackass. Revivants trained their weapons on the tiny Joe figure and opened fire, blazing away on full auto, their rounds chewing out chunks of concrete, metal, and glass. To the left, John disappeared into the building, carrying Millie.

"What a putz," I remarked. My words dropped into the sudden silence with the weight of steel plates falling on the floor.

"No," Millie said. "What you did, Joe... that was heroic. Don't diminish it with your typical flippant remark."

"Heroic!" I laughed. "Man, that bullet ripped out a chunk of brains after all, 3M. My pants are too dark there, or you'd see where I peed myself."

"You saved us, Joe," John intoned. With his too-serious face, the words came out like a cancer diagnosis.

I shook my head. "You guys are loony."

"Shut up, Joe," Millie ordered.

"Yes, ma'am."

"We wanted to know," she continued, "if you would consider another little outing."

Every eyeball in the room fixed on me. Rogers regarded me over steepled fingers, and Alex nodded when I met his stare. John's smile was encouraging. Millie said nothing, and her face gave away even less. Somebody ran a vacuum in a room nearby; its drone cycled up and down.

"An outing?" I said. "You mean like a picnic?"

"No," Millie told me with a shake of her head. She curled her hair back over her ear. "I don't think it will be much of a picnic at all. I can't tell you anything about it until you agree to go. If you don't want to, that's fine, no hard feelings. I'm sure Franklin can use your help for as long as you want."

Meaning I would never get any closer to the Children of Liberty than I was right now. I could hang out here and wire buildings or fix the plumbing or do one of a thousand jobs that needed doing in Cabrini territory, but I'd never see the secret rebel base that was my ticket from under Ramirez's thumb.

"Uh..." Here it was, the moment of truth. Ramirez wanted me inside, and it seemed as though the Children were opening the door and letting me in. All I had to do was say yes, and I'd be part of the gang, secret handshake and everything.

"What's wrong?" Alex asked.

"I, uh... I'm not sure if I buy in to the whole party line, y'know?" *And I don't know if I have the guts to squeal on you to Ramirez.*

"There's no party line." Alex's brow creased, and he leaned forward. "You're free to believe what you want, that's the power of the founding documents of this country. All we want to do is free people from the tyranny and slavery of the welfare state. In 1929—"

"Alex," Millie warned. "No lectures, okay? You promised."

"Sorry." He shrugged at me. "Occupational hazard."

"It's time to pick a side, Joe," Rogers stated.

"Joining up is a commitment," Millie said. The fire in her eyes could weld steel; their actinic flare burned hot and true with the flame of a righteous, deeply held commitment. "Let's be clear about that. It commits you to opposing the government of the United States as it's currently constructed. We fight for three things: civil liberties as promulgated by the Constitution, personal responsibility, and the right to succeed or fail without government oversight. We believe in taking care of each other without a centralized authority telling us how to do it."

"Wow," I said at last, having to physically force myself to back away from the nuclear fission glowing from within the short woman. "I thought you said no lectures."

"Joe." Millie busied herself with packing away the vid player. "You saw what they did to us. You saw how the media treated it. Can you deny the government has grown beyond anything intended by the original framers of the Constitution?"

"No." I topped off my cooling coffee with a fresh hit from the pot. "No, I can't deny that."

"Are you in or out?" Millie challenged.

"I'm in," I said.

And won't Ramirez be proud of me? Good doggy.

Twenty-Five | The Secret Rebel Base

"COME ON." FRANKLIN Rogers slapped his thighs and stood. "I've got things to do, and you people are clogging up my space."

Rogers circled the table and laid a bone-crushing handshake on me. "Thank you, Joe," he told me, holding my biceps at arm's length. "You really made a difference here. Those kids on your crew got more from you than you'll ever know."

"I, uh... well..." For the second time that morning, I could think of nothing to say.

"Follow me," he said with a grin.

Rogers led the way from his office, down the hall to the elevator vestibule. A cluster of people gathered there, centered by Momma Rose, who opened her arms and engulfed me in an outrageous hug.

"You take care of yourself, y'hear," she ordered. "I don't want to know about you gettin' in no trouble. I'll come after you and jerk a knot in yo' fool head, boy."

I breathed in the scent of fresh bread and hyacinth soap and tried to speak past the thickness clogging my throat. "Have to catch me first."

Momma Rose stepped back and shook a finger at Millie. "You take care o' dis boy. He don't look like much, but he got the makin's to be something special."

"Well," Millie said, "you're at least half right."

"I—Hey!"

"Don' listen to her," Monique said. "We know you ain't nothing special any way atall."

"C'mere, you skinny wench."

I said my goodbyes, from the pencil-thin Monique Bordelon to the economy-sized Mycroft "Bears" Osborne. By the time I was done, my eyes were blurry.

"Is you cryin'?" Monique challenged.

"No," I sniffed. "I'm allergic to Domino's perfume, is all. You people try not to electrocute yourselves while I'm gone. I'll be back to check on your sorry asses, and if I find you all burnt to a crisp, I'll kill you. Understood?"

Millie, Alex, John, and I piled into the elevator. When the doors closed, Millie slid back a hidden panel under the push button controls, revealing a thumb reader. She touched it, and the mechanism whirred to life, sending the car downward with a lurch.

"Where're we going?" I rubbed my sleeve across my face. I avoided everyone's eyes, examining a water stain on the wall.

Alex chuckled like a mad scientist. "Our hidden lair."

The elevator clunked to a halt, and the doors slid back to reveal a concrete tunnel lit by square ceiling panels every ten meters. A cool, musty smell puffed into my face. Gray and utilitarian, the corridor terminated at a metal door, made tiny by distance.

"Downtown Chicago," Alex, the history teacher, explained, "is undercut by several levels of tunnels, from the uppermost pedway to the deepest tunnels at more than 100 meters. Parts of the pedway are still in use, if you're brave enough to venture there, but the levels below that were sealed off some time ago for safety concerns. Flooding was the biggest issue, as some of these tunnels were dug in the 1800s." He flashed a smile. "We moved in about twenty years ago and did some remodeling."

Our footsteps echoed along the hall. Millie and Alex led the way, and I kept pace with John's stride at a two-for-one ratio.

I cut my eyes at the big man. "Tunnel, huh? Who'd've guessed?"

John's cheek showed a spot of color, and he stared straight ahead.

The door had no lock on our side, and Millie heaved it open with a simple lever handle. On the opposite side, someone had welded brackets for doorjamb braces, like the ones on old-timey wooden forts. Once we were through and the door closed, John slotted two thick metal bars into the brackets, one top, one bottom, effectively locking the door. Getting through it would take an explosive device or a laser welding torch.

"What," I teased, "you don't let Franklin come visit?"

"Sure. As long as he calls ahead," Millie told me.

The tunnel we were in now was considerably older than the one leading to the elevator. We stood on a narrow walkway, surrounded by dank concrete walls, grainy and blackened with age, overhanging a trench that held rusted iron rails laid over rotting ties. Bare bulbs hung from jerry-rigged sockets, spaced far enough apart to give the tunnel that dark, scary-movie, rats-up-your-leg feeling. Someone had strung exposed Romex in the not-too-distant past to provide electricity for the bulbs. The work resembled a Saturday morning kid's project. A smell of wet mustiness overlaid everything.

"We're in a subway?"

"Very astute, Joe," Millie said with a wink. "I see you've lost none of your keen observational skills."

"An abandoned section of the CTA's underground rail system," Alex explained. "We're borrowing it for an access tunnel."

"This way." Millie marched off, and I followed, with Alex and John behind me in single file. I hugged the wall to my right. No way in hell I wanted to fall into the rail bed. It was dark down there, with no easy way back up, and doubtless inhabited by flesh-eating rats. Rodents of Unusual Size, indeed.

We hiked without talking for what I estimated to be about eight or ten long city blocks, until we stopped at another metal door, as featureless as three others we'd passed. Millie tugged the handle, and it opened without a squeak. She held it long enough for me to catch the edge, then passed through into a stairwell without waiting. I trailed after her blond mop as she bounced down the stairs—down being the only direction available.

"This looks new," I commented.

"It is," Alex said from behind me. He had to raise his voice to be heard over the noise of all four of us clanging down the metal treads. "We cut the shaft about ten years ago and replaced the original ladder with stairs after that."

"Where's it go?" I yelled back.

"Next level down is the freight tunnels."

"Jesus, how many freaking tunnels are there?" I muttered.

"What's that?"

We rounded the final flight and Millie waited at the bottom, holding yet another steel door open. I threw a glance back at Alex and raised my voice. "Nothing. Just wondering if we're gonna see any minor demons, or, you know, guys with pitchforks—" I passed Millie and entered the freight tunnel and stumbled smack into a wall of muscle with a tactical weapon aimed at my right eyeball. "Oh, shit!"

"Not a pitchfork," Millie said. "An LM44 automatic rifle with All-Use optics, capable of firing over 40 rounds of self-propelled ammunition in under two seconds." She grinned when I burned her with my fiercest scowl. "Joe, meet Sergeant Patrick."

"Uh," I said. "Hi?"

The rifle's muzzle held rock-steady, and sweat broke out on my forehead.

Should I let him sniff my hand?

After a suspended heartbeat or two, Patrick snapped his weapon back to port arms—or whatever they call it when they hold their rifle crosswise—and nodded to me. A mix of charcoal gray and black, his camouflage fatigues blended into the dark background. However, his heroic jaw and glacial eyes did not. He tracked those diamond-chip blue eyes to Millie, and they lost a fraction of their chill. "Miss Mac-Cauley. John, Alex. Cams picked you up on the way down. Wasn't sure about this one."

Meaning me.

"Joe's with us now."

Patrick failed to jump with glee. "Everyone's ready," he droned.

"Good," Millie grunted and led the way again, the shortest among us obviously in charge.

There was no walkway in this tunnel; we traveled at grade level. Although all the rails were gone, impressions cut in the floor showed where they once lay. I stayed in the middle, between two of the grooves. Water dripped from the ceiling and seeped from the walls to collect in trickles, which flowed along each side, as the middle of the floor was slightly humped. The stagnant air had an earthy, wet smell and was cool enough to make me glad of my jacket.

Like a nice, chilly grave, whispered the nasty voice in my mind.

Stop it, Nasty Voice. I hate you.

Alex appeared beside me. "These tunnels flooded back in 1992. One of the reasons we have them to ourselves these days. The entrances were sealed off back then due to the danger, and most people forgot about them." He shrugged. "We pumped them out, but still get some seepage from somewhere, not really sure where."

"Oh, good. And me without my swim trunks. Where the hell are we, anyway?"

"Under Orleans Street, somewhere near Illinois, I'd imagine."

I jerked a thumb over my shoulder. "And is that the only entrance?" If it was, Ramirez would pay hell getting his troops through that hole, after fighting his way through Cabrini-Green to get there. So it wouldn't matter what I told him.

"Oh, hell no. These tunnels go all over the city. There's a dozen entrances that we use, all of them hidden. Probably a hundred more sealed, or locked."

"So the feds could cut in pretty much anywhere."

He inclined his head. "I suppose so. If they knew where we were."

Great. Peachy.

"And so what's, uh"—I made air quotes—"the *outing* thing we're doing? Spelunking? 'Cause I gotta tell you, I didn't realize till this very minute I'm, like, claustrophobic."

"Hah! No, the mission's above ground, but I better wait for Millie to brief you in."

"And when will that happen?"

"About... now." Alex gestured ahead, and I realized Millie had disappeared through an opening in the tunnel wall. Brighter light glowed from inside, and when she went in, men's voices rose in greeting. John and Patrick halted behind us. "Come on," Alex urged. "Let's go see the boys with toys."

"Toys, huh?" Somehow, I didn't think he meant Legos.

I drew a deep breath, let it out...

... and nearly gagged on the wall of testosterone in the room.

Millie stood at the far end, studying a row of overhead photographs tacked to the wall, close-up pictures of some blocky buildings. The pictures were heavily pixilated, indicating they'd been enlarged from a very distant shot, like a satellite. Between me and her, a battered conference table of circa 1980 vintage was covered in maps and cups and pencils and crap. Eight barbarians from the steppes of Cimmeria—mighty thews, festooned with weapons, urban camo, and badass—ringed the table.

"Yikes," I blurted. "Where's Wonder Woman?"

Only silence and a palpable sense of imminent destruction greeted me. They entirely missed my witty reference to the Justice League.

Maybe Millie was right about the sorry state of modern education; it appeared none of them had studied the classics.

Patrick brushed past me and joined his clones at the table, his LM44 auto-whatever slung over his shoulder. John flanked me on my left, and I considered using the big man as a human shield. These guys made even Godzilla seem as meek as a puppy in a bowl of marshmallows. Where were they when Ramirez had me against the wall?

"Joe," Millie said, "meet 1st Squad, 2nd Platoon, Charlie Company, 3rd Battalion of the 1st Marine Regiment, United States Marine Corps."

"The Marine Corps? I thought they were—"

"Disbanded in 2032?" Millie said. "Officially, that's true. The US government, in a cost-savings measure, gutted the Marine Corps and turned their mission over to the remaining troops of the Army. Some... felt that wasn't a prudent decision."

"Wow. A secret army in a secret lair. This gets better and better."

"We only have one platoon here at the moment; the remainder got delayed in travel." Millie pointed out each man in turn and said their names, "Privates Smith, Lilyhorn, Benson, Lance Corporal Jackson, Corporal Appier, Privates Perlmutter, Charles, Wix, and you've met Staff Sergeant Patrick. Marines, meet Joe. He's the guy I told you about, who saved our butts at the Drake and wiped out an armed security guard."

"I... didn't do that much," I mumbled. I refrained from adding, *By hitting him in the back with a door and whacking him with a fire extinguisher.* The soldiers in the room oozed skepticism and suspicion like heat waves from hot tar, so maybe less confession would be better. "Could've used you guys there, that's for sure."

"The marines weren't dispatched until it became obvious Homeland was in a shoot-first mode," Alex explained. "Typically, they remain on bases in—"

Patrick cleared his throat, stabbing Alex with dagger eyes.

"—in undisclosed locations," the history teacher continued without a beat.

"Anyway," Millie resumed, "our Marine detachment will assist with this mission."

"Which is?"

"Have a seat, Joe." Millie waited until the three of us by the door found chairs at the now-crowded table. I squeezed in between two marines, Wix on one side and Lance-something on the other. Our blond pixie leader remained standing and produced the vid player from a dress pocket. "This is the mission."

I cocked an eyebrow.

"The building you see here"—she pointed to the blown-up photo behind her—"is a server farm in Schaumberg, roughly fifty kilometers away. It is operated by Homeland, so it exists outside the NSA's Vigilance system."

She paused to let that sink in. My mouth opened and closed. Reopened. "You mean... no filtering of the content?"

"Exactly. Anything we post from there goes out raw and unedited. The government can't stop it." Millie broke out in a sunny smile that turned her into a teenager. She held up the flat, palm-sized box. "We plan to infiltrate this facility, take over a server, and publish this video showing the massacre of peaceful citizens. The truth will finally reach the people." She paused, clearly pleased with how earth-shattering she found the idea.

"So," I said.

"What do you mean, 'so'?"

"John Q. Citizen watches a vid of Homeland killing innocent civilians. What happens then? Somehow I don't see, first of all, that a ton of people are going to believe it's real, or B, that it'll generate this huge tidal wave of change." I hated seeing Millie's smile disappear, but her cockamamie idea had no legs to stand on.

An impish smile played at the corners of her mouth. A cat who ate the cream and blamed it on the dog. "But that's not the only video."

Ah-fucking-hah. Brain, meet Joe. It wasn't hard for me to look mystified—it's sort of my default expression—so I schooled my face to remain dumb and confused. Ramirez wanted a video file recovered, one he assumed the CoL were planning to manually duplicate. Only, they had a different plan, and it involved unblocked servers and direct Internet access.

Holy Mother of the Web. Ramirez would give birth to live fuzzy kittens when he found out. What would he do to Ding and the girls? Were they doomed to continue their miserable half-life without control of their own bodies? And Chelle? Was she gone for good, or did the short prick from Homeland really mean something when he said her situation might be temporary?

Millie had continued speaking while my mind ran down a dozen narrow, twisty alleys. I blinked and caught up with what she was saying.

". . . recorded by an operative inside the president's cabinet, who obtained this footage during a closed-door session last year—"

"Hold it." I threw up a hand. "The United *States* president?"

"Yes, Joe," Alex intoned, serious as an actuarial table. He lifted his chin to Millie. "It would be best if you just played the recording. Let Joe see for himself."

The blond woman's lips crimped in a determined line. She touched the vid player and stepped back as an image popped up on the table. It showed a meeting room with President Ross Johnson and a bunch of serious people I didn't recognize gathered around it. No, take that back—the VP lounged a few chairs to Johnson's left. He looked half asleep. The camera was positioned at head height to a tall man, showing the table from one corner. We could only see the backs of those seated close to the camera, and the ones at the far end were a little fuzzy. Closed captions displayed the speakers' names and what they said. However, Millie touched the player, and the volume rose so we could hear their actual voices.

President Johnson: Okay, people, let's keep moving. I want to be driving a Titlest before the end of the day. Marciela, you're up.

Health and Human Services Secretary Zapata: For my first item, the Gen VI B-Mod packs have been distributed to all clinics and doctor's offices across the nation. Beginning in—

President Johnson: Remind me?

Zapata: The new B-Mods to prevent obesity, smoking, and to curb aggression, Mr. President. We found a sixty-eight percent reduction in negative social behavior among the test group, and the decision was made—

President Johnson: Gotcha. Continue.

Zapata: Ah, beginning in this upcoming school year, all children will receive the B-Mod dosages with their Dip-Tet inoculations. We predict coverage of over ninety-seven percent of all school-age children.

Education Secretary Contreras: Amazing. In ten years or less, we could practically wipe out smoking and heart disease. With a few little nanobots.

Zapata: Yes, ah...

President Johnson: Yvette? You have the legal side of this locked down? Don't give me chapter and verse, just a yes or no answer.

Attorney General Lemieux: Um... yes.

President Johnson: Good. Marciela, anything else?

Zapata: One more thing, Mr. President. Phase Two of the Elderly Relief and Reclamation Plan is prepared for your signature. That's the one where all federally funded clinics and hospitals will begin offering incentives to the terminal and elderly to accept early Revivant status. This will significantly reduce the strain on our health care infrastructure by removing those with the highest medical expenses from the system. Estimates vary on the savings—

"Turn it off," I choked out.

Millie touched a button, and the playback disappeared. "Are you sure, Joe? There's another twenty minutes of briefing here."

"Yes," Alex chimed in with a sardonic grin, "you shouldn't miss the part where they intend to replace all the military and law enforcement paramilitary troops with Revivants. It's a great cost-saving—"

"Stop," I told him. "Enough already."

Stale sweat and burnt coffee scented the room. My eyes locked with Millie's for a hundred years during the next few seconds. For some reason, she wanted either my approval or agreement. Why? Why would she give a damn what I thought? It sounded to me like the feds had all the bases covered. Best thing to do would be to find a hole (or a tunnel) and hide out until the shock waves passed. What could the fourteen of us accomplish?

I said, "Do you really think this little vid is going to—what?—ignite folks to... to overthrow the government?"

Alex cleared his throat. "Some of us believe there is a sleeping giant in the American populace"—he indicated Millie with a tilt of his head—"who will wake up to their own enslavement once sufficient evidence of the chains is brought forth. Others argue that it's too late for incremental change; that nipping away at some rotten branches will not solve the problem, which has grown too big, too complex, and too protected for uprooting. And yet a third position"—he touched his own chest with a thumb—"believe Americans are so unenlightened, so uncaring, and so self-absorbed that nothing we say or do will precipitate change. We must simply hunker down and wait for the inevitable implosion. Once that happens, the rotted tree of liberty burns to the ground. We arise from the ashes and rebuild."

"Sounds like a plan to me." I tapped a riff on the table. "Where do we hunker? And when's lunch?"

"Joe." Millie pinned me with a sad puppy look. "Do you know how many people will die if we allow the system to 'implode' as Alex suggests?" She didn't wait for my answer. "Millions, Joe. Millions and millions. Think about it. Federal law enforcement disappears. Welfare, veterans' benefits, and healthcare go belly-up without money. Over two-thirds of the people in this country receive some form of government assistance. What happens when that goes away?"

"Melodramatic much?"

"Joe, cities will burn." She ignored me; I should be used to it. "Local law enforcement won't be able to stem the riots on their own, not without the National Guard. What happens if our foreign enemies overcome their own internal issues and invade in force? The Chinese have invested heavily in this country. There're rumors some of our own leadership have made plans to defect there in the event of a total collapse. How hard is it to imagine a few million Chinese troops being dispatched to help 'keep order' or 'protect their assets'? You think our current military, unpaid, unfunded, and without leadership could stop them?" She ran out of steam, but not fire. The propane flame in her eyes burned as bright blue as ever. "How can we stand by and let that happen without *trying*?"

The marines shifted and shuffled but remained tight-lipped. Alex stared at the table, spinning a pencil in circles, while John's gaze promised he'd charge hell with nothing but warm piss and a blanket if Millie told him to. Millie straightened. "I don't know what releasing the video will accomplish. But I think the American people deserve to know the government plans to inject nanos into their kids and turn Grandma into a Revivant as a cost-saving measure."

And exactly what difference would that knowledge make? The feds held all the cards—all the troops, all the drones, all the advanced weaponry, artillery... And with Revivants for troops, none of the conscience of the American soldier. The concept of revolution was as outdated as the black-powder musket.

"Well," I heard myself saying, "should be a walk in the park. Break into a secure government facility, hold it long enough to upload a video, and save the world. I'll get my cape, and we'll get started."

Twenty-Six | Why Me?

A DOWNTOWN PARKING garage concealed an exit from the Bat Cave. Shortly after 2:30 a.m., the team—I wanted a catchy name like The Retaliators, or Millie's Marauders, but nobody else would go along—left the garage in three vehicles. Millie and I drove a ratty Dodge Defiant hybrid electric-diesel sedan with holes in the floorboard, and the marines boarded two vans, one driven by John Marsh, the other by Alex de Galvez.

Or actually, Millie drove the car while I learned to pray.

"Drive much?" I reached for the chicken strap over the door and found it broken, snapped clean off. Obviously Millie had passengers in this car before.

"I'll have you know I'm a very good—" A delivery truck signaled and started to change lanes in front of us. "Get out of my way, moron!" Millie accelerated and shot ahead of him.

I focused on breathing.

With Millie attempting to break the land speed record to Schaumburg, we made it to the staging area, an open parking lot of a closed, long-defunct electronics store, well before our two troop vehicles. She turned into the lot and crept through the grunge to the far left corner of the vacant building before continuing around the rear to the alley, where she turned right. We crawled to a deserted, junk-strewn wasteland adjacent the store's loading dock. A feral cat—or I hoped it was a cat—bounded away, flashing past our headlights. Millie braked to a stop facing a chain-link fence and shut the power off.

Weeds as tall as the car's roof grew through cracks in the asphalt and provided at least some cover should a Homeland squad car cruise back here for a look-see. At three in the morning, Schaumburg slept, and the only people out were cops, bad guys, or drunks rolling home with their vehicles on autopilot. Two people in a parked car would draw attention from anyone in uniform, which was the last thing we needed. Out of superstition, we crunched down in our seats, eye-level with the dash, as if that would save us from roving patrols.

We were dressed in similar dark clothes; Millie had switched from her summer dress to black jeans and a gray T-shirt. Alex had produced a similar outfit for me, with regular blue jeans and a navy tee. Which was now stuck to my back with sweat.

Facing us hulked a bi-level parking garage and beyond that a place called the Affiliated Data Center. Three stories tall, with thin arrow-slot windows, the ADC building resembled a cube with one corner cut off. The chopped side faced the street and featured the main entrance portico with four plain cylindrical columns supporting an overhang. A narrow drive split the building and the fence line on the other side. At least, the surveillance photos said all that was there. From here, all I could see was a fence and a garage.

"Affiliated with what?" I asked.

"Excuse me?"

"It says 'Affiliated Data Center.' What's it affiliated with?"

"I... I don't think it's affiliated with anything," Millie said. "I think it's just a name."

We'd lowered the windows to let in a cross-breeze, which carried the itchy smell of weeds and a baker's dozen hungry vampire mosquitos. I smacked my hands together as one floated past my face. I had to wipe the greasy black bug carcass on the Dodge's upholstery.

"Stupid name," I groused.

"What?"

"Never mind. How far ahead of Staff Sergeant Conan and his Barbarians did we get?"

She held her palms up. *Who knows?*

I slapped another mosquito. "Why me?"

"Why you, what?"

"Why am I along on this little adventure? Don't get me wrong, nowhere else I'd rather *be*! Fuck. Missed."

"You came looking for me, remember? Followed Tim to find me?"

"Yeah, but you could've left me pulling wire in the Green until hell froze over. Or had Franklin hang me from a lamppost."

"He wouldn't do it," she said. "I asked."

"Hey!"

She flashed a smile.

"So?" I asked again after she didn't speak for a while.

"Joe, of the fourteen million people in the Chicagoland area, about ten percent of those align with our views, politically speaking. There'd be more, but the—ahem—no-education system has left people clueless about basic economic theory."

"Yeah, yeah, yeah."

"Anyway, about ten percent of the politically aligned are committed enough to support the cause with money or material. Of that group, about eight *thousand* are full-time active members, living off the grid, hiding in various spots around the city. You didn't see them, because we didn't go that direction, but there are over four thousand living in the tunnels. What I would call the core group. Everyone has some task: childcare, education, sanitation, security, logistics, what-have-you."

I smacked a black bug between my palms. "Hah! Got you that time."

"Am I boring you?"

"No, no. Please continue. I love politics." I wiped mosquito guts on the side of the seat.

"The organization is run by an elected council. I'm council chair, elected at large. Sort of a mayor, if you will—Stop bowing, you look ridiculous. As chair, I have a staff through which I enact the policy decisions of the council. Like a mayor might have a city manager, right?"

"Absolutely." I yawned. A humid breeze drifted through, bringing a second's respite from the stifling air. "Manager."

"That post is currently vacant. My last manager left to help the Detroit group get reorganized."

"Uh-huh—Hey, wait a sec!" I popped up in my seat so I could aim a better glare at the blond woman. "You don't see *me* in that job. Do you?"

"I didn't, at first." Millie leaned over to check the time on the dash clock: 3:40. "At first I had you pegged for a worker bee, someone who could fix pipes or wire lights. Franklin sent me reports on your progress." She leveled a sincere look at me. "Joe, he was amazed. He hoped to have three buildings wired for solar by the end of a month, and he would have been happy with one or two. You finished ten in four weeks and, he said, you'd have another twelve wrapped by next month."

"I... well..."

"You have no idea how extraordinary that is, do you?" Millie squirmed in her seat to face me. "Joe, you're smart as hell. You're organized. You cut right to the chase without a lot of bullshit. You get things done. And when you're not hiding under that prickly sweater of cynicism, you're pretty fun to be around."

I drew a breath. Let it out.

"Here's how it is," Millie continued after my pause. "I have Alex and John as top guys. John's more of a follower than a leader. If I give him clear instructions, he'll do exactly what I say, without question and without stopping. Which is a problem, because when things go off plan, he's terrible at improvising. I love the guy, but he's not a leader. Of course there's Alex. Smartest man I know, but every task requires an hour's discussion on all the ramifications and possible consequences. Alex would argue the appropriate way to flush a toilet, if you let him."

"Heh. True." Crickets sang, and a mosquito whined in my ear. "So you mean to say, out of—what was it?—four thousand people, you can't find a go-to guy in the bunch?"

Her blond hair stirred when she tossed her head. "No, there are some. But there's always politics to consider. Some of our members are fringers, people who're more twisted than a strand of Christmas lights. Loners. Potentially violent and way too confrontational. Or they're aligned with one sub-group or another. I would like someone outside the politics. Someone who doesn't give two shits about whether or not embryonic cell therapy is an invasion of the fetus's right to privacy, or whether the right to free expression should allow you to walk around nude with your balls painted red."

I laughed. "I've always considered blue balls my default color."

Millie sighed and shook her head. "The stupid debates we get into sometimes..." I studied her profile by moonlight as she stared through the windshield and tucked a curl of hair behind her ear. "Besides, Joe, I need someone I can..."

Oh, shit. Don't say it.

"... someone I can trust." Her eyes swiveled to me. "Are you that guy?"

Ah, dammit.

Light washed the inside of the car and paralyzed me for a heartbeat. The second I swiveled for a look, the headlights cut off, and our vans drifted to a single-file stop at our rear bumper.

"That's us," Millie stated, shifting to all-business mode. "Go radio hot."

"Uhhhh..."

"Tap your earbud comm. Once for hearing only, twice for full voice-audio link. Like this."

"Oh." I tapped my bud once, glad to be doing anything besides lying right to her face. Was my status as potential turncoat relevant at this point? Ramirez said find the copy lab. Well, there was no copy lab. And I couldn't inform him about the raid, even if I wanted to. How could he blame me if the Liberty folks got their message out?

"*. . . ual to Eagle, do you copy? Talon Actual to Eagle—*"

"Eagle here," Millie's voice echoed in stereo, from right next to me and in my ear at the same time.

"*Eagle, Talon Actual. We clear?*"

"Good to go."

Men spilled out of the vans and jogged into a loose perimeter, muzzles pointed out. Thankfully.

"Ready to go play commando?" I asked.

Millie grimaced. "I wish we were just playing, Joe."

The clamshell rear doors of the last van in line stood open. Sergeant Patrick and three marines clustered around the opening. As Millie and I gathered behind them, Lance Corporal Jackson opened a toolbox-shaped plastic case. The contents sparkled under a hooded light held by the sergeant.

"My little beauties," said the lance corporal. Iron-hard, with oil-black skin and a shaved head, the corporal couldn't have been more than nineteen or twenty. When he grinned, I realized he'd dyed his teeth red.

He removed two devices from inside the box and handed one each to the waiting privates, Charles and Benson, and retrieved another for himself.

"Are those game controllers?" I wondered aloud.

"For a very deadly game," Patrick said.

"You and John Marsh... brothers from different mothers, right?"

The three marines powered up the handheld units, and glowing screens fizzed to life, hovering over the controller. At the same moment, a thin, high-pitched whine came from the case, and three jewel-like objects rose to hover at eye-level. Each the size of a black-eyed pea, the suspended motes danced as the soldiers twitched their controllers.

I squinted and leaned in. "Bugs? We're attacking the feds with bugs?"

"Micro-drones, Mr. Warren." Patrick switched off his light, leaving only the barest reflected glow of the controllers to provide any illumination.

"Are they"—I slapped the side of my neck, squishing something wet there—"any good at killing mosquitos?"

"All UMDRAV checks clear," Lance Corporal Jackson said. "Systems nominal."

"Deploy," ordered the Sergeant.

"Deploying, aye."

The three bugs zipped away, zooming up then curving toward the ADC building, their whine trailing away with them.

I had to ask, "What's an umdrav?"

"Unmanned Micro-Drone Reconnaissance and Assault Vehicle," the sergeant droned.

I mouthed the words to Millie, who shrugged.

"Watch the screen." Patrick gave us space to crowd behind LC Jackson and see the 3D projection hovering over his controller. It glowed with unnaturally saturated colors, but otherwise the image was crystal clear. And vomit-inducing. The little bug bounced and dipped through the air like a roller coaster designed by an acid-dropping sadist.

Nothing made sense at first, until I caught a glimpse of the doors to the Affiliated Data Center. After that, I was able to focus and follow the micro-drone's flight from its own "eyes."

"Become the bug," I intoned.

Millie elbowed me in the ribs. "You *are* a pest. Now be quiet."

"Helppp meeee," I whined in a tiny voice.

"Sshhhh."

The building rushed at our faces as the micro-drone dove toward the front door. I cringed when the twin panes of glass loomed, growing to gigantic proportions in a heartbeat. Jackson wiggled his thumb, and we zeroed in on the middle split, which didn't look big enough to slide in a piece of paper. It was like riding a magnifying glass to a close-up inspection of the mullion then taking a tour between the chrome-plated edges.

"Almost there..." The lance corporal threw in some body English, twisting around like he was the one doing the crawl through the tight space. We popped through the other side, and Jackson jiggled the zoom. The screen filled with a view of the lobby.

As big as a doctor's waiting room, with a cherrywood desk centered between two interior doors, the lobby was staffed by a single guard. A low table, some guest chairs, and a sofa used up the rest of the space. Nice, conventional pictures decorated the walls. Seated at the desk, the guard wore a black jumpsuit with the Homeland patch on one sleeve. The drone circumnavigated the room at ceiling height before pausing in a hover, high above the guard's left shoulder. The man at the desk scanned the ceiling with narrow eyes, no doubt wondering where he put the mosquito spray.

"Do it," Patrick murmured.

"Do what?" I swiveled from the sergeant's unsmiling face to the lance corporal's. The other drone pilots were juking and twisting their own controllers, engaged in different tasks.

"Aye aye," Lance Corporal Jackson acknowledged. He touched something, and a targeting reticule appeared on the screen. Some minute adjustments and the marine laid the circle and crosshairs on the guard's neck. "Target acquired. Delivery probe enabled."

The screen blurred with forward motion and filled with the tan flesh above the guard's collar. The drone smacked home, directly impacting the skin, like some miniature kamikaze dive-bombing super-mosquito.

"Direct hit," Jackson said without inflection. "Full load delivered."

"Pull out," said Patrick.

"Pull out, aye."

I popped off, "Don't you think it's a little late for the rhythm method?"

The picture wobbled, then steadied as Jackson fiddled with the controls. The guard was now facedown on the desk.

"Did you kill him?"

"No, Mr. Warren," Patrick assured me. "Merely tranquilized. Unless he has an allergic reaction to the trank, he should be fine." The sergeant checked with his two other drone pilots, who had penetrated the building through other... orifices. "Report."

"One roving patrol," Benson said. A light-skinned boy from the farmland, Benson had the palest eyebrows I'd ever seen on a human. "East corridor. Confirmed control center door, same corridor."

"Nada, Staff Sergeant," Private Charles said with a head shake. "Offices, all dark. No activity in the west corridor."

"Okay, Benson, zap the roving patrol and recover the bugs. Good work." Patrick clapped Jackson on the shoulder. He addressed Millie. "Ready to go huff and puff on the door, ma'am?"

The fighting elf straightened, and her jaw firmed. "Let's do this."

"Oh yeah," I chipped in, "but afterward you guys have to show me how to fly one of those things. I've always wanted to be a fly on the wall."

"What wall?" Millie asked.

"Are you kidding? The girls' locker at Saint Andrew's Catholic school. *Ow!* Stop hitting me."

"Well, stop being such a dick." Millie marched away to join Patrick and the remaining marines.

"What are you laughing at?" I said to Jackson.

"Man"—he chuckled—"she got you pegged, is all."

Twenty-Seven | The Truth... Will Get You Shot At.

TO AVOID TRIPPING ANY sensors in the fence, the marines used an extending contraption that resembled a stepladder, only wider across the top. With some grunting and swearing, four guys wrestled the bridge into place, stamped home a couple of power-driven stakes in the feet to hold the bottom steady, and called it done.

"Fire Team 2, with me," Patrick ordered. "Fire Team 1, hold the back door open."

The sergeant and four marines swarmed up and over the ladder. Millie and I followed when they signaled the all clear. In a loose formation we trotted to the garage, hopped the low wall, and continued across the open space inside. Our pounding feet seemed loud in the confines of the concrete parking structure.

On the far side, Patrick held up a clenched fist, and everyone stopped and sank to one knee. My head swam from the extra shots of high-octane adrenaline being pumped into my bloodstream. Sounds were clear yet oddly distant, and I had a hard time keeping my thoughts in a straight line.

"Talon 2," Patrick murmured.

Private Perlmutter scuttled up next to his boss. Perlmutter had a strong Middle Eastern influence baked into his DNA. His dusky skin stretched over sharp, heavy facial bones and was accented by dark hair and eyebrows.

The sergeant said something low in the private's ear, and the youngster bolted away as if shot from a cannon. He zigzagged across an open expanse of concrete and ornamental grass, jogged up the front steps and paused briefly at the front doors. A second later, he rolled to the side and covered his eyes. Light flashed at the center joint of the entry doors, followed by a mild pop. Smoke wreathed the lock before drifting away.

Perlmutter tugged the door open and disappeared inside.

"Move out," Patrick growled. He bolted forward, and we followed, jogging with the marines in a diamond formation.

A scorch mark blackened the center mullion of the double doors, and the electric strike had melted to slag. The glass-paned door swung freely when Patrick jerked the handle. The six of us scuttled inside and split left and right. I paused by a planter containing a fake tropical tree.

PFC Benson crouched by the guard Jackson had injected with his weapon of miniaturized dope. Benson secured the man's hands with zip ties and laid him out beside the desk before taking the guard's chair. Glowing screens lit his face from the underside. His eyes flicked to Patrick, and the sergeant acknowledged with a thumbs-up gesture.

The interior looked exactly as it had in the drone's eye view, except smaller. Something I'd missed earlier: above the reception desk hung an antique clock with a dial as large as a car tire, with ornate metal hands and a sepia face. The time was off. It read 11:55, with the second hand clunking its way through the bottom of the dial and laboring up the home stretch.

Tock.

Tock.

Tock.

Patrick touched Millie's arm and murmured, "Objectives secure, ma'am. We have zero casualties and have encountered only light resistance. Fire Team 1 is holding the route of egress, and Lance Corporal Jackson and Private Benson will hold the lobby. The civilians Alex and John have the vehicles prepped and positioned for evac. We are on plan and on schedule. We are green to go, ma'am."

"Let's do it," Millie ordered. "Lead the way, Sergeant."

"Aye aye, ma'am." He pointed at Charles and Perlmutter and issued terse orders. One man ghosted to the left interior door, the other drifted right. To Jackson, he said, "Lance Corporal, get us some eyes in the sky."

Jackson fired up another toy from his box. I held the door open a crack at his direction, and a larger copy of the micro-drone—this one the size of a sparrow—buzzed through the gap and angled into the sky. I let the door swing closed and edged next to Millie.

"Where is everybody?"

She shrugged. "I don't know. It seems... too easy."

"This is the part where I say, 'It's quiet in here,' and you say, 'Too quiet.'"

Both interior doors were locked. Charles and Perlmutter, working in almost perfect synchronization, removed patches the size of Band-Aids from breast pockets and slapped them over the door strikes. Twin tabs were jerked, and both men spun to the side and faced away.

Pop! Pop!

Smoke and sparks spewed from the patches, then dissipated. When the PFCs tried the doors again, they swung open. Perlmutter and Charles vanished through the smoke while Patrick held up a fist, signaling us to hold fast.

We waited.

Tock.

Tock.

Tock.

The atmosphere was surreal.

When I played this scene in my head before we left Chicago, I envisioned blaring lights, sirens, automatic weapon fire, screams, death, destruction, and heart-pounding action. Instead, it was like we were visiting the dentist. Three-thirty in the morning, we were committing a vast number of major felonies, and nobody seemed to notice. Except the clock, which recorded each frame of our lives with a steady beat. Sounds were muted. Lights dim. All we needed was canned music over the internal speakers.

Tock.

Tock.

Almost midnight.

"That's not freaky at all," I muttered.

"What?"

"Nothing."

Three hundred or so slamming heartbeats later, a deep voice spoke in my ear. Millie jumped at the same instant—I wasn't the only one with edgy nerves.

"*Talon Actual, Talon 3.*"

Patrick said, "Actual, go."

"*Control center 100 meters, left corridor. Copy?*"

"One hundred meters, left corridor, aye. Break. Talon 4, Talon Actual."

"*Four, go.*"

"Recover and fall back to the lobby. Hold position with One and Two."

"*Recover and fall back to lobby, aye. Hold with One and Two, aye.*"

Patrick tapped his ear and said to us, "This way."

We followed the wide-shouldered marine through the left-hand door at a trot. The ugly beast of a clock chimed a single ding as I passed it.

Midnight.

Beyond the lobby door lay a bland hallway, lined with a collection of offices, conference rooms, a break room, and toilets. For a government facility, I was deeply disappointed. Where were the chains? The iron maidens? The desiccated bodies of tax-evaders hanging by hooks?

A door opened behind me, and I spun around. A beefy guy in a black suit wandered out of the restroom with a magazine flimsy in hand. His eyes popped wide the instant he spotted us. The agent's hand swept down and came up with a pistol.

"Drop it!" Patrick's voice pounded my earbud and my eardrum at the same time. "Now!"

The wafer-thin magazine fluttered loose as the Homeland agent cupped his shooting hand to brace it. A low-pitched chatter rattled behind me. The guard's head shattered, and he slumped to the floor like a split sack of kidney beans.

"Holy fucksticks, dude!" At my feet, the dark-suited Homeland agent sprawled like he wanted to make a snow angel in the floor. Blackish-red blood puddled the tile around his head, and a handgun lay at his fingertips. He was thirty years old, tops.

"I didn't even hear shooting," I said.

"Suppressor." Patrick's voice came drifting past me.

Millie sucked in a deep breath and gripped my arm. "They... Joe, don't forget they fired first. At the Drake. Remember Goldie." Her face had gone creamy pale, and her eyes were wet. It sounded more like something she was saying to reassure herself.

"Yeah." Well, if she could handle it, I could too. I swallowed the queasiness and led her away from the body and into the nerve center of the server farm.

A perfect circle of workstations ringed the room, probably ten in all, with eight screens in dormant mode. PFC Perlmutter held his rifle on two dweebs pressed against the right wall. They both appeared to be dispensed from the geek pharmacy. Nerd Tablets, for daily use.

To prevent computer dysfunction. See a Level II Tech if you experience downtime lasting more than four hours.

Directly opposite the door, the screen at the twelve o'clock position was active, as was the one at the nine o'clock position to my left.

"All secure," Perlmutter reported.

"Confirmed. Restrain the civilians," said Patrick. To us, "You have ten minutes, Eagle. We will maintain security."

"Roger, aye aye, sir." I pointed to the open workstation on my left. "I'll take this one."

She signaled agreement and marched to the unit directly across from the door while Perlmutter zip-tied the nerds and questioned them about the number of guards on duty. Terse masculine voices chattered in my ear as the sergeant confirmed status with his scattered troops. I tuned them out and set to work.

I had a simple job: load the massacre video to as many external sources as possible. News—blog news, not network news—social media sites, and download servers. In other words, vomit the thing all over the Net.

While I was doing this, Millie did the same thing with the cabinet meeting recording.

The input layout of the workstation was more advanced and had more gizmos and doodads than ones I had used before, but the premise remained the same. I touched holographic controls and opened Google. I had a list of thirty sites and had to get through them all in the time allowed, so I had to prioritize.

"Let's see," I said to myself. "Start with Mark Scourge's site..."

The background noise faded as I focused on entering data and syncing the video player with the workstation's input field. Not that there was a lot of chatter; aside from an occasional laconic report by the marines or sniffles from the control room geeks, sounds were rare. Quiet intensified. At one point, I imagined I could hear the ticking of the lobby clock as it struggled from one second to the next—*tock*...

tock... tock—but in the end convinced myself it was only an echo in my head.

The air conditioner was set to nut-freezing. I clamped my fingers under my crossed arms to keep them from turning into icicles, and my nose started running. Despite the temperature, a bead of sweat tickled the side of my neck.

Every minute, Patrick called out the time remaining. I had made it through ten sites when his monotone "Six minutes" came through my earbud and from the sergeant himself. He knelt by the door and watched the corridor. Perlmutter kept a close eye on the techs, in case they broke out in some fighting style they learned from *Call of Duty: The New Millennium*. Millie pattered away at her server, shoulders hunched. I had an unnerving urge to go rub the tension out of them for her.

Great timing, asshole. Secret mission and you want to give your new boss a back rub.

Did she really mean all that bullshit about wanting me to help? To get things organized and jobs done? It seemed farfetched—

"*Talon Actual, Talon 1!*" Something in Jackson's voice sent a tingling down the back of my neck.

"Actual, go," Patrick radioed.

"*Convoy of numerous emergency vehicles, converging this pos. Repeat, beaucoup bogies, flashing lights and sirens, inbound this pos.*"

"Dammit," Millie cursed. "We must have tripped a silent alarm somewhere."

"Or somebody didn't check in when they should." Patrick regarded the two techs for a long moment, possibly considering how quickly he could extract the information. Or how to use them as human shields? "All right, ma'am, it's time to unass the AO."

"Agreed," Millie said. "I'm done anyway." She left her workstation, and with a few key strokes, I did the same.

"Talon 1, Actual," Patrick barked.

"Talon 1, go."

"Set charges at the gate, fall back to front lobby, regroup with Talon 2 and 4, hold position. Await further."

"Aye aye. Bogies are rolling hot, ETA five mikes."

"Roger that. Haul ass."

"Aye-fucking-aye, boss." Talon 1 sounded more than a little breathless, as if he were talking and running at the same time.

"All right, people, listen up." A glacier couldn't have been colder, or more formidable, than Staff Sergeant Patrick. I was glad he was on our side. "Homeland QRF will be here in five minutes. I suspect the alarm we tripped contained a video stream, so they know they have armed intruders. They're bringing the house. We will exit the building through the back door, follow the walkway to the east—left as you exit—and enter the parking garage at maximum speed, with suppressing fire being laid down. From there, we will cross the garage at the lower level, same as the entry, protected from incoming fire. Team One will cut the fence to speed our egress. We won't bother with the scaling ladder. The escape vehicles will be there, waiting. Understand?"

We nodded, and Patrick flicked a glance at Perlmutter. "On point, Marine. Eagle to follow, then Feather. I will bring up the rear."

"Aye aye," belted out the lean, dark-eyed Perlmutter. He flashed through the door and pivoted left. Disappeared.

I swallowed something mean and hairy that wanted to come right back up. Millie stood beside me as we waited for Patrick to give us the signal.

"Go," the sergeant ordered.

I exited first with Millie crowding right behind me. Perlmutter paused at the end of the hall, by another security door. He slapped an exploding Band-Aid to the latch, and it burned through the lock in a puff of smoke. Behind me, a flash of heat and boom shook the hallway. Sergeant Patrick had dragged the two techs into the hall. Smoke billowed from the control room.

"Thermite grenade," he answered my raised eyebrow. "Control room is slagged. Move."

We rushed to follow Perlmutter, who had disappeared into the next room. I peeked inside, and the marine beckoned me onward. It was the server room. Rack after rack of stacked servers, humming and whirring and clucking to themselves.

The radio crackled in my ear. "*Talon Actual, Talon 1.*"

"Actual, go," Patrick radioed.

"*Two tangoes have dismounted vehicles, are at the barrier. All Talon elements in the lobby.*"

"Roger. Hold position."

"*Holding.*"

I glanced at Millie and indicated the racks of servers. "Did we bring any more thermite thingies? We could fuck over the Homeland people pretty hard."

"Who's a revolutionary now?"

I laughed. "Bomb-Throwing Joe, that's me."

Patrick came up behind us. "We don't have very long before—"

A low *boom* shook the building.

"—they try and open the gate."

"That would be Homeland cops blowing up," I surmised. "Correct?"

The sergeant bared his teeth in a feral grin. "See how they like that shit for a change."

We hurried along the outside row of servers, following Perlmutter's crouched shuffle-run. He held his weapon at the shoulder, and his cheek pressed against the stock, flicking the weapon to point down any opening we passed before returning it forward.

An exit sign glowed above the door at the end of the row. Perlmutter paused, waited for a go-ahead from his sergeant, and shoved the emergency exit handle. The alarm went off the second he shoved through, screaming a falsetto note of anger. Millie pushed past me when I hesitated before crossing the threshold. If there was a line of gun-toting Revivants on the other side, I'd rather find out *before* going through. Millie was made of sterner stuff, apparently.

Nothing blew up, so I shoved out past the closing door and found Perlmutter, kneeling at the far corner of the building, peering around the edge.

"Talon 1, Actual," Patrick growled. When the back door swung shut, the screaming alarm diminished in volume.

"*Talon 1, go.*"

"Report. Any contact?"

"*Negative, Actual. Two tangoes down at the gate, appear Kilo-India-Alpha. Estimated twenty-plus tangoes are dismounted and fanning out across my front, inside the fence. They are advancing in overwatch. Be advised, they will have us flanked in one, maybe two mikes.*"

"Withdraw through the back of the building, post haste, Talon 1. Repeat, all elements to withdraw through the rear exit."

The marine repeated his instructions.

"Did he say twenty-plus?" I hissed.

Millie nodded. "Yes."

"That's a lot of guys. Hey, did you know my code name was Feather? What's that about?"

"The first choice was Bird Shit."

"Oh," I said. "Feather's good."

Twenty-Eight | Retreat? Hell, Yeah!

WE HUDDLED NEXT TO the building, as deep into the shrubbery as we could squeeze. Perlmutter remained rooted, with me crammed up against him, tight enough he could probably tell I was circumcised. Millie crowded my back, and Staff Sergeant Patrick held down the rear.

Perlmutter craned around to get my attention and pointed to the parking garage. "You know what that is?"

"Sure. It's a big structure where cars live during the day."

"No, dickhead. The gap."

"Yes," I said. A short wall protected the first floor of the garage; above that it was open to the bottom of the second floor. Between us and that gap lay an expanse of landscaping and a driveway, a good eight-second sprint. I figured I could make it in four.

"When I give the word, you two are going to run like hell for the gap. Jump over, don't stop. Jump and roll, okay?"

"Jump and roll, got it. Why are we still waiting? I'm ready for jump and roll right now."

"For the rest of the team to catch up," Patrick said. As soon as he did, the blaring back door popped open, and the three rearguard marines tumbled out in gun-shifting synchronization, each covering a sector as they exited. "Private Perlmutter, covering fire!"

Perlmutter leaned around the corner, and his rifle stuttered. It made less noise than a sewing machine, but it had an effect far out of proportion to the sound. Yells and commands burst from the Homeland troops when Perlmutter hosed them down with his LM44. A crackle-pop of return fire spat and sputtered, bullets zinging off the tarmac and dusting the wall over Perlmutter's head. He ducked back.

I glared at Millie. "You know, hanging around you is like playing duck in a shooting gallery."

Patrick gestured, and the marines behind him fanned forward. Lance Corporal Jackson belly-flopped at the edge of the building and ripped off controlled bursts at the enemy position. Privates Charles and Benson stacked high and low at the corner where Perlmutter had been and engaged as well. Perlmutter reloaded and held his weapon at the ready position. Sparkly lights winked from the garage.

What the hell was that? Muzzle flashes. Fire Team 2 had the Homeland troops in a crossfire.

The sergeant slapped Millie and me on the shoulder, one at a time. "Go!" he roared in my ear. "Go, go, go!"

I grabbed Millie under the arm and jerked her up, dragging the compact woman around to my right side, away from the incoming fire. Her mouth set in a grim line, eyes blazing, the blond pixie resembled a fierce Sidhe warrior more than she did an underground leader. All she needed was an elven bow and silver arrows.

We ran.

Sounds muted by the roaring in my ears, I couldn't hear the slapping of our feet on the pavement, or the furnace-bellow gasping from my lungs. Our route to the garage appeared more of a tunnel than an open space. I held Millie's sweating hand in mine, our mismatched tempo throwing me off, but I was determined not to let go of her. Hot, zinging bullets slapped by me, some close enough I could see the air distortion when they tore past.

I screamed one long, impassioned word: "Ssssshhhhhiiiiiiiiiii-itttttttttt!"

Then we were at the garage, and hands hauled us over the low wall. I dropped to the oily floor, pebbles stabbing my back, and sucked air, waiting for the blackness to recede.

Don't pass out, don't pass out.

Corporal Appier leaned over me. "Are you hit? Did you get shot?"

I shook my head, grit crunching against my hair. "No... I'm good. Millie?"

"Fine." Millie bent double, hands on her knees, panting.

"We need to move out," Appier yelled. "They're getting their shit together over there and bringing down some heavy fire."

He was right. The wall we'd vaulted appeared to be disintegrating under a sandblaster. The feds were pelting it with a streaming hose of incoming rounds that spewed concrete and sparkled with ricochets spalling rock.

"What about—?" How in the hell would Patrick and Fire Team 1 make it past the lethal barrage?

"Don't worry. We got this." Appier belly-crawled to his three marines, who were popping up, burping out small bursts of fire, and ducking back down. "It's time, boys. Light 'em up." The corporal double-tapped his ear. "Talon Actual, Claw 1."

The soldiers fiddled with a switch on their rifles, peeked over the revetment, and steadied their weapons on the ledge.

"*Go for Actual.*" Patrick's voice droned in my ear. He sounded as excited as a man ordering takeout.

"Cover going downrange. Bring it home, boss."

Pom-pom-pom.

"Grenade launchers," Millie yelled in my ear.

Flashes lit up the night, followed in an instant by flat cracks that thumped me in the chest.

"Again!" Appier commanded.

Pom-pom-pom.

Another series of hard bangs slapped the air and thudded into my breastbone. For a second, I almost felt sorry for the guys on the receiving end of this little slice of hell. They were simply guys doing a job, everyday working stiffs like me. I couldn't indict the entire agency because of Ramirez and the system that produced him. Could I?

On the other hand, they hadn't seemed reluctant to gun down unarmed civilians using undead troops as surrogate executioners. And Ramirez wasn't a part of that, so were all of Homeland's agents as warped as he? Did they know they would soon all be replaced by Revvies?

Pom-pom-pom.

Fire Team 1 crashed over the wall. They tumbled in graceless heaps, all panting harder than perverts at a peep show. At least I wasn't the only one stressed by outrunning a river of speeding bullets.

White lightning banged again, flaring against the underside of the garage deck above us. I rolled onto all fours and scrabbled over to Millie, who had sense enough to use a support column for cover. I squeezed in next to her. The acrid fumes of burned accelerant clouded the air with a misty gray fog, and my ears were ringing, which made hearing problematic. Somehow, even with all that, I felt pretty damned glad to be alive. Almost giddy.

"Can we go somewhere just once without getting shot at?" I shouted.

Her expression would best be described as perplexed. "You're asking me out? On a date? Now?"

What? "I—no! I mean, ah... No, that's not what—"

"Let's go, people," Sergeant Patrick boomed. "They've pulled back for the moment. We need to hustle before they regroup."

Millie poked a finger in my chest. "We'll discuss this later, Joseph Warren."

"Ah, yes, ma'am."

Women. Always thinking about sex.

The marines leap-frogged to the far wall in cover teams. The garage wasn't that big, so everyone made the fence in about four leaps. The chain link made a *ching-ching* sound as we slipped through.

John and Alex had turned the two vans around and opened the back doors.

"Everybody mount up," Patrick ordered.

"What about the car?" Millie asked.

"Leave it."

"Are you sure?" I said. "In her hands, it's a lethal weapon."

"Eagle in here." Patrick guided Millie into John's vehicle on the right and all of Fire Team 1 piled in behind her. The sergeant slammed the doors and pounded the back twice. Stuffed in the driver's seat, John twisted around, showed a *thumbs up*, and stomped the accelerator.

Patrick climbed into the passenger seat of Alex's van, and the rest of us clambered into the cargo space like a herd of cattle off to market.

"They'll figure out where we went sooner or later," the sergeant told de Galvez, loud enough for the rest of us to hear. "Pull out slow, with no lights until you know our cover's blown, then haul ass."

"Alex," I said, "you know what haul ass means?"

"Run like a jagged streak of hot burning cheetah?"

"That's it, buddy." Squashed against the divider, on the passenger side, I had a limited view through the gap of Alex's wide-toothed grin. The old professor seemed to be enjoying the shit out of this.

"Let's roll!" He shifted the gear lever, and the electric-powered van coasted forward at a walking pace.

"You might try rolling a little faster, *mi amigo*." I craned forward to see through the windshield as Alex kicked it up to a jog, and eventually to a weak run. We made the left at the store's corner. A brick dividing wall blocked the alley, so we had to make a run for

Golf Road. Ahead, the night sky flickered with a multihued patina of bright lights.

"Keep crawling," Patrick urged. "They're all over at the ADC building, sneaking up on the parking garage. Nice and easy, and they'll never see us."

We broke cover, and the light show intensified. I stuck my head all the way through the gap and peered past Alex's nose at the red-blue-white-yellow emergency flashers blocking a big chunk of Golf Road to our left. The way ahead remained clear. No sign of John's van; he must have gunned it out of the lot and made the road. All we had to do was play mouse and sneak out past the big, bad cat and we could do the same.

Tonk-tonk-tonk-tonk-tonk. A row of holes stitched the cargo compartment over the heads of the seated Marines.

"Floor it!" Patrick barked. "We're taking fire! Everybody down!"

The van surged ahead with all the muscular acceleration of an old man's wheelchair. Behind me, the marines dogpiled together. I crouched as low as I could get and still see out the front. If I buried myself under Marine Hill, I would be blind and deaf to whatever fate had planned.

"Can't this thing go any faster?" I yelled.

"I'm giving her all she's—*Uhh*!" The driver's side window starred, and chips of glass exploded inward. More bullets hit the door and punched through. Alex jerked and grunted again. He clenched his arm against his side and grimaced in pain.

"Are you hit?" Patrick barked.

Alex hissed, and his head bobbled loosely. "I'm okay," he gasped.

The speedometer needle crawled up the dial... 50 kph... 60 kph...

Thwap-thwap! The van shuddered as more rounds punched through its thin-skinned sides and hit something in the cargo space. A marine yelped in pain. We rocked and bumped over pitted pavement, and the motor whined at its highest output. Golf Road grew closer, like a bad dream where you ran but couldn't gain any ground.

A white streak of light burned toward us in an arrow-straight line.

"Missile!" Patrick yelled.

A cart-return island saved us. The ancient structure bloomed in fire when the missile impacted a metal pipe, less than twenty meters away. The van rocked through the shuddering boom. I lost sight of the fireball as we sped past.

"Come on, baby. Come on." I chanted under my breath while holding on to the partition walls. "A little bit more..."

Alex had gone pale, and his face twisted into a mask of pain. He breathed in sharp gulps and listed away from the door, his left arm clamped against his side. He kept his foot jammed on the accelerator. 70 kph... 75...

"Slow down," Patrick cautioned. "You'll never make the turn."

"Can't," Alex gasped.

In truth, we were rocketing toward the curb cut, flying over weeds and debris. As top-heavy as the van was, a sharp turn at this speed would likely tip us over. More rounds thunked into us, sensed but not seen.

"Alexxxx..." I gripped the partition edges and squinted my eyes shut. We barreled to the edge of the lot, the van juddering and wallowing at more than 80 kph.

At the last second, Alex slammed his foot on the brake. The nose of the van dipped hard, nearly throwing me into the center console. He slewed the wheel right, palming it one-handed, and the boxy vehicle bounced and skidded, tires squalling.

We tipped...

tipped...

hung...

and fell back to four wheels.

"Yeah, baby! Way to go, Alex!" I slapped his good shoulder. "Punch it, bro, punch it!"

Alex punched it, and the electric motor whined a protest song.

Cool as a rock star, the sergeant said, "Keep it floored. We'll be out of range in under a minute. We'll need to ditch this vehicle as soon as we're out of sight. The feds will be all over the roads ahead looking for it." He craned around, peering over my head. "Anybody hit?"

"Private Charles caught a round in the butt!" Bensen yelled.

"Brain damage?" the sergeant asked, a tiny smile curling his lip. His eyes widened, and I spun around to see what spooked him. Through the van's rear windows, another arrow-streak of fire burned toward us—

God smacked the back of the van with the biggest hammer in His toolbox. We flipped into the air, and my world tumbled. Freefall. We floated, and, for a moment in time, I lived in a suspended state, processing images like pictures from a still camera.

—Patrick, hands braced on the dash—

—straight down, the concrete road filling the windscreen—

—a machine screw, frozen in space—

Then the van hit, nose first, and white lights exploded in my head.

Twenty-Nine | Hello Again... Naturally

I WOKE UP WHEN AGENT Ramirez slapped my cheek. "Joseph? Joseph?"

"Déjà vu," I mumbled.

"Indeed. Seems we've been here before."

"Except this time I'm strapped to a chair. Whassamatter? You don't trust me?" My body ached from head to toe. A quick inspection suggested no serious damage—a minor miracle considering I was blown up by a rocket and slammed around a tumbling van. "What happened?"

"The vehicle carrying you and your terrorist friends was intercepted by a man-portable missile on Golf Road, in Schaumburg. Do you remember that?" The agent's eyes were bloodshot, and his tie hung askew. He stifled a yawn.

"Yeah, gotcha. What about the... others?"

"Two dead, five injured. Including you. Very lucky you survived at all."

"Who died in the crash?" I asked the question to gain a few seconds. The sticky clouds filling my brain were clearing, but I needed time to think.

"Who cares who died? What did you think you were doing?"

"What you told me. Getting inside the Children of Liberty."

He snorted. "Children, indeed. A stupid plan that has done nothing but stir up more trouble. Did you know there are already riots in DC? Those videos have sent people into the streets. Riots, Warren. A lot of people will die because of what you did tonight." He rubbed his eyes. "Why can't people simply behave? Why must they be so... so deviant?"

"Ummm... free will?"

"Don't make me laugh. We'd be better off with a nation of B-Mod Revivants."

A paintbrush dipped in ice water washed my spine. He sounded like he meant it.

"So, Joseph. I suppose finding the video file location is moot. Where is the MacCauley woman? Where's her base of operation?"

"What about Ding? Deandre, Signe? And Chelle? What happens to them now?"

"Stop wasting my time."

"They're gone, aren't they?"

"No coming back from B-Mod, Joe. Once injected, forever implanted." Ramirez straightened his tie, seemed to pull himself out of his funk. "Now, answer my question and at least you can walk away. I'll only ask you this once: Where are the Children hiding?"

My tongue stuck solid, and a baseball-sized lump settled in my windpipe. Here it was, laid out clear as a pane of glass. I could tell Ramirez everything I knew. About the entrance to the tunnels inside Franklin's building and the one in the downtown parking garage. How the Children had more than four thousand men, women, and children living underground, under the feet of downtown Chicago pedestrians. I could give everything up and babble away all my secrets. Ramirez would invade the tunnels and massacre the entire population. Game over for Millie and John. What happened to me? Did I live or die? Would I care?

The alternative answer?

"Fuck you, Ramirez."

I never saw him move. My head rocked, and my cheek burned from the slap. A high-pitched whine started in my ears.

"Shit, Ramirez," I slurred. "Girl scouts hit harder than that."

Smack! My head snapped to the opposite side. Now I had cheek burns on both sides.

"Joe," he chided. "What's gotten into you? Your time playing soldier started a spine growing down your back? Huh?" He slapped me again. My head bounced like a tennis ball being volleyed from side to side.

I spat blood between my feet. "You trying to hit me or fuck me, Ramirez? I've had rougher foreplay."

A hard fist cracked my nose, and pretty lights sparked behind my eyes. My head jumped straight back this time.

"I don't have time for this. Bring him in," Ramirez ordered. I paid attention to the room for the first time. Me, in a straight-back plastic chair, arms and feet strapped down, sitting across from Ramirez in a similar chair, not strapped down. Duh. Stark room, no other furniture, a single light directly overhead, centered between the two of us. A hulking figure by the door, now leaving.

"Cheery place," I said. "I like what you've done with it."

"Tell me what happened, Joe." Ramirez seemed sad, almost regretful. "Did the cute little MacCauley woman pussy-whip you? Did you convert to the cause? What did they say in the old days? Did you drink the Coca-Cola?"

"Kool-Aid, you prick. Drink the Kool-Aid." My head hurt. I rolled it in a circle to loosen my neck.

"Tell me where they live, and I'll make it easy."

"What does it matter? The video's out."

"My orders are to eliminate the Children of Liberty, regardless of the video. Traitors to the core, each and every one of them."

The door opened, and two goons carried in a slumping Alex de Galvez. Bloody bandages wrapped his bare upper torso, and his face was black and blue with purple all over. Agent Maravich trailed in behind carrying another plastic chair. He set the chair next to Ramirez, and the goons deposited Alex hard enough he grunted and his eyes popped open. Alex focused on me and tried out a weak smile.

"Hello, Joe," he rasped.

"It seems," Ramirez said as the two goons left, "all the insiders of the CoL have been injected with blocking agents that counteract the effects of our strongest truth-eliciting drugs. Using synthetic material to gain information has proved fruitless. Likewise, hypnotic blockers have defeated the... less pleasant ways of gaining information."

"So you're fucked. Sounds great. Can we go now?"

Ramirez's lips compressed in a thin line. "Hardly fucked, sir. Hardly. I still have you."

"Kiss my skinny ass, Ramirez."

"Atta boy, Joe," Alex mumbled. His eyes had closed again, and he slumped in the chair, held upright only by Maravich's hand on his shoulder.

"Do you see what my companion is holding?" The agent waved a lazy hand. Maravich showed me an injector with a vial of blue liquid loaded in the delivery chamber. "That's Gen I RVT 0287-A. The earliest working version of Revivant nanobots. They were never meant for human hosts. Do you want to know what happens if Agent Maravich injects them into Mr. de Galvez?"

I jerked against the restraints. "You fuck. Don't do it."

Alex opened his eyes in alarm. He stirred, and Maravich's hand tightened on his shoulder.

"Mr. de Galvez," Ramirez said, "will experience a lifetime of pain as the nanobots convert his living tissue to their own needs. They will invade his limbs, causing agonizing paralysis. From there, they will creep into his stomach, claiming his liver, kidneys, and bowels. All the excess waste in the body will be expelled as the nanos clean the system. His lungs will be commandeered, as will his heart, as the microscopic devices reprogram the nerves to react to their input instead of the brain's." Ramirez leaned forward, and the overhead painted his face in a Phantom of the Opera Halloween mask. "Then they will find that very brain they have just shut off from the rest of the body, and they will alter the neural pathways to suit their programming, creating a janitor, or a soldier, or... any number of useful citizens. Did you know there is a growing sex industry using Revivants? Seriously! I would not have believed it myself, but hey, to each his own, huh?"

"Don't." I wasn't proud of the note of whiny pleading I heard in my own voice, but I was powerless to change it. "Please don't."

"You can stop it, Joseph." Ramirez leaned back and held his palms up. "It's simple. Tell me where the Children abide, and Mr. de Galvez may avoid this fate. He will not be forced to feel his own body being eaten away from the inside, one millimeter at a time."

"No, Joe," Alex whispered. Tears flooded his cheeks and dripped from his chin. "Don't do it. It's not worth it."

"Goddammit, Alex." My heart thudded, and heat rushed into my face.

"One last time, Joseph. Where are the Children of Liberty?"

"I..."

"No," Alex pleaded. "Don't say anything."

"Ramirez..."

"Yes, Joseph."

My throat worked as words tried to form in my head. What could I say that would get us out of this? All my life, I'd been quick with a snappy comeback. Words came easily; I used them like a weapon. The only words in my head were: *Tell him they're in the tunnels!* My eyes locked on Alex's. The rest of the room blacked out, leaving only the connection between his liquid dark pupils and my own. Across that gap, as powerful and real as a megawatt of electricity traveling on 10-gauge steel wire, his... I don't know what else to call it except soul... jumped from him to me. It filled me with strength, like a direct charge of the power inherent in our shared humanity. Our hope for the future. Our passion for life and our willingness to die for the people we...

Loved.

"It's okay, Joe," Alex whispered.

"Well," Ramirez demanded. "Time's up. Where are they?"

"I'll tell you," I sighed and slumped, the connection from Alex de Galvez broken. How could I do this?

Ramirez leaned forward again, transforming himself again to the Phantom of the Opera. "Yes?"

"Everyone's down at the dog shelter. Watching your mother pump out a new litter."

Ramirez eased back with a long, sibilant sigh. He shook his head, as if disappointed by an unruly child. It's a look I recognized because I'd seen it all my life. Except from Alex, who beamed enough approval to light a fire in my heart.

"I'm sorry, bro," I told him, and meant it.

"It's okay, Joe. I'm proud to have known you."

"Enough of this shit." Ramirez grunted. "Hit him."

"About time," Maravich said. He jabbed the injector to Alex's shoulder and hit the trigger.

Alex lasted five excruciating minutes. He screamed the whole time. I held his gaze as long as he could manage.

When it was over, Ramirez said, "Joseph, I have to say you surprised me. It's too bad, really."

"Whatever. Suck on it."

"I wonder..." He paused so long I cranked my head up and cocked an eyebrow. "I wonder if you have been with the Children long enough to get your inoculations against our truth agents. How about it, Joseph? You remember getting any injections?"

Oh shit. Nobody gave me any shots. Did they?

My answer must have been written on my features. The short Homeland agent's face broke out in a genuine smile. "I thought not. Wait here, will you? I'll be right back."

LIGHTS.

Ow, that hurts.

Questions. Why are they asking me questions?

Shut up.

Go away.

What? I don't understand.

I need to puke.

Oh, fuck, just kill me, okay? Get it over with.

No.

No, I don't know. Stop asking me.

Wait, what's that? Get aw—Ow! Oh... Um, that's nice. Everything's all floaty.

What? Sure. Why didn't you say so? Yeah, that's easy.

IN MY DREAM, SOMEONE was screaming.

A racking, bitter, horrid scream that never stopped. It was dark, and I couldn't tell who was wailing. *Shut up, I'm trying to sleep.* But they wouldn't. The shrieking paused for a moment, only so the tortured soul could draw breath to reload the scream machine.

Fuck this. Wake up and tell 'em to can it.

I cracked my eyes open. The howling continued.

Bright overheads. Reek of chemicals. Bleach overlaying a smell of shit. And a sound of pure, animal agony ripped from the core of a human soul. An ice demon gripped my heart in his frozen fingers and squeezed. I shivered and clenched my groin to keep from wetting my-self. The type of pain required to induce that level of anguish...

I shifted, and paper crackled. Eyes squinted against the white light, I peered through fluttering eyelids. A hospital room? More like a ward. Six beds. I was at the end of the row, on an examination table. Sterile environment. One wall with a row of cabinets and a counter-top. Medical crap all over the counter. Against the far wall, one of the beds was tilted upright, and, strapped in place, Private Perlmutter shrieked in mortal agony. Next to him stood Agent Maravich, hold-ing an injector and pursing his lips in deep concentration as Perlmut-ter screamed his guts out.

"Stop it," I commanded Maravich. Or I tried to. My voice came out kittenish, more of a mewl than a roar.

I levered up to a sitting position, and my movement must have caught the agent's attention. He shot me a grin and said, "Your turn next, Warren."

Perlmutter stopped screaming, like a faucet being turned off. A glassy, faraway look came into his eyes, just like a... just like Alex.

"A Revivant." Panic raked my throat with grimy claws. "You killed him and made him a Revivant."

"Eh, not quite." Maravich shrugged. "More like: I made him a Revvie and killed him."

"You're a sick fuck, you know it." My voice burred, rough and raspy. Aches and pains woke up and begged for attention. My left shoulder grated when I shifted that arm, pain slicing from the joint to my ribs. My guts hurt, as if a heavyweight boxer had been pounding my midsection for a few rounds, and I couldn't be sure my legs would hold me if I tried standing.

Pain won't bother me long if Maravich injects me with nanobots. Suck it up.

I flexed my muscles and breathed through the pain. I'd been banged up enough before. The sensation of working through pain was nothing new. Pain was nothing but a message from pissed-off tissue. Shut off the communication and block it out.

The burly agent busied himself unstrapping the former Private Perlmutter and settling his feet to the floor. He snagged a horseshoe-shaped collar from a rack and slipped it around the soldier-turned-Revivant's head. Maravich crossed to a virtual keyboard on the counter and typed a series of commands.

Perlmutter twitched and ventured a step, followed by another. In a second, he marched to the door like a wind-up toy. Maravich tapped a key, and the door buzzed open in advance of the marine's jerky steps. The dead marine exited, and the door swung shut behind him, locking with a click. Maravich entered some more commands, and it sounded as though another door opened and closed.

"Now for you, Mr. Warren." Maravich sharked his teeth. He threw the used injector in a medical waste bin. There were four others exactly like it lined up on the counter, filled with blue liquid. "Why don't you come on over so I don't have to drag your ass kicking and screaming. Sooner started, sooner done."

I cleared my throat. "I talked, didn't I?"

"Like a schoolgirl," Maravich gloated.

I have to get out of here.

Thirty | Fight the Government, They Said. It'll be Fun, They Said

MARAVICH DEMONSTRATED a complete lack of concern that I wasn't cuffed. Not for the first time I wished I'd been blessed with a Sergeant Patrick body, an alpha male's alpha muscles straining my shirts and power oozing from my pores. I'd clean the floor with Agent Maravich and six more like him. Despite my month of hard work and good food, the Homeland agent outmassed me by a couple of buffaloes and a small sheep, plus whatever drug they hit me with left me feeling weak as chicken broth.

"C'mon, Warren. Get over here so I can strap you down; I ain't got all day. Ramirez is gearing up to take down your buddies, and I want to be there, just in time to arrest Little Miss Millie." He sneered. "She'll enjoy the company of a real man for a change."

"A real man? Who? You?" I snorted. "I don't think so."

Maravich narrowed his eyes and shambled in my direction.

"Tell me," I sneered, "when you raped Signe, were you able to get it up? Or'd you have to pretend she was a guy?"

"Fuck you, Warren," the agent grated.

"Maravich, you're living proof that there's life after abortion." I jumped down and rushed to the end of the exam table to meet him head on. "You fell out of the psycho tree and didn't miss a branch on the way down, did you?"

"Keep talkin', asshole," he snarled. Flaming redness boiled up from his neck and soaked his face. He seemed so hot I worried his hair might catch on fire. He coiled a fist to knock me into next week...

And I punted him in the nuts.

"Oof!" he grunted.

Even kicked in the cojones, Maravich was quick. A massive fist blurred into my face, faster than a camera flash. I flew backward, hit the bed, and crashed to the floor. *It'd be nice not to be hit in the face anymore.* I fought through the dizziness and climbed to my feet. The Homeland agent hunched over, glaring bloody murder and mayhem.

"You're dead, fucker," he growled.

"So I've heard."

I flew at him and landed a shot to his cheek before a piledriver right slugged me under the ribs and blasted out all my wind. I tagged him again, but it was so weak I might as well have kissed him. His crossing left caught me in the ear, and my head rang like a bell. I met the floor again. Patted it like an old friend. *Missed you, buddy.*

Maravich lifted me by the shirt and slung me across the room. I crashed atop the row of beds, flipped upside down and went over the side, taking a mattress, sheets and all, with me. My hip screamed from where I'd collided with the bedframe, and dizziness struggled with nausea to decide which would be first to kill me. Resting under the loose bedding seemed like a really good idea. I lay on my back in the dark and let my spinning head whirl to a stop.

The agent ripped away the bedding, exposing me to the cold, sterile light.

"Get up!"

I played dead. Maravich dragged me up by the armpits and held me at arm's length, like a puppy who'd wet himself. I let my head loll to the side and mumbled something.

"What?" he snapped. "What'd you say now, you smartass prick?"

I poked him in the eyes with my thumbs.

"*Argh!*"

This time when he threw me, he wound up like a discus and really put his back into it. I sailed through the air and smashed into the line of cabinets with a horrendous bang. My head bounced off the wood, and more sparkly lights bloomed inside my head. I slid off the cabinets, hit the counter, and scrabbled to stay upright.

I fell on my ass. A cascade of medical supplies avalanched on my head.

Maravich flung me onto my back and loomed over me. He clutched my shirt in both fists and jerked me up.

"You little cockroach." His breath choked me with an onion-and-rotted-meat smell. "You're done, you hear me? I'll beat you to damned near death, then I'll fill your ass full of nanobots. How's that for a long-term plan, huh?"

"Hey, Maravich?" My breath whistled through my blood-clotted sinuses.

"What?"

He saw the injector in my hand. His eyes bulged, and he tried to untangle from my shirt, grab the injector, and push away at the same time...

. . . and failed at all three.

Too late, asshole. I jabbed the point into his thigh and squeezed the trigger. The injector hissed and dumped a full load of Gen I nanobots into Agent Maravich of the Homeland Security Agency.

Five minutes later, he became Revivant Maravich of the You're Fucked Agency.

I laughed while he died. Before the nanos ate his brain, I said, "That was for Signe and Deandre, you prick."

AGENT RAMIREZ ENTERED the office of Special Agent George Crispo without knocking and almost planted his fists on the man's desk. Crumbs and crud littered the walnut surface. Ramirez sneered and remained standing.

Crispo ran the Armed Response Team for Homeland Security's Midwest Division from an office in Homeland's Buffalo Grove complex, fifty kilometers from downtown Chicago. With seventeen years in the Agency, Crispo had never held a field assignment. With a fringe of curly hair circling his pointy head, the lifetime bureaucrat resembled a penis with glasses.

"Crispo." Ramirez kept his voice low and mild, as it freaked people out. "Why have you been ignoring my phone calls?"

The special agent regarded him over the top of his half-glasses. "Ramirez, it might have escaped your attention, but there's a wee little crisis in Washington. I can't get anybody on the phone or email, and the rumors don't sound good."

"In *Washington*?" Ramirez let his jaw drop. How could someone so stupid rise to a position of such authority? "In case it escaped your attention, Special Agent, we have a crisis right fucking here. Terrorists hit our data center in Schaumburg last night. They murdered an agent inside, and three from the Quick Response Force died retaking the building. Eight men are in the hospital. What part of crisis does not apply here?"

"Yes, w-well," Crispo stuttered. He leaned back in his chair and tugged his collar. "I need approval from the director before I can authorize the kind of force you're asking for. All my Z's? That's sixty zombies and ten controllers. And then the response teams? That's over forty men. You know how much that kind of deployment will cost?"

Ramirez slid out his ID case and held it at Crispo's eye level. He dropped his voice from menacing to viperish. "What does this say?"

When Crispo didn't respond, Ramirez continued. "It says Special Agent in Charge, Counter-Terrorism, Central Division, Ramirez, Angel. That's me. I am responsible for protecting the homeland and preventing acts of terrorism from the Great Lakes to the Rio Grande, the Mississippi to the Rockies. Look up the regulations. Section 8: Counter-Terrorism. Chapter 12, Duties and Authority. In that chapter, you will read that in the event the SAIC CT—that's me—determines there is an exigent threat to the security of the nation that is material and manifest, the SAIC CT has the authority to commandeer resources and personnel, up to but *not* including nuclear devices, to mitigate or preempt the threat."

"I—I'm familiar—"

"Shut up, I'm not finished." Ramirez put his ID case away. "Terrorists have attacked our facility. We know who they are, we know where they are, and we know they will scatter if we don't act immediately. Therefore the threat is exigent, material, and manifest. You have one option here, Agent Crispo. Furthermore, I have written authorization to use any and all means necessary to eliminate this threat. Pick up the phone and release all of your Z-units as well as your Armed Response Teams that are currently based here. If you have more deployed elsewhere, you will relocate them to the staging area I designate. Are we clear?"

"Ramirez, come on, I need—"

"Crispo, if you respond with anything except, 'Yes, Agent Ramirez,' I will shoot you down like the pencil-pushing prick you are and find out if your subordinate can follow regulations. One more time. Will you release the teams to me?"

The special agent rocked back in his chair as if struck. "You're insane," he hissed.

"It would be best if you kept that top of mind when I request resources."

Ruddy spots broke out on Crispo's cheeks as the older man tried to stare Ramirez down. Whatever he saw in Ramirez's eyes, it must have convinced him the counter-terrorism agent meant exactly what he said. Crispo touched the EarRinger comm unit dangling from his left earlobe. "Get me the duty officer. We need to deploy... No, not in a minute, *now!*"

MARAVICH IMITATED A toppled statue, rigid and solid, lying at my feet. I prodded him with a toe. Nothing. He would remain in that position until somebody programmed the nanos in his system to perform a function. I prayed for shit sweeper. There was a sidearm on the agent's belt; I tugged it free and examined the weapon. It looked nothing like Grandpa's Smith & Wesson. Flat, black, and covered up with knobs and levers, the weapon was beyond my ability to operate. One thing it did have, that I recognized from countless vids, was a SmartGrip. The pistol would read its owner's identity through the grip and fail to fire for anyone not coded for it, so for me, the pistol was nothing but a fancy club.

At the sink, I washed my face with shaky hands and dried off with paper towels. The silence of the room ate at my nerves, and the dead agent's eyes followed me around like a painting in a horror movie. I dragged a blanket off one of the beds and draped it over his body.

I had killed a man. I felt... disconnected, like it happened to somebody else. Should I send up a prayer, maybe? *Say, uh, sorry, Big Dude of the heavens, but I kind of killed a guy here. He was a dick, so I don't think you'll have to make space up there in heaven, but, uh... you know? Amen.*

The command console displayed a floor layout diagram with icons and labels. The lock icon for a room labeled TREATMENT stood out in red. I touched it. The lock buzzed, and the door opened, exactly as it had for Perlmutter. I stuck my head into the hall.

"I've been here before," I muttered. And it dawned on me. I was in the basement of the Huateng Tower, the same place Ramirez and his clowns had nailed me during my escape from the robbery. The elevator at the end of the hall looked very damned familiar. I guessed it made sense. Where else would Maravich find a ready source of Revivant nanos but the basement workshop of the mad scientist? I closed the door and went back to the console. Five other rooms on the diagram were labeled. INVENTORY, LAB 1, LAB 2, STORAGE, and DETENTION.

"Detention sounds interesting." I tapped the icon, and a message popped up. ENTER CODE. "Well, that won't work."

The detention room was two doors down on my right. I wedged the treatment room door with a bedpan so it wouldn't lock behind me and scooted down the hall. The stylized R of Renascentia's logo adorned the outside of each door in the hall. I banged on the R of the detention room with the flat of my hand.

"Hey! Anybody in there?"

After a pause, a voice rumbled, "Staff Sergeant Patrick, US Marines. Who is this?"

"Santa Claus," I yelled back. "Hold on, I'll get you out. Wait... You're not dead, are you?"

"Ahhh... That's a negative."

"Good enough for me."

A thumb reader on the mullion glowed red. I touched my thumb to it, and it still glowed red. "That was smart, Joe," I grumbled. "Sure, they keyed all the locks to your thumbprint. Dumbass."

Nothing for it.

I trotted back to the treatment room and rummaged through the drawers until I found a surgical kit, tore it open, and extracted a wicked-sharp scalpel. I flipped back the blanket covering the right

hand of dead Agent Maravich and... did what had to be done. Carrying his freshly liberated thumb in a wad of paper towels, I went back
to the detention room and pressed the digit against the reader.

Buzzzz-click.

Sergeant Patrick and Lance Corporal Jackson rushed out the second the lock clicked.

"Hi, Sarge," I told him. "Good to see you guys."

"Warren! How'd you get the lock open?" Patrick's ice-chip eyes
lasered into me, suspicion tightening his face.

"Oh, I had a hand." I tossed Maravich's thumb away, and the
sergeant tracked it as it left a bloody trail down the hall.

A microscopic smile cracked his lips. "Well done, soldier."

"We're still in a world of shit. Homeland knows about the tunnels, and, last I heard, they're gearing up to rain down blood and
death."

"Have you seen the other team members? Benson? Perlmutter?
Charles?"

"Perlmutter's... dead. Maravich..." My hand fluttered down the
hall. I didn't know how to tell him Perlmutter was hanging out in
one of the adjacent rooms—probably the one called INVENTORY,
awaiting programming. "Maravich said there were two others killed
in the blast. I, uh... damn. I watched them murder Alex de Galvez as
well."

"Fuck." Patrick looked mad enough to chew rock and shit sand.
"Do you know where they put our gear?"

"Um. Hold on."

I retrieved Maravich's thumb and brought it to what should be,
according to the diagram, the storage room. The lock disengaged
and—hallelujah—the team's weapons and gear was stacked inside.

"All right, Warren," the sergeant said. "Well done again."

"Don't go gettin' all mushy on me, Sergeant."

The marines slipped into harnesses loaded with the Home Depot of military hardware. They slung weapons over their shoulders and strapped pistols to their hips. There was plenty to go around, as three of their buddies wouldn't need their gear any longer. Patrick stuffed a lethal load into a gym bag with a Renascentia logo and handed it to me. "Carry this."

Jackson followed that with a wicked-ass machine gun. "Here, you might need a friend."

"Uh, yeah..." Settling the gym bag's carry strap over my shoulder, I examined the stubby firearm. No longer than my forearm, it had two pistol grips, fore and aft, the latter having the trigger. A blocky box squatted on top, near the back end, containing what appeared to be a miniature display screen that showed a magnified view of its point of aim. "I give up; what is it? A Bifluvian Death Ray?"

"SMG60." Jackson flashed his red teeth in an evil grin and re-trieved the weapon. He demonstrated as he spoke. "Look, it's easy. Safety, trigger, sights, magazine. Set the safety *here*, to Burst. Depress the trigger slightly, and you'll see a green dot in the sight picture." He held the gun up for me to see; sure enough, a green dot glowed in the center of the box's screen. "Put the dot on the bad guy's belly, *squeeze-don't-jerk* the trigger, and the bad guy goes buh-bye. Lather, rinse, repeat. At twenty-five percent magazine capacity, the sighting dot will flash yellow. At empty, it will turn solid red. When that hap-pens, press *here*, drop the magazine and pop in a new one."

Jackson set the safety and handed the weapon back, whereupon I accidentally practiced the magazine release. The lance corporal caught the narrow metal box of cartridges before it fell to the ground. He sighed and allowed me to reinsert it.

"With self-propelled ammo," Jackson said, "there's no bolt to throw, no cartridge cases to clean up, and virtually no recoil. That's it. You now officially a New-nited-States Moh-reen. Semper Fi."

"If you ladies would care to join me," the sergeant said. Patrick didn't wait; he powered ahead with long, purposeful strides, and I trailed behind him. Lance Corporal Jackson, an armload of his munitions tucked against his chest, fell in next to me and clapped his free hand on my shoulder.

"You know," he said, "I'm starting to like you, Feather. You still a dick, but you a dick in a good kind of way."

"Thanks, Corporal." I held up the SMG60. "Let's hope I don't have to use this thing for real."

"God wouldn't be that cruel."

AGENT RAMIREZ HIKED across the Homeland complex to a square, featureless building with a sign out front that read BLDG 1410. The security on 1410 was an order of magnitude higher than the other buildings on the campus; not only did he have to thumbprint the reader on the outer door, he had to authenticate with a retinal scan, then wait for the security officer to release the mantrap inner door.

The officer directed Ramirez to an elevator. He descended to the eighth sublevel and exited to a single room with a glass divider, behind which drowsed a clerk. Above the glass, a sign proclaimed: Evidence Room.

"What can I do for you, Agent Ramirez?" the paunchy middle-aged clerk asked, once the agent had shown his ID.

"Last month, we busted six Mus—ah, radicals in Kansas." At Homeland, religious profiling of non-Christians was frowned upon; if the clerk reported him, it could be a blot on his record. "In their possession were a number of canisters of aerosolized Vx. Has that been destroyed?"

"Let me check." The clerk tapped his screen with a two-finger tattoo. "Ah, no, still here, waiting for the HazMat team to pick up."

"Good." Ramirez allowed his feral grin to break through. "How much is there?"

The clerk blinked and focused on his display. "Um, says here six canisters, twenty kilos each, with air disbursement nozzles."

Ramirez ran the math in his head. A dose as small as ten milligrams was fatal to a human. One hundred and twenty kilos equated to... twelve thousand grams, so the eight canisters represented enough Vx to kill twelve million people, under optimal dispersal conditions.

Like say, in a tunnel.

"Give me all of it," Ramirez ordered.

Thirty-One | Stand for Something, or Fall for Anything

RAMIREZ TRIED ONE CITY department after another and finally dug up a retired city engineer who claimed to know about the abandoned freight tunnels. Two agents retrieved the man from his home in Naperville and drove him to the Homeland complex in Buffalo Grove, running code three the whole way. At 1:09 p.m., the escorts delivered Alvie Brockbank to the warehouse staging area where the TAC teams and the Z-squads were assembling.

The old man shuffled, and his damp eyes kept wandering from the digital maps projected over a planning table to the rows of Revivants and paramilitary agents. Scrawny and chicken-necked, the former engineer was dressed in a puke-green work shirt and brown canvas pants. Instead of a side-to-side comb-over, Brockbank's ran from back to front.

"The tunnels?" he repeated after Ramirez asked him a question. "Which tunnels?"

"The tunnels under the city."

"There's, ah, there's bunches of tunnels down there. There's more air under parts of downtown than there is dirt. Six, some places seven, levels. As deep as a hundred feet... ah, thirty meters."

"Where are they?" Ramirez gritted his teeth. The clock was ticking, and every second meant his quarry would be scattering like an upended bucket of cockroaches. "I have an old map from the web overlaid on the street grid, but it is nearly useless."

"I expect so. That map shows the old freight tunnels. Lots of old fiber and cable laid in them now, but I don't know that anybody's updated a map since Obama was in office."

"The city people said you used to go down there and do maintenance from time to time. How did you get in? I know one entrance is here"—he tapped a spot near Oak Street and the Chicago river—"but it's inside Cabrini territory, at the bottom of an elevator shaft. Not a tactically advantageous place to assault. I need options."

"Options," the old man said, but more to himself. He scratched his bristly chin and narrowed his eyes, leaning across the table to peer at the glowing map.

"Are there any grade-level entrances?" Ramirez asked.

"Grade-level?" Brockbank shook his head. "Not anymore. Never were, best I can remember. Everything at that level was by elevator or ladder only. The old cable car tunnels under the river, yeah, they had them some street level entrances. Had to, so the cable cars could go down 'em."

"But not the freight tunnels?"

"No, not the freight tunnels."

"So, how—"

"Hold on a sec, let me think." Brockbank traced routes with a shaky finger, nose close enough to the map it nearly pushed through the projection. He mumbled so low, Ramirez only caught bits and pieces. "There's LaSalle... Washington, okay... goes under the river there... How'd we... oh, yeah..."

The approach of Captain Reed, leader of Armed Response Team Eight, distracted Ramirez from considering how to hurry the old man along.

"All teams locked and loaded, Special Agent," Reed reported. A taller-than-average man with hawkish features, the captain towered over Ramirez. The special agent eased back to give himself room.

"And the Z-Squad controllers?"

"Loaded in the Mobile Response Vehicle. Z-Squad lead reports all telemetry online and functional. You will have ten independent squads of six Z's each."

"And the special material?"

Reed shifted his feet and looked away, finding something outside the warehouse to focus on. "Loaded with the Z's, sir." Reed hesitated before blurting, "Sir, have you heard about this so-called video circling the Net? I haven't seen it, but some of my guys are getting calls from their folks—"

"A bunch of trumped-up crap these people have put out to cause disruption. Focus on the mission, Reed."

"Yes, sir."

"Excellent." Ramirez dismissed the team leader and turned to the engineer. "Brockbank? How about it?"

"Well, it's been a while since I been down there, but seems to me there was a stairway put in back in '18 or '19 under the old CTA building on Lake, right next to the Clinton-Green Metro stop. You know the place?"

"Yes."

"You take the elevator to the basement," Brockbank said, "and there's a vault door, take some getting through. You'll need tools. Open that door and there's a staircase that'll take you allaway down to the old freight tunnels, then on down to the deep tunnels."

"Get in the van with the TAC team," Ramirez ordered.

"Me?" Brockbank's chin quivered. "Why me?"

"Because if that door's not there, old man, you'll be the first one I shoot."

THE TWO MARINES AND I made it back to Franklin Rogers' headquarters by hailing a cab. The driver eyed the military equipment with something less than enthusiasm, but carried us to the edge of Cabrini territory without complaint... right after Patrick stuck a pistol in his ear. We jogged six blocks from the drop-off, as even threat of death was insufficient to get the cabbie to cross the Cabrini-Green border.

My body hurt down to the DNA level. Getting blown up, beaten, drugged, and, oh yeah, beaten again had left my face puffy and swollen. Aches radiated from my ribs, my hip, and my belly. Even my eyeballs hurt. Within two blocks, my lungs clawed for air, and I squeezed one palm against the stitch in my side. Patrick and Jackson jogged ahead of me, and I allowed the gap to widen.

Besides the physical pain, dread weighted chains of guilt around my soul. I had betrayed the Children's hiding place. And I killed a man. A vicious, pig-nasty sonofabitch, but still a human being. For all my tough talk about murdering Ramirez, the reality of blood on my hands squatted on me with the mass of a small planet.

I squinted at the painful glare of the sun, broiling high overhead, well past the midday mark. Winded and sweat-drenched, I slowed to a walk as we approached Franklin's three-story apartment building, across an open lot. Balconies overlooked a playground where kids shrieked and laughed. A toddler in grass-green corduroy training pants crabbed the wrong way up the slide, ignoring the protests of the girl at the top.

"You look like recycled shit, man."

I glanced around and found three Cabrini sentinels had ghosted alongside without me noticing. Lean young wolves in ghetto clothes and a motley assortment of weapons, the sentries would have once scared me blue.

"Pass the word, DeShawn," I told the guy next to me, "things are about to get real here. The feds are coming."

"One if by land, two if by sea?"

"Exactly." During my month in Cabrini, I'd borrowed some of Franklin's books. The lines from Longfellow's old poem came back to me now, something I'd read late one night that I didn't remember until DeShawn jogged the brain cells into alignment. "'The fate of a nation was riding that night; / And the spark struck out by that steed in his flight, / Kindled the land into flame with its heat.'"

"Right on, Joe." DeShawn clapped me on the shoulder and ignored my grimace. He seemed quite happy at the prospect of a firefight. "It's time for some revolution, *bay-bee*."

DeShawn and his buddies escorted us to a cafeteria at a school a block away from Franklin's headquarters. No kids were around, which confused me until I remembered it was Saturday and all the urchins would be out for the day. Rows of tables filled the middle of the room, with impossibly small chairs stacked on top, creating a forest of silver legs. At one end of the room was a stage with a curtain, while on the opposite end was the serving line, closed off by metal shutters.

I laid the SMG60 next to me and stretched out on the edge of the stage. I fell asleep in about one point three seconds. Like passing out, only faster, and without the stigma.

RAMIREZ, CAPTAIN REED, and the Z-Squad commander, Stephan DiNunzio, traveled in the back of a swaying command vehicle—a box truck outfitted on the inside with comm gear and map screens, computers and weapon racks. The ART captain wore his helmet but kept the HUD visor raised while Ramirez outlined the game plan. DiNunzio wore a business suit and a complex communication and control device. Apparently grafted to the side of his head, the boxy appliance sprouted antennae and flickered with LEDs in Christmas colors of red and green. Under a muted green overhead light, Ramirez pointed out the building Joseph Warren had identified during chemically-enhanced interrogation as the entry point to the Children of Liberty's rabbit warren of a home base.

"They'll expect us to hit here," he explained, "at this building on Oak and LaRue. This is the headquarters of the Cabrini separatists, commanded by an ex-army major named Rogers. I suspect it would be ruinously expensive to take this building and ingress the target through the elevator; however, I want them to think that is our objective. You, Captain"—Ramirez indicated Reed—"will take seven of our ten Z-Squads and two of our four ART units, and our armored vehicle. That will give you twenty living soldiers and forty-two Revivants, along with seven controllers. You will fake an assault on this building, using whatever means and methods you think most effective to pin down the enemy and give them the impression this is our main thrust."

"From the northwest," Reed said. "Between Cosby and LaRue. Minimizes their sight lines and allows us cover for the approach."

"Remember this is all Cabrini territory," Ramirez cautioned. "Expect all these buildings to either be fortified or booby-trapped."

"Understood."

"While you and your teams feint here," the agent continued, "DiNunzio and I will take the remaining forces and penetrate the tunnel complex here, through the Lake Street CTA building's basement. We will advance along the west-to-east axis under Lake Street. The mass of tunnels will be to our south, but with any luck we'll catch the defenders in the flank. We will bring all the... special weapons with us, strapped to a single Z-squad. The Z's will, ah, deploy the gas throughout the tunnel complex once we've spotted the enemy."

"Problem," DiNunzio said. Middle-aged, middle-sized, and middle-ranked, the Z-Squad commander would disappear in a crowd of four.

"What?"

"The comm system for the zombies will be fucked. With our van at street level, we can do two-three kilometers without a repeater. More if we can bounce off a cell tower. Underground? In concrete tunnels? Be lucky we can make eighty-ninety meters. No signal and the Z's revert to hardcode program."

Ramirez frowned. "What about your mobile controllers? I remember doing a CBT on a handheld Z-controller."

DiNunzio pulled a face like he'd bitten a shit sandwich. "You want my guys to walk behind a cloud of Vx? Yeah, let me see if I can get some dumb fuck to sign up for that. Jesus, Ramirez, they'd be dead in ten seconds."

"We have hazmat suits," Ramirez noted. "And bulletproof riot shields."

"Oh, yeah, right," DiNunzio snorted. "Makes all the difference."

"The assault team members will be suited up. I don't see the problem."

"The problem, Special Agent, is my guys are techno-geeks, not field ops. We hired kids who're good at video games to run the Z's, not a bunch of Jack Reacher types."

Ramirez compressed his lips, and an eyelid twitched. "Fine. Give me the handheld unit, and I'll run the Z's myself."

"*Ten minutes*," the driver's voice carried over the internal PA system.

"Everybody understand their job?" Ramirez checked with Reed, who showed him a thumbs up. DiNunzio scowled as though he didn't know where to spit out the taste in his mouth. After a long pause, he nodded.

"Excellent," Ramirez said. "Good luck and Godspeed, gentlemen."

BUBBLES OF CONVERSATION danced along the edge of my semiconscious mind, bouncing off the cocoon of blackness wrapped around me. Waking up would require a commitment to endure not only the physical pain of my battered body, but the emotional trauma of explaining how I'd compromised everyone's safety. Nope. Better to snooze for a while longer than have to face...

A warm hand touched my shoulder, followed by a woman's voice. Millie's light scent, akin to wildflowers and summer breezes, caressed me. "Joe?"

"Mmm, murgle sterff?" I stretched and regretted it when a dozen pain signals fired across my network of neurons and overloaded the system. "Oh," I hissed. "That smarts."

"Oh, Joe." Millie knelt on the stage and helped me sit up. "They really worked you over, didn't they?"

I avoided responding and instead focused on the group clustered at a nearby table. Franklin Rogers I recognized right away, along with Sergeant Patrick and Momma Rose. John Marsh was there, overloading a plastic chair next to a woman I didn't know in battle fatigues. A half-dozen other people I vaguely recognized were gathered there as well. The murmur of conversation stilled, and every face turned in my direction.

"I gave it up," I blurted. "They hit me with drugs and... I, uh..."

"We know," Millie said. Her hand stayed on my shoulder. "My fault, not yours. I rushed you into an operation without thinking it through."

I stared a hole in the floor and spoke through the broken glass in my throat. "They killed Alex. I watched him die."

Millie hugged me with arms stronger than I expected, her compact body pressed against me. I wiped my cheeks against my sleeve and tried not to sniffle. Sniffling would mean I...

Goddammit.

I hated crying in public.

"We started evacuating our people as soon as we realized your team was lost," Millie said in my ear. "We couldn't know for sure, so we took the precaution."

Franklin spoke up. "Listen up, Joe, and we'll download our plan. Lots of things are happening in the world today, and you need to be up to speed quickly."

"Embrace the suck," Patrick told me, not unkindly.

"Aye aye, Sergeant. Embracing now." I touched my eyebrow in a wry salute and gestured for Franklin to continue.

"Millie, if I may?" the major said. At her gesture, he continued. "Objective One is owned by the Children of Liberty. They will continue to evacuate the tunnels through the southern routes. Lieutenant Gonzales"—Rogers indicated the woman in fatigues I hadn't met before—"will take her marines and screen the evacuation. Inevitably, a bottleneck will form at the State and Roosevelt, and the Polk and Canal exits, so people will back up into the tunnel system as far north as Van Buren or Washington. Millie's team will sweep forward, collect the stragglers and keep her people moving." Rogers paused and exchanged a look with my warrior elf. "Your people, your plan, Millie. Any changes or updates?"

"Negative."

"Objective Two," Rogers said, "is the defense of C-G against a probable incursion by Homeland, targeting our Oak Street headquarters. After MacCauley's people leave, we will blow the connecting tunnel from the elevator to their Orleans Street entrance. This will effectively block their rear from attack, should Homeland breach our defenses. Which ain't fucking likely." Rogers twisted his lips into a wolfish grin.

"Franklin, you don't have to—"

"Millie, honey," Momma Rose spoke for the first time, "you know we been over this already. We tired of these people stompin' into our homes whenever they feel like it. They come around this time, we gonna slap the daylights outta them."

Millie chewed her thumbnail and compressed her lips in a thin line, keeping her eyes fixed on the tabletop. I knew that look. It spelled trouble with a capital Oh Shit.

Rogers held up three fingers. "Objective Three is to secure our borders and provide shelter for Millie's displaced population against the uncertainty of the near-term future."

I must have projected my puzzlement via telepathy, because John said, "In the last several hours, Joe, the cabinet meeting video has blown up around the world. Millions of downloads. People are in the streets, mad as hell."

"We think the president means to declare the government insolvent or declare martial law," Millie stated.

"Holy..."

"Yeah, exactly."

"Pursuant to Objective Two," Rogers said, "we have fortified our HQ based on Plan Turtleshell. Our civilian population has retreated to deep basement shelters and hardened buildings throughout our territory. One of our two companies of light infantry has taken up defensive positions along Hobbs and LaRue, while the remainder waits in reserve. If, or I should say when, the Homeland boys show up, we will treat them to a breakfast of firepower like they've never seen." Rogers paused to examine the faces around the table. Every person shared faces set in grim determination. "With God's grace, we will not only knock the feds on their ass, we'll send them back to the special pit of hell that spawned them. Questions? No? Then let's execute the plan."

Chairs scraped, and I eased off the stage and helped Millie down. She popped off a string of orders. "John, Joe, you're with me. Lieutenant, gather your people and deploy scouts along Kinzie and Canal.

I want to know if Homeland has found another way in before they jab a gun up my ass."

"Aye aye, ma'am," the marine officer said. She flicked a gesture at Patrick and they departed at a trot, breaking through the knot of Franklin's people at the exit.

I hesitated. "Millie, I..."

"Joe." She fixed me with her welding-torch eyes. "The past is the past. There's a long way to go before our people are safe, and it's our job to make sure they come to no harm. This is your chance to be the kind of man I think you can be. Are you with me, or not?"

My answer surprised me more than anyone.

"Let's go."

Thirty-Two | I'll See Your SNAFU and Raise You a Clusterfuck

RAMIREZ TRIED FOR THE third time in the last hour to reach Maravich, without result. He left another message and disconnected. *Screw it. He'll have to catch up on his own.*

He rode the elevator to the basement of the CTA building with the second group of ART team members. His eighteen Revivants and three controllers waited near the vault-like entrance to the freight tunnels, while Alvie Brockbank, the retired engineer, hammered on the rusted wheel that should—in theory—unlock the door.

The living personnel wore black hazmat suits with the hood thrown back to conserve the oxygen in their narrow backpack tanks. Twelve of the zombies carried automatic weapons, and the other six wore a different type of tank strapped to their backs, metallic canisters without paint or adornment. A hose ran from the top of each tank, under the Revivants' right arms, to a wand with a flap trigger. To Ramirez, they looked exactly like exterminators with bug spray devices.

And they have a similar mission.

Finding volunteers to join the assault had not been as difficult as DiNunzio predicted. Ramirez approached the Z-Squad human controllers, also dressed in hazmat gear, the instant the elevator doors opened. "Bishop," he said to the tall, skinny kid with zits, "your Z-team will be on point through the tunnels until we locate and pin the enemy. The AR team will provide personal security for you while you maneuver. Understood?"

"Yah, brah. No problem." The techie carried a handheld device—though handheld was stretching the definition as the unit dangled from straps around the kid's neck—and wore a pair of wraparound VR glasses.

Ramirez addressed the second controller, who was also tall, skinny, and spotted with flaking acne. "Crenshaw, your team will remain behind until called. If we hit resistance, your group will lead the way with full-body riot shields."

"Gotcha."

The third Z-Squad controller fidgeted in place like he wanted to take a piss. Shorter, rounder, and Asian, but with an identical map of pimples, the kid could not have been older than twenty.

"Rao, your crew will follow behind Crenshaw's team. Your Z's have the important job of sweeping the tunnels clear of vermin using the... bug spray."

The kid swallowed before stuttering an acknowledgement.

With a final slam and a curse, the wheel lock broke free, and Brockbank chortled in victory. "Got you that time, you bitch... showed you who's boss, didn't I? Just have to give it a spin—uhhh!" The old man grunted and turned the squealing lock, retracting the bolts. With a solid kick, the door burst free. A shower of rust fell from the frame and pattered across the floor, bringing with it the smell of musty water and damp concrete.

"There you go, boss," the engineer said. "Like I promised."

Ramirez went through first and found the top landing of a metal staircase that creaked and moaned when he trod on it. It switchbacked into the underground darkness and disappeared. He activated his shoulder-mounted light, and the beam stabbed the gloom with a white bolt. "All right, Mr. Bishop, you're up. Get your Z's down the hole and let's find these traitors."

"Fuckin-A, man."

The squad of Revivants marched forward as a unit, shuffled into single file, and crossed the threshold onto the landing. Their filmy eyes didn't flicker as they clomped down the metal treads, moving like so many sleepwalkers on a midnight refrigerator raid. Ramirez shivered and waited for the procession of dead to march past before following them into the tomblike darkness.

IT TURNED OUT MILLIE drove an electric golf cart much like she did a car: at full speed and without formal introduction to the vehicle's braking system. I could reach out and touch the walls on either side, and John Marsh would be decapitated by the arched ceiling if he stood up from his backseat position. Zipping through the narrow-gauge passages in a MacCauley-driven cart was a bit like being shot from a gun. Wide-spaced bulbs painted us with short bursts of yellow light.

Every so often, we'd reach a joining of several passageways, and Millie would shoot off to the left or right, guided by a confident sense of direction. Actual street signs affixed to the walls flashed by too fast for me to read, and within minutes she'd confounded my sense of direction. I was as lost as the battle of Pearl Harbor.

Millie tromped the brakes and nearly vaulted me through the nonexistent windshield. We skidded to a stop a meter from a line of people jamming the tunnel ahead of us. Those in the rear turned and stood straighter as Millie jumped out and approached the group.

"How fast are you moving?" she asked.

A man in a tattoo body suit and not much else said, "More like how fast we ain't moving. Seems like we've been standing here for over an hour."

While Millie and Tattoo caught up on old times, I wandered back to a crossing tunnel and found a sign claiming we were under Canal Street at Madison. The weight of my stubby submachine gun dragged at the shoulder strap, making me as self-conscious as a man buying feminine products. By carrying around a gun like some modern-day cowboy, I might as well paint *IDIOT* on my forehead.

But I felt better having it. More in charge of my own destiny.

The marines were nowhere to be found, having taken their own carts and dispersed through the underground system on a plan known only to them. We had communication, of a sort, depending on line of sight and the range of the nearest repeater, so I caught scattered bits and pieces of chatter as Gonzales and her crew sifted through the tunnels.

"Hey, John," I called out. "Where'd you say the exit was?"

The giant shuffled to me, stooped over to avoid banging his head on the bare bulbs. "There are two down this end of town. The one directly ahead is at Polk. Parallel to us is State Street, and there's an exit from State at Roosevelt. Not far from where we met—outside the Office of Benefits and Welfare."

In this section, the tunnels were laid out in a grid pattern that mirrored the streets overhead. I closed my eyes and pictured a Chicago street map. "That's... nearly a mile away. What the hell? We'll be here for hours moving these people out."

"Guys"—Millie hustled back to where John and I stood—"our signal strength is crappy down here. I'm going to the front and find out what's going on. Can you hang back and keep in touch with Gonzales?"

After Millie jogged away, John said, "You think we should take the cart and get closer to the marines? We might get a better signal."

"Good idea. While we're at it, let's lose the cart keys so Millie can't find them."

ROGERS HAD LONG AGO rigged every building in Cabrini territory with video cameras and networked them so that he could maintain an overall view of any conflict from his command post. He swiveled in a leather chair positioned in front of a massive display screen, divided up into a score of smaller pictures surrounding a larger segment in the middle. With a flick of his fingers, he could call up any video feed and drop it into the expanded view, or sequence through any number of pictures on a rotating basis. He'd also configured analytics for certain events—such as a human figure carrying a weapon—that would autoflag a flashing callout and draw his attention to a particular screen.

That latter feature was going somewhat crazy right now as twenty-plus Homeland agents advanced from cover to cover along Cosby Street, led by a phalanx of parading Revvies, unconcerned with either cover or concealment. The front rank carried riot shields the way a marching band carried banners.

"Well this should be interesting," he muttered.

"Sir?" A junior aide named Dixon occupied a station to Rogers' left, a comm mike jutting in front of his lips.

"Nothing. Just an old man rambling on." Rogers flitted from screen to screen for a few more moments. "The enemy appears to be well within the engagement envelope, Mr. Dixon. Please give 2nd and 3rd Platoon the signal to fire."

"Yes, sir." Dixon keyed his mic. "2nd Platoon, open fire. Fire at will. 3rd Platoon, open fire. Fire at will."

Smoke boiled from windows along Cosby, and muzzle flashes twinkled. There was no audio, so Rogers studied the action in silence. The living elements of the Homeland force scattered for cover, leaving the non-living troops to advance alone. The rear ranks of the Revivant squads opened up with automatic weapons, all six of the walking dead in a squad firing in the same direction, targeting the buildings sheltering Rogers' resistance fighters.

He chuckled, and Dixon flicked a worried glance his way.

"It's okay," Rogers said, "I haven't lost my mind, son. Just thinking how one man's resistance fighter is another man's traitor."

Dixon frowned. "That's true, sir."

The Homeland agents huddled behind cars or at the corners of buildings while the Revivants advanced along an axis that would lead them to Rogers' Oak Street headquarters. On their current trajectory, the RVTs would come under minimal direct fire from the Cabrini fighters. The ones in front stumbled a bit when a round impacted their shields, and the following Revivants would jerk or stagger from a direct hit, but very few fell out of line. In minutes they would reach his headquarters' blindside and be sheltered from the Cabrini shooters.

"Dixon, please advise 1st Platoon to redeploy along our northwestern edge. And get me Lieutenant Claybaugh on the line. I'll need to brief him on what to expect."

"Yes, sir."

Dixon repeated his commands while Rogers frowned at the screen and spoke under his breath. "Now would be a good time for some grenades; blow the legs right out from under these bastards. Maybe I'll ask Santa to bring me some next Christmas. In the meantime, how do I kill something that's already dead?"

"—*ontact!*" the radio fizzed in my ear.

The stuttering burp of gunfire echoed through the tunnel. I tapped the brakes and allowed the cart to roll to a stop, turning my head like a radar dish to try and locate the sound. More staccato bursts rattled like a drummer with palsy.

A voice I didn't recognize blurted out, "... *omeo Ac... Romeo 7, contact, grid... ference G4, Golf Four, co...?*"

"*Copy Golf Four, Romeo 7,*" Lieutenant Gonzales's voice came through much stronger. She must be closer.

"*Romeo Actual, Romeo 7. Estimated six... advan... heavy incoming fire... inned down.*"

"*. . . they're not dying!*" a new voice chimed in.

"*Pull it together, Romeo 2,*" Gonzales ordered. "*Help is on the way.*"

"Shit, they got around Rogers somehow." I nudged the big man beside me. "Where are we?"

"LaSalle, north of Adams."

In our quest to find Gonzales, John and I had wandered farther east than I'd realized. My nose was running from the chill in the air, and dried blood clotted my sinuses. I snorted and spat the gunk out, trying to breathe through my nose. The chatter of small arms fire continued echoing through the underground passage. "Okay, here's what we'll do. Take the cart back to the line and send one of the fastest guys to run up and tell Millie we're about to take it up the ass here."

"Take it up the ass," the big man repeated, nodding.

"Don't use those words, John. Tell them the feds are in the tunnels, and John"—I paused with a hand on his arm—"whoever you pick as runner, pull him aside and tell him quietly. Let's not start a panic."

"What about the gunfire? You can hear that for miles down here."

"Tell 'em ... hell, I don't know. Just tell them not to panic, okay? The marines have everything under control."

"Okay."

"Then come back and find me," I told him as he switched over to the driver's seat and I hopped off. The golf cart sagged heavily from one side to the other when he settled. "I have a feeling I'll need you, and this cart, before we're done."

John waved and backed into the nearest juncture, where he spun the wheel and hummed away. Leaving me alone in a dimly lit tunnel. With people shooting at each other not far away. Towards whom I started marching.

"You're an idiot, Joe," I told myself. Even my whisper echoed.

I checked the SMG60 as I walked. Safety, trigger, sight, magazine. Should I set it to Burst now? Or wait until feds were climbing into my shorts? If I turned a corner and bumped into one of our people, could I avoid shooting them? *Damn good question.* I left the safety on and continued forward.

Voices buzzed and chattered through my radio earbud, excited shouts in the arcane language of war. A strong burst of fire hammered the tunnel; the string of overhead lights flickered, and a fat dollop of water hit the top of my ear. I checked the ceiling for cracks. My luck, somebody would set off an explosion down here and the entire tunnel would flood like it did back in the 90s.

"Look on the positive side," I told myself. "Ahhh... Nope. Can't. There is no positive side to drowning under tons of river water."

I trotted through the passageway, the scuff of my shoes amplified by the narrow walls and complemented by the thrumming bass of automatic weapon fire. It sounded stronger to my left, so I turned that way at the Madison tunnel, which had been converted to sleeping quarters. Cots lined one wall, partitioned by blankets that now hung limp, shoved aside in the rush to evacuate. Each tiny "room" was smaller than the jail cell where I'd first met Millie and John and...

Alex.

Lieutenant Gonzales's voice boomed in my ear. "*Fire Team Bravo! Move forward along route Fox Three-Two. Try and find their flank.*"

"Aye! Fox Three-Two, flank."

I poked my head around the corner and found Gonzales crouched over a map with Corporal Jackson and a marine I didn't know. They huddled against the wall in the north-south Franklin Street tunnel, about halfway between Randolph and Lake. The lance corporal glanced up and motioned me forward.

"What's going on?" I yelled in his ear. The stuttering flashes from an entire army of small arms lit up the walls and shuddered deep in my chest.

"It's a clusterfuck is what," Jackson groused.

Gonzales barked orders, alternating between the map unfolded against her knee and staring into the middle distance. It took me a second to realize she used a helmet with a Heads Up Display. I'd seen them in vids and VR games; an entire encyclopedia of information could be displayed in front of her eyes. Depending on where she directed her gaze, vital statistics or the individual helmet cams of her troops would pop to the forefront. Whenever I tried to use one in a simulated HUD in a VR game, I'd be swamped in information overload in seconds.

"I know what 'fuck' is," I said, "but define 'cluster.'"

The corporal showed me his own map and pointed out landmarks with a grimy finger. "The feds busted in here, somewhere on Lake Street, west of the river. They were advancing due east along Lake when our guys ran right into them, here at Clinton. We lost three men trying to break contact and establish a perimeter."

Gonzales ordered, "Hack their legs out from under them, Sinacola! I don't care if they die or not; you cut their legs out, they ain't moving."

"Fucking RVTs," Jackson said. "We got our ass handed to us by a bunch of cold meat."

"Shoot the controller gizmo on their heads," I offered.

Gonzales flashed sour eyes with a message that very clearly told me to stay out of her kitchen and let her cook. "They learned that lesson; they're wearing helmets over their controllers."

"The federal agents are using riot shields. We're chopping the zombies to dog meat, but the live agents are about as hard to kill. They pushed us back almost to Wacker." Jackson indicated a spot by the Chicago River.

"Dammit," I spat. "They're already past Canal. If they turn right on Canal, they'll run smack into the backs of the people lined up there."

All of us paused to listen as the volume of fire scaled down to a few cracks, like the last kernels in a popcorn bag before drying up entirely. After a full minute of breathless silence Patrick's voice came over the radio in my ear. "*Romeo Actual, Romeo Six.*"

"Go, Six."

"*Romeo Actual, be advised the enemy advance has halted for the moment. No movement. All Revivants are combat ineffective at this time. I have six Whiskey-India-Alpha—two of whom are combat ineffective—and one Kilo-India-Alpha. Jacobsen.*"

"Jacobsen? Fuck!" The muscles in Gonzales's jaw worked, and I imagined I could hear her teeth grinding. "Romeo Six, Romeo Actual. Hold until further."

"*Romeo Actual, Six. Hold, aye.*"

Gonzales studied the map on her thigh with an intense frown then slapped the folded sheet with the back of her hand. "This is impossible! There's too many holes to plug with thirteen men. It's like that game where the rats pop up and you try to smack them down, but you can't reach all the holes."

"Sounds like my old apartment." But the lieutenant was right. The old freight tunnels ran in a grid pattern; if we blocked one tunnel, the feds would go to the next. Or the next. There was no way we could keep ahead of them and know which way they would jump.

"Blow the tunnels behind us," Jackson said.

"No!" Gonzales shouted it the same second I did. I let the lieutenant explain. "We blow the wrong place and these tunnels flood. Explosives are out, but we do need some barricade material. Suggestions?"

The corporal and I exchanged a look while the other marine stayed out of the discussion and kept watch. I shrugged. "I have a golf cart, Lieutenant. We could tip it on its side, but I don't think it would block the whole tunnel."

"Where is it?"

"Ah, well, John Marsh has it now."

"And where is he?"

"Uh. Well. Not here." John would have gone back to the end of the Canal Street queue to deliver his message. I'd told him to come find me, but I didn't tell him where. If he came directly back along Canal and kept going, he'd run smack into the bad guys.

I explained this to Gonzales, who shook her head with a pinched-lip expression of disgust.

"Let me see your map, Jackson." Gonzales snatched it from the lance corporal's hand. "We have to protect the evacuees, right? One exit line is on State, one is on Canal. On State, we put a couple of guys here, here, and here." She pointed out the three intersections before the Polk Street exit. "If one pair spots trouble, the others relocate to back them up. On Canal, we need to stop the feds from making a straight run up our butts. Put the rest of the guys across the river, Randolph and Canal, and maybe a spotter on Clinton, in case they try an end around." Her eyes focused on her HUD, and she rattled out a series of orders with grid references.

I ignored all the radio babble and said to Jackson, "I have to make sure John doesn't drive smack into the feds. I'll be at the Canal-Randolph intersection."

"Safety, trigger, sight, magazine," the lance corporal said. "Oh, and the sight uses all spectrums of energy—thermal and IR as well as visual. Use it in the dark, okay? And, hey, point it at the enemy and do *not* shoot my ass by mistake."

"I make no guarantees, Corporal. Besides, who's the dumbass gave me live ammo?" I jogged off without waiting for his response.

Safety, sight, magazine, trigger...

Thirty-Three | Hangman's Coming Down From the Gallows

"STALEMATE," REPORTED an Armed Response lieutenant named Singh to Agent Ramirez. "Bishop's Z's are down, and our guys can't advance. Too much incoming fire, shields or not. We've got two dead and six wounded."

The agent stood erect in the middle of a mainline bypass tunnel adjoining the Lake Street line, surrounded by crouching ART troops. Grime and filth covered the walls; he'd already brushed against one side and smudged the shoulder of his black hazmat suit with concrete dust. He wiped at the blemish while Singh whined about the resistance.

"Maybe your guys are too chickenshit to advance," Ramirez said, "but the Z's do not care. Send an agent back to bring Crenshaw and Rao forward. In the meantime, send a team to our right, down Canal, to find a clear route to the enemy's flank. If we can turn the corner on them, we will hose them with Vx. Tell everyone to mask up too. If a stray round hits a tank, we need to be protected."

Singh hesitated, his face twisted like that of a man who'd eaten a bug and didn't care for the crunchy bits. "Agent Ramirez... are you sure?"

The Homeland agent felt his cheeks tightening to a death-mask. He touched the butt of the pistol strapped to his waist, and his voice chilled to a notch below *frozen corpse*. "Do I look indecisive to you?"

"Ah, nossir."

"Why are you still standing in my way?"

Singh saluted and ran.

Ramirez scrubbed the grime on his shoulder. "Damn," he muttered. "This will never come out. Should have told that idiot to bring a damp towel back with him."

FRANKLIN ROGERS ABANDONED his easy chair and joined Lieutenant Claybaugh and 1st Platoon behind the sandbag barricade that blocked off LaRue at Hobb Street, on the north side of his headquarters building. Dixon trailed behind him, carrying a canvas tote bag.

The platoon laid down a steady stream of suppressing fire that utterly failed to suppress the undead enemy. Their rounds sparked and flared from the Revvies' shields, which were now abraded to the point of being opaque. The approaching army of marching zombies closed to fifty meters.

"Lieutenant," Rogers shouted over the din. "Hold your fire! You're wasting ammo."

"Yes, sir!" Claybaugh relayed his order, and the Cabrini fighters hunched behind the sandbags and reloaded. Rogers read a tremor of disquiet in their expressions—not fear, by any means, but a measure of concern that, if left unchecked, would spawn panic and poor judgment. Not only had these boys been untested in a straight-up fight, the enemy they faced couldn't be killed or deterred by the soldiers' most determined efforts. It was bound to be... discomfiting.

Rogers injected his voice with a buoyant inflection. "Men, you know what we have here?"

"Dead fuckers walking, sir?" suggested a private with a diamond nose clip.

Rogers chuckled. "Exactly. But besides that, the enemy is attempting to recreate the Han Dynasty's mobile infantry square, a formation that was very effective *two thousand years ago*! Also popular during the Napoleonic Wars. How did the French defeat an infantry square, Lieutenant?"

"Uh, artillery?"

"That's the best answer, but absent artillery, what other method was used?"

The lieutenant, clearly nonplussed at being quizzed on history during a full-scale assault, blinked and opened his mouth to answer. No sound came out. The stamp of marching feet crunched across the remaining few meters: the Revivant squads had reached the intersection and were crossing Hobb, a distance of under ten meters.

"Ahh, I don't know, sir," Claybaugh managed, darting a glance over the barricade. "Shouldn't we be..."

"In a moment, Lieutenant. Dixon, hand out the toys." Rogers paused while his aide opened his carry-all. "The answer, gentlemen, is twofold. One, the French would use charging cavalry to break the square." The major's lips skinned back in a hungry smile. "Then they'd get in close and cut the enemy to pieces. When I give the word, we're going to chop these bastards down."

"Sir?" The earnest Claybaugh fingered the bright steel blade of the hardware-store machete that he received from Dixon. His brows knitted in confusion.

Rogers touched his comm and said, "Now, Mr. Dupree."

I SETTLED WITH MY BACK against a concrete wall. I had a good view north along the Canal Street tunnel. Most of the lights were out in this section. A rare bulb hung over the intersection, and a few more shone at random intervals. To the north, after the first ten meters, there was nothing but Dracula-loving darkness. The silence settled around me, disturbed only by the rare, distant clang or the closer drip of water plinking to the floor. I strained my hearing, hoping for the hum of an electric motor signaling John's return. I had called him on the radio three or four times and got only static.

"Where are you, man?" My harsh whisper spooked me, coming out much louder in the confined space than I intended.

The cool air chilled my sweaty forehead. I leaned my head against the bricks and dampness seeped into my hair. I sniffed and daubed my runny nose with the back of my sleeve, something my mother used to get on me about. Gone seven years now, it was hard to remember her face, but that tone of voice she used when she caught me sopping up a runny nose with a sleeve... Man, you'd have thought the lottery board was coming by the house any minute to give out winning tickets, but only to the people with clean sleeves.

What would Mom think of me now? Would she be proud—

A metallic noise *skritched* from the depths of the tunnel, a miniscule shriek as tiny as a fairy's death-cry. It unmistakably emanated from the dark hole to the north, in the direction of the federal troops. The bad guys, or at least the ones who wanted to kill me and make me a janitor, were coming my way. Unless John had somehow gotten ahead of me...? No, that didn't make sense. The big man had the electric cart; he wouldn't be sneaking back down the tunnel. He'd be tear-assing away at full hum, squashed into the driver's seat like a bear in a kiddie car.

Where were the marines? They should have joined up with me by now. Gonzales knew I was the weakest link; she wouldn't leave me to hang here alone. How far away could they be? I reached to tap my earbud and stopped myself a millimeter short of touching it. If I called them on the radio, it would give away my position.

I snaked across the concrete floor on my stomach, SMG60 cradled in front of me, cringing at the cold cement. My balls shrank up, trying to hide themselves somewhere safe and warm. I poked my weapon around the corner of the junction, pointed into the blackness. Since the opening was on my left, I had to expose more body than I wanted in order to see down the passageway.

A shoe scuffed.

Shit. What did the corporal say about the gun in my hands? Trigger, safety, something, something, IR-something else. I examined the weapon as if I'd never seen it before. Found the magazine release button again, by mistake. Caught the ejected mag before it hit the ground. Fumbled and clicked it back home. Where was the—? *Ah. Safety, set it to Burst.*

Now, look down the sight and depress the trigger a tiny bit and—Holy fucknoodles! I bit back a girly scream when the optics lit up with images of ghosts creeping toward me. Three figures, painted in multi-hued auras with assault weapons cupped against their shoulders, soft-footed from the northern end of Canal, hunched alongside the curved walls. Instinct—or paranoia—told me these weren't my marine reinforcement.

Despite the chill, sweat ran down my face as I lined up the green dot on the closest agent.

AN ENGINE ROARED ON Hobb Street. Franklin Rogers switched his helmet HUD to a camera feed from a nearby balcony, giving him a bird's eye view of the action. A diesel-powered dump truck powered in from the right, billowing black smoke from its exhaust. It jumped at every gear change, like an eager puppy. The Revivants, having piled into the intersection at LaRue and Hobb, were grouped tighter than a rack of tenpins at the Tri-County Bowling Lanes in DeKalb.

The RVTs, not being able to perceive or interpret the sounds of the oncoming vehicle, reacted slowly to the threat. Two of the rows had begun a ponderous turn to their left when the diesel's squared-off nose smacked home. The grill slammed into the dead with a smattering of soggy *thunks*, cutting a swath through the shambling parade, crackling over bodies with its massive wheels until it cleared the intersection. Brakes locked, tires smoked, and the truck squalled to a stop. The driver revved the engine, ground the gears, and backed up, this time hitting the front ranks of the Revivant formation. More bodies staggered and fell, several crunched under the machine's worn tires.

"That's it, men," Franklin roared. "Up close and personal! Get in tight so they can't move."

Howling, 1st Platoon leaped over the sandbags, Franklin in the middle of the scrum. His heart thudded in his chest like a battered war drum, and a familiar pain stitched his hip when he climbed the barrier. Old age sucked, to be sure. The kids flew past him, swinging their machetes in long, looping, vicious arcs that thudded into dead, nano-driven flesh. Magenta "blood" sprayed from the Revivants, who stumbled around in confused chaos.

The big diesel backed from the intersection and revved up for another forward run. It plowed through the remaining semi-organized mob of zombie soldiers on the far side of the intersection, slower this time, as the driver hadn't had the chance to get up a head of steam. He stalled against a mound of bodies, downshifted and hit the accelerator. Black smoke poured out, and the dump truck ground up the ghastly hill.

The boys of 1st Platoon swarmed into battle as if the enemy were dummy targets on a training range. Blades glittered, and magenta nano-blood rained.

A Revivant stumbled close, and Rogers buried his machete in the thing's neck, half-severing the head. It required two more swings to cut through the leathery tissue. Both parts of the dead—or dead again—body fell to the pavement, splashing Rogers' boots with gore. The major stumbled back to catch his breath; those few swings had taken more out of him than he cared to admit.

Nothing like a hand-to-hand fight to get the blood pumping.

A fist of invisible force slugged him in the chest and blew Rogers backward. A splash of heat washed him from head to toe. The sound wave of a crushing explosion slapped his ears. The major bounced off the sandbags and fell on his face.

Wagging his head, ears ringing, Rogers forced himself to stay conscious, stay engaged. His helmet was gone. He tasted scorched fuel on the back of his tongue, and his sinuses burned with the stench of charred metal and rubber. Rogers' vision swam. Blurry images became clearer—much too slowly. He blinked and focused, and fought his way to a standing position.

Flames engulfed the dump truck.

"What the hell?" he croaked.

One of his men, a skinny kid with fevered eyes, pawed at his arm and pointed. Over and over he shouted, "Tank! Tank! Tank!"

The major followed the kid's finger, and his jaw clenched. At two hundred meters, a black armored vehicle with a short-barreled cannon rolled down LaRue on four oversized tires. Even as he watched, the gun belched smoke, and another shell whistled in.

THE THREE FIGURES SLINKING toward me weren't marines—they couldn't be—and yet I hesitated pulling the trigger. I held the green targeting dot on the first agent on my right. Why? He was closest. Tiny numbers in the sight read out the distance as sixty-three meters. Sixty-two... sixty-one.

Why hadn't they seen me yet? Didn't they have super sights like mine?

My damp cheek pressed into the SMG's graphite stock, and I battled the sick panic in my gut. I wasn't a soldier, or a warrior, or much of a fighter, for that matter. The only thing I could punch was a time clock. My singular experience firing a weapon had flopped bigger than the Broadway musical remake of Rambo.

Fifty-eight meters.

Cold soaked into my belly from the tunnel floor. Small tremors made my targeting dot dance against the backdrop of the oncoming agent. His rifle, held low, swung up toward his face. Assuming he had a thermal sight too, he'd spot me the instant he checked it. I'd be the quivering lump of queasy flesh huddled behind the shelter of the tunnel corner. Fifty-four... fifty-three.

The leader froze. He yelled, "*Cont—*"

—and I shot him. Flame burped from the SMG's muzzle, a quick flicker that lit the passageway like a camera flash. The leader staggered and triggered his weapon high, stitching the ceiling with a long ripple of fire. Concrete shattered and dust billowed from the impact. He twisted and fell, wounded or dead, with his rifle clattering beside him.

The agent to the leader's right dove to the ground while the trailing agent hugged the wall. Both leveled their weapons. I hesitated. Which one? My target dot waffled in the middle and settled on the one against the wall because he was a better target. Bullets whapped the air by my ear, and more chewed into the concrete near my nose. I snapped off a quick, shaky burst and rolled behind the wall.

With no need to stay quiet, I screamed into my comm. "Gonzales, I'm under fire! Send some reinforcements!"

Cement splattered as more rounds chipped the corner. I poked the SMG around the edge and fired blind, ripping off a couple of quick triple-shots before jerking it back.

"*Romeo Actual to unknown speaker,*" Gonzales's voice blared in my ear. "*Is that you, Warren?*"

No, it's fucking Santa Claus. "Yes, goddammit!"

"*Position and situation, Warren. Report.*"

"On the ground and scared shitless, Lieutenant." I snapped off another blind shot to keep the Homeland guys from rushing me. "Ah, hold on. I'm, ah, I'm at the corner of Canal and Randolph. Three feds headed my way from the north on Canal. One may be down. I think I got one."

"*Hold position, Warren, help is on the way.*"

"Aye, roger... whatever the fuck, just get here."

A rectangular metal canister clinked past the tunnel mouth, bounced twice, and came to rest in the middle of the intersection. My many years of video game training kicked in. *Flash-Bang!*

I rolled away, screwed my eyes shut, and clapped my hands over my ears. The light from a thousand suns flared, and a sound wave kicked me in the head with the force of a diesel piston.

Thirty-Four | Tanks for the Memories

THE BITTER TASTE OF blood filled Rogers' mouth, and smoke choked his lungs. Dust and gravel pattered around him; the last round from the government tank had struck home on the third floor of the building at his back. A brick had clipped his shoulder, and another had hit him square in the butt.

He couldn't find his helmet.

The tank, more of a glorified armored personnel carrier, had a stubby 5-inch gun protruding from a small turret. Rogers guessed Homeland had modified a four-wheel M1117 to fit their needs, as the vehicle normally carried a grenade launcher-machine gun combination. Small arms fire from 2nd and 3rd Platoon's position in the complex of apartments along LaRue sparked against the APC's left side, while the main gun pounded 1st Platoon to hamburger.

The Revivants were being ripped apart by their own incoming fire.

Another shell hit the sandbag barricade to Rogers' left. The concussion bounced him in the air and made his head ring like a pennywhistle. Dixon? Where the hell was Dixon? Oh. Dixon was splattered across the outside of the sandbag wall in several separate chunks.

Rogers hauled a gasping private to his feet. Covered in brick dust, the kid reminded the major of someone dressing up for Halloween in a zombie costume. "Get everyone back!" he roared at the private, who blinked red-rimmed eyes and saluted. The major set him free

and looked up in time to see four of Gainer's 2nd Platoon break cover
from the apartment complex and rush the APC. Three carried Molo-
tov cocktails.

Automatic weapons opened up from the Homeland agents' position, and one of the Molotov-carrying kids sprawled on the sidewalk. His flaming bottle skittered across the street. The APC lurched
forward. Two of the resistance fighters leaped on the vehicle's flank
while the third—Rogers recognized the kid called Domino—scur-
ried aboard the sloping front, near the forward windows. Domino
waved his hand in front of the bulletproof glass, and the major gog-
gled. The young soldier was spraying the view ports with black paint.

"No, son, don't," he croaked.

The remaining resistance fighters lit the wicks of their own Molo-
tovs, smashed them into the turret and jumped away, only to be cut
down by direct fire from the concealed feds. The flames boiled away
the paint atop the APC and spewed inky smoke. At best, Rogers figured, the crew might get a little toasty, but the fire would cause no
sustained damage.

Blatnik from 4th Platoon landed next to Rogers and grabbed him
by the upper arm. "Sir! Are you okay? We need to pull back!"

"Get some more vehicles, Lieutenant," the major barked. He allowed the younger man to help him up and over the sandbags.
"Maybe we can box this thing in and cook it in place."

The M1117 shifted gears, leaped back with a sudden jerk that
sent Domino sprawling in the street. Skidding to a stop, the APC's
barrel declined to aim at the scrambling soldier, tracking him with a
fluid ease.

"Get outta there!" Rogers bellowed. "Lieutenant, get that kid
to—"

The APC's gun belched flame and smoke, and the space containing Domino ceased to exist, evaporating in a thunderclap of annihi-
lation. Greasy smoke boiled from the superheated pavement.

The APC's engine revved, and the vehicle surged forward, splitting through the debris cloud and leaving twin curls of smoke in its wake. With a roar, the armored vehicle sped toward Rogers, its weapon cranking around to settle on him like the eye of a vengeful god.

IT WAS LIKE MY ENTIRE head—crown to chin, ear to ear—had been shot full of Novocain, like I had a giant puffball atop my shoulders. Sensory input came by way of a distant, faulty messaging system. Shooting lights flickered in random patterns through the marshmallow between my ears. Triplicate images vibrated—three tunnels, three swinging light bulbs, and six clowns in black suits—bracketed by a vignette effect.

I was on my back.

My back was cold.

For some reason, I needed to be really, really concerned about the scary motherfuckers in Halloween costumes with automatic rifles dancing around at the end of my vision-tunnel. Why? Uh... something about...

. . . About...?

No. Lost it.

Three of the black-suited agents said, "Here's-here's-here's one-one-one."

"Kill-kill-kill-him-him-him," rumbled the other guys.

Poor schmuck. Who'd they want to kill? Hate to be that guy.

Rifle muzzles swam in and out of focus. Funny how big they looked from this side. "Hey," I wanted to say, "is that a big gun, or are you happy to see me?" It came out "Heyzattabegunhappieseeme?"

Triple giants appeared behind the clowns and slammed their heads together like in a cartoon. A weird buzzing sound came from my chest. Laughter? While I was laughing, the triple-giant picked up a group of clowns by the ankles and whirled them in a big circle and let fly. They went waaaaaay far away, and I didn't see them anymore. Sad clowns. The giants grabbed a handful of clown heads and pounded them into the ground near me, which I got to watch. That was even more fun, because I really didn't like the clowns too much.

A million-billion years later, a single giant face loomed over me, blocking everything else out.

"Joe? Joe?" the giant said. "Joe, are you okay?"

I waved John back, rolled over and threw up for a while.

"The hell happened here?" Lance Corporal Jackson said.

I let John do the talking and contented myself with turning my stomach inside out. "I found these two Homeland guys about to shoot Joe. I, uh, stopped them."

"Another one down," I rasped through an acidic throat. "Tunnel. Down there." Pointing, so they'd understand it.

"Check it out, Pelham. Martens, zip-tie that guy over there," Jackson ordered. Boots thudded away. "What happened to you, Joe?"

"Flash-bang."

"Ah. Yeah, that stings a bit, I'll bet."

I snorted something nasty and spat. "Water?"

"Sure." A canteen filled my hand. "Don't backwash nothing, Warren, you hear? I like you, but not that much."

"Bite me," I told him, but nevertheless splashed water in my cupped hand before tipping it into my mouth and rinsing it out. My ears rang, amoeba-like spots bobbed in front of my eyes, and a giant bowling ball squatted on the end of my neck. Other than that, everything was peachy. John helped me sit up, and I didn't vomit any more. Progress.

Lance Corporal Jackson had three marines with him. One, presumably Pelham, trotted back from inspecting the tunnel and reported the agent I'd shot was dead.

Jackson showed me his red-tinted teeth. "Good job, Warren."

"Yeah, woo-hoo. Go me." I'd killed two federal agents in one day. Pretty soon my face would be on Homeland's Most Wanted website.

"What about the other one?" the corporal asked.

"Restrained," Private Martens reported. "Breathing."

"Good, bring him here and then get set up on the intersection," Jackson ordered the two privates, who *aye aye*'d and dragged a bound, black-suited agent by the ankles from the place John threw him. By where the guy landed, he'd flown a good twenty meters via John Marsh Airways before crashing into a wall. They dropped him near us, then went back to settle by the corners, one on each side of the Canal Street tunnel. The corporal knelt by the other Homeland agent—the one whose head John had bounced off the floor a few times. "Is this guy dead? And why are they in CBW gear?"

"I don't know if he's dead," John admitted. "I hit him pretty hard."

"CBW?" I asked.

"Not hard enough," Jackson said. "He's still breathing."

"Will somebody tell me what the hell CBW means?"

"Chemical and Biological Warfare," the corporal explained. "Allows them to work in a compromised environmental situation."

"A what?"

"Like one covered in anthrax."

THE ARMED RESPONSE Lieutenant Singh and the Z-Squad controller, Rao, followed Agent Ramirez to the intersection of the Lake and Canal Street tunnels. Behind them, being driven by commands from Rao's control panel, a single Revivant carrying a Vx canister marched in glassy-eyed silence. The remaining five nerve-agent zombies had been disconnected from the network and idled in a side tunnel several dozen meters to the rear. Having all their nasty Easter eggs in one basket didn't seem like a wise idea.

Ten agents jogged up from an adjoining tunnel, having been ordered to break contact and assemble at the intersection. The remaining AR officers kept the marine force pinned down to the east. This gave Ramirez eleven men, plus Rao and his "bug sprayer."

Ramirez ordered all living personnel to mask up, given the presence of a single tank of Vx in the enclosed space.

"One stray round could ruin everyone's day," the agent said. No one hesitated to seal their hazmat suits. Rao twitched his nose behind his mask like it itched while Singh signaled the black-garbed agents to fan out and form a perimeter.

Inspecting the narrow path ahead revealed nothing special—another tunnel with rusted rails disappearing into the diminishing distance. Grimy concrete, curved walls coming to an arched point overhead. Fewer lights than most. Ramirez shrugged and mentally tossed a coin.

"A scout team went this way," he stated over the command channel. "A few minutes ago there was a ton of chatter and some small arms fire. We have lost contact with the team." Ramirez touched Singh on the shoulder. "We are committing everyone here, one big push. Advance teams will probe for resistance. When we find a concentration of terrorists, the bug sprayer advances and wipes them out, then we move forward again. Questions? No? Good. Let's go."

At the Homeland agent's signal, the ten-man AR detachment split into tactical overwatch teams and dashed ahead. Rao followed a few moments later, with the Revivant clumping along behind him and Ramirez bringing up the rear. His breath lightly fogged the bottom of his face shield.

Shadows flitted along the walls, and the agent's heart thudded harder. He had forgotten to pop a stick of gum before locking down the suit; the lack of THC was making him jumpy. "Well, with any luck," he told himself, "this won't take long."

He switched his comm on and broadcast to the team, "Good hunting, gentlemen."

The release of the video was on him. Proctor had already called him six times, and he'd ignored all six calls. The only way he could save anything from this mess would be to eliminate the Children of Liberty. After that, they would see about restoring order and discipline to the American people. The tumult over this... little snag... would die out soon, as all such incidents did, once the people's quick temper boiled off. A small group of the political minority would make the right noises about reforming Washington, and the people would go back to leading their lives.

Without the terrorists fanning the flames, the spark would die out.

America would be safe again.

GONZALES SHOWED UP with five privates and Staff Sergeant Patrick, all of them out of breath and panting. The lieutenant directed two men to continue beyond Canal, to hold the next intersection to the west, and squatted next to John Marsh and me. She swore in a colorful, multilingual way.

I arched an eyebrow. "Bad day?"

"This place is a cunt-busting maze. I hate this underground fighting bullshit." Gonzales had shaved the sides of her head to stubble and left a thicker patch on top; when she slipped off her helmet and scratched her head, it stuck up in spikes. "Corporal. Report."

While Jackson brought his commander up to speed, I used John as a ladder and levered myself into a standing position, hunched over with my back to the sloped wall. The stun-grenade-induced calamity inside my noggin had abated somewhat, and I could almost think again. Neurons were firing faster than horse-and-buggy speed, for a change.

"Where's the cart?"

"I left it with Millie. I ran, which is why it took me so long." The big man shifted beside me. "What do you want to do, Joe?"

"Go to sleep in a warm bed." I twisted my head in a big circle, and my neck crackled. "We better get back to Millie. She'll have all kinds of chores saved up for us by now."

"*Contact!*" yelled a marine, and in the next instant the tunnel filled with hammering guns and streaks of burning light.

"GET BACK! GET BACK!" Major Franklin Rogers ordered. Soldiers of Blatnik's 4th Platoon, and company medics, had poured from the Oak Street apartment, piled over the barricades and sought to separate the savaged remnants of 1st Platoon from the Revivant corpses littering the intersection.

The feds' armored vehicle roared forward, shrugging off the pinpricks of lightweight automatic rifles from the resistance. Black diesel exhaust billowed behind the lumbering four-wheeled monster. Rogers' fighters retreated in good order—some dragging wounded comrades while the others expended hundreds of futile rounds in sheets of buzzing fire at the oncoming APC.

Rogers grabbed the last pair of retreating troops by their collars and jerked them backward over the barricade. "Get inside!" He risked one last quick glance to make sure his men were clear, knowing the shell with his name on it was already loaded in the cannon's breech. Why hadn't they fired?

The APC idled in the middle of the intersection, its four mammoth tires astride a carpet of the... terminated... Revivants, listing slightly left due to the uneven nature of the piled corpses. The barrel of the big gun was so perfectly aligned with his nose, Rogers imagined he could see all the way down to the conical tip of the high-explosive round nestled therein.

Which still didn't fire.

"What the hell?" Rogers muttered.

He and the tank watched each other, neither moving. A breeze sliced through the smoke and cooled the sweat soaking Rogers' neck. The reek of blood and shit and burnt gunpowder hung heavy, despite the breeze.

Lieutenant Blatnik appeared beside him; Rogers becoming aware of him only when the younger man spoke. "What are they waiting for, sir?"

"I... I don't know."

The major squinted and tried to see through the half-painted window glass of the driver's viewport, without the slightest luck at all. A squeal of metal came from the vehicle, and a hatch atop the turret rose up, tipped, and fell open with a clang. A moment later, something popped up that perplexed Rogers more than anything else in his fifty years of military actions.

"Is that...?" Blatnik said, clearly stunned.

"It is, Lieutenant." Rogers put his hands on his hips and shook his head in disbelief. "It's a white flag. Apparently, the feds want to parley."

WITH THE VOLUME OF fire the marines poured into the Canal Street tunnel, I could not figure out how a single human could survive more than a second. Marines burned through magazine after magazine, calling out observations, orders, and status updates without pausing the symphony of destruction they played at maximum volume.

"I'm out."

"Target left, engaging."

"Reloading."

"Gonzales," I yelled to the lieutenant. "We're heading back."

She waved without looking at me. Two marines poured fire down the tunnel until their magazines ran dry, then swapped place with two others to reload. Gonzales snuck a peek around the corner and jerked her head back when a bullet clipped the concrete a gnat's ass over her helmet. Somehow the feds were coming on, even in the face of withering fire from the marine positions.

"Zombie coming, engaging."

"Come on, John. Let's you and I slope on outta here; leave the fighting to the pros."

"I agree." The giant fell in behind me so we could walk in the center, where the ceiling was higher. At that, he still kept his head ducked low to avoid the occasional dangling bulb. "What do you think—"

A shriek from the rear cut through the small arms chatter, and the blood in my veins turned to frozen slushie. Three marines thrashed on the ground, convulsing, choking, obviously unable to breathe. The remaining soldiers backpedaled away from the intersection; Lieutenant Gonzales the exception. She started forward, but Staff Sergeant Patrick grabbed her battle harness and hauled her back.

"Gas! Gas! Gas!" he screamed.

Private Pelham, on the far side of the intersection, ripped a grenade from a strap on his chest and yelled, "Frag out!"

"Pelham, no!" Patrick bellowed.

The private skidded to a stop in the middle of the intersection, cocked his arm to throw, and the gas hit him like an invisible freight train. He dropped the grenade halfway through a weak throw and collapsed next to his stricken comrades. The egg-shaped explosive wobbled along the rail toward the cluster of marines scrambling in our direction. John and I witnessed a slow-motion disaster, helpless as if we watched a plane falling from the sky.

Lance Corporal Jackson screamed out, "Grenade!" and launched himself through the air. He belly-flopped, covering the weapon with his body. Light flashed under him, and a dull thump bounced the corporal in the air. He didn't move again.

"Get back," Gonzales ordered. She consulted her map while being half-carried by the tall sergeant, who dragged another marine to his feet by his battle harness. "Fall back, marines. Regroup, ah... regroup grid location... grid location Charlie Two-Two."

I forced my feet to unstick and tugged a fistful of John's shirt. "Shit, John. The feds are gassing the tunnels; we need to get our people out *now*!"

We ran.

Thirty-Five | I've Been Working on the Underground Railroad

MURPHY'S LAW. RAMIREZ toed the dead body of his Z-Squad controller. A ricochet on a bad-luck trajectory had zipped in and taken off the back of the young Asian's head.

Of his original eleven *living* agents, three effective bodies remained. Eight killed taking one intersection. *One* intersection. Four from the terrorist's direct fire and the rest from punctures of their CBW suits that allowed penetration of his Vx. Incredible. The Revivant was pretty chewed up as well, barely able to stand on legs shot to ribbons.

Ramirez unstrapped the Z-controller from Rao's body and slipped it over his own head. It took some fiddling, but he finally managed to activate a second Vx-loaded zombie and march him forward through the tunnels to join up with the remaining team. The feds hunkered in the intersection formerly defended by the terrorists, shifting and cutting glances his way, unhappy at advancing further into such stiff resistance. Well, tough fucking titty. Life sucks, then you die. Then you live again.

"Move out," Ramirez ordered. He keyed the Z-controller, and Revivant #2 shambled into the darkness of the Canal Street tunnel, followed by a hesitant cluster of AR agents.

"WHERE ARE WE?" I GASPED, pressing a palm into the stitch in my side.

John huffed behind me. "I don't know," he admitted between pants.

"Great. We're lost."

I stopped at an intersection and hunted for a sign, but nothing jumped off the wall and screamed, "You Are Here, Stuuuuuupid." This entire section of tunnels under the downtown streets had been stripped of signage; cleared rectangles showed through the grime where they had hung. Entire sections were without lighting. We were as lost as a preacher at a peep show.

At times, gunfire flared or echoed from a distance. I had no idea how the marines fared against the feds. Were they holding them back? Was the gas wafting through the tunnels, unseen and silent, waiting for me or John to blunder into an invisible cloud and die?

"This way." I pointed to a direction with a scattering of light bulbs, and we shambled into a wind-sucking jog.

THREE RUNNING FIREFIGHTS had whittled Ramirez's remaining forces to himself and a pair of zombies. One agent dropped with a bullet through the facemask of his visor, the second fell within minutes. The third agent had run screaming when a near miss ripped his suit, and he freaked out about the Vx contamination.

In whittling down the resistance, Ramirez had burned through four of his original six Z's. The Revivants had been chopped up by incoming rounds beyond the point they could continue. He dumped them and activated new ones as needed.

Like driving a new car out of the garage every time you wreck one.

Ramirez controlled a pair of fresh units, maneuvering them ahead of him along the Canal Street route, using their optics to probe ahead and spring any traps planted along their route of march.

Six resistance fighters were down, either shot to death or victims of a lethal dose of Vx. They died bravely. Stupidly and stubbornly affixed to a useless cause, but harder to kill than a cold virus. Ramirez stepped over the body of a dead female officer, Gonzales by her nametag, the latest victim of the lethal nerve agent. Such a waste.

The viewer embedded in the control unit showed the scene facing his zombie's optics. A thrill zinged through Ramirez from head to crotch when he spotted people clustered at a juncture of several tunnels. According to the rangefinder, the traitors gathered in a long line eighty-six meters ahead of his current position, and less than forty meters away from his pair of zombies.

Through the IR-enhanced optics, he identified a small figure gesticulating and acting very much in charge.

"MacCauley," he breathed. "My lucky day, indeed."

He tapped a series of keys that brought both Revivants' full tanks of Vx online and prepped the spray nozzle that would expel the gas under high pressure. By experimentation, Ramirez had found forty meters was the very limit of the tank's range. Twenty was better.

"A few more seconds..."

FRANKLIN ROGERS ORDERED two chairs and a table set up in a clear space in front of the federal agents' APC. He met the Homeland officer, a Captain Reed, and shook the slender man's hand. Rogers grabbed one chair while Reed accepted the other.

"Major Rogers, I'll get right to the point here." Reed towered above two meters in height, tall and outrageously thin. He reminded Rogers of Ichabod Crane playing dress-up in a black jumpsuit.

"Please do." The major schooled his features to calm. He waited at parade rest in the shadow of a wheel-mounted cannon that could easily vaporize him in less than a heartbeat, and behind him, troops from 4th Platoon circulated among the wounded and dead, gathering bodies and triaging those still alive.

Calm.

The Homeland agent spoke first. Without preamble, he consulted his phone and said, "I've seen evidence that suggests we"—he waved a hand to indicate his waiting troops—"will be phased out in favor of Revivants. A number of other measures are underway that I personally find repugnant. I'm told the president has declined to address the questions raised by the leaked video."

Rogers blinked and opened his mouth. Words stalled and refused to come out.

"My superiors just informed me," Reed continued, "the president intends to declare martial law and use the military, staffed by zombies, to enforce the law."

After a long pause Rogers said, "I can only say I'm surprised it didn't happen sooner."

"Frankly, I agree." The tall captain scrubbed his face with both hands. "This is not the venue to debate the politics of the situation, Major."

"True enough."

"Instead..." Reed regarded the surrounding devastation with... remorse? "I don't have the moral right to ask this question, but I owe it to my men to make the effort."

"Ask what?" Rogers' mind wandered away from the immediate, already turning through ideas and contingency plans. He became aware of the distant scream of emergency vehicles haunting the surrounding city and smoke pillars blotting the sky. The rioting and looting had grown. He focused on Reed. "Spit it out, Captain."

"We would like to join you."

"Say again?"

"Homeland has kept tabs on you for a long time, Major." Reed shrugged, and his hands fisted. "Many of us have cheered you on from the sidelines as we watched you rebuild the American ideal here in Cabrini. It was only the scuzzballs in Washington who put us on the other side of the fence." The Homeland captain leaned forward and searched Rogers' eyes. "The United States of America is dead. It's time to start again."

JOHN MARSH AND I STAGGERED around a corner and nearly bumbled into a short man dressed in a black moon suit. My eyes bugged out when the man turned and I got a look inside his face-mask.

"Ramirez!"

"Warren!" The Homeland Security agent acted fast. His hand swept down and back up, holding a blue steel pistol, and triggered a round. A hammer hit me in the hip and spun me to the ground.

"You shot me, you fuck!"

"And I'm going to shoot you again," Ramirez reported. He lined up the pistol on my nose, and his finger curled on the trigger.

John leaped in front of me the instant Ramirez fired. The giant grunted and stumbled back a step. Ramirez shot him again.

"John! No!"

Two more rounds punched John in the chest before a huge paw swatted the gun from the agent's hand. The weapon bounced away and clattered somewhere into the darkness. John toppled with the stiffness of a redwood, collapsing at the stubby agent's backpedalling feet.

"John!" I tried to scramble up, but something was wrong with my right hip, and I fell again. Pain lanced my side. I gurgled a wet scream in response.

"This is even better than I could have hoped for," Ramirez told me. He tapped some keys and shuffled to the side of the tunnel. I panted and squeezed a hand into the patch of wetness to the right of my groin. John shifted a bit, groaned. Went silent.

"Goddamn you to the bottom of the shithouse, Ramirez." At the end, all I had left was curses. The marines were nowhere to be found. Millie and her people were at the mercy of this maniac. The feds had won, and the Children of Liberty would be eradicated by lethal gas as soon as the psychopath finished me off. "I hope demons buttfuck you for all of eternity."

"Pretty weak, Joseph. I recall you once had a sharper tongue."

Two Revvies stumped out of the darkness, marching side by side. One reminded me a lot of Larry, the janitor-turned-killer from the Huateng Tower.

Ramirez danced out of reach and placed me in a sandwich between him and the Revvies. Ramirez spoke without taking his eyes off his controller. "I think I'll hose you down with a little Vx, Mr. Warren. Maybe a tiny dose. Just enough to ensure you die of asphyxiation over an extended period of time."

"Wouldn't your mother be proud of you now, Ramirez?"

"In fact, she would—"

"Joe!" a new voice called from behind the matching pair of Revivants.

"Millie! Stay back. He's using nerve gas!"

She ignored me—what else is new—and shoved past the shambling hunks of meat to crouch at my side. I was reminded how strong she was when she damned near lifted me to a sitting position with one arm. "What have they done? Oh, John," she cried when she noticed Marsh's body.

"MacCauley," Ramirez crowed. "This gets better and better. Let me see now. This button first."

The Revivants stepped forward and raised the nozzles of their spray guns.

"Agent Ramirez," Millie rapped out, "you don't have to do this. I heard from our people up top, and the video is out. The country is in turmoil. If we don't work together, our enemies will waltz in while we're at each other's throats."

"If the country is in turmoil, it's your fault, MacCauley."

"Hey Ramirez," I said. "You know something?"

The agent focused on me, a tiny smile curling the corner of his mouth.

I shifted against Millie, easing the banshee scream of agony flaring from my hip. "In the Huateng Tower, Mr. Yamadut taught me one thing: You can't keep a dead man down."

"What the hell are you talking about, Warren?"

"Revivant," I barked. "Code Alpha-Foxtrot-One-Seven-Niner."

"Okay," the dead men grunted in unison. They dropped the spray nozzles and cocked their heads at the same precise moment.

"Kill that sonofabitch!" I roared and pointed at Ramirez.

"Okay. Kill." The Revivants shuffled in a loose turn and started for Ramirez, who stabbed keys on his control over and over with increasing vigor.

"Warren! What did you do?"

"A little present from Larry the Dead Guy. Enjoy the afterlife, you dog-butted psycho."

"Make them stop!" Ramirez screamed. He backed away until the wall brought him up short.

"Don't think I will. I'd run if I were you."

He ran.

Epilogue

THE MEDIC HELD UP HIS scanner and said, "You're going to need a new hip, Mr. Warren. The ball joint is shattered."

"No problem," I said. And it really wasn't. They'd shot me up with a heavy dose of something really, really good. The guy could have said I needed my dick removed and I would have agreed to the procedure. "No problem at all."

I waited in an aboveground triage tent. They wanted to do a patch job until I was well enough to undergo the hip-replacement procedure. I had absolutely no idea where I was or what time it was or what planet I was on. I floated on morphine clouds and dreamed of painkiller lollipops.

Millie showed up at some point and placed a cool hand on my forehead. Next to her appeared a heavily bandaged Staff Sergeant Patrick, who glowered at me as if I was a malingering private. People rushed around, doing important things. I smiled and enjoyed the feel of Millie's soft palm.

I closed my eyes for a second, and the next thing I knew daylight streamed in the open tent flap. Patrick and Millie had been joined by Franklin Rogers and Momma Rose. The four of them hovered over me like a squad of angels... or judges.

"Who died?" I croaked, instantly regretting my own smart mouth. *Too many good people*, was the answer. "Sorry, that was stupid. Did we get Ramirez?"

Millie leaned over and tucked the sheet around my shoulders. "Ramirez got away. We put down the two Revivants you... activated?... and secured all the Vx, but the tunnels are a write-off until we can detox them. We're not even sure how to do that."

"The good news," Momma Rose soothed, "is that John Marsh is hanging on."

"What?" My eyes popped open wide. "The big guy's alive?"

Happy smiles confirmed it.

Well.

Shit.

I blotted my eyes with a sheet and tried to blink away the blurriness. "So is the fight over?"

Rogers turned grim. "No, young man, I'm afraid it's not. The United States has all but collapsed. We have rioting, looting, mass murder, and crimes both petty and horrific with which to contend. The country's burning, my friend, and it's anybody's guess how long until the Chinese, or Russians, or hell, who knows, the goddamned Costa Ricans march across the border and try to take over."

"The American experience is on the brink of extinction, Joe," Millie said. Her blue eyes flared brightly. "The freest people on earth, the most powerful nation in the history of the world, the greatest ideals of men like Ben Franklin and Thomas Jefferson, have all but been destroyed by self-serving greed and stupidity."

"You need a band to give a speech like that." I grinned.

Millie's smile faltered at birth. "I don't know how we're going to get back what we've lost."

"Get it back?" I squeezed her hand in mine. "We don't have to get it back, we just have to get it right. We fuck up, we fix it. That's what Americans do."

About the Author

Scott Bell holds a degree in Criminal Justice from North Texas State University and has enjoyed careers in asset protection as well as sales. With the kids grown and time on his hands, Scott turned back to his first love—writing. His short stories have been published in The Western Online, Cast of Wonders, and in the anthology Desolation. Yeager's Law is his first published novel, but there are two more due for release next year, and more on the way.

When he's not writing, Scott is on the eternal quest to answer the question: What would John Wayne do?

Also by Scott Bell

An Abel Yeager Novel
Yeager's Law
Yeager's Mission

Standalone
Working Stiffs

www.ingramcontent.com/pod-product-compliance
Lightning Source LLC
Chambersburg PA
CBHW032139190626
46814CB00005BA/1755